Praise for *The Last Voyage of the Marigold*

"A mesmerizing, can't-put-down read… a thrilling tale on the high seas."

—Christine DeSmet, mystery author, screenwriter, and writing coach

"Journey through a story of mystery, thrills, and adventure."

—Mary Davidsaver, author of *Clouds Over Bishop Hill* and *Shadows Over Bishop Hill*

"Be prepared. This thriller delivers action and twists that will keep you turning the pages to the exciting conclusion."

—Shawn Wilson, author of the Brick Kavanagh mystery series *Relentless* and *Duplicity*

Other Titles by Pearl City Press

Married, Living in Italy by Misty Urban

The Last Voyage of the Marigold by Dan Moore

The Adventures of Bobby, Iowa Farm Boy by Bob Bancks

Penny and the Woodland Fairies by Bob Bancks

Silent Sam and Other Stories by Alan Arkema

Books by Writers on the Avenue

Winter Holidays in the City of Pearls

Climbing the Hill of Life

From River to River

Everything Old is New Again: 30 Years of WOTA

Roads We've Taken

Escape on the Silk Road

DAN MOORE

Muscatine, Iowa

Published in the United States by Pearl City Press
An imprint of Writers on the Avenue

This is a work of fiction. All characters, incidents, and events are products of the author's imagination or are used fictitiously with no relation to actual persons or events.

For permission to reproduce selections from this book, contact Pearl City Press pearlcitypress@writersontheavenue.org

10 9 8 7 6 5 4 3 2 1

ISBN-13: 978-1-7369498-8-7

DEDICATION

For my wife, Kathy

THE SILK ROAD

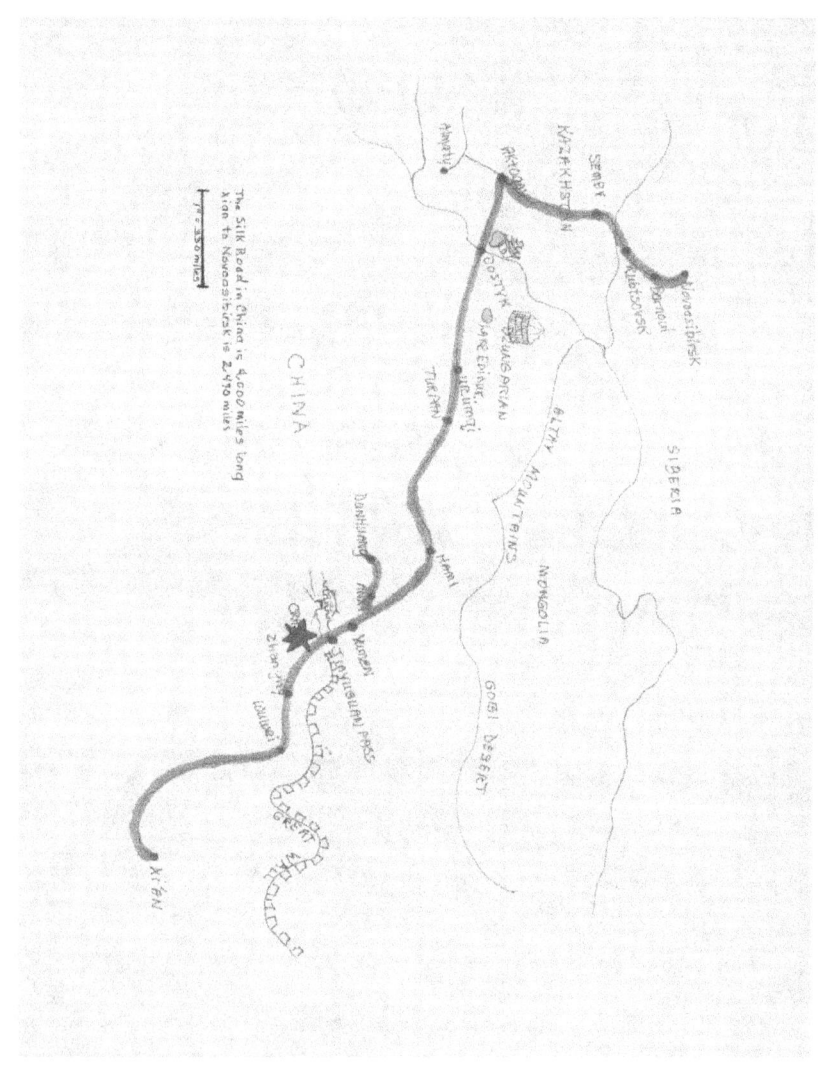

Contents

Contents vii
Prelude 1
Chapter 1..5
Chapter 2..19
Chapter 3..31
Chapter 4..41
Chapter 5..47
Chapter 6..57
Chapter 7..64
Chapter 8..67
Chapter 9..84
Chapter 10..92
Chapter 11..98
Chapter 12...111
Chapter 13...123
Chapter 14...131
Chapter 15...135
Chapter 16...152
Chapter 17...159
Chapter 18...170
Chapter 19...182
Chapter 20...189
Chapter 21...192
Chapter 22...199
Chapter 23...201
Chapter 24...219
Chapter 25...221
Chapter 26...224
Chapter 27...236

Chapter 28 245
Chapter 29 255
Chapter 30 257
Chapter 31 260
Chapter 32 273
Chapter 33 285
Chapter 34 288
Chapter 35 295
Chapter 36 310
Chapter 37 314
Chapter 38 327
Chapter 39 345
Chapter 40 348
Chapter 41 354
Chapter 42 356
Récession..366
Author's Note 368
About the Author...369

Escape
on the
Silk Road

Prelude

"SEE, MARCO? THERE, in the distance—palm trees!" Niccolò Polo called to his son. "It's an oasis! I told you not to despair."

Marco shielded his eyes against the intense desert glare, squinting to make out no more than a darkened smudge at the base of the distant dunes. He gripped his camel's saddle, posted up between the two humps, and tried to identify it. His Uncle Maffeo pulled his camel alongside his brother and clapped his back.

"I think I see it! I see something," Marco exclaimed.

The other members of their caravan strained to see what he was so excited about. It had been almost three months since they'd departed the windswept central Asian steppes and snow-enshrouded mountains to the west and set out across the dry desert expanse.

Prodding his camel, Marco brought his beast to his father's side. "We've done it! You said there would be water at the base of those mountains. How much farther now to Khambaliq?"

Ever since his father and uncle had returned to Venice in 1269 with wondrous stories of Kublai Khan's Cathay, Marco had pestered them to take him with them next time. Almost four years later, one and a half years into their present journey, he was anxious to visit the desolate

1

places his uncle and father had described and to reach the great Khan's palace.

"Be patient, Marco. We'll rest by the Flaming Mountains for a few days and reprovision. We still have over a hundred days before we reach Khambaliq and Shangdu. There is still much to endure."

Their return to Cathay was at the behest of Emperor Kublai Khan himself. The emperor had been intrigued by Niccolò's stories about Western religion and had even given them a passport, an engraved golden tablet, affording them safe passage anywhere in the Khan's vast empire.

Under the Khan's protection, they were to bring him learned Christians and oil from Jesus' Holy Sepulcher in Jerusalem. With the oil safely stowed in their baggage and two friars in tow, they now neared the end of their quest.

Marco's face brightened as they entered the shaded expanse of the oasis. The respite after their months of hardship was a godsend. Where there had been nothing for so long—no civilization, no means of support—there were now people with food and shelter.

Those who lived at the oasis made their livings dealing with a few chance traders and wandering Buddhist pilgrims who dwelled in caves carved in the nearby hills. Here the incessant sand dunes gave way to the empty Hexi Corridor, a barren panhandle extending from the Taklimakan Desert to the Yellow River further east. The hard-packed gravel and sands of the Gobi Desert lay to the north. Travelers who dared enter this region were funneled through this windswept, arid wash, narrowest at its western approach, before reaching Cathay proper.

"I told you the journey would be hard, but it will be worth it," his father said to his son's delight. Then the older man's countenance changed to one of caution. "This has been the easy part of our journey. Travelers leaving Cathay find the return journey twice as difficult."

Chapter 1

Tegh and his roommate finished eating and went outside to enjoy the early fall air. The restaurant was popular for its simple, inexpensive fare. With the pressure of exams and papers behind them, they had two weeks to relax before restarting the academic grind.

Tegh asked, "It's so nice, what do you want to do?"

"It's too early to go back to student housing," his roommate said. "Let's head over to the plaza. I heard there are some students gathering regarding the latest postings on the government billboards. I want to hear why the government feels the need to spread their propaganda on university square? Our campus is supposed to be a place for the free exchange of ideas, not for the government to plaster restrictive policies all over the place."

Tegh looked at Mingze, his roommate from southeastern China who was three beers into the evening already. "Keep your voice down," Tegh said. "There are most likely people listening who would consider your thinking too radical for public expression."

"Come on, Tegh," Mingze insisted. "I'm just saying what a lot of us are thinking about the State's constant infringement on how we think and speak. Besides, you're a Mongolian, not a native of China, so you don't see the government tactics for what they are."

"And what would those—?" Tegh stopped, realizing that rationalization wasn't going to assuage his friend's alcohol-tainted reasoning. "I get it. Still..." He shrugged. "You know, I'm tired. I'm heading back to the room. Go on, but be careful."

Tegh walked the several blocks to his dorm, hoping his roommate wouldn't draw attention to himself. Tegh had noticed Mingze's political restlessness before, and listened to the closely guarded opinions expressed by other grad center students concerning recent government dictums. Tegh hoped the fresh autumn air would mellow their enthusiasm. *I just want to finish my studies and go home.*

A half hour after returning to his dorm, loud pounding at his door startled him. Before he could reach it, two burly men burst into his shared apartment. A Ministry of State Security guard flipped on the overhead lights as the other one surveyed the room.

Seeing that Tegh was the only one there, he demanded,

"You're under arrest for conspiring in subversive activities. You will come with us *now.*"

Tegh made a move to bolt through the door, but a second guard grabbed him. Struggling, Tegh demanded, "What's this about? What have I done?"

The guard tried to bend his arm behind his back, but Tegh shook him free. "What are you doing?"

The other guard said calmly, "Resisting only adds to your crimes."

Realizing his struggle was futile, Tegh faced him. "I've done nothing except go to dinner and return here."

"You were seen only a block from the square where

protestors like you are being detained as we speak."

Thinking quickly, Tegh said, "And if your cameras or informant were carefully checked, you would know I didn't accompany those students. I left and returned directly here, where I've been ever since."

The guard in charge looked at the one who was now opening desk drawers and rummaging through shelves in search of incriminating material. He stopped and shook his head.

"You may or may not be telling the truth," the guard in charge said. "In any case, you're coming with us."

Tegh thought, *this is outrageous. But if I protest, regardless of what they think I've done, that will be enough to get me deeper in trouble.* Tegh grabbed his backpack. "Look, if I'm going somewhere, let me take this—my identity papers and visa."

The burly guard started to snatch the backpack away, but the other guard shook him off, saying, "That's fine. Let's go."

They ushered Tegh out the door to a waiting MSS security van and locked him in the back. All alone on a bench seat, Tegh wondered, *why isn't the van moving?* Then he heard one of the guards calling on the radio.

After several static-filled conversations, the van jerked into motion.

"Hey, where am I going?" Tegh yelled.

"To the airport. Your roommate has been detained for subversive activities and is being questioned. You're lucky you weren't with him. Our precinct captain says that since you're a foreigner, your visa's been revoked and you're being expelled."

"Wait a minute, you can't—" Tegh caught himself,

suddenly understanding the hopelessness of protesting.

Twenty minutes later, the security van pulled to a stop at a side entrance to the Xi'an Airport departure terminal. Two waiting MSS guards took charge of Tegh, barely giving him time to grab his backpack before they traipsed him through a door that bypassed normal security and led him down a windowless corridor. Reaching an unmarked door, a guard nudged Tegh into the sterile waiting area with several rows of chairs.

"Sit here," a guard in the room said.

Tegh looked around. He could see the main terminal departure lounge beyond a set of double glass doors at the far end of several long rows of scoop-seated plastic chairs. He sat partway down the second row from the front. The only other person there was an elderly Chinese man sitting in the first row, a few seats from the door guard. His head was down and he didn't look around.

It had happened so fast, Tegh hadn't had time to consider his pending fate. Patting his backpack, he thought, *wherever I'm headed, at least I managed to keep my passport, cell phone, and money. As soon as they let me, I'll call home to Ulaanbaatar.*

XI'AN CULTURAL CONVENTION CENTER

THE TWO POSED for a selfie with their backs to the fountain inside the convention center. The LED marquee behind them advertised an international clothing manufacturers convention, which they'd travelled from Germany to attend.

"Hurry up, Fritz, we haven't got all day. I want to get back to the hotel and write down my ideas about the exhibits while they're fresh in my mind."

"Betta, you're too impatient. What's the hurry? Between the two of us, we can remember them well enough. Besides, I snapped photos with my phone when no one was looking. You know, that integrated loom and finishing machine. It's perfect for the reinforced action wear…"

"You what? With all those signs forbidding photographs, you took pictures anyway?"

"Betta, stop worrying. People sneak pictures all the time. I even picked up a couple of souvenirs." Fritz held up a button with a corporate logo of an impish figure and a small rectangular device imprinted with a figure of the sun with a stylized solar flair and the words Sunku.

"You stole them?" Betta said incredulously.

"No, they were on the table across from that computer-controlled loom you were so interested in. I figured it was advertising swag. It's not like I—"

Fritz didn't finish before three policemen approached, one demanding his cell phone.

Fritz snatched his hand from their reach. "Wait a minute. I'm a German citizen. You can't do that."

The policeman in charge said sternly, "Do you speak English?"

"Yes, but…"

"Give me the phone. Both of you, come with me to the police station. You are being detained for industrial espionage."

Fritz slapped the guard's hand away from his phone and another guard raised a baton threateningly.

Betta screamed, "Don't hit him."

The guard stopped, arm still raised, as Fritz offered up

his phone. The guard scrolled through Fritz's pictures of convention display machinery. As he did so, Fritz stuffed the swag in his lower cargo pants pocket.

Looking at the phone and shaking his head, the guard said, "You've engaged in forbidden activity. Follow me, please."

The guards ushered them out a side door and forced them into a panel van.

"Where are you taking us?" protested Betta. "You can't do this."

The guards slid shut the van door and the two young Germans heard a tap-tap on the roof, apparently a signal for the van driver because the van started moving.

"Fritz, see what you've done," Betta said. "How many times have I said you aren't home now? You have to pay attention."

"Betta, I don't need your badgering. We've more important things to worry about."

She barked, "Like where they're taking us and what's going to happen?"

"Betta. Please, just concentrate on what we're going to do next and not what's happened."

They'd sat silently for about fifteen minutes until they felt the van pull to a stop. A guard slid open the side door and motioned them out.

As he stepped from the van, Fritz tried to shake free from the guard's grasp and he struck Fritz's shoulder with a baton.

As Fritz jerked back in pain, Betta screamed, "Do as he says, Fritz."

For a moment, the two stood awkwardly and stared at what appeared to be an airline terminal, but there were no airline logos like Lufthansa or Swiss Air. One of the guards nodded towards two other guards waiting by the terminal door. After a brief discussion, the guard from the van saluted, climbed back in his van, and left.

"You will follow me," the guard said in English.

Fritz, craving a smoke after not having had one since the convention center, tried to take out a cigarette. The guard said sternly, "No smoking," and pushed him towards the terminal.

Betta said, "Just do as he says, Fritz."

"Come on, Betta, I don't need—"

"In here," the guard said, prodding them with his baton and holding open a door.

They went down an unadorned corridor and entered a large waiting room, not unlike an airport departure lounge, except the walls were bare and there were only chairs fastened together in long rows with a set of large glass doors at the other end.

Their guard said, "You will wait here."

"Wait for what?" Fritz demanded.

The guard raised his baton, and Fritz held up his hands in appeal. Thinking fast, Fritz pulled several Chinese yuan from his pocket and held them up to the guard, saying, "Look, you're mistaken. Let us go and…"

The guard swatted Fritz's hand away, the bills fluttering to the floor, and said, "I will add bribery to your charge of stealing intellectual property. These are serious offenses in the People's Republic. You are lucky you're only being expelled and not imprisoned."

"But…" Betta objected, but the official cut her off.

"Young woman, you're lucky you're not in jail. Your offenses are more than worthy. Thank what little good fortune you still possess that you're going home. Do I make myself clear?"

Betta shrank back.

While the guard was preoccupied with Betta, Fritz picked up the money from the floor and tried to stuff the bills in his cargo pants pocket, but the button and plastic stick with the sun logo were in the way. He removed them, still holding the money, and stuck the button on the strap to his backpack, then shoved the small plastic souvenir into the cigarette pack in his shirt pocket with the money.

He followed Betta to the middle of the next to last row of chairs. Looking around, she saw a lone guard sitting next to the door through which their escort had just departed. Two rows in front of them sat a single Chinese man in the front row.

Fritz fidgeted, catching himself from pulling out a cigarette.

"Will you stop that, Fritz? Aren't we in enough trouble?" Betta said.

"What else am I supposed to do?" he said.

"Wait!" she replied.

XI'AN AIRPORT

STEVE APPLEGATE PLEADED with the ticket agent at the China East Airlines arrival desk. "I'm supposed to be on the Aeroflot flight from Irkutsk to Tokyo. Things got all messed up in Russia and I was put on a flight here instead. Please, can you reroute my ticket to get me home to Ohio in the United States the easiest way possible?"

The clerk, with limited abilities in English, asked him

to wait and left the counter. Shortly, an airline official, accompanied by a guard, replaced her at the counter. The airline official said, "Mr. Applegate, show me your ticket?"

Steve handed it over and watched as the man punched several keys on his computer. The accompanying guard asked Steve, "What was the nature of your stay in the Russian Federation and why have you come to the People's Republic of China?"

Frustrated, Steve said, "Look, I'm not in China by choice. I should be in Tokyo, on my way to Los Angeles and then Cleveland, Ohio. And who are you to be asking, sir? You're not with the airlines."

He replied curtly, "The Ministry of State Security has a need to know the nature of your business."

Steve looked at the airline clerk for a hint of sympathy, but the clerk ignored him, busying himself with his computer instead. Steve said, "If you insist, I was working for a non-profit in Russia on a civil engineering project. When Russia invaded Ukraine, my government urged Americans to leave the country. So, I booked a flight, but it seems the Aeroflot folks have somehow mixed things up and gotten me on a flight here instead of Tokyo as planned. So, here I am trying to re-book to America the easiest way I know how."

The MSS guard displayed no emotion regarding Steve's misfortune. After a pause, he said, "Wait here. I must check." Then turning to the airline clerk, he said something, which Steve didn't understand, and stepped through a door behind the ticket counter.

A few minutes later he returned and said, "Mr. Applegate, you will please follow me."

The ticket clerk handed Steve a boarding pass, but before Steve could read the destination, the MSS guard again said, "Please follow, Mr. Applegate."

Steve held up his boarding pass. "Will this get me all the way home?"

The guard said over his shoulder, "You're temporarily the guest of the People's Republic of China, Mr. Applegate. We can't become involved in whatever disputes your government may have with the Russian Federation. I have been instructed to place you on the next flight leaving China. You don't have permission to remain."

"But..."

Steve's reply was lost by the sound of the guard actuating the automatic double glass doors to a waiting room off the main departure lounge. The guard motioned him in. The undecorated waiting room contained several long rows of uncomfortable looking chairs.

"Have a seat here, Mr. Applegate. Someone will come for you when your flight's ready."

Steve blurted, "But a flight to where? Where are you sending me?"

Without emotion, the MSS guard ignored him and walked to the back of the room where another uniformed guard was seated by an exit. Stopping briefly to say something to the door guard, Steve's escort left through the back door.

Steve looked around. There was a couple sitting in the next to last row, both looking at him but saying nothing. And there were two single Asian men, one just beyond the middle of the second row and the other sitting directly in the middle of the front row. Steve scooted down the second aisle, stopping a few seats from one gentleman, and sat almost directly behind the man in the front row.

The room was silent.

Suddenly, the back door opened. Two new MSS guards came in and stopped directly in front of the forlorn man in the front row. The first guard stood with his boots touching the seated man's shoes while the second guard barked orders in Chinese. When the seated man didn't immediately respond, the first guard jerked him to his feet by his collar, giving rapid fire orders.

Struggling to maintain his balance, the accosted man started to object, but quickly lowered his gaze and shrank protectively when the guard hit him with a baton across the shoulder.

The man sitting in Steve's row jumped up and yelled at the guard, who backhanded the would-be Samaritan on the neck with a baton. Wincing, the other stepped back from baton-wielding guard, exclaiming something not quite as vociferously as before, but still sounding like a plea for the guard to ease up.

A third MSS guard arrived, stopping next to the two guards and their charge and standing directly across the chair from Steve. The new guard barked something at the man held by the guards and then motioned for the man farther along in Steve's row to sit back down. Turning back to the two guards, he bellowed, and the two guards frog marched their target out of the waiting area through the back door.

The guard giving the orders reached across the chair for the backpack sitting beside Steve, who put his hand on the guard's arm and said, "No, that's mine."

The guard glared at Steve in defiance. Steve held his

gaze in a standoff of only a few seconds, but which seemed longer.

Finally, Steve relaxed and slid his hand from the guard's to the luggage tag. In as calm a voice as he could muster, Steve said, "You can read my name on the nametag. It belongs to me."

The MSS guard stared at Steve, recognizing that he was a westerner, but not backing down.

Steve slowly held up his boarding pass and pointed to the name on it and then to the backpack's nametag, which was imprinted with small American flag. "See, the same."

For the longest few seconds, neither man moved. The impasse was broken when yet another uniformed guard, this one with gold braid on his cap brim, approached. He spoke sternly to the guard confronting Steve. The guard released the backpack and followed the newly arrived senior guard out the back door.

The MSS door guard, who was standing alone and looking around as if he should do something, motioned for Steve and the Asian man to sit. Seeing the guard look beyond them to the back rows, Steve turned and saw the couple, a young man and woman, sitting back down and whispering between them.

Rubbing the side of his neck where he'd been struck, the Asian man asked, "You're an American?"

Surprised that he spoke English, Steve said, "Yes, do you know what that was all about?"

He said, "The best I could tell, the man was being held on a state charge and an order must have come to move him. But I must say, you were very lucky their supervisor showed up, otherwise you'd have been carted off too. No one talks back to the MSS, much less touches them, and gets away with it."

Pointing to the red welt on his neck, Steve said, "I see you got swatted for your troubles. How come you're still here?"

"All I did was to point out that he was complying with what they wanted, so give him a chance."

"But, why didn't they—"

"Because I'm not Chinese, I'm a foreigner, like you, here on a deportation order."

Steve said, "But I'm not—"

A male voice behind them interrupted, "That explains it."

The two turned and looked at the young man sitting next to a woman.

"Did you take some illegal pictures, too?" he continued.

The woman slapped his shoulder, saying, "Fritz, give it a rest."

Hearing what he thought was English spoken with a German accent, Steve asked, "Why are you two here?"

The woman offered, "My careless partner took photos at an exposition despite the warning posters."

Steve said, "Well that explains—"

They were interrupted when the door guard snapped to attention and a Chinese official in civilian clothing entered, flanked by two MSS guards. Addressing all four of them in Chinese, he spoke in a commanding voice. The man sitting nearest Steve translated for their benefit. "He's from Immigration Control and he's directing us to follow the guards to our aircraft."

Grabbing his backpack, Steve asked the lone man, "You seem to know what's going on. What's your name?"

"Please call me Tegh. The rest would be too hard for you to pronounce."

"Steve, Steve Applegate, and you two?" Steve said, turning to the couple.

"I'm Lizbetta VanderKellen, Betta to my friends. And this is my business partner, Fritz Steiner. Where are we going?"

Steve looked at his boarding pass but couldn't read the Chinese writing. He held it up for Tegh to read.

Tegh said, "Evidently to Samarkand, and we'd best move along before they get antsy." He pointed to the guards motioning them towards the jet way.

Chapter 2

CHINA EAST AIRLINE FLIGHT 1822

FOLLOWING THE MSS guards, Tegh led the other three down the ramp and through the entry door of CEA flight 1822. Another guard awaited them where a flight attendant would have normally greeted passengers and directed them to file down the two adjacent aisles towards the back of the aircraft. Passengers looked at them and seemed to wonder if these prisoners, for what else could they be with that much attention, were the reason for their delay on the tarmac.

Steve followed Tegh down the right-hand aisle without saying anything, while Betta kept up a constant harangue of Fritz as they moved their way down the other.

"Will you just be quiet, Betta. I don't need this," Fritz said as they passed the business class section.

"You should have thought of that before you decided to break all their rules," she said.

Their bickering kept up in what Tegh thought could be called stage whispers until the guards halted them at the last row of seats. The center four seats had been cleared and the passengers reseated elsewhere in the partially filled cabin. Stowing their backpacks in the overhead bins, they sat in the middle row backed by the aft bulkhead, Steve and Fritz in the middle with Tegh and Betta on the aisles. With them secure, the two guards marched forward and a flight attendant secured the cabin door.

As Tegh followed the guards' progress forward and off the plane, he saw dozens of heads craning to get a glimpse of the captives they were to share this flight with. He thought the flight delay, the menacing abruptness of the guards, and the sudden arrival of the four persons under escort must have been discomforting. *They must be wondering who we are and why the escort.*

He was brought back to the present at hearing Betta and Fritz continue their barbed comments, which drew more questioning glares from passengers seated two rows in front. Steve turned to comment, but Tegh stopped him with a finger to his lips and whispered, "Best not say anything. I don't know what will happen if we talk." Betta and Fritz must have heard him and at last became quiet.

Just as suddenly as the guards left the aircraft, the attendants busied themselves ensuring the passengers were secured and the plane taxied. Tegh thought, *I hope my display in the waiting lounge when I pleaded with the guard won't come back to harm me. So far, I've been fortunate.*

Tegh's experience was that when someone stood up to the MSS, things didn't turn out well. Now here he was. In a matter of less than a few hours, his carefully orchestrated world of student life had been turned upside down, and he had no idea what his future held for him.

As the plane accelerated, passengers were pressed into their seatbacks and the aircraft lumbered off the runway in Xi'an, China, bound for Samarkand, Uzbekistan. The engines whined as the big plane clambered for altitude, filling the cabin with noise. When the background din lessened as the undercarriage retracted, Tegh noticed passengers fidgeting in their seats, some chancing furtive glances around. From the looks on their faces, he assumed their collective moods were returning to normal, normal for folks on their way to vacation, business, or visiting relatives.

The aircraft levelled off and the engines quieted to an incessant background roar. The seatbelt sign clicked off and flight attendants busied themselves with refreshment pushcarts. Individual conversations sprang up and passengers, except the last row, acclimated themselves for the long flight.

As flight attendants efficiently served refreshments, Tegh wondered, *will our isolation continue? Are we allowed to move about the cabin? Can we use the WC? Will we get refreshments or a meal?* By his own personal time standard, it had been some time since he'd been free to do any of that.

Watching the flight attendants go about their service, Tegh noticed passengers settling in to watch individual seatback entertainment screens, view their individual laptops, or don sleeping masks. Those at window seats watched the sun gradually settle over the mountains ahead. In the back row, however, Tegh could see the other three were uncomfortable, as if they were still under surveillance.

"You can make yourselves comfortable," he said, unbuckling. "The guards are gone and we're on our own now. As far as the Chinese authorities are concerned, we're no longer their problem. We'll be out of Chinese airspace shortly and then on to our separate ways home."

"Good," Fritz said. "I have to use the bathroom. These

bastards don't appre—"

Betta interrupted, "Fritz, stop complaining and try to make the most of it. We wouldn't be in this mess if it hadn't been for you."

Fritz scowled.

"Betta, don't treat me like a child. You're the one who wanted us to attend that trade expo. I was only trying to do what... Oh what the hell!" He unbuckled and brusquely stepped sideways past her knees into the aisle and headed to the WC behind them.

Betta looked to her right where Steve and Tegh were watching. Before she could offer an apology, Steve said, "No need to explain. I've seen couples argue before. Hey, being grabbed by security guards in a foreign country is upsetting enough."

Betta smiled in disgust. "Ha! You think," she pointed to the empty seat beside her and then back to herself, "that he and I are a couple, that we're married?"

Steve looked sheepish as she continued. "Definitely not. We're simply colleagues starting a new enterprise for making active wear, you know, outdoor clothing. The expo in Xi'an was for clothing manufacturers around the world to see what Chinese industry had to offer."

Tegh interjected. "And your friend Fritz got carried away with what he could take back as far as technology, right?"

Betta said, "Unfortunately."

Fritz reappeared and unapologetically worked his way back to his seat. Before any of the others could speak, the flight attendants reached their aisle and handed them soft drinks and box lunches.

Fritz mumbled something unintelligible, but his body

language, as far as Tegh could tell, was unappreciative. He looked at Steve and then Betta, avoiding Fritz's belligerent attitude, and said, "We should eat. I don't know about you, but this may be all the hospitality we're afforded until we reach our destination."

Taking him at his word, they opened their boxes and ate. Later, after giving their trash to the flight attendant, Tegh stood and opened the overhead bin, pulling down a pillow and blanket. "I suggest you do the same," he said. "It will be a while before we reach Samarkand."

Almost ninety minutes into the flight, most of the vacationers had forgotten, or at least had dismissed, the disquieting events that had interrupted their departure and had absorbed themselves in their private affairs. Tegh noticed Betta and Fritz had thankfully settled into an uneasy truce.

Without warning, the plane nose-dived. Tegh clutched his armrest and watched in horror as people, not fastened securely, grasped for anything to keep from slamming into the cabin's overhead, as inertia drove them upward. Then, he felt the plane's nose violently jerk up, as the pilot desperately tried to regain control. He saw folks hurled downward onto their seats, other people's laps, and the floor. Screams filled the cabin as passengers searched vainly amidst the chaos for something or someone to save them. Tegh, witnessing the utter displacement of those seated in front of him, held on as tightly as possible, thankful his seatbelt was securely in place.

Betta, to his left, screamed. Steve thrust his arms to either side reflexively, pinning Tegh, Betta, and Fritz to their seat backs. Betta grabbed Steve's arm in a death grip, desperately holding onto something.

The plane pitched forward again, descended, and fishtailed violently as the aircraft corkscrewed from the heavens, unresponsive to the pilot's efforts. Overhead bins popped open and their contents pummeled passengers. As debris fell, Tegh dodged a yellow plastic breathing mask that danced crazily in front of him. He thought to grasp it, but was afraid to release his armrests. Then, he was pressed hard into his seat as the aircraft suddenly pitched up, almost level, as if the pilot had miraculously regained control. Then the plane yawed violently before—WHAM!

Wisps of pungent, greasy smoke tickled Tegh's nose and he twitched. Eyes still shut, he heard nothing except a distant crackle and the susurrus rustling of loose cloth nearby.

What's that?

The cloying smell of burning kerosene rolled by.

Smoke!

Tegh snapped his eyes open and sensed the volatile stench of burning. His nose hairs tingled and one eye watered. He tried to sit up straighter, but couldn't.

What's that flapping sound? Fabric? Something's holding me. Why can't I move?

His arms were free, but he peered into empty blackness. He grappled with his seat belt, finally lifting the edge of the buckle which popped free onto his lap. He looked left. Two men and a woman were seated just beyond.

Do I know them?

It slowly came back to him. Tegh looked right.

That's the aisle.

There were two empty seats and an oval window just beyond on a wall curving up. A lifeless body was sprawled in the aisle.

I'm in an airplane.

Tegh traced the curved surface with his eyes as it arched above, then across to the left, and down again, only to be obscured by the unmoving man seated to his left. He leaned forward and put his feet down. Nothing.

The floor, the ceiling, the seat in front of him, everything that should be there was gone. Tegh looked ahead and up and could see a gray-brown landscape with stars above. Bright pinpoints of light twinkled overhead as wispy clouds moved across.

My plane's crashed. I'm sitting in an airplane seat, but the plane's gone.

He looked behind him. There was an aisle leading back to a door that read Lavatory in English and Chinese. Part of the plane's tail was still there. But the everything else was missing.

The man next to him moaned. Tegh remembered.

His name is Steve. Guards forced us onto the plane.

Tegh turned towards him, kneeling backwards in his seat, and shook him.

Steve's head nodded. "Uh, what… where… What's that smell?"

The breeze shifted and the acrid air wafted away.

"It's me, Tegh. The plane crashed. Are you okay?"

Steve flutter-kicked his legs and moved his arms. He looked at Tegh kneeling on the seat cushion next to him. "Yeah, I hurt like hell, but I'm okay… I think. Whoa!" He tried to get up but his seatbelt caught him.

Tegh said, "Easy. Things aren't normal. I think the tail section broke off. That's where we're sitting. In front of you is a long drop to the ground. Check the two next to you to see if they're alive."

Steve shook the shoulder of the man strapped in next to him. He came to yelling something Steve didn't understand.

Tegh said, "His name is Fritz and she's Betta." Looking at Fritz, he said slowly, "Can you speak?"

Fritz looked, first at Steve, then at Tegh. "Yes. Yes, where are… what's happened?"

Tegh said, "You were in a plane crash."

Fritz's eyes widened. "Get me out of here! I've got to get away! Don't let them take me!" He slumped back, exhausted.

Tegh leaned with some effort across Fritz and shook Betta, who jerked awake, eyes wide, and clutched his arm.

"Easy," Tegh said. "Just sit there and collect yourself. Let's see if you're okay."

She stared at him, seeming to recognize he meant well.

Tegh said, "Okay, sit still while I check out what's going on."

She looked first at him and then across the aisle to her left and the rows ahead. A body, restrained only by a seat belt, slumped into the aisle. She screamed.

Steve said, "I'm pretty sure they're dead. You might want to console your friend here." He pointed to Fritz. "Keep him calm."

Realizing the Betta and Fritz were most likely in shock, Tegh said, "My name is Tegh. Remember? I'll help you to the ground once I figure out what the conditions are."

Carefully, he eased himself forward, searching with one foot extended below him for purchase. Within in short order, he stood on a broken piece of flooring that was sturdy enough to bear his weight. Turning to the others, he explained the situation. "Feel with your feet and hold on to whatever piece of the plane you can grab to support yourself. Be careful, there's lots of jagged metal."

Still agitated, Fritz pleaded, "Don't let them take me."

Tegh said, "Hang in there, friend. I'm with you, but first let's get clear of the plane.

"But the guards are coming for us," Fritz insisted.

"Okay, okay, but first things first." Turning to Steve, Tegh said, "It's Steve, right?"

"Yes, Steve, Steve Applegate."

"All right, Steve, you come first. Step onto that cross beam and climb down to the ground. Hold my hand till you find your support. I'm standing on the ground, so it's okay once you get here."

Carefully, Steve rested his weight, first on one piece of wreckage and then another, until he made it down.

Tegh next worked his way to Fritz. There was a moment of confusion as Fritz excitedly shifted to German until Tegh coaxed him back to English.

"Step down easy, Fritz. Feel with your foot before putting your weight on it."

With cumbersome movements, Fritz made it to the ground and pleaded with Tegh and Steve, "I don't want guards messing with me anymore."

Steve held up a hand in a peaceful gesture. "Okay, okay."

Ignoring Fritz, Tegh moved to help Betta. "Can you move?"

She reached her arms up and wiggled her fingers. She kicked one leg, then the other. Tegh saw a bump on her head where flying debris had hit her. One leg of her yoga pants was ripped and he wondered what other damage she might have suffered.

"Okay, that's good. What's your last name, Betta?"

"VanderKellen, Lizbetta VanderKellen."

"That's right. Okay, Betta, ease yourself forward and I'll help you down. Step carefully."

She put weight on one foot and screamed. Losing balance, she fell forward, with her full weight on Tegh. She was almost as tall as he, and it was all Tegh could do to hold her upright.

Tegh called out, "One of you give me a hand. We'll have to help her to the ground and find out what's wrong. I think she injured her ankle."

As they eased her down, Fritz kept insisting they had to flee the scene as quickly as possible. Tegh and Steve tried to calm him by focusing him on his surroundings, to no avail. Betta, however, whispered something to him in German which finally worked.

Finally, the three stood with Tegh, looking around in the darkness and taking in the scene. China East Airline flight 1822 had crashed onto the barren slopes of western China.

The plane had hit flat, ripping off the nose, forward cabin, and both wings as it scraped hundreds of yards along a rock-strewn hillside. The tail and rudder, the last recognizable portions of the aircraft, had come to rest, nearly upright where the four now stood. Fires burned in the wreckage's wake along a long swath that ended at the surviving tail section.

Tegh looked at the destruction and thought how the explosion, the rent metal, and what must have been a panicked cacophony was now absolute quiet. Cocking his head, he heard the licking hiss of flames in the gathering night farther down the hill. The wreckage was a blackened smear on a slope. To the east was a desert landscape and to the west he saw snow-tipped mountains. A gentle breeze worked its way upslope from the valley floor and pushed smoke in their direction. Night stars danced above.

Tegh shook his head as he realized their good fortune to have survived. He now understood that the aircraft's tail had been cleaved from the rest of the plane. The lavatories, the galley, and the bulkhead behind where they had been sitting remained. Immediately behind and above that, however, was a huge hole where the roof had been. Through it loomed the plane's tail rudder with its China East Airlines logo.

Chapter 3

TEGH STOOD AND stared with the others. Along the slope behind them, for a good quarter mile, fires burned where once had been the starboard wing. Tegh recognized the acrid stench of burning aviation gas as it wafted through the shifting night air.

Beyond the miracle of being alive, he assessed that his only ailments, and those of the two men, were contusions, aches, and pains from having taken the equivalent of a beating. Betta, however, was limping on an injured ankle, wincing with each step. Otherwise, she seemed to be okay.

With a look at each of them, Tegh sensed they were thinking the same thing. *What do we do now?*

Tegh said. "We can't stay here. We've been deported from China. I for one don't want to wait around to find out what sort of the welcome we'll get when searchers arrive."

As Fritz lit a cigarette, Betta said, "We're German. Surely, they'll transport us to a hospital and then to our embassy."

Fritz exhaled a cloud of smoke that billowed and mixed with the vapor from his breath in the chill mountain air. "Did you forget, Betta? The Chinese came up with a flimsy excuse to kick us out."

"There was nothing flimsy about it, Fritz. You were just flaunting their rules ..."

Tegh said, "That's enough, you two. You're not solving the problem."

His abruptness caught Betta off guard, but Fritz pointed his cigarette at Tegh. "I agree with you on one thing. I don't trust the Chinese, precisely since we don't know exactly who it is that would be coming to help us." And then he added, "And I especially don't trust that you're not one of them."

Steve stepped between the two men before things escalated. "Fritz, you're still in shock. Take a breath, buddy, and chill. We all want to survive and get out of here the best way possible. We can only do that if we stay calm."

Betta clasped Fritz's hand. "He's right, Fritz. Listen to him."

When Fritz tried to return her gesture, she let go. Frustrated, he pulled his hand back and regretted coming to the Xi'an Expo as much as the thought of trusting these two strangers. He took a long drag on his cigarette.

Tegh, seeing Fritz's conflicting emotions said, "Minutes ago you were screaming not to let the Chinese capture you. Now you're blaming me for being one of them. Well, I'm not. Like you, I'm not predisposed to trust that a friendly Chinese agency will rescue us. I don't have a crystal ball to tell you who will come to the crash site, or what reception we'll get. I do recommend getting away from the immediate vicinity, if for no other reason than to observe from a safe distance who shows up. Then we can make a final decision."

Fritz faced Tegh. "What makes you such an expert?

Look, I don't know what's going on, what really happened, or what's in store for me. I'm more than confused. You're Chinese. For all I know, you could just be saying these things to get in good with the authorities when they come."

Tegh remained calm. "You've been through a lot; I get it. But looks aren't everything. I told you, I'm not Chinese. I'm a Mongolian. I was grad student studying in China. And for some reason, the Chinese authorities thought I was protesting with other students. That makes me, whether true or not, an enemy of the state. Welcome to the world's largest socialist dictatorship. As I said, waiting for rescue is not the best thing for us.

"Face it, all of us were escorted under guard to that plane." Tegh pointed at the smoldering wreckage. "I don't know what your full stories are, but I for one don't want to hang around. In the eyes of the Chinese, I'm an outsider, a dissident, and persona non grata, accused of unlawfully associating with a protest. In China, that's a cardinal sin. I can't loiter to find out what happens."

Steve said, "For me, I don't know how I got in this mess. I'm an American. And sure, my country and China don't get along too well, but those guards were a little too quick to lump me in with you three and force me onto this flight.

"Hell, I was supposed to be on a different flight in the first place. To top that off, my father's a general on active duty in the Marine Corps, a fact which the Chinese can easily use as political leverage. You know, sins of the father passed on to the son. So, you're darned right I'm worried about what they'll do to us. I agree with Tegh."

Fritz puffed slowly on his cigarette, then directed his

comment to Betta. "What about you? You still pissed off at me? You think we should throw in with them?"

Betta stared right back at Fritz. "You're damn straight I'm pissed at you. Not only for taking those selfies, but you tried to bribe that official, Fritz. I don't know what's going to happen, but I think hanging around here isn't our best option."

Tegh said, "You tried to bribe a guard?"

"Yeah, typical Chinese bullshit," Fritz said. "It was ridiculous, but what could I do? They had my phone with the pictures and I ..." His voice trailed off.

Tegh filled the silence. "It's lucky you're not in jail."

For the first time, Betta flashed a look of sympathy as Fritz tightened his jaw and crushed his cigarette with his shoe. "Look, we're the victims here, not spies. Maybe running's not the best idea. I say we wait to get rescued."

The others stared at him incredulously.

Tegh said, "Well, you can wait, if that's what you want. But I don't want to spend my time in a Chinese prison while they sort things out. I say we get as far away as possible, and the sooner the better."

Tears welled in Betta's eyes as she said, "How would they explain it when they can't find our bodies?"

Without hesitation, Tegh pressed his point. "They'd claim our bodies were consumed by the fire. Look, we don't have time to debate this. We need to distance ourselves from the crash site. Each of us is healthy enough to walk out of here, though you may need some help, Betta. So, we should start while it's dark."

Betta looked at Fritz. "What do you say?"

Seeing her waver, Fritz reconsidered. "Well, if you're willing, I'll go along." Looking directly at Tegh, he said,

"But I'm still not sure I can trust you."

Tegh made no attempt at rebuttal.

To break the tension, Steve said, "How bad's your ankle, Betta? Can you walk on it, or do we need to carry you?"

Betta said, "If someone can wrap it tightly, I'll be all right."

Tegh realized a compact had been struck. "All right, we have a decision. We'll move away from the crash site. We don't know where we are, where to find food, water, shelter, or in which direction to head, so before we trek on, I recommend we scrounge as much from the wreckage as we think we might need and can carry."

For the first time, Fritz acquiesced. "What do you want us to do?"

Steve didn't hesitate. "Check suitcases and stuff from the overhead bins for anything useful. There's bound to be things of value that survived."

Having made a decision and buoyed by their own survival, they set to gleaning the aircraft wreckage. Using emergency flashlights they found on the bulkhead outside the lavatories, in less than an hour, they had salvaged dozens of items. They found a treasure of foil wrapped dinners in the galley. A baggage container ejected from the plane's underbelly contained luggage and clothing. Additionally, they found a great deal of money. They took time out to change into shirts, long pants, serviceable shoes, and jackets. And what they couldn't wear, they packed as changes of clothing into the rescued backpacks.

Fritz, Tegh, and Steve sorted the money into mounds of individual national currencies. Steve pointed to the piles of yen, rupees, and several other national currencies.

He said, "Just take the dollars, euros, and yuan. The rest we don't need."

This caught Fritz's attention. "We're not going to take all the money?"

Stuffing the useful bills into a backpack and leaving the rest, Steve said, "Can't spend it anywhere we're headed."

While the men picked through baggage, Betta searched the tail section cabin. Miraculously, she found that the overhead bins above their seats had survived unopened. Rummaging through, she found their backpacks along with their passports. "Ah, we're in luck, guys."

Out of necessity, she opened the lavatory door to see if the toilet was still intact. Somehow it was, which prompted her to realize they'd need toilet paper, and for her, tampons. She opened the locker door and found a sufficient supply of each. Next, she searched the flight attendants' station and pried open a door. Inside were cartons of cigarettes, matches, a first aid kit, dozens of small liquor bottles and even an airline flight map. She stuffed a flight attendant's carryon bag full.

Finally, they took a moment to consider if there was anything else they should do before abandoning the crash site. Concerned with how much time they'd spent searching the wreckage, Tegh said, "If we're going to put distance between us and the crash, I suggest we get going. Betta, do you need help?"

She tested her foot, crying, "Uhh! I don't know."

Fritz put her arm over his shoulder. "Here, let's see how this works."

They stepped off in a modified three-legged-race gait.

"Unh! That's a lot better. I may not be fast, but at least I'm moving. Okay guys, stop gawking and get a move on."

They headed west, well below the mountain ridgeline. Within a few hundred yards they found a well-worn game trail, which made Betta's going more tolerable.

The stars blazed above in an eerily black sky. With no contaminating glow from towns or cities, they could easily see their footfalls and made relatively good time, considering Betta's condition, stopping every so often to let her rest. On the move again, Steve and Tegh alternated with Fritz as Betta's human crutch.

Finally, Tegh said, "The eastern horizon is starting to brighten. My guess is the sun will be up in about an hour. We'll need a place to rest so we're not walking in the open during daylight."

"I could use a rest," Betta said.

Tegh nodded and said, "Okay, let's stop here and eat. We can't risk a fire. Someone might see the smoke, but we can at least get Betta off that ankle."

They pulled airline microwave dinners from their backpacks and ate for the first time since the crash.

"Even cold, this tastes good," Betta said.

"Yeah, whoever thought we'd be saying that about a TV dinner," Steve said.

When finished, Steve picked up the trash and said, "I'll go downslope and bury this. We don't want a wayward hiker finding evidence of our being here."

Fritz lit up a cigarette and asked, "Who'd be out in this desolate landscape?"

Tegh said, "There are shepherds throughout this region. They're always moving their flocks to find summer grazing in these mountains. We've probably been following one of their trails for the past few hours." Thinking about their exposed condition, he said, "We should rid ourselves of any items the Chinese might use to track us. We should keep only what we absolutely need."

"Like what?" Fritz asked.

"Laptops and cell phones, anything with a GPS component. But keep your passports."

Betta asked, "How do you propose we get rid of them?"

"Go up the mountain a few hundred yards and bury them," Tegh said. "They'll never look in that direction. It's hard scrabble and it's difficult to track someone on that. The crash is well behind us and below the ridgeline. If they even suspect we survived the crash, they'll probably look downhill from the wreckage."

Fritz grumbled at having to part with his cell phone and tablet, but reluctantly agreed as he pulled the last cigarette from the pack in his shirt pocket. As he did, he felt something else in the pack. Shaking it, a plastic stick fell into his palm. On it was an odd logo of the sun with both Chinese and European writing: Sunku. He fidgeted with it for a moment.

"What do you have there?" Steve asked.

Fritz pulled on the ends of the stick and it separated. "It looks like a flash drive."

"Where'd that come from?" Betta asked.

Remembering, Fritz said, "I picked it up from one of those demonstration booths at the expo," he said. "I forgot I had it."

"Well, you'd better get rid of it with the rest of our hi-tech stuff," Steve said.

As they set about disposing of their modern technologies, Steve stepped away from the others and went several yards below the opposite side of the crest. He turned on his phone and, to his astonishment, he had a single signal bar. He realized it was a calculated risk to energize a device which could be geo-located. But he figured the Chinese had already determined where the plane had crashed and a brief stray electrical signal wouldn't attract attention. He dialed the international carrier number for his father. The phone on the other end rang several times and went to voice mail.

"Leave a message," was the curt greeting.

Steve didn't hesitate. "Dad, if you get this, I'm okay. I'll let you know more when I can."

He broke the connection and removed the battery and SIM card, which he threw as far down the slope as possible. Then he dropped the phone and crushed it beneath his heel before climbing back up the ridge to rejoin the others.

Chapter 4

TRANSPORTATION INVESTIGATION HEADQUARTERS, XI'AN, CHINA

LIN CHU, THE First Director of the MSS Transportation Investigation Division in Xi'an, was starting yet another day in his bureaucratic purgatory. A mediocre career security official, he'd been relegated to this backwater station to retire quietly, out of the spotlights that were the MSS Beijing hierarchy. Lin had accepted his fate and held little hope of returning to the good graces of senior officialdom.

As an experienced manager, however, he was up to the task of directing the MSS Department of Transportation's mundane activities. China was the third largest country in the world and had a massive transportation system that moved a billion people every month. Lin knew the department's inner workings well. But the reality remained: in the hierarchy of the national government, no Beijing functionary cared what went on at Transportation, as long as they didn't rock the ship of state. Foreign Service, Military, Agriculture, and Industry—those were what the government bureaus deemed important, not the ticket takers and schedulers in Transportation.

As he started yet another routinely busy workday, Lin hoped everything would operate as smoothly as possible and not mess up his plans for a quiet last few months before he could retire. Though a minor functionary in a very big bureau, Lin enjoyed the few perks of his position, like the occasional use of the vacation villa. More importantly, however, he abhorred the interminable meddling by senior functionaries. Once, he'd been an ambitious bureaucrat, seeking chances to climb the ranks. But now, he was satisfied with only making the well-oiled functions of his department work efficiently.

Lin stood in front of dozens of his workers until they quieted. Today his address was short. "We do important work. Give your best effort. Something must be wrong out there with all the traffic were responsible for, so let's find it." Silently he mused that it was inevitable that complex systems such as the one he was responsible for failed, crashes occurred, and people were injured and killed. But he silently hoped, not today.

With unimpressed resignation, the workers returned to their monitors, schedules, and teletypes as the bustling grind of routine business resumed. And that's the way the day proceeded—routine. Routine, that is, until just before the end of the workday when the undercurrent of office humdrum was interrupted and the duty officer's printer came to life. It spit out a terse, one-paragraph report as its alarm bell dinged. A preoccupied watch officer, looking forward to shift end, listlessly tore the printout from the machine.

When he scanned it, however, his eyes widened. He immediately walked to the small office just off the work floor bullpen. Excitedly, he said, "First Director Lin, there's been a plane crash. China East Airlines reports air airliner out of Xi'an crashed in the Qilian Shan in Gansu Province."

After years of toiling in lowly assignments and with the reality of his limited competence having all but set in, Lin recognized this event as a glimmer of hope. This wasn't just something else Lin would have to resolve to preserve his anonymity until retirement. No, this was his chance to get back in the mainstream—his chance for reprieve. Resolving crises was something he was good at.

The only problem with the dispatch was it meant he'd have to deal with the incessant questions from his boss the minister, whose only concern was in keeping the heat off himself from the higher ups in the Beijing. Lin was quite content with the way his job usually went—no hassles. As a matter of personal pride, Lin silently vowed, *I'll prove to the general that I'm capable.*

Lin rattled off questions to his staff. "Do we have a passenger list? Has someone checked if there was anyone of importance on the manifest, anyone who should demand special attention from the ministers?"

"I have that being pulled now, sir," the watch officer replied.

The phone rang on First Director Lin's desk and he picked up. As soon as heard the voice, he was filled with dread. "Yes, sir, I will, sir. No, we have not, sir." He put the receiver down and looked up. Lin's eyes glistened with the purpose he'd prepared his entire career for—an opportunity he thought would never come.

"Get me the MSS watch commander on the phone. No, have him come to my office. It seems we have unaccounted-for deportees to recover."

He inwardly gloated. The phone call from headquarters reported that four passengers were missing; and from conditions at the scene, they couldn't be presumed dead. The passenger manifest listed them as unescorted foreigners under expulsion decrees and no longer welcome in the People's Republic.

The contempt Lin silently reserved for his bureaucratic bosses was replaced by a glimmer of hope. *Fortune has given me an opportunity — the ticket I needed. If I can locate the fugitives, I'll be in line for the long overdue recognition I deserved for my steadfast loyalty over the years. But, one misstep and I'll be cashiered to an even worse ignominy than I've endured. If I complete this task successfully, the MSS Director himself will know that I, First Director Lin Chu, is the one who thwarted this threat to China's internal security.*

Turning to his watch commander, Lin said, "Watch Commander, I'm going directly to the crash site to supervise the investigation to ensure our field workers follow proper disaster protocols in recovering remains. Then, I'll lead my team in tracking down the four missing persons."

But, the elation on Lin's face faded as he read a headquarters' dispatch one of his watch standers handed him. It read, "General Wu Xi arrives tomorrow to take personal charge of the investigation."

The stakes for him had just been raised. It was rare that a general officer showed interest in the Investigation Division of the Transportation Directorate, much less left the headquarters building for a field visit. Lin thought, *this is a big deal. I must not allow this bureaucratic fool to steal all the credit.* Then, unconsciously he muttered, "Why does he need to bother the local commander with such a trivial task as finding bodies?"

No one replied, but he had their attention. Rereading the notes on his desk monitor, Lin addressed the office.

"One of the missing persons is an American, the son of a US military general. Two others are German nationals accused of trade sanction violations. And the last fugitive is a Mongolian Uighur sympathizer, involved in civil disorder at Xi'an University. They all face additional charges of," and here he read from the text of a message, 'resisting arrest and assault on security personnel'."

First Director Lin Chu took rapid stock of his situation. Was it possible that, of all the people on that plane, these four persons actually survived? If they did, could this be an infiltration plot? *This just may be my opportunity to resurrect my promotion prospects and rise above this outpost.*

This further steeled Lin's determination to embrace the opportunity and give Minister Wu Xi—a man who was all business with party connections, a man who loved the perquisites of power—no, not give, but serve up to the general these missing individuals on a silver plate.

As he contemplated his resolve, the private phone on the First Director's desk rang. Picking up he said, "This in Lin Chu."

A stern voice on the other end said, "First Director, this is General Wu."

Lin's heart sank.

"I was just informed by our counterintelligence directorate that one of those missing from that CEA flight is wanted for espionage."

"Espionage? I don't understand, General. I was told…"

"It seems that the German attending the trade expo in Xi'an stole a flash drive from one of the exhibits. The software contained on that device was dual purpose, developed by the Sunku Corporation. Besides its commercial utility, it is also used in the guidance system software for some missile applications. It is imperative that we track this agent to ground and regain control of that device."

Chapter 5

HILLS ABOVE THE GANSU CORRIDOR, WESTERN CHINA

THEIR ELECTRONICS BURIED and any traces of disturbed ground brushed away, they returned to their backpacks and sat down to rest. Suddenly, Fritz said, "If what we want is to distance ourselves from the wreck, then resting where we've disturbed the ground isn't a good idea. I'm just saying, let's move a farther along."

A tired Betta looked pleadingly at him, but it was Tegh who said, "Actually, Fritz makes a good argument. This is desolate countryside and our chances of being spotted are slim."

"Especially if we stay below the ridgeline so we won't be silhouetted against the skyline," Steve said.

Tegh said, "Good point, Steve. The farther we get from the crash, the better are our chances of getting out of here."

Steve asked, "So Tegh, exactly where is 'here'?"

"Exactly? I don't know, but we're in the Qilian Shan Mountains and that's the Gansu Corridor," Tegh said, pointing to the valley below. "It's a six-hundred-mile finger of arid land leading from central China to the western regions of the country. Over to the north is the Gobi Desert and to the west is the Taklimakan Desert. This is some of the most sparsely populated countryside in the world."

Betta looked at her business partner and said, "Fritz, it's not often you come up with a good idea, but you make sense." Then, she begrudgingly hobbled to her feet and put on a brave face as her bad foot touched ground. Steve moved to help her and she put an arm around his neck.

Tegh said, "Okay, fellas, let's get a move on like Fritz said."

With each man taking turns in helping her, they moved out. With the sun now high in the sky, Betta was overjoyed when Tegh finally raised his hand to stop.

"I see a gully wash down there where we can find water. Beneath that rocky outcropping should be a good place to stop."

Fritz helped Betta down and got her settled while the others made themselves as comfortable as wilderness circumstances allowed. Using backpacks for pillows and extra clothing for shade, they soon fell asleep, exhausted from the events of the last eighteen hours.

With an early afternoon sun in the sky, Betta awoke with an urge to go to the bathroom. She nudged Fritz. "Help me get up so I can go to the bathroom."

Not very quietly, he got her to her feet, waking the others in the process.

"What's wrong? Is Betta okay?" Steve asked.

"I'm all right, gentlemen," Betta said now embarrassed. "It's just that I need a little help, and some privacy!"

"Oh," chorused Steve and Tegh.

A few minutes later, they dug through their packs for food.

"No sense in trying to get any more sleep," Steve offered, holding up an airplane dinner. "We might as well eat while this stuff is still fresh. Chicken stir fry, anyone?"

They ate cold airplane leftovers and when finished, Betta asked, "Shouldn't we get going again? I'm sure they've discovered the crash site and are looking for us."

They looked to Tegh, but it was Steve who commented. "This is the heat of the day. I'd think waiting a couple more hours until the sun's lower would be to our benefit. This area is as arid as I've ever seen and I'm guessing our chances of finding more water are slim. So, let's top off everything we can carry while we can. And lastly, Betta, waiting a few more hours will give you more time to recuperate."

It was Fritz, surprisingly, who said, "It makes sense. Let me know when it's time to go.

Betta said, Fritz "Good to see you going along for a change, Fritz."

With nothing to do but wait, Fritz lit a cigarette and asked, "Tegh, with you being a student, what did you do that was so bad to rile up the government? You're Chinese, right?"

Tegh, not the least bit put out by his question, said, "I grew up in Mongolia, about eight hundred miles northwest from where we're sitting, but I was born in China, the only son of a Uighur goat herder. As a youngster, I walked across land much like this, taking livestock to market with my father.

"Being Uighurs, we moved to Mongolia to avoid Chinese persecution when I was eight. My father wanted me to get an education to afford me a chance to do something besides herding goats. So, off I went to Almaty, Kazakhstan, for my secondary education, where I lived with my great aunt's family. While in school, I became enamored with Chinese folklore.

"To further my interest in my heritage, I attended Xi'an University for graduate work. It was there that my roommate got sidetracked into political activism. Believing I was someone who abetted his actions, the police rousted me from my room. I told the MSS I wasn't involved in my roommate's activities, but when they found some of his pamphlets in the flat, they forced me to leave China. That's how I came to be on our China East Airlines flight. When I argued with that guard in the detention lounge, that didn't help my cause. It further branded me as a dissident."

His explanation was matter-of-fact and unemotional. Betta nodded her understanding, but Fritz raised a skeptical eyebrow.

Seeing this, Tegh added, "You're from the West and may find this hard to believe, but all four of us have the same problem. We each broke political rules, which may seem harmless to you, but in China that's not—"

Steve interrupted. "But I didn't do anything except get put on the wrong flight."

Tegh fixed him with a knowing look. "But you stood up to their head guard. And no matter how innocent or justified you may think that was, in China, it's not tolerated. That's why we have no reason to believe we'll be treated other than as dissidents if they find us. So, I suggest we work together on what we're going to do to avoid being 'rescued'."

It was quiet for a moment as a rustling breeze blew up the mountain. Then Betta squared her shoulders and looked Fritz in the eye. "Stop being a putz. We're in this together, so you might as well contribute to the solution."

Fritz couldn't meet her stare as he stubbed out his

cigarette. Betta patted his shoulder.

Suddenly, the quiet was interrupted by an alien trampling sound coming from the nearby scrub brush. Just as surprisingly, a young man appeared and came to an abrupt halt. He was startled at encountering four strangers. Everyone remained stock still, unsure of each other's intentions.

At first, Betta thought this was just another survivor, someone from a different part of the wreckage who had miraculously lived through the ordeal and had stumbled across them. His dirty garb didn't arouse her suspicions, since they were all looking disheveled now. It was Tegh's sudden outburst, however, that put fear in her and made her realize this boy might not be friendly.

Tegh barked, "Stop right there. Who are you?"

Though he wasn't carrying a weapon, Betta could tell the boy was cowed by Tegh's larger stature.

The teen responded slowly. Tegh translated. "He's a shepherd and saw the light come from the sky and disappear into the hills. He says he lives in a small herders' village in the foothills east of here."

Tegh demanded, "Are you alone?"

"Shi, yes, I came to see what happened. That's all. My name is Kulin."

Skeptical of his story, Tegh shook his head, needing more information. He explained this to his companions, then began interrogating the shepherd.

The boy explained, "My father tasked me to round up the last of our summer grazing sheep from the hills. I'd made a field camp and had just put my dinner on the fire when I saw the plane crash higher up in the mountains. This morning, I followed the burning smell and found the smoldering wreckage. I searched the plane but couldn't find anyone alive. It was then I saw your tracks and followed, until I heard voices."

Tegh turned to them and said, "I believe him." He fished through his backpack and pulled out a candy bar. Offering it, he said, "Here. Go ahead, it's okay." He waggled the chocolate.

Fritz started to object, but Betta nudged him.

Kulin looked at the candy bar as if it were a mythical treasure. He took it and ate greedily.

Fritz looked with alarm at his cohorts. "If this kid can find us, then there's no telling when the authorities will be here. And what about him?" Pointing at Kulin, he said, "It's mighty coincidental he shows up after the crash just as we're trying to leave."

Betta's brows shot up. "Oh my God, Fritz! Will you give it up? He's a shepherd boy. Look at him. Does he look like the Stasi?"

She spoke in German, so neither Tegh nor Steve understood, but they couldn't help but notice that her remonstrance had the desired effect of silencing his objection. Fritz sulked, lit a cigarette, but said nothing.

Steve offered, "So, we're good here?"

Fritz took a long drag and blew a smoke cloud, but didn't reply.

Steve said, "Okay, now what are we going to do?"

Tegh raised a conciliatory hand. "This kid, as you call him, is experienced in tracking lost sheep among the rocks and scrub. It's no wonder he found us. But, it's only been a short while since the crash. It will take authorities at least another day to find the crash site and several more to sort through the wreckage to determine, if they ever do, that someone's missing."

Steve said, "But that still doesn't solve our problems of what we should do now and what to do about him?"

They were searching each other's faces for an answer when Kulin said, "What are you going to do?"

When Tegh translated, they laughed at the irony.

Finally, Tegh said, "Fritz's initial recommendation of getting farther away is still valid. Come dusk, we'll continue in the direction we were heading, travel through the night, and camp again at sunrise." He looked at Betta with her ankle propped up and said, "I'm still worried about Betta's limitations."

Betta readjusted her foot and winced. "I think it's getting better, or at least it doesn't feel worse."

Steve offered, "If there were some sturdy branches in the gully we can use for a splint. Fritz, go see what you can find. Sit tight, Betta." He turned to Tegh. "Can I talk with you a minute?"

Betta sat in obvious discomfort as the men stepped away, out of earshot.

Steve said, "Tegh, her ankle's bad. It's not just swollen; there's an ugly red streak working up her calf from the ankle. She may have a cracked bone."

"What do you recommend? We can't stay here."

"Hey, I'm good at first aid and that's about it. Immobilizing it and keeping her off it is all we can do. I'll wrap it tight and splint it, but she shouldn't walk on it."

"How about a crutch? If Fritz can find a sapling, maybe we can get as much of her weight off it as possible."

"Okay, but let's not let on to her or Fritz about how bad we think it is."

Steve worked on Betta's ankle, wrapping it as tightly as

he could, Betta yelping every time he took a turn.

Watching the men's faces react to her grimaces, she said, "Look, fellas, it's a bad sprain; it's not broken. I can carry on. I just have to be careful."

Proud of her resolve but skeptical of her ability to do as she said, the men put on a good front.

By now, the sun was approaching the top of the mountains to the west and it would be dusk soon. Tegh took a moment to explain to Kulin their intention to move westward for as many miles as they could in the dark and would appreciate it if he would help them as a guide.

Kulin said he understood, but explained that his father was expecting him back by now and that he had to get home. Going with them put him not only farther away, but also made his eventual return that much more difficult to explain.

As Tegh explained their new dilemma, Fritz said, "What do we care? What do we need him for? We've made it this far without him. Let him go, we'll do fine."

Steve gave Tegh a what-do-you-think look when Betta interjected. "What's gotten into you, Fritz? Why don't you believe the boy? Of course he'd be a big help, he knows the area."

As the four of them discussed what to do, Kulin, hearing their ever-rising voices, edged cautiously a few steps away, momentarily forgotten.

Suddenly Betta said, "He's walking away. We can't let him go! Tegh, tell him not to!"

Kulin stopped.

Picking up on Betta's plea, Tegh said to his fellow survivors, "Look, our position is precarious. We just survived a plane crash. Though we're not as mobile as we'd like, we need his help. If nothing else, he's another strong hand to help with Betta."

Betta said, "What?"

It was Steve who explained to her without going into detail, "Betta, you really shouldn't put any weight on that foot." Then looking at Fritz, "Tegh's right, we're better off with him for as long as we can talk him in into it."

Pointing to Kulin, he added, "All your arguing is scaring the only person who has a clue where we are and who might be able to help us. I suggest you win him over, Tegh. And maybe, just maybe, we can get out of here in one piece before the police arrive and do who knows what to us."

It got very quiet. A breeze wafted crisp desert air with a barely perceptible scent of scrub pine. Betta nodded her agreement and, without waiting for Fritz to speak, Tegh addressed Kulin.

"Kulin, we'd like your help to get our bearings as to where we are and in which direction we should head. If you could, we would appreciate it."

The boy asked, "Do you have another candy bar? I haven't eaten since this morning." A broad grin broke across his face as Tegh reached into his backpack.

Betta breathed a sigh of relief. "Okay, crisis averted."

While the boy unwrapped the candy bar, Tegh explained what they needed. As Fritz lit up another cigarette, Tegh told them what Kulin had said.

"He says moving farther west is a good idea. Opportunists frequent—"

Fritz looked up. "Opportunists? Who the hell are they?"

Tegh paused slightly. "Bandits looking for a chance to enrich themselves at others' expense. People like that exist the whole world over. Now, Fritz, if you'll stop being an ass, let me finish telling you what he's said."

Fritz started to say something, but Betta stared him into submission.

Tegh went on. "Kulin says many people frequent these mountain trails and they surely saw the crash. Some could be here before the evening is out. To be safe, he suggests we head up the mountain to a col only a few miles from here."

Steve looked to Betta. "What do you think, Betta, up for it?"

Betta said, "As if I have a choice." Then she said to Fritz in German, "Promise me you'll trust this fellow and stop being such a schmuck."

Duly chastised, Fritz nodded.

Tegh reached into his backpack, pulled out more of their salvaged goodies, and gave them to the boy, who grinned, readily accepting the gifts. "I can help you until the morning after next. Then I must return to help my father get our sheep down the mountain to the winter pasture. Otherwise, he'll send my uncles looking for me."

As they trudged up the rough terrain, Betta asked Tegh, "Why is he agreeing to help us?"

"Two reasons. One, shepherds have a universal code of hospitality, and two, they have an equally pervasive dislike for the central government's authority over herdsmen such as Kulin's father. That, and the chocolate bars, will insure his silence on—Betta, are you all right?"

Chapter 6

FRITZ AND STEVE quickly got Betta standing again.

"Just silly me," she said, taking a moment to catch her breathe.

Seeing no damage was done, other than to her pride, Tegh said, "We'll slow it down a bit. Getting there is more important than how fast we do it."

Kulin kept them a hundred yards below the ridge, but Tegh was concerned they weren't making progress he'd hoped. Though Betta had taken to the crutch fairly well, it was very tiring for her and they'd have to let her rest more frequently.

As darkness fell, a waning sliver of a moon kept them company while they picked their way across unfamiliar terrain. Kulin confidently led them along the myriad of herding trails, which made the going at least easier for Betta, since she didn't have to pick her way through scrub and over rocks.

Just before sunrise, they stopped against a stony overhang. This modest rock purchase offered a respite thanks to a freshening wind coming from the valley floor. As they made a makeshift camp, Tegh pointed to the valley below.

"That's the Gansu, or Hexi Corridor. We're in the Qilian Shan, and those mountains across the valley are the

Flaming Mountains of the Bogda Shan. It's gusty here because the two mountain ranges funnel the prevailing winds along the valley. The sun will warm us soon, but for now, we should huddle for warmth. We still can't chance building a fire that might give us away."

For a while, idle chitchat kept their minds off their chilled and exhausted condition. Steve knelt to check the bindings on Betta's foot. As he did, she asked, "Why'd the plane crash?"

With a touch of sarcasm, Tegh said, "It's a Russian plane run by the Chinese. Besides being an old plane, the maintenance probably wasn't up to par."

"Wish I had known that before I let that Aeroflot lady sell me the ticket," Steve said, cinching Betta's ankle wrap tighter.

"Ouch!" she protested.

Steve patted her calf. "Sorry."

"You didn't have a choice, Steve?" Fritz asked.

Standing up, Steve said, "To be honest, I was so anxious to get going, I didn't ask."

Looking up from the cold airplane dinner Tegh handed her, Betta asked, "Tegh, what were you studying in Xi'an?"

Tegh liked the question, thinking, *maybe this is my chance to dispel Fritz's distrust of me.*

As he recounted how he'd come to Xi'an, Kulin stared at the foil wrapped tray he'd been given and wasn't sure what it was. Seeing Betta and Fritz peeling back the foil and eating with their fingers, he followed suit.

Steve asked, "Tegh, what's your fascination with the Silk Road?"

"I'm fascinated by ancient Chinese culture: The

Grand Canal, Great Wall, and Silk Road to name a few. More important than the goods they traded on the Silk Road were the ideas that flowed into China. The road stretched 7,000 miles east-west between Xi'an and Istanbul, with the first recorded account coming from a traveler in the fifth century BCE. China prospered from this trade which fostered commerce and helped Chinese rulers concentrate power into an empire."

"Too bad your studies got interrupted the way they did," Betta said, setting aside her finished tray.

Fritz made no comment as he too finished and lit up a cigarette.

Tegh continued. "The hardships of the Silk Road—bandits, thirst, terrain, and weather extremes—were conquered by ancient traveler's lust for adventure, wealth, alliance, and missionary zeal. Eventually the emperor made Chang'an, as Xi'an was called then, the capital of China thirteen hundred years ago."

Seeing Fritz's attention drift off, Tegh stopped, saying, "Forgive me, I'm getting carried away."

Betta said, "No, go on, it's fascinating. Other than Marco Polo, I'm clueless about Chinese history."

They laughed as Fritz said, "And he isn't even Chinese."

Tegh noticed Kulin looking around, lost without a translation. "No, we should get some rest. It was a long day."

Steve, yawned and stretched his arms. "I agree, today was no walk in the park."

"Fine by me," Fritz said, pushing his backpack next to the rock face. "I'll just put my back up against the rocks and get comfortable."

Seeing Betta wince as she tried to lie back, Steve asked, "You okay, Betta? It looks like your ankle's bothering you."

"I'll be okay with my weight off it," she grunted. But she accepted Steve's arm to ease herself back. He rummaged in his pack and found a salvaged first aid kit with a cold pack. He broke the internal chemical seal to activate it. "Here, I'll wrap it in place while you rest."

He stretched the wrap tightly across the cold compress, prompting Betta's protest. "Ouch, ouch..."

"Sorry, but I want to make sure the wrap holds the compress tight. Icing a sprain is the best thing for it."

He finished and pulled her pants leg over the top of the wrap. "That'll throb, but it should feel better come morning."

As they settled in, Steve caught Tegh's eye and motioned for him to step away for a moment.

Whispering, Tegh asked, "How does it really look, Steve?"

"The red mark hasn't moved. I guess that means it's not getting worse. I'm amazed she's able to tolerate it. I just wish we could get all her weight off it for a few days."

Not wanting to arouse suspicion with a prolonged absence, they returned to the overhang for some well-earned rest. Stars popped in and out of passing clouds. The sun would be up soon.

Near midday, Kulin tapped a sleeping Tegh's foot and motioned for him to follow. They made their way to a ravine that cut its way down the mountain where he'd seen a trickling stream. They filled their salvaged water bottles and hiked back to where the others slept. On the way, Tegh queried Kulin if there were someplace nearby where they could buy provisions. Kulin, well acquainted with the landscape, told him of one and as they returned to the group, Tegh reached a conclusion.

Shortly, the others were up and rummaging through backpacks for food. Tegh announced his proposed course of action. "Kulin says the town of Jiuquan is close by where we can replenish our food. While you rest, he and I'll go down the mountain, buy food, and investigate what, if any, reaction there's been to the plane crash. We should be back by early afternoon."

Alarm crossed Fritz's face. "You're leaving us! Why don't we all go to town? Is it safe being here alone, just three of us?"

Trying to allay his fears, Steve said, "Fritz, what do you think would happen if three Europeans walked into a small town in the Chinese backcountry and started poking around? Wouldn't that attract attention? For crying out loud, it's a remote village in Nowhere Fucking China. We'd stand out like sore thumbs. Tegh speaks the language and at least looks Chinese."

Tegh could see Fritz wasn't being contrary, but was truly worried about being left behind. He calmly said, "You can't remain anonymous, Fritz, but I can."

This had the desired effect and Fritz blew a cloud of cigarette smoke skyward as his way of acceptance.

Sensing a little more reassurance wouldn't hurt, Steve said, "Fritz, Tegh's got a good idea. For us to move out without getting a sense of where we are, what's around here, and who may be looking for us would be foolhardy. This way, he can check the rumor mill and determine exactly where we are."

Fritz seemed to be mollified now as he opened a new pack of commandeered cigarettes and lit up. The smoke curled through the dark stubble of his two-day beard as he gave a satisfying exhale.

Steve added, "Make sure you bury all those butts. If someone is tracking us, finding foreign cigarette filters would be a dead giveaway."

"Yes, Master," Fritz responded in mocking sincerity.

Seeing the impasse was broken, Betta said, "We shouldn't make any plans until Tegh and Kulin return from their reconnoitering trip. When we do move, by then we'll have the best information possible."

"Agreed," Steve said. "Let them scout out the town and pick up food and survival supplies. But as Fritz has been saying, we're still too close to the crash site. It's been just over a day. We still need to move farther away and let things settle down."

After pulling a few hundred yuan from their currency stash, Tegh and Kulin grabbed a water bottle each and headed down the mountain, following the natural contours of the ravine.

They'd been gone for several minutes when Betta discovered something while rummaging through their salvaged equipment. Examining the first aid kit, she found a GPS device. "Look what I found," she exclaimed.

Steve and Fritz moved closer and examined the small piece of electronics. She pushed a button and a dim green glow appeared on the tiny screen. Steve immediately said, "Turn it off until we absolutely need it. Better yet..." He grabbed it, yanked out the batteries, and threw them downhill. "There, now we won't have to worry. If we ever get somewhere safe, we'll get new batteries."

Fritz said, "Are you crazy?"

"Look, Fritz, I'm not trying to piss anyone off, but GPS devices can be remotely accessed, allowing someone to track our precise location."

"And how exactly do you know that?" Fritz challenged.

"Because my father's in the military and they do it all the time. He taught me a lot about situational awareness and I think it bears paying attention to. Maybe this gizmo has such a feature or maybe it doesn't. I don't know. But we shouldn't take the chance."

When Fritz started to raise and objection, Betta grabbed his forearm, and the strength in her fingers surprised him. "Ffrrriiitttzz," she said, drawing out his name. "We don't need this right now. Listen to what Steve's saying. It makes sense."

She felt the tension in his arm subside as he said, "I thought—"

"We need to pull in the same direction. So, what do you say?" Her voice softened, but her comment was no plea.

"What do you say, Fritz?" Steve offered his hand.

Fritz pulled away and took out another cigarette.

To put an end to the awkward moment, Betta said, "I wonder how long they'll be?"

Chapter 7

RESIDENCE OF MG WARREN APPLEGATE, SHAKER HEIGHTS, OHIO

THE PHONE IN THE study was on its third ring when a man with closely cropped gray-speckled black hair answered. "Hello." He accented the first syllable and let the 'o' of the second one drop off.

"Warren? This is Brad Gearity. Sorry to call at this hour, but I have bad news."

Brad Gearity was the Commandant of the Marine Corps. He had been Major General Warren Applegate's protégé several years earlier when the two had served together in Okinawa. At that time, then Brigadier General Applegate had been Colonel Gearity's division commander. But the colonel's outstanding leadership style and extraordinary performance record had impressed the Marine Corps' hierarchy into promoting him rapidly. Now, Warren's former pupil had risen to the top spot in the Marine Corps, effectively his boss.

"Yes, General, it's no problem. I'm used to late-night phone calls. I'm on leave in Ohio and just watching the football game on TV. Your news can't be as bad as the season's going for Cleveland. What can I do for you, sir?"

Always the professional, Warren Applegate deferred to his former pupil. But in the back of his mind, he knew the call wasn't about Marine Corps business.

"It's about your son Steven. I know from our embassy in Moscow that he and the other US citizens working there as NGOs heeded the State Department's evacuation warning to leave Russia when we levied sanctions on the Russian Federation. The Aeroflot flight he was supposed to be on was scrubbed and he was manifested on another carrier. It seems he was on that CEA flight that crashed in western China." He paused to let the message sink in.

Warren Applegate remained stoic. "Do we have any details? I knew Steven was on his way home, but I didn't know which flight. The cell phone coverage from over there is pretty screwed up. A call triggered my answering machine last night, but no message came through."

"Good to know. I'll get NSA to check that out, Warren. Our ambassador in Beijing tells us the Chinese officials have reached the crash site. The first reports are that there were no survivors. We've asked for permission to allow our National Transportation Safety Board to send investigators over to assist. So far, the Chinese haven't responded. To be honest, the Chinese don't have a good track record when it comes to cooperation of this sort. The first satellite photos I've seen show the plane broke up on impact and there was a lot of fire."

Warren Applegate had dealt with disaster notifications his entire life. But this was the first concerning his immediate family. Fighting decades of professional training at hearing the news, he sucked in a breath. "You don't smell anything like foul play, do you, sir?"

"They're not reporting any, and we've got nothing from our National Security Agency or satellite intelligence that would hint otherwise. The plane went down in a very remote region, south of the Gobi Desert in China's Gansu Province."

To a layman, the geographical reference would have meant nothing, but to the thirty-one-year veteran who'd spent most of that time in Asia, Major General Applegate was all too familiar with the rugged, remote terrain that the Commandant mentioned.

His lip quavered and it was all Warren Applegate could do to hold back his emotions. "Well, sir, I guess you've done all you can. We've both been through drills like this before. If I could ask, sir, let me know when you get anything new."

"You know I will, Warren. I'm sorry to have to bring you this news. I'll get you personal updates every day. I promise."

The line went dead. Warren replaced the receiver and stared out his study window. Surprisingly, he didn't doubt that Steven could have survived. A father never gave up hope, even a stoic like him. His next thought, however, was less hopeful. *At least I don't have to tell Gladys.*

His wife was in home hospice care, dying of cancer. Her bouts of lucidity were infrequent at best. In his long career, he had faced the specter of telling many a mother of the loss of her Marine Corps son. It was never easy. But this time, it would have been a burden too much for her to bear. Reluctantly, he decided to spare his beloved wife another hardship to endure—that one of her last thoughts would have to be of the passing of her son. She didn't deserve such news during what life remained for her.

Chapter 8

JIUQUAN, WESTERN CHINA

TEGH AND KULIN followed the rill down the mountain. In the steeper spots, they used clumps of brush to ease down embankments. As they carefully worked their way, Kulin explained that Jiuquan was by no means a modern town. From the boy's description, it was simply a waypoint on the national highway from Wuwei in the east to Yumen in the west. Kulin added that there was a military garrison north of the town, for what purpose, he didn't know.

Looking at the airline map he'd salvaged from the wreckage, Tegh realized Wuwei was two hundred miles to the east. While a city like that would certainly have most of what they needed, it was in the wrong direction. Yumen, as big if not larger than Wuwei, was over a thousand miles to the west.

Remembering what he could about Jiuquan from his grad studies, the little town they were approaching was one of ancient China's last outposts before the desert region. Tegh thought its remoteness made it a place less likely be discovered by police. With the staple supplies they could acquire in Jiuquan, they'd be able to reach Jiayuguan, a big city thirty miles west, in a few days, according to the map. Once there, travel options would be available.

Reaching the foot of the slope and within sight of the outskirts of town, Tegh decided on something he'd been wrestling with ever since Kulin had stumbled into their camp. He should caution Kulin not to mention their whereabouts to anyone they might run across in town or even to his relatives and friends when he returned home.

The boy took Tegh's admonition in stride, saying only that he understood because he and his father didn't care for the local police either. So as not to dwell on it, Tegh said, "Kulin, Betta's ankle is still bothering her. When looked at it last night, it was still swollen. I'd like to buy her some sturdier shoes."

The boy surprised him by saying, "Why have her walk? Why not buy her a horse?"

"A horse? How much would that cost?"

"Not much this time of year. I'm sure there's a farmer willing to part with one. Fall's coming, and for him, it would mean that much less fodder he'd have to stock up for the winter. Right now, farmers could use the money."

Tegh realized his guide was savvy about livestock. "I'll need your help negotiating."

"Do you have yuan?"

"A little," Tegh lied, not wanting to reveal how much he really had. Kulin was friendly, but he was still a stranger, and common sense dictated caution.

With that behind them, Tegh and Kulin proceeded to a market at the edge of town. From the animal dung littering the street, Tegh surmised there were animal pens nearby.

Rounding a corner, Tegh confirmed what his nose was telling him. There, bordering the main road into the town, was a livestock corral half-full of goats and sheep. Kulin pointed to the back of the fenced area where two horses were tied.

"He's not going to want to sell his ride home," Tegh cautioned.

Kulin only smiled. "He wouldn't have them here if they weren't for sale. In this land, everything's for sale for the right price. Wait here."

Tegh watched as Kulin greeted the farmer. After a few back-and-forth niceties, he could tell the two were negotiating in earnest. A singsong, expressive haggling went on for several minutes before they both grinned. Kulin turned to Tegh and said, "He's anxious to sell. Five hundred yuan for the small mare."

Tegh did the mental math. That was about €150 or $225, which seemed high. He turned his back and counted out 250 yuan and pocketed the rest. With yuan in hand, he handed Kulin the money. "Tell him this is what I can pay."

Kulin was obviously delighted that Tegh was playing the bartering game.

The farmer frowned, his face furrowed in dismay, as well as years in the sun, and said something to Kulin who gave the new offer to Tegh. "He says he can't go less than four hundred yuan."

Without hesitating, Tegh said, "Tell him 370 yuan and that includes her saddle and saddlebags."

When Kulin translated the offer to the farmer, he gave the impression that what had been offered was an insult, but he accepted.

Leading their new purchase down the street, the two perused the offerings of the wet market where merchants displayed their goods under makeshift awnings in front of stores. Produce, dry goods, and household utensils were in abundance. With no refrigeration, live chickens, ducks, and geese were tied by their feet and fluttered in the dust along the road. Mutton and goat carcasses hung in varying degrees of disarticulation from meat hooks, attracting flies as well as women eager to make purchases for their evening meals.

The aroma from mounds of brown, yellow, and red spices offset the repugnance of the offal. Patrons crowded their way through the maze of shopping stalls and the air was filled with the patter of merchants and shoppers striking bargains. Tegh found the collective energy of the shoppers invigorating.

Tegh explained, "Kulin, I must purchase enough fresh food to last for the next few days."

The two threaded their way through the stalls, stopping here and there to buy what they needed: dried beans and peas, vegetables, and three scrawny chickens. Seeing that Tegh intended to load his purchases on the horse, the merchant wrung the necks and plucked the birds for him.

Tegh thanked him and they moved on to tables stacked with ripe melons and onions, fresh smells that were tantalizing compared to the livestock pens and butchers' stations.

While Kulin filled the saddlebags, Tegh asked the vendor, "Where do you get the fresh fruit from in this dry countryside?"

The man replied, "It comes in fresh twice a week from Turpan, in the western desert."

Amazed at the old man's revelation, Kulin asked, "Desert? You farm the desert?"

The farmer explained.

"Turpan is in the Great Depression at the base of the Tien Shan mountains. Snow-melt gives us grapes and melons from there all year long."

Salting those facts away, Tegh surveyed what else he had for sale, finally settling on a small kettle, a ladle, and two water skins. From an adjacent stall, he purchased some Double Happiness Chinese cigarettes for Fritz and a jacket for himself, similar in style to what the farmers wore.

Leading the mare away, Kulin said, "That was very good. You drove a much harder bargain than I could have."

"I'm from horse country. Bargaining for horses is our way of life. Besides, I could tell that that first farmer really wanted to sell a horse."

As they walked towards town center, they passed beneath a single streetlamp in front of a small railway depot building. The teller's window was closed, and would probably remain so, Tegh figured, until just before the next train arrived. Tegh examined the railroad map beside the posted timetable schedule. The tracks ran from Lanzhou in the east for two thousand miles to the west and Urumqi, paralleling the national highway.

A female railway attendant in a rumpled uniform sat in an anteroom at desk with her feet up. Seeing the saddlebags and their stuffed backpacks, she said without moving, "Must check bag!"

A soldier standing idly out front, obviously intimidated by the woman, offered to show them to the baggage room, but Kulin explained they were just checking the schedule. Though a member of the official state authority in China, Tegh could tell by his disheveled appearance this security man was a far cry from the MSS guards he'd encountered in Xi'an.

A cloud of dust and diesel exhaust fouled the air when a heavy coal truck rumbled past. Kulin asked the soldier if the road continued to the center of town. He said it did. Kulin thanked him and they continued on. The railway attendant never moved her feet from her desk.

The landscape consisted of scattered birch and poplar trees edging meager fields of cabbages, hay, and beans. A few people walked on the shoulder of the road, while others rode bicycles or led donkey carts. All were lean, wiry folks—no chubby children or fat matrons. But what caught Tegh's eye was a sprinkling of people who didn't manifest characteristic Asian traits. They had green eyes, prominent noses, and natural reddish-blond hair.

Several blocks farther on, they came to a bus station that offered peasants a cheaper travel option than did the train. Like the train depot, it was closed and would remain so until a few minutes before the next scheduled arrival or departure.

Now they found standard building storefronts with window displays of dry goods and farm implements. Clothing was arrayed on racks in front of stores to entice passersby.

In the town proper, more people were in evidence and the main street was choked with the dust of increased bicycle and vehicular traffic. What breeze there was blew a settling ash from residential coal and dung fires. A single hotel dominated the main street. Curiously, Tegh noted chirping birds roosting in its porch eaves in attempts to avoid the heat. A man sat on his haunches on the porch, eating a melon slice and spitting seeds. His canvas pack lay next to him. Tegh tied the mare to the porch railing. Sensing a treat nearby, his horse stretched her neck to nudge the squatter's haversack, looking for some tidbit.

They entered the hotel. In the lobby sat four people at a table to one side. A man seated with three others noticed the newcomers and invited Tegh and Kulin to join them for tea, a traditional hospitality. As they sat the man said he was the town doctor. He introduced a nurse, a midwife—much older than the nurse—and a soldier. From the soldier's laid back demeanor, Tegh assumed he was much like the guard at the train station, that is, not so much an emissary of the central government, but more like an unfortunate civil servant biding his time in a remote duty station.

Looking at the meagerness of the possible medical support the three others offered, Tegh guessed the doctor and his staff offered minimal medical care: preventive practice, minor illness, and common injury treatment. Anyone suffering more serious issues would undoubtedly have to be transported to a provincial hospital where better trained doctors and staff resided. A faint antiseptic smell permeated the air, which made Tegh wonder if he actually practiced medicine in a portion of the lobby.

To put the three locals at ease, the doctor explained that conversing with strangers would bestow on each of them good jinn and grace, for which they would gain face. Tegh thought it would also break the monotony in a place where he guessed visitors weren't that common.

The three nodded their understanding, but did not offer a greeting. Gaining tacit acquiescence, the doctor served tea along with some stale biscuits.

Looking around the lobby, Tegh saw it contained unupholstered, wood-slat furniture, some farm scene black-and-white photos, and a few crocheted items for decoration. Along two lobby walls, a wainscoting of white tiles, painted with a single-line of blue tulips and bordered by scalloped arches, provided the only color in what remained a dun-colored background surrounding faded furnishings.

The soldier vigorously nodded his thanks, causing his black cowlick to bob up and down. He looked amiable enough in his army great coat and soon added to the meager conversation by lamenting there wasn't much to do in the town. He'd come here straight from basic training and was charged with standing his post at the various commercial businesses in town, looking for what, he wasn't sure, admitting that being this far from Beijing, he'd yet to run across anything out of the ordinary.

Tegh thought, *good, that tells me the authorities, at least here, aren't looking for us.* Then, in attempt to spur conversation, Tegh asked the doctor, "Why do I see Chinese people with blondish-red hair?"

"Mmm, yes, they're most certainly Chinese, but their ancestors were foreigners, descended from captured Roman Legionnaires in 55 BCE. Over the centuries, their survivors left a part of themselves embedded in successive generations."

Tegh said, "I've never come across that in my university studies."

Seeing his interest, the doctor said, "Yes, western China has many interesting things about it. My nurse and midwife were assigned here thirty-four months ago by a central public health committee. We know not only Western medicine—antibiotics and general surgery—but also Eastern holistic practices—acupuncture, indigenous-inspired medicinal remedies. We borrow from each discipline as needed to serve our patients."

As he listened, what struck Tegh odd was a door behind the doctor which he guessed lead to his clinic. Even though the doctor said he was schooled in scientific methods, there was an astrological chart posted next to his office door. *Ah, do no harm,* thought Tegh.

As the doctor went on, Tegh suddenly had a thought of how to remedy their situation better than simply with the food supplies they'd gotten. "My helper's mother has a severe ankle sprain and…" He described the swelling on Betta's ankle, the purplish hue, and the angry red streak that had appeared, careful to reveal any other details. "…ankle wrap and splinted it. Is there anything else we should do?"

The doctor listened carefully to Tegh. Then he turned to his nurse, who listened to his instructions and left the table for the star chart-festooned clinic door. While she was gone, the doctor asked if they wanted more tea. By the time he'd finished replenishing cups, she returned holding a capped paper cup and paper packet.

The doctor thanked her and said to Kulin. "This will help your mother. The cup contains salve which you should apply liberally twice a day. Put a small amount of this powder," he said, holding the packet, "in tea or water when she arises in the morning and just before bedtime. I think you will see improvement in a few days."

Kulin nodded his thanks.

Tegh sniffed at the salve in the cup and recoiled at its

offensive odor. Handing it to Kulin, Tegh reached in his pocket and removed some yuan, but the doctor held up his hand saying, "No need for that, my friend. That is what we are here for."

"Well, on her behalf I thank you," Tegh said.

To fill an awkward silence, Tegh asked, hoping he might glean some recent news, "What are the villagers like?"

"They are people, how do you mean?"

"I mean, how do they amuse themselves; how do they make a living; what do they do for fun?"

"Fun? Our lives are dedicated to building the frontier, to making progress."

"But progress towards what?" Tegh pressed.

"The goal they set for us," the doctor replied.

"Who are they?" Tegh finally asked in frustration.

The doctor shifted his gaze between Tegh and Kulin without expression. His eyes betrayed no sense of misunderstanding. They simply didn't hint that there would be an answer to Tegh's query.

The midwife took out a small cigar from her skirt pocket, but before she could light up, the doctor said, "Laotaipo, not in the clinic. Go out to the porch. Since when did you switch from cigarettes to those little brown cigars?"

"Since I decided to have some fun like the young people just suggested."

As she stood, the soldier reached into his coat pocket for his own cigarettes. "I could use a smoke too." Turning to Kulin he said, "I see your horse tied up outside, want to go give him an apple while these old people talk?"

Kulin stood and followed the midwife and soldier

outside. Tegh wondered what the lad was up to.

The doctor said, "You will pardon my midwife, please. She seems to feel at ease with younger folks."

The nurse gave a soft grunt of disapproval of the midwife's actions and turned her attention to Tegh, offering to pour more tea. Tegh nodded agreement. Then the nurse asked a seemingly innocent question. "What brings you to our frontier outpost?"

Tegh knew she couldn't possibly have suspected his real reason. Thinking quickly, he replied, "Auntie, I was studying Chinese art in Almaty and decided I needed to see the real thing, rather than simply read about it."

"You won't find much art here," the doctor interjected. "But in Jiayuguan to the west, you'll find examples in the caves painted by Buddhist missionaries centuries ago."

Although Tegh knew of such examples, if not those specific ones, he feigned interest. Seeing this, the doctor said, "The road you're on now passes through Jiayuguan and extends west to Aleppo on the Mediterranean Sea. For thousands of miles, it skirts deserts, climbs mountains and crosses great rivers."

"You make it sound like that ancient road still exists."

"But it does. The road allowed people to eke out a bare subsistence year after year. Great Wall remnants still exist on the ridge tops bordering the road to the north. The Gansu Corridor was the only way into or out of China. All other routes were prohibitively impassable."

When the nurse cut in to explain other nearby historical sites, Tegh didn't give her his undivided attention. Instead, he was more concerned at having Kulin out of his sight and talking with a soldier.

Seeing Tegh's distraction, the doctor asked, "Is

something wrong?"

"No, no, it's just that he's my friend's boy and I don't want him outside alone with strangers. Besides, he and I must get going. "Thank you for the tea." To the nurse, Tegh said, "I'm sure our friend will benefit greatly from the medicines you've provided.

They didn't get up but smiled warmly as Tegh rose and left.

Outside, Kulin was sitting on the porch, the mare craning her neck to take bits of apple he offered while the soldier sat next to them, enjoying a cigarette. The midwife sat on a weathered bench in the shade nearby with her cigarillo.

Tegh pointed to the soldier, who was looking down the street, and asked Kulin, "Everything okay?"

Kulin said, "He's just bored to death with garrison duty in this town."

"We need to be heading back. There's still a few things I need to pick up."

As Kulin turned to say goodbye to the soldier, Tegh said softly, "No, just get the horse and let's go. I want to leave as little of a lasting impression on the locals as possible. I don't want them remembering us."

The two led the mare back the way they'd come. The soldier never turned around, so interested was he in watching two women farther up the street. A block away, the two found a merchant with clothing and other life essentials out for sale. Tegh sorted through knit caps, shirts, pantaloon trousers, and undergarments.

As he held several selected items up for inspection, Kulin said, "These would be good for your friends to wear. Much better than what they wear now."

Tegh made his purchase, this time not bothering to haggle on price.

But the merchant, determined to make as much as he could from the strangers, asked, "Do you need shoes?"

Tegh nodded and the man motioned for them to follow him. Leaving the mare tied to a hitching post, they turned onto a street that paralleled the main road and walked until they came to a store with shoes in the window.

The merchant said, "Be careful. Don't stare at the shoemaker. He has only one good eye and is very sensitive. To make notice of someone's deformity is considered bad luck."

Tegh thanked him.

The cobbler fitted Tegh with an over-the-ankle boot that snugged his foot quite well. When it came to paying for them, the cobbler, sensing that Tegh wasn't local, hinted that he could give a good discount if he paid in other than yuan.

Tegh held up a €5 note. The cobbler titled his head for a better look with his good eye and said something to Kulin, perhaps thinking the youngster was an easier mark. Kulin said, "He wants more."

Tegh pulled out an additional €5 note and the shoemaker's face broke into a broad grin. Now that the stilted formality of business was concluded, the merchant asked Tegh where he was headed. Tegh realized the cobbler would remember their encounter. While pondering his response, Tegh struck upon an idea for planting the seeds of deception.

"I'm looking for a ride east to Zhangye, which is only three hours by train, but your depot is closed." Tegh knew the city was supposedly Kublai Khan's birthplace, not an unusual destination for a visitor to the region.

The cobbler said they should have no trouble in catching a ride on one of the trucks that passed frequently on the highway, if they didn't want to wait for the train.

Tegh thanked him and they headed back to retrieve their horse. Standing there was the young soldier they'd left at the hotel. Thinking quickly, Tegh knew there was no way the lad wouldn't remember them, should authorities ever ask him, so he decided it best to make a good impression. Remembering the young soldier had been smoking a cheap brand of Chinese cigarettes, Tegh offered him a pack of a European brand he'd salvaged from the plane, which the young man gladly accepted.

A confidence hopefully won, Tegh engaged him in casual conversation. Though it was apparent the soldier harbored no sense of concern at seeing strangers in town, Tegh remained wary. He learned that the soldier was part of the garrison at an army installation just north of town. Listening carefully, Tegh never heard him mention a recent plane crash or of efforts by authorities searching for foreigners.

The soldier did, however, impart one bit of useful information. He told them that a new directive from the central regional government permitted local police stations to issue visas for travel to China's western neighboring nations, from Kazakhstan to Turkmenistan. Immediately, Tegh realized that egress from China to the west had just been made easier.

BY EARLY AFTERNOON, Steve, Fritz, and Betta were starting to worry.

Betta, said with much concern, "I hope nothing's

happened to Tegh and Kulin."

Steve said, "They're fine, I just know it. You must remember they're on foot and it's several miles down to the town and now the same distance uphill to get back. So relax."

As usual, Fritz was taking out his anxiety on a cigarette, almost a pack consumed already that day. "Hope you're right, Steve. I still don't believe that kid is on our side if the police start questioning him, candy bars or not."

"Come on, Fritz," Betta entreated. "Think of something else."

Steve, afraid he was going to say something he'd regret, asked, "Are you two going to be okay here alone? I'm going to reconnoiter the surrounding area from up on the ridge."

Fritz stopped puffing his cigarette and looked warily at Steve. "You're not leaving too, are you, Steve?"

Steve dismissed his comment saying, "No, I just need some alone time. I won't be gone long."

Fritz tossed his half-smoked butt to the ground. "Hey, it's no fun for us either, Steve."

Steve offered with a hint of sarcasm, "Fritz, if it's okay with you, I need to be by myself for a bit. I'm just going to the top of the ridge to get my bearings. Stay here with Betta."

Betta, always the pragmatic one, said, "Stay with me, Fritz, while I nurse this ankle. The swelling's subsiding, but it's turning a beautiful shade of purple. Besides, you and I haven't had much time to talk. We've been on the move ever since the crash."

Her tactic worked and Fritz sat down next to her as

Steve trudged away. Fritz pointed to her elevated foot. "It's a good thing you spent so much time hiking back home. All that exercise toughened you up. Who knows how you'd have fared if you weren't in shape."

"Sure wish we were home now." Betta wasn't reminiscing; she was simply being honest. "These mountains are unnerving, and not knowing where we are is getting to me. Hey, do me a favor and see if there's some cream in that backpack to put on my face and neck. My sunburn's starting to hurt."

Fritz rummaged until he some antiseptic cream. "This is all I could find. At least it'll add moisture to your skin."

She dabbed the salve on the bridge of her nose, tops of her ears, and cheeks. She unbuttoned the top three buttons of her shirt to expose her shoulders. "Put some on my neck and shoulders, will you? Be careful, they're sore."

Fritz wasn't surprised by her boldness. More than once he'd watched Betta strip near naked for a swim in a Bavarian mountain lake. Not a shy girl, she wasn't provocative, just practical. Fritz had always hoped their relationship could have progressed beyond being collegial business partners, but she'd never given him any reason to foster even the hint of promise.

As he slathered her reddened skin, he asked, "Do you believe can we really trust the kid, Kulin?"

"Of course we can. Ouch."

"Sorry, I'll press more softly."

"Umm, that's better. Certainly, we can trust him. You saw his face when Tegh offered him the candy and money for his father. He's definitely on our side."

He stopped rubbing.

"What?" she said.

"Oh nothing, just thinking. Not important." He continued his ministrations, patting her shoulder lightly when he finished.

"Thanks," she said, shrugging her shoulders back into her shirt. "I wish I'd had the presence of mind to scrounge up a wide-brimmed hat from the passengers' luggage."

Just then, Steve returned and Betta asked, "What did you find?"

"More rocks, scrub brush, and gravel as far as I could see." He said. "It's pretty desolate. I couldn't see any evidence of search parties walking around, so that's good. I guess fortune is in our favor...for now."

Fritz said, "I was just asking Betta what she thought our chances are that—"

He stopped, and all three turned towards the strange sounds coming from just below the crest of the hill in the direction of the gully.

Chapter 9

HILLS ABOVE THE GANSU CORRIDOR, WESTERN CHINA

WITH A CLATTER of hooves, Tegh and Kulin appeared leading a horse with bulging saddlebags.

"I guess that answers your question, Fritz," Betta said.

Kulin had a big grin on his face as Tegh said, "Greetings. Wait till you see what we brought back."

Both men went over to greet their return and Steve said, "Well, don't just stand there, let's see what you got."

Tegh pulled off the saddlebag with the clothes, saying, "Kulin says you guys need to change into clothes that look more like what the locals wear. Try this stuff on. I hope it fits."

Steve and Fritz quickly shed what they'd been wearing since leaving the crash site and donned their new clothes, voicing their thanks at what he'd brought.

Betta, however, voiced mock concern. "I'm not thrilled with the look of these baggy pants," she said holding up a pair.

Tegh cautioned, "Don't be critical, Betta. Try them on. It's best you not draw attention to yourself in those Western-style clothes."

She laughed. "I don't care if it's Western, Eastern, or from a Shakespearean-cast costume. I don't suppose you thought to buy me clean underwear?"

Fritz and Steve smirked as Tegh explained apologetically, "It was difficult to figure out the size for you know… for what you needed… Well, they did have a lot of…ladies' things, but I wasn't sure how to describe your…" Tegh cupped his hands to his chest in a lame attempt to express himself, only to go speechless with embarrassment.

Fritz immediately offered, "Unmentionables?"

"That's a good way to say it." Tegh laughed, accepting the verbal rescue while Betta enjoyed his dilemma.

In mock disdain, she said, "Just like you men to think only of yourselves while we women have to suffer."

But her face lit up when Tegh brought out the bundle with her new underwear.

She held them up, only mildly curious at seeing the disparity in the sizes he'd brought.

Tegh said, "I bought three sizes of each, you know…"

She beamed and winked at him. "Something here will work. At least they're clean." Then, seeing he was still flustered, she added, "I'm just teasing you. Thank you, Tegh."

On impulse, she said, "Come here." He bent over for a hug.

Switching gears, she said, "And you brought us some food, and wow, a horse."

Tegh heaved a sigh, only too happy to be off the subject of her underwear. "I do have some good news. Kulin found out from one of the people we talked with that there's nothing circulating in town regarding search parties. There is a rumor, however, that the army found the crash site, but from what he could gather, the claim is there were no survivors."

He carefully didn't mention what he'd confided to Kulin about not tipping his hand regarding their presence in the hills. Instead he added, "And just to steer any questions anyone might have had regarding Kulin and me, I said I was looking for a way to catch an eastbound train back east to Lanzhou. The line in Jiuquan is the main east-west link in this part of China running from Xi'an in the east to Urumqi out west."

Steve shook his head. "That's a lot of geography for me."

Fritz said, "Me too. All I want to know is, where are we headed now? I'm still nervous we haven't put enough distance between us and the crash site."

"Jiayuguan," Tegh said, "is a big city thirty miles west of here. Once there, we can take a train or bus and make better time in reaching the western Chinese border."

Suddenly, what Tegh had said about laying a false trail registered on Fritz. "Hold on. Shouldn't we have discussed this heading east stuff before you went blabbing it to the locals?"

Tegh sighed. "I had to say something before they asked me or Kulin too many questions."

Fritz said, "Yeah, but I've been thinking —"

Tegh cut him off. "Look, I'm positive we didn't raise any suspicions. And if the authorities ever come asking questions, they'll just say they met two men travelling east. Besides, Kulin learned something else."

This got Fritz's attention, still not sure he trusted the boy. "Yeah, what?"

Deciding not to reveal that it was a soldier who had told Kulin, Tegh said, "The Chinese government is making it easier for people to obtain exit visas for entering countries to our west. That means getting into Kazakhstan will be that much easier."

Fritz countered. "I'm still uncomfortable with—"

Betta cut him off. "Fritz, quite being paranoid. What's wrong with you?"

Fritz said, "I know what Tegh said, but—"

Steve shook his head. "Tegh's right, Fritz. To your initial comment, moving farther from the crash site is good, but our best bet should be to get out of China as quickly as possible. So, let's agree that Tegh and Kulin did well and get moving as soon as possible."

"I agree," aid Betta offered. "Without Chinese visas, none of us really wants to remain here. Fritz, you and I have already been told to leave. Who knows how they'd react at finding Tegh, a known dissident, wandering around the countryside with us."

Fritz shook his head, still not completely won over with Tegh's having discussed any train travel while he was in town without discussing it with the group first.

Steve shifted tacks. "It sounds like the Chinese authorities don't believe anyone survived the crash, which means no one's looking for us right now. But, who knows when they'll figure out, if they do. And if they do, how will they know that those survivors would be us? So moving on is our best bet. I for one don't relish the prospect of being interrogated about how we came to be in the People's Republic."

Tegh said, "Steve's correct. We don't need to deal with Chinese officials. They dislike outsiders." Then, looking at Betta, he said, "We got you a horse, Betta, so you don't have to test your ankle and we'll make better time. It's already late afternoon. I recommend we rest some until dark, eat a good meal, then move west under the cover of darkness.

"And another thing, if you remember, Kulin's already said he could only help us for a short time before he had to return to his village."

Hearing Tegh's translation, Kulin took that as his cue to leave. But before he could say his goodbyes, Steve dug into his backpack and handed him a few hundred yuan. "Here, tell your folks you sold a goat or something. That should head off questions about what you were doing these past few days."

Kulin flashed a toothy grin and pocketed the money. Waving goodbye, he made his way spryly towards the east, in the direction they'd come. As he disappeared along the mountain trail, Tegh commented, "If he should encounter any searchers, they will surmise he made the trail in the brush and won't be suspicious. He's perfect cover for us."

Then, changing the subject, he said, "I think we can risk a small fire tonight for cooking, as long as we keep it small."

"Amen to that," Betta said with a grin.

While Steve built a fire, Fritz and Betta got out the last of the airline dinners to cook on the rocks next to it.

Betta said, "That will at least warm them up."

Tegh walked the mare a few yards away and hobbled her.

Within an hour, they were sitting cross-legged before a modest fire, enjoying their first warm food in a while.

Tegh looked at them. "You know, these blousy clothes are at least more comfortable."

Betta said, "But I wish you could have brought me a pair of boots. My ankle's still throbbing."

"I thought of getting all of us boots, but I would have only been guessing at the size," Tegh said. "Oh, that reminds me." He dug in a saddlebag and pulled out the salve. Without explaining about the doctor, nurse, and midwife, he said, "I was told this poultice will help the swelling."

Betta took a whiff of the container. "Ew," she said, recoiling from the smell.

"Don't knock holistic medicine, Betta," Tegh said. "Native remedies have worked for centuries, long before modern medicines came along."

Not convinced, she said, "I'll need a little help."

Fritz stubbed out his cigarette and bent to remove her bindings and splint. To her credit, Betta didn't seem to be in as much pain as the day before.

"It's looking better," Fritz observed, turning his head to avoid the noxious odor as he scooped a finger full of the purple salve and spread it liberally on her heel and ankle. "I think we'll have you sleep on the other side of the fire tonight, though. Wow, this stuff really stinks. At least you won't have to walk, Betta. You've got a horse to ride. Looks like there's room for you and the equipment."

Accepting this consolation, she said, "But we'll have to wrap it really tight again. That would still help."

Tegh and said while digging back into a saddlebag, "Oh, I forgot. I'm supposed to mix this powder," he held up the paper packet, "in some tea for you to help with the pain I guess."

"Oh joys," Betta said. "I hope it tastes better than this salve smells."

Tegh poured some hot water into a cup and mixed in the powder. "Here."

She drank it as the others watched for her reaction.

"And?" Steve asked.

"And nothing," she said. "It just tastes like tea." Taking a last gulp, she added, "Here's hoping my ankle will be good enough to walk on later."

"Walk?" Tegh said. "That's why we bought the horse. And with you on horseback, we'll make better time. Getting your weight off that ankle for another day or two will help it heal."

Betta gave an appreciative smile. "Okay, I guess we have a plan. I ride and you guys walk. Sounds good to me."

Fritz wiped his hands on a tuft of grass and then placed the cup of salve back in a saddlebag. "What's the name of this town again that we're headed for?"

Tegh said, "It's called Jiayuguan, and it's big enough to have travel options besides walking."

"Maybe we can exchange some of our foreign currency into Chinese money without drawing attention to ourselves," Steve said.

Tegh shook his head. "Exchanging money would require presenting a passport. We don't want to do that unless absolutely necessary."

Steve and Betta nodded their heads. Fritz took out the wads of bills from the saddlebag and separated them into dollars, euros, and yuan. The others amused themselves watching as Fritz tried to keep track of the sums in each of the three growing piles.

Finally, he said, "I'm betting we've got enough Chinese money to get whatever we need for a while. We've got well over a thousand euros worth here."

"I agree," Tegh said. "And we'll get more once we get to Jiayuguan and sell the horse. Then we can hitchhike or take a bus or train. Dressed like locals we'll blend in more easily. Our only concern will be to lookout for police check points and road blocks."

The others nodded solemnly, realizing it would be a while before they were completely out of the woods.

Steve broke the momentary silence. "My sense is that buying tickets on commercial transportation will be less risky than hitchhiking. And the farther and the faster we get away from Jiayuguan, the better." He poked the fire to await the Fritz-storm. The fire crackled, but no one said a word.

"Okay, then, west it is," Steve said, throwing the stick in the fire and sending up a cascade of sparks.

As Fritz stuffed the money back in a saddlebag, he said, "What the hell is this, these markings?"

Tegh looked at the symbols embossed next to the saddlebag's tie-down strap and recognized the Chinese military property symbols. *That rancher sold me a stolen horse.*

Chapter 10

HILLS ABOVE THE GANSU CORRIDOR, WESTERN CHINA

NOT WANTING TO alarm the others, Tegh shared his suspicions about the markings, saying only that they were the livery's logo—where the harness, saddle, and saddlebags had been made. Tegh knew that horse theft wasn't tolerated in a region where thousands made their living with livestock, and he hadn't had the common sense to ask for a bill of sale. No wonder the farmer was so willing to let him haggle down the price.

Tegh's mind raced with the thought that right now the Jiuquan police were hunting for a horse thief. *I'll be lucky if the search stops when they question that rancher.*

Not realizing Tegh's quandary, the others were satisfied with his explanation and turned their attention back to the dying fire. Tegh gave a furtive glance at the faces huddled around the campfire and realized they had enough to worry about and he shouldn't burden them with his dilemma. For the sake of something to talk about, Tegh suggested they reflect on what they'd been through during the past forty-eight hours and talk about how they were feeling now.

Rather than ask if they wanted to, Tegh started right in. "Thinking back to the plane crash, the engines sounded funny just before I was slammed into my seat. After that, I don't remember anything until I regained consciousness sometime after the crash."

"That's how I remember it," Fritz said. "The engines started making loud noises and then we hit."

Silence ensued as the other two hesitated. Tegh looked at Steve as way to urge him on, but he remained quiet, staring ahead at the glowing fire.

Betta, sensing his private moment, scooted her backside next to him and softly touched Steve's forearm. "Steve, I know it's difficult, but it would be good for you to tell us what you're thinking."

Steve felt her thigh press against his leg and the gentleness of her touch. He gave an audible exhale and patted the top of her hand. "Thanks. I'm okay. I was just thinking about how I was looking forward to getting back to the States and seeing my family. I'd been working as an NGO on an urban development project in Irkutsk, near Lake Baikal in Russia. I'd been there for over a year when the Russians invaded Ukraine and our State Department put out an urgent evacuation warning for US citizens, forcing me to make hasty arrangements to leave. At the last minute, Aeroflot cancelled my flight and put me on the flight to Xi'an. I was minding my own business waiting for my flight to Tokyo when two MSS guards shoved me in with you guys."

Tegh encouraged him to continue. "Did you have any close friends working your project?"

"Yeah, I guess as close as fellow workers working a long way from home can be. We hadn't known each other before hand, but yeah, we hung together pretty well." Then Steve gave a laugh.

"What?" Betta said.

"I just remembered getting to the airport in Russia.

There were four of us and we were all excited about going home. The night before a Brit friend of ours threw a Last Night in Russia party. Alex, he was the Brit, was an expert on inland fisheries working with his Russian counterpart on the Lake Baikal ecosystem. Anyway, there was lots of vodka and we all drank too much. Charlie, our group's Spanish civil engineer, was hungover pretty bad when we got to the airport. He was on that Xi'an flight, but we got separated at the ticket counter. In the hubbub of boarding, I didn't see him again." His smile disappeared as he drifted off in thought.

Betta patted his shoulder. "I think your friends sound like a good bunch."

Seeing that Steve needed a break, Tegh asked Betta, "How about you? We only know your recent history."

"I grew up near Stuttgart in what the allies called West Germany. My mom was, still is, a schoolteacher and my dad works in a public relations firm. I guess that's where I got my appreciation for the business world. After college, I worked retail jobs until realizing I could do a better job at designing outdoor wear than what the current companies were doing. So, I decided to go out on my own."

Tegh noticed Fritz was remaining aloof and urged him into joining the discussion. "Come on Fritz, it won't hurt you to share a little."

First lighting a cigarette, he said, "I lived in a village between Leipzig and Dresden, not far from the Czech border. I was raised by my mother and two older brothers because my father..." His voice trailed off.

Betta nudged him. "Go ahead, Fritz. You've been through this before."

Resignation clouded Fritz's face. "My father, he wasn't around. All my mother would ever say on the matter was he was an enemy of the state and that I was the happenstance of one of her conjugal visits with him in an East German prison.

"Anyway, I did well in school and loved sports, especially soccer. I played well enough to make it onto the regional soccer club when reunification came. A semi-professional soccer club in Munich brought me there where I played while taking business courses at university. I soon realized my soccer prowess paled in comparison to the stiffer competition I was now facing.

"I dropped sports, graduated, and began a career in clothing design. I was looking for a way to start my own line when I met Betta. And that's what brought us to China—to find new manufacturing ideas at the Expo in Xi'an."

He stopped and tapped a newly extracted cigarette lightly on the back of his wrist. Finding matches in his pocket, he lit it and took a long drag, tossing the spent match into the fire. With the embers all but dead, the others realized he'd emotionally rejoined the group. It had been a long day, but a good one. They lay down next to the stones encircling what was left of the fire for what little warmth it might offer and went to sleep.

In the dead of night, Steve got up as quietly as he could and picked his way through their small encampment, looking for a likely place to relieve himself. He'd gone a dozen yards when he heard Tegh whisper from behind.

"Where're you headed?"

"I gotta take a leak."

"Yeah, me too."

They finished and turned back to where they'd been sleeping. With their eyes fully adjusted to the dark under a full canopy of stars, walking was easier than the outbound trip.

"Mind if I ask you a personal question, Tegh?"

"Not at all."

"How come you don't wear a cap like I see some of the Chinese do?"

"You mean, Uighurs?"

"I don't know who they are, just that some wear them and some don't."

"First of all, I'm Uighur. But as a student in the heart of China, I chose not to draw attention to myself, despite what the authorities said when they came for me."

"Makes sense."

As they stepped their way towards the campfire, Steve said, "I thought you did a good job handling Fritz yesterday."

Tegh stopped, surprised by Steve's comment. "Thanks. I know everyone was mixed up from the shock of the crash. Being stranded with strangers in the middle of nowhere, in a foreign country no less, must be unsettling. And then a shepherd boy comes along, no wonder suspicions flared."

"Anyway, I thought you handled it well. Fritz is a bit of a bully. He'll bear watching."

"That's quite an observation coming from an American. You folks have a reputation for getting your way."

Steve muffled his laugh, fearing he might awaken the other two. "I don't think it's just Americans who push their weight around. We don't have a monopoly on that. The presidents of Russia and China are doing a pretty good job of that in their own right."

"You make a point. But with totalitarian regimes, it's easier to do than in a democracy. They have absolute control over their economies, military, and manpower and can pursue any adventure they choose. The situations in Ukraine and Taiwan being my case in point."

Steve, impressed with Tegh's grasp of the world situation, said, "Well, democracy can go a little haywire on occasion, especially if the leadership makes it sound like they have a panacea at the same time things at home look tough."

Tegh took Steve's measure under the starlight and liked what he saw. "Let's hope our leaders don't screw it up and leave nothing for us to enjoy."

"Enjoy is the right word, Tegh. Right now, I'm going to enjoy a few more hours of sleep while it's still quiet."

Chapter 11

NIGHT VISITOR, HILLS ABOVE THE GANSU CORRIDOR, WESTERN CHINA

FRITZ WAS THE first awake as the hint of dawn crept across the valley. He stirred the coals, coaxing sparks from the fire and producing the hint of a red glow from the embers. He threw on a few sticks to rekindle the flame and watched the modest blaze build. Then, feeling the urge, he made his way to the trail leading from camp in search of a place to relieve himself.

As he rezipped his trousers, he was startled by the sounds of something moving towards him from the rocks above. His first thought was it sounded like the rustling of clothing. Then he recognized the unmistakable sound of footfalls. Straining his eyes in the dim light, Fritz made out the image of a man, some hundred yards distant.

The grayish figure wore loose fitting pantaloons, a cloak pulled tightly around his shoulders, and a knit cap stuffed over his ears. He was carefully side-stepping his way down the mountain side, dislodging loose rocks as he made his own path and making no effort to disguise his presence.

Fritz shuddered, unnerved by the specter of this approaching shadowy figure in the near-darkness. The sounds of the interloper's heavy treads got louder.

Regaining his courage, Fritz stepped as stealthily as he could, and followed the lambent flicker of the campfire coals back to where the others lay, careful not to make a noise that would draw the intruder's attention. With the first rays of the morning sun, he could make out the lumps on the ground at the campsite. Recognizing Tegh, he stooped and nudged him. Tegh raised his head and Fritz quickly put his fingers to his lips indicating, shh.

Tegh looked up in confusion, but didn't make a sound because now he heard the noise, too.

On all fours, the two crawled behind some scrub for cover. The intruder was closer, still working his way downhill, probably only fifty yards in the direction of the trail. Tegh repositioned to a crouch and reached for his backpack. He knew they'd salvaged no weapons, but perhaps the mag-flashlight could be of use.

He motioned for Fritz to stay put and tiptoed to the mare, approaching so as not to startle her. She remained stock still. The last thing he wanted was for to her nicker. He slowly brought his open palm to her muzzle and let the horse catch his scent. She curled her lips, expecting a treat, but there was none. She made not a sound as Tegh ran his other hand over her withers, patting gently.

For the next few minutes, the scrambling sounds of the passerby slowly diminished downslope to the east of their campsite, not thirty yards away. Neither men nor animal moved a muscle except to keep their ears as keenly attuned as possible. Finally, Tegh returned to Fritz and whispered for him to get the other two up and to caution them to remain silent. By all indications, the stranger hadn't seen them and, thankfully, the breeze was blowing to the west so he hadn't smelled their smoldering night fire.

The group quietly gathered their gear in haste. As Tegh retightened the saddlebags on the mare's saddle, he wondered if the intruder could have been a policeman looking for the stolen horse and the thief.

As silently as possible, the small band, three walking and one riding, headed west, away from where their predawn visitor had disappeared. They stayed far enough below the ridgeline so as not to silhouette themselves against the sky. After an hour, Tegh held them up.

Betta whispered, "You want to tell us what's going on, Tegh?"

"We had a visitor pass by our camp."

She gasped, "What!"

It's okay," Tegh said. "He completely missed us, didn't notice a thing."

"B-b-but," she stammered.

"Think it was the shepherd coming back?" Steve asked.

"No, the silhouette I saw was too big to be Kulin," Tegh said. "My guess? At the very least, he was a local from a nearby village on his way down to Jiuquan. Or at the very worst, he was a bandit looking for easy prey."

"*What?*" Betta all but screeched.

Tegh didn't reveal the possibility that it could have been the police looking for whoever had stolen the horse. Instead, he held up his hand in a calming gesture.

"Don't worry. From the way he was kicking up dust, he had a definite destination. And if he was a bandit, he wasn't expecting to encounter anyone this far up the mountain. I don't think he'll be of concern to us anymore."

A shaken Betta asked, "Are you sure?"

"Yes, I'm sure. The way he was moving downhill, side-stepping to control his momentum, he was on his way somewhere specific. Still, we're fortunate he didn't stumble onto us."

"Why don't we take a few minutes to take care of any personal business?" Steve said, pointing towards some scrub brush where Betta might find privacy. "Then we can get going in earnest. The sooner we get clear of the hills and closer to civilization, the better off we'll be."

As they resumed their trek, both Steve and Tegh could see Fritz's demeanor had changed. His conversation was more convivial, beginning a kinship with the group. Gone was his all too prevalent animus.

At first, Betta had difficulty getting used to the mare's gentle bouncing. But after half a day, she'd become accustomed to riding horseback. When they stopped for their afternoon break, she swore that her backside and thighs would never be the same. Partly in response to her complaining muscles and partly to show she could hold her own among the men, she wondered, *maybe I should test my ankle. That godawful smelling slave seems to be working because the pain's dulled to an ache and the purplish coloration has receded beneath the splint wrapping.*

But, she decided against it.

After twelve arduous hours of Betta's jostling under a hot sun on the trail, and with twilight approaching with surprising suddenness, they stopped and made camp. Though only just before six, with mountains to the west, darkness came early. They made camp at a modified stone shelter—simply three stone walls, perhaps four feet high on a side with a woven reed roof held in place by heavy rocks, about three-yards square in all.

Settling in, they reviewed their plan. After consulting

their nearly useless airway map, they estimated they'd come about eighteen miles that day and the trek to Jiayuguan would probably take them another two across the ridge's scrabble and tufted brush.

Looking at the primitive stone structure, Betta asked, "Who built this?"

Tegh said, "Shepherds bring their flocks up here in the summer when the grass is green and plentiful. They built temporary shelters like this to sit out bad weather. The good news is, we can have a good-sized fire tonight. These stone walls will shield anyone from seeing the campfire."

Several yards away, they found a percolating spring-fed stream running between two finger ridges. There was a pre-autumn profusion of flowering shrubs and grass for the horse to eat along its bank. Tegh cut up an onion, a few carrots, and sliced up the chicken from the larder he'd bought in Jiuquan, and fashioned them into a reasonable stew.

As comforting as the warmth of the fire was at cutting the gathering chill, its light invited unwanted guests in the form of thousands of insects, most bent on vengeful bloodlust. To combat their pesky onslaught, they drew scarves around their exposed necks and faces and rolled down their sleeves. But it did nothing to stop the ground-dwelling sand fleas. Against them, there was no defense.

After dinner, to take her mind off the incessant biting, itching, and scratching, Betta asked Tegh, "What's Mongolia like? It must have been different from anything we grew up with."

Tegh smiled, happy to hear of her interest. "It was very satisfying. Our lives centered around livestock. I knew my grandparents well, since they lived with us. In fact, they were the ones who insisted I learned of my heritage, a lifestyle that was much dependent on horses.

"Grandfather taught me about the horses' spirits, speaking of them with a kind of reverence and saying that their spirits lived in their hair. Hair plucked from their horse's tail and woven into a spirit banner brought good luck and protected from danger.

"The horse was the ancient Mongol's livelihood, his food, and his means of survival. Mongol Horde armies were astounding for their size, consisting of thousands of soldiers and even more horses. Mongol ponies are so valued, that, to this day, they can't be taken across any border without special permission. In 1206 CE, Genghis Khan…"

For a good half hour, Tegh related how the Mongol hordes had unified China and conquered most of the known world at the time.

"That's interesting," Steve said. "I was always fascinated by stories of Genghis Khan. And now I get to know one of his descendants."

Tegh added, "During the time of Pax Mongolica, east-west trade flourished along the Silk Road, the very same road we're travelling along now."

"Wow, Tegh, you must be very proud of that," Betta said.

Tegh said, "Every Mongol is. If you were to visit Mongolia today, you'd still see the evidence of their reliance on and reverence for horse culture. But I must admit, I never took a liking to kumys, which is fermented mare's milk."

This brought a laugh.

Tegh continued, "Any herder you encounter will be gracious and willingly share food and drink, without payment. To accept money means to lose self-respect. You'd also find that today they do most of their ranching from Datsun pickup trucks."

They laughed again.

Then giving a big stretch, Steve said. "We should get some sleep. We have another long day tomorrow."

With their horse hobbled, they huddled together in the protection of the stone hut. The fire burned down to a comforting smolder. However, the bugs never relented in their onslaught.

By Tegh's estimate, they covered twenty miles the next day, stopping finally when twilight demanded and settling in on the northeastern, or morning side of the mountain. They gathered rocks, built a stone fire circle, and cooked another hot meal.

As soon as the sun had dipped below the ridge behind them, it grew noticeably colder. Soon they were huddling closely, warming themselves by the fire. No one complained about the brisk air because the bugs were gone, unable to thrive in the cold.

"Betta, how was the saddle ride today?" Fritz asked.

"I'm getting the hang of it. I think she's been in this countryside before. She easily picked her way across the rocks and was actually very gentle."

"I'm glad you're doing better," Tegh said. "That salve must be helping."

Betta said, "For as bad as it smells, it seems to be doing the trick. The discoloration is almost gone. I might try walking on it tomorrow."

"No you won't," the men chorused in objection.

Tegh said, "We've got just one more day till we reach Jiayuguan. I think you should give that ankle as much time to heal as possible."

"Listen to the man, Betta," Fritz said.

Surprised at how agreeable Fritz was being, Betta acquiesced. "But if I have to sit on my bum, how about some more stories, Tegh."

"Yeah, Tegh," Steve said. "You have any more tales of the Silk Road?"

Tegh looked a little surprised. "I figured you'd all be tired of them by now."

"It's not like there's anything else to do," Fritz deadpanned.

While Tegh started his spiel, Steve built up the fire to ward off the chill. The three sat entranced as Tegh described the incredibly rugged western Chinese terrain, its vast deserts and surrounding barrier mountains. When he paused after describing Chinese inventions, such as paper, printing, and gunpowder, Fritz said, "Hold up, I gotta dig out some more cigarettes."

Rummaging through a saddlebag, he held up a small paper-wrapped package and said, "What's this?" Opening it, he said, "Is this candy?"

Tegh said, "Oh, I completely forgot about that. Kulin saw the confections and asked me to buy some. I must have overlooked giving it to him when he left. Go ahead, take some and pass it around."

As they enjoyed the unexpected sweet treats, Fritz said, "It sounds like there was a lot of back and forth traffic on the Silk Road. How long did it take to get from Istanbul to Chang'an?"

Tegh said, "Actually, Fritz, very few actually

travelled the full extent of the Silk Road. Marco Polo was a notable exception because—"

"You mean Marco Polo was real," Fritz interrupted.

"Most certainly," Tegh said. "He accompanied his father and uncle on their second trip, this time under the protection of Kublai Khan himself. In fact, when the older Polos returned home, Marco Polo stayed an extra twenty-five years at the Khan's behest, travelling all over the empire as his personal emissary."

"Just imagine," Fritz said, "all of that happened and I didn't know anything about it."

Betta threw a stick on the fire, sending a burst of sparks skyward into the still night. "You know, I always wondered where all those silk robes the European royalty wore came from."

"It's as if an entire other world existed and we never even knew about it," Steve said. He stood and clapped his hands together against the chill. "Anyone else tired? I know I am. Sunrise comes early in the mountains. I just hope we don't see any more unwanted passersby."

When Steve woke, the others were still curled up, sound asleep. Steve blinked at the pre-dawn light, unable to sleep any more on the rocky ground. He brewed water for tea over the waning embers of their campfire. The calendar was closing in on the fall, so to ward off the chill, he stoked the fire.

Looking across the barren landscape spreading endlessly towards the northwest, he saw a haze forming that would soon shimmer with the rising heat of the day off the valley floor. He stared into the nothingness.

Having worked near Lake Baikal in Siberia, he'd heard stories of the privations endured by the occasional travelers who had ventured to western China. He thought back to a dinner hosted by a Russian colleague of a story he'd heard of how few were the ones who survived this unique topographical gauntlet he stared at, this corridor that stretched before him.

Steve cupped the mug of tea in his palms to warm them. As he took another sip, he was surprised by the crunch of footsteps and turned to see who it was.

"You're up early, Tegh."

"I heard you trying to keep the pot from rattling while heating the water."

Steve smiled. "Evidently I didn't do too well. Join me?" He raised his mug.

"I'm good. Have you figured it out?"

"Figured what out?

"Whatever it was that had you so lost in thought."

Steve pointed to the mountains. "Why's there no snow on the peaks over there?"

"It's way too dry in the summer," Tegh said. "Come winter, though, and those peaks will be well covered."

The two stood silently and gazed across the miles of hard rock scrabble covering the valley that so many travelers had used over the millennia.

"The Silk Road certainly is a marvel," Tegh finally said.

"Humph," was all Steve could muster.

Their travel that day was uneventful. With several days off her feet, Betta felt the need to test her ankle, against vociferous objections. For short stretches, she dismounted and led her mare until discomfort force her back in the saddle. By late afternoon, as the shadows settled across their trail, they got their first glimpse of the outskirts of Jiayuguan.

"I think it best that we enter the city in daylight," Tegh suggested. "I recommend spending the night on the mountain and plan for what we may encounter tomorrow."

Not hearing any objection, they built their camp for the night stacking rocks as a shield against the wind as well as from being observed at a distance. All four lent a hand in preparing dinner with their remaining food from Jiuquan. After eating, they warmed themselves by the coals.

Seemingly from nowhere, Fritz said, "I got to ask, Tegh. Did Marco Polo really travel this way?"

Betta kidded him by saying, "You've been saving that up since last night, haven't you?"

Tegh, however, recognized Fritz was honestly interested and answered.

"Not only was he real, but he, his father and uncle eventually arrived at the Dunhuang oasis, the Silk Road crossroads of the southern, central, and northern routes. From there they travelled through Anxi, Jiayuguan, Zhangye, Xi'an, and finally to Shangdu, more famously known to westerners as Xanadu, where Kublai Khan had his summer court."

Fritz asked, "Is that the same Jiayuguan we're going to tomorrow?"

"It most certainly is, Fritz. And for the next two and a half decades, Polo travelled China at the Khan's behest before returning to Venice in the year 1295. The most famous account of his adventures was written by Rustichello, whom Polo met in prison upon his return. You see, Fritz, Marco Polo did exist."

"That's amazing," Fritz said. "Just think, I'm going to

stand exactly where Marco Polo did over seven hundred years ago."

As pleased as he was at getting the four of them safely this far, Tegh wondered what police presence they'd find waiting for them in Jiayuguan, and whether those police would be looking for four exiles from China who'd survived a plane crash, or worse, a horse thief.

Chapter 12

THE NEXT MORNING, they broke camp and descended the Qilian Shan foothills towards Jiayuguan, a city of three hundred thousand people. For an hour, they walked the mare and her rider haltingly down the steeper parts of the slope until they reached easier ground that eventually would give way to the valley floor.

Tegh pointed to a distant ridge of mountains to the northwest. "Those are the Horse Hair Mountains, the Heli Shan, the northern wall of the valley or throat of the Gansu Corridor. Okay, enough sightseeing. What we need when we reach the town proper is find a place to clean up, rest and, most importantly, stay out of the public eye."

With easier footing for the horse, they made better time, passing open scrubland where occasional herdsman had horses and sheep grazing. But as they approached the city, Steve realized that three men leading a woman on a horse looked out of place. Finally, he said, "Hold up a minute."

"What's wrong?" Fritz asked.

"Nothing's wrong, it's just that we don't blend in right now, despite our clothing. Leading a horse is bound to draw attention."

Tegh agreed. "You're right. How do you feel about walking, Betta?"

She said, "It's at least tolerable. I'll just have to work out the stiffness, though I'm not sure how many miles I can go."

"This area seems rural enough. We ought to be able to find a rancher who could use another good mount," Tegh said.

Twenty minutes later, they saw a home set back from the road that had an animal enclosure behind it. Besides goats and some pigs, two horses stood, head down and munching the sparse grass. Tegh said, "All right Betta, now's the time to try out that ankle for real."

She dismounted and stepped gingerly. Then, as she flexed up on her toes, she winced.

"You okay?" Fritz asked.

She nodded without saying anything, her grimace betraying what she might have said.

Steve handed her some water while Fritz lit up. Taking the horse's reins, Tegh walked the mare to the house. A woman raking next to house's foundation looked up. Guessing the stranger had business with her husband, she motioned Tegh towards the corral around back. Several minutes later, he reemerged and walked back to the others, this time without the mare.

"Well, how'd you do?" Steve asked.

Tegh held up a handful of bills and smiled. "We're now two hundred and forty yuan richer, and he wanted all the tack, too."

"Not bad," Fritz said.

"Considering what Kulin and I paid in the first place, it's really good."

What Tegh didn't mention was what he'd worried the whole time he was making the transaction. In a rural area where livestock ownership is a natural way of life, the fact that the authorities might be looking for a stolen animal as valuable as a horse was his real concern. But, the farmer was only too happy to strike a bargain, especially one he hadn't been looking for. And to get a sturdy mare with all her tack thrown in, that was too good to be true. The subject of a bill of sale never came up. And with that behind him, he was glad he'd never brought his true concerns to the light of the others.

A much relieved Tegh said, "Let's find us a place to rest in the city.

They had gone a mile or so when a carryall van pulled to the side of the road and the driver rolled down the window. Tegh stepped forward and the driver asked if they wanted a lift. Seeing commercial markings on the side of the van and figuring it was safe enough, he said, "Can you drop us near the city center? Our car broke down and my uncle is going to meet us."

The driver agreed and the four of them got in. Tegh sat in the front seat and engaged the driver in conversation for the remaining half-hour trip into the city. It turned out, the driver was a farm equipment salesman and regularly made the three-hour trip from his home to Jiayuguan. He was only too happy to have the company.

Seeing the marquee for a hotel, Tegh told him this was a good enough landmark for his uncle. Tegh thanked the man and they waved as he drove away. Looking around, the could see five hotels within two blocks. While the three waited on the street, Tegh entered the Wumao Hotel. It wasn't top of the line but suitable for their needs.

He asked for a single room to avoid having to produce multiple passports. The receptionist took no notice of the others when they joined him at the elevator.

In the hall, Tegh told Betta, "You get the bathroom first to clean up. It's down the hall. The rest of us will use it after the hot water tank refills."

Once refreshed, they found a restaurant with a menu in a window with limited English translations. They were hungry, eagerly anticipating something that wasn't two or three days old and cooked over a campfire. Over a hearty lunch, they huddled at the table to make plans. Tegh unfolded the railway service map he'd picked up at the Jiuquan train depot and laid out their options.

Betta stopped him as Tegh began. "I'm getting these Chinese cities mixed up in my mind."

"Take a minute to orient yourself with the map," Tegh replied and circled the city names, which stretched east to west, like a string of pearls along the national highway.

"Okay, that's a little clearer," she said.

"Good, we're here and there's still hundreds of miles till we reach the western border. We'll have to make the trip in segments, switching types of transportation to make us less conspicuous."

Fritz asked, "Why are we switching? Won't going back and forth between bus and train travel increase our chances of being discovered?"

Steve and Betta looked to Tegh for an answer.

"Fair comment, Fritz."

Tegh traced his finger along the Gansu Corridor, which stretched through western Xinjiang Province to China's borders with Kazakhstan and Uzbekistan.

"The government built dozens of towns along this

route, just like Jiuquan where Kulin and I got supplies. They built them for the sole purpose to encourage westward expansion of the population, despite the inhospitable terrain."

To Steve's and Betta's surprise, Fritz seemed satisfied, at least until he asked, "Why not go north into Mongolia? That looks closer to where we are, plus you lived there."

Steve and Betta flinched, fearing Fritz was stirring up trouble again.

But Tegh simply said, "Good question. There are two reasons not to. First, the Gobi Desert stands in the way, and secondly, there's no transportation infrastructure, much less population centers to support such travel. By going west, however, we'd be traveling a road people have followed for two and half millennia—the Silk Road. Plus we'll have two choices for transportation—bus and train, both of which lead to Hami, our next logical resting place. From there, we either go south, skirting the Taklimakan Desert to Kashgar and into Pakistan, or continue west to Urumqi and then Kazakhstan.

"The southern route through Kashgar, however, means crossing the Himalayas. That's some of the most desolate and dangerous landscape imaginable. The border regions of Pakistan, Tajikistan, and Afghanistan are fiercely tribal, and thus too dangerous for us."

"Why not go through India via the Karakorum Highway?" Steve pointed to another possible route.

"That's an even longer journey and again, the border provinces aren't places outsiders should travel."

Fritz looked confused. "But isn't Pakistan a Western ally?"

"Yes, but those tribal regions are controlled by bandits

and warlords. We could be detained for ransom, or killed, or both," Tegh replied. "Besides, the route skirting the southern edge of the Taklimakan Desert is rudimentary at best. There's no rail or bus traffic, and the road is discontinuous in many sections, having succumbed to desertification. The lack of water is a serious problem along the entire route—no rivers and few oases."

"That sounds like a non-starter," Betta said. "So, the northern route it is?"

"It's the quickest way to Kazakhstan or Uzbekistan, both of which are nations where we'd all have a legal allowance to be."

Steve shrugged.

"Unfortunately," Tegh continued. "To reach Uzbekistan or Kazakhstan, we must travel via Urumqi, a city of several million situated a hundred miles east of the border. I don't know how large the People's Liberation Army's or the Ministry of State Security's contingents are in Urumqi. In general, though, we should be okay. The more remote the locale is from Beijing, the more autonomous the citizenry is from central authority groups like the PLA or MSS. All in all, I think our chances of travelling trouble free are best if we take that route."

"How formal is the border crossing into Kazakhstan?" Fritz asked.

"I don't know for sure. My experiences at border crossings to and from Mongolia lead me to believe that the Kazakh guards were lax when it comes to border security."

"Okay, I guess it's west to Hami," Betta said.

A perplexed expression suddenly crept across Fritz's face. "What if we get stopped? It's hard to imagine we can embark on a thousand-plus-mile journey and not run across a policeman or security person somewhere."

Betta looked at Tegh plaintively, for once agreeing that Fritz had a point.

Surprisingly, Steve agreed. "It would help if we had a reason to be here, an alibi if you will. We have to have some story to offer in the event we get asked."

Betta's eyes brightened and she snapped her fingers. "Right, right, I know. Why don't we pose as journalists covering China's lost treasures?"

Caught up in Betta's enthusiasm, Fritz chimed in. "Sure. We could say we're working for a German travel magazine and writing a book about Silk Road art. That would give us a plausible excuse for being here."

Tegh liked it. "There are plenty of ancient religious artifacts and pilgrims' cave paintings to provide believable reasons for us to be exploring. None of that would raise suspicions and cause guards to question our presence, much less connect us with the plane crash."

Steve, relieved they had a consensus, said, "Okay, that all sounds plausible. But we need to work on our appearance so we're not conspicuous and as easily identified as outsiders. The clothes are a nice touch, but you need to get your hair trimmed, Fritz. And Betta, that flaking nail polish on your fingers and toes has to go."

Tegh said, "While you're doing that, I'll check out the bus schedules."

The men found a barber shop to take care of the hair issue. When they emerged, they looked significantly more presentable. Betta searched the storefronts for a nail salon or pharmacy to no avail. Finally, she had to settle on a hardware store where she bought some paint remover for her nail polish. Next, the group bought local clothing from a street vendor.

Betta privately thought, as she looked at her clothing choices, *it's not fashionable, but at least I can find things that fit.*

When Tegh met back up with them, he had a sheepish grin.

"What's so funny?" Betta asked.

"When I was at the bus station," Tegh said, "a local policeman asked me what I was doing."

Betta had a sudden case of dread. "What's wrong?"

"Nothing. I said I was with fellow journalists researching local architecture and art."

Looks of alarm appeared on their faces, and Fritz asked, "So we now have a policeman with a reason to remember a group of wandering journalists?"

"Far from it," Tegh said. "He proceeded to become my unwitting travel agent, advising me as to which local sites to visit while here."

They breathed a cautious sigh of relief.

"So, what did he recommend?" Steve asked.

Tegh said, "Apparently, Jiayuguan marks the end of the Great Ming Wall as it existed in the year 1372. He referred to this region as the Mouth of China. Everything beyond here is Outside the Mouth, the limits of old Chinese civilization and the beginnings of barbarian lands. Just to the west is the narrowest part of the Hexi Corridor, which he referred to as the path for exiles, fortune hunters, pilgrims, and common folk seeking a new start in life."

Fritz stubbed out a cigarette. "What's the Hexi Corridor?"

"Gansu Corridor, Hexi Corridor—they're one and the

same," Tegh explained. "In ancient times it was called the Hexi Corridor; today, it's the Gansu Corridor."

"Humph, it's very confusing," Fritz said.

"About the policeman," Steven said. "Isn't he going to get curious?"

"I thanked him with a pack of cigarettes, so I don't think so," Tegh said.

Fritz piped up. "Just as long as he doesn't have second thoughts and he suddenly thinks we're spies and not journalists."

"Oh, Fritz, you're just worried about losing a pack of smokes," Betta chided.

"I wouldn't worry," Tegh said. "Chinese police everywhere harbor at least a taint of corruption. That pack of cigarettes will stand us in good stead. This guy may be corrupt, but he's also naïve."

Steve persisted. "But to Fritz's concern, now we've been seen. If security guards come through asking questions later, this cop might tell them we were here."

Tegh mulled this over, then snapped his fingers. "I know what we can do. We'll leave a false trail, just like Kulin and I did in Jiuquan." He gestured to their map. "Instead of going directly west to Hami, we could take the bus southwest to Dunhuang via Anxi, like we're headed down the southern route. Then, we backtrack by train to Anxi before continuing northwest to Hami."

"Hami, Anxi, Swami—I'm getting confused," Fritz complained.

Tegh pointed to the map. "Look here. Dunhuang is a historical tourist attraction, a perfectly plausible place for photojournalists to visit. We wouldn't stand out among all the foreign tourists. If investigators do come there asking about us, they'll discover we're heading southwest to Kashgar and Pakistan."

Fritz puffed away without comment.

"I don't think we should leave a money trail by buying tickets," Steve cautioned.

Fritz blew a cloud of smoke across the map. "I agree with that."

"That's okay, I didn't purchase them yet," Tegh reassured them. "Let me think."

"I know," Steve said, interrupting Tegh's thoughts. "We could hitchhike?"

Betta's scowled at the thought of thumbing a ride. But Fritz nodded.

Tegh said, "That's an excellent idea, Steve. We could hitchhike as far as Anxi and then buy bus tickets to Dunhuang. After a day or so in Dunhuang, we'll take the train back to Hami. If the Chinese army does get wind of us, they'll think we're heading east, back towards Lanzhou. Meanwhile, we'll take the northern route from Hami to Turpan, and then on to Kazakhstan and safety."

"I like it," Steve said. "We'll leave no audit trail by hitchhiking, but we'll have a bus ticket into Dunhuang and a train ticket back out to confuse them."

"It's not only them who will be confused," Betta grumbled.

"This is all well and good, but I'm getting hungry," Fritz said, stubbing out his cigarette.

Tegh offered, "I recommend we buy some liuyuan, or chicken on a stick."

"Then it's a plan," Steve said. "Hot food and a good night's sleep will do us good. Let's relax at the market while we eat. Tomorrow morning, we can head down the road and distance ourselves farther from the crash site. There's no need to spend a day sightseeing here, cover story or not."

The next morning after breakfast, Tegh told them to gather their things while he checked for directions to the main highway. It wasn't twenty minutes later until a winded Tegh came in as said, "Come on, hurry, we have to leave *now!*"

They did as Tegh said, rapidly taking the side street exit from the hotel lobby. Tegh led them along a parallel road to the main street and then turned at the next.

"What's happening, Tegh?" Betta pleaded.

Reaching the next street, he had them turn the corner. Now well out of sight of the hotel and certain no one was following them, he explained.

"Remember that farmer I sold the horse to yesterday?"

Steve said, "Yeaaahh."

"While I was asking a man at the newspaper stand the best way to reach the national highway, I saw him talking to a policeman. He was pretty loud and upset because someone had sold him a stolen horse yesterday."

Fritz said, "So?"

"Remember when you saw that embossing on the tack that came with the mare? Well…"

Tegh took no more than a minute to explain what had been bothering him since first recognizing the markings on the horse's saddlebags.

"You knew it was stolen and you didn't tell us?" blurted Fritz.

In his own defense, Tegh said, "I didn't know it. It was more like I suspected it."

"But, you didn't tell us," Steve said.

"What were we going to do? Betta was in no condition to walk and we needed a horse," Tegh said in his defense. "Look, we can stand here and discuss recriminations, or we can get out of town like we were planning. That farmer talking with the police doesn't know my name, but he could certainly recognize me. And the longer we stand here, the more likely he'll find us. Right now, he's only two blocks away. As soon as we're out of here, the better."

Chapter 13

ANXI, WESTERN CHINA

WITHIN SIX BLOCKS they'd found the on ramp to the national highway. Five minutes later, an accommodating westbound trucker stopped and offered them a ride. As they pulled away, Fritz leaned over to Tegh and said, "You should have just let the damn horse go and not sell her. We didn't need the money."

Six hours later they reached the town of Anxi where the national highway divided. The truck driver pulled over, saying he was heading on to Hami after he refueled. This gave them pause to consider if they were going to go ahead with their plan to reach Dunhuang or continue with the truck driver, essentially off the grid, all the way to Hami.

It was Fritz who broke their impasse. "We thought this through once and it's a good plan. As journalists in Dunhuang, we can hide. We've got no plan for Hami. I say, bid this guy farewell, thank him, and let's get on with what we said we were going to do."

Tegh gave the driver two hundred yuan for gas and mentioned they'd decided to stay in Anxi for a few days. He didn't say anything about continuing to Dunhuang.

Much smaller than Jiayuguan, Anxi offered few amenities for visitors to choose from. Their pick of restaurants was limited to two. Fritz and Betta entered one while Tegh and Steve went separately into the other, the thought being they wouldn't look like a group travelling together should a policeman take notice.

The restaurant Fritz chose had a menu in the window with English subscripts. After a quick glance, Betta said, "Why don't I just order for us. Everything is noodles and something. I guess it's chicken, goat, or mutton. I'm choosing chicken, any objection?"

"No, that's fine."

Betta pointed to their choice, holding up two fingers for the waitress to indicate it was for them both. The woman scribbled something down and headed for the kitchen.

"What's going on with you?" Betta said. "Ever since our conversation about going east or west, you've been in a crappy mood. Now suddenly, you're the one making the rational suggestion to stay with the plan. You're not having a nervous breakdown or something, are you?"

"For goodness sakes, I'm trying to be nice, Betta. I'm just don't want to draw any attention to us by offering information to strangers, like that policeman back in Jia... whatever the name of that last city was. And then there's that horse Tegh stole. He—"

"He didn't steal it. The farmer in Jiuquan did. Tegh didn't even suspect anything until we saw those markings on the saddlebags and harness. Besides, that's behind us. There's no way any police report of persons unknown in Jiayuguan could ever follow us here."

"That may be true, but I got nervous when I saw Tegh and Steve wavering when the truck driver offered to take us to Hami. I don't like changing things around that we've all decided on. And lately, you seem to be agreeing with anything they say."

"So that's what your new attitude's about? You're jealous?'

"Don't be silly. We've been partners for almost two years. We've made plans. Hell, we travelled all the way to China to attend that outdoor clothing expo. Now that we've been kicked out of the country, your idea of doing this thing together seems to have vanished."

"Well, excuse me! We had a little matter of a plane crash to deal with. So pardon me if my, I mean our, plans got messed up." She crossed her arms and sulked. But after a few seconds her expression softened as she realized she agreed with him, at least in part. He was correct that their business venture, as she had originally envisioned it, was over. The stress of the entire matter, including her failure to consider the danger in placing any trust in a representative of the Chinese government, albeit a local policeman, was eating at her, too.

She also recognized Fritz's attachment to their relationship was more than business. His were feelings she didn't share, and that was a problem. Certainly, they'd been together during the planning stages for their enterprise. What nascent business deals didn't involve some amount of close collaboration? Their relationship had never been intimate, although he certainly hinted at it enough. Typical male.

Then it dawned on her. *That's the issue. He can't accept things have changed. He sees two new men competing for my attention and honestly believes that somehow, suffering in a plane crash was trauma enough to patch over our differences and allow us to continue with our business dreams together.*

Before she could chase her train of thought further,

their waitress returned with steaming bowls and two bottles of soda. A quick taste told her the drink was a cola of some sort. "I wasn't sure from the bottle," she said to Fritz. "The writing's in Chinese."

"It's wet and sweet, that's all that counts," Fritz said, picking up a skewer. "Well, this looks like chicken kabobs on a bed of noodles, fine with me. Whoa, its hot!" He chewed gingerly, not fully closing his mouth to keep from burning the insides. Finally, it became manageable and he added, "Not bad, but it could use some seasoning."

Betta smiled at his antics, but took his discomfort to heart and blew on her food before taking a bite of her own. "You're right; it is a little bland."

Seeing some small bottles on the front counter and hoping one was soy sauce or a reasonable facsimile, she pointed them out to their waitress. The girl nodded and brought one over.

"Here goes nothing," she said as she dashed several drops on her noodles and chicken. Taking a bite, she pronounced, "Not bad, not sure what this is, but at least it adds flavor."

They enjoyed their meal, never returning to their initial conversation.

In the other restaurant, Steve was thankful to have Tegh as his translator. There was no mystery to what they ordered, two bowls of a clear broth containing meat-filled doughy pastries with soppy green vegetable floating on top.

To Steve, it looked like wonton soup, but with an entirely different taste.

"Do you like it?" Tegh asked.

"It's fine, not what I expected, but good." After taking a few more spoonfuls, Steve waved his hand to fan his mouth. "Wow, that's got an after taste."

Tegh smiled at his displeasure. "I'll make you a fan of real Chinese food yet." Then changing the subject, he asked, "Have you noticed a change in Fritz?"

"Yeah, I thought it was just me. Fritz seems to be coming around to being a team player, but something's bothering him and it's not about our escape plan."

Tegh finished the last bit of his soup and said, "If you ask me, I don't think he's comfortable with anything to do with police. What he doesn't understand is that in China, we're going to encounter the PLA and the MSS a lot, no matter where we go."

Steve asked, "Do you think the authorities have figured out we're missing and unaccounted for from the crash?"

"Three times now, in Jiuquan, Jiayuguan, and here, I purposely made checks at the transportation depots to see if there was hint of the national police searching for someone. I couldn't detect a hint of it. The exception being the stolen horse fiasco, but that wasn't the police, that was just the farmer trying to convince a local cop of his problem. Who knows if he'll be successful."

"The matter of the horse is a small 'if', Tegh. But in the matter of searches after the plane crash it, may be a while before we're clear of that. Just in case there are searches for us by the PLA or MSS, I think your plan to plant the seeds of disinformation regarding the directions we're heading is prudent."

Tegh tilted his soda bottle towards him as thanks.

"On the other hand," Steve said, "how do we get Fritz

to feel comfortable around cops?"

"It may be that we can't. Maybe going forward, I simply won't include him when I share information that has to do with contacts with government authorities."

Steve blew on his spoon. "Maybe not the most honest thing to do, but it's practical."

An hour later, while three of them waited outside the bus depot, Tegh purchased four tickets to Dunhuang on a bus that would depart in an hour. To keep from attracting attention, Tegh recommended they sit separately under the covered outdoor waiting area. If they had to use the facilities, they should go individually to the unisex, three-quarter enclosure behind the station.

"I was wondering where the bathroom was," Betta said.

When she returned, she proclaimed, "You boys are lucky. I can't wait to tell my mother about the comfort of using an open slit trench I had to share with other travelers. Thank God I had the presence of mind to salvage toilet paper from the plane."

The men looked at her sympathetically, but judiciously didn't reply.

Not knowing how long they'd be on the bus, Steve went to a food vendor's pushcart across the street. The wagon chef was making wheat stretchers by massaging a lump of dough, drawing it out, and then using his fingers in a cat's cradle to strand the dough into noodles. He boiled them in a soup broth with fried mutton, peppers, onion, and tomatoes. Steve bought two cardboard containers to share aboard the bus.

Their ride arrived forty minutes late. Continuing their

subterfuge, they took separate seats among the dozens of other passengers. Their fellow riders were a cross-section of everyday Chinese who shared a common circumstance: none could afford even the least expensive third-class train ticket. Baggage was either stored on an above-the-seat ledge, or tied between two rails on top of the bus.

They endured the cramped seating arrangements, confident that, should anyone come looking for them back in Anxi, they would find a cold trail.

Chapter 14

AS THE FOUR survivors were leaving Anxi, Lin Chu was sitting in the small police station in Jiuquan when his harried section chief said, "First Director Lin, I have news on the missing plane crash victims."

Taking the offered print out from the anxious man, the First Director cautioned him, "They are not victims, Fu Chuyu. They are fugitives of the state. Don't forget that."

"Yes, First Director, my apologies." The young man slinked away, firmly chastised.

Lin Chu read the printout with gathering interest as his eyes moved down the page. He reviewed the last three paragraphs to make sure he hadn't misread them and smiled. Rushing into his private office, he dialed the phone quickly.

The phone finally connected with the front desk of General Wu Xi's hotel. "Give me General Wu's room. And hurry. It's urgent."

A room extension picked up and a groggy voice answered. The general was still in bed at 9:30 in the morning after flying into Jiuquan just after midnight. "What is it?"

The Regional MSS Security Administrator sounded annoyed, but Lin Chu couldn't hold back his enthusiasm.

"General Wu, sorry to bother you, but we have a solid lead on the fugitives."

"What?" General Wu was fully awake. "Tell me you have them in custody."

"Not exactly, General, but I'm certain they've been positively identified."

"By whom? Where?" demanded the General.

"As you know, we interrogated the Jiuquan train depot matron and she remembered seeing two vagrants several days ago checking the train schedules and walking up the street, only to have them walk by again, this time leading a loaded pack horse. Further investigation turned up a midwife at the hotel who said a Uighur and a shepherd from the hills had been asking questions."

"Uighur? This is the first I've heard of this." The general sounded eager for details. "How did she know he was a Uighur?"

Lin was aware that capturing the fugitives would be a big boost for him professionally. But, if they also turned out to be Uighurs, that would certainly get the attention of his, and the general's, higher ups.

"All she said was they looked Uighur. She did confirm that the two had left town heading east with a loaded pack horse, like shepherds often do when moving their flocks."

"So they're grazing sheep in the fields outside of town?"

Though the general sounded excited, Lin knew he was confused.

"No sir, well, I don't know about them, sir, but—"

"What do you know, Lin!" The General now pressed First Director Lin for clarification. "We're looking for four foreigners from the plane crash. Tell me exactly why you think these two are part of the ones we're looking for. Did she see a passport, or signs of injury?"

"Not exactly, sir."

"Then exactly what did she say, First Director?"

"One of them asked for some salve for his mother's ailment, which—"

"Ailment. Did she mean injury?" The general was insistent.

"She wasn't clear on that, sir, but she did say mother. And she observed that the older one's shoes weren't the kind worn by a herdsman."

"Shoes? You want me to devote my time and resources because he wore the wrong shoes?"

"General, my men searched the grazing fields within five miles of town in all directions. There was no sign of them. That means they weren't who they claim to be. They weren't shepherds. They must have headed further up into the mountains. They wouldn't have gone back towards the crash, so they must be travelling west. I radioed the MSS chief in Jiayuguan. He's conducting a search of the city as we speak. If they're there, we will have them in custody shortly."

"Shoes, sheep..." the general mumbled to himself. Then, the general said, "Lin, you better hope your colleague in Jiayuguan has better luck than you've had. I've come all the way from Beijing thinking this would be an easy proposition to pick up four injured fugitives. Now you tell me they're harboring at least one subversive Uighur in their midst. You must bring this to an end. And quickly." He slammed down the phone.

First Director Lin called to his section chief. "Fu Chuyu, gather a detail. We have work to do."

Chapter 15

DUNHUANG, WESTERN CHINA

THEIR BUS TRIP from Anxi took all evening and night, stopping frequently, sometimes in the middle of nowhere, to discharge a passenger or two into the dead of night. Being a local transit line and not an express, it carried everyday people to places of business or, more probably, to visit relatives.

It was mid-morning when they pulled into the depot at Dunhuang. In a desert valley heat that belied the early hour, the bus emptied. Hungry from subsisting on nothing but their last candy bars and the wheat stretchers Steve had bought, they found John's Info Café only a block from the station. The restaurant was cheap and had menu pictures in the window for passersby to see. While they ate, they surveyed the comings and goings of locals and tourists in the central town square across the street.

Sated from their meal, but still feeling the worse for wear from their long bus trip, Betta announced, "I don't know about you men, but I need to bathe and sleep."

Fritz said almost immediately, "Sounds like the best idea I've heard in a while."

"Wait here, Tegh said. "I'll look around for a hotel."

Checking the two blocks he could see in either direction, there were four to choose from: the Feitan, the Dunhuang, the Sun Grand, and the Five Rings. The last three appeared to be upscale, thus more conspicuous. Tegh entered the Feitan and checked in, offering up his passport. Five minutes later, he returned to the restaurant where the others were sipping tea and said, "We're all set. The hotel is only three doors down, just off the town square."

Betta stood up. "Don't have to ask this girl twice."

Half an hour later, the three men were in the lobby wondering how much longer Betta was going to be. Fritz, tired of hearing Tegh's explanation of how important it was for them to get out among the tourists and become lost in the flow of people, said, "I'm going up to check on her."

Climbing the stairs to the second floor, he knocked on Betta's door. "Come on Betta, we're all waiting downstairs."

A muffled "Go away" came through the door.

He tried the knob and the door opened. Stepping in, he saw her, already in bed, covers pulled up to her chin.

"What do you want? I'm dog tired. You guys go ahead."

Fritz sat on the foot of the bed and patted her covered feet. "Look, as much as Tegh drones on sometimes, he says staying here makes it too easy for someone who might be looking for us to find us. If we get out there and mingle in the crowds, we'll be harder to spot."

She fluffed the other pillow over her head and said something unintelligible. Tegh, reached over and pulled the pillow off. Then, digging a finger in to her side to tickle her, he said, "Come on Münchkin, get up."

She squirmed and giggled, giving a mock defense. "Okay, okay. Now get out and let me get dressed."

He stood and said, "I'll be waiting out in the hall. So no taking time for make up and figuring out what outfit to wear."

He ducked as she threw a pillow in his direction. "Get out!"

Betta and Fritz joined the other two in the lobby a few minutes later, drawing a comment from Steve. "Good to see you could make it Betta. Feel rested?"

She threw him a nasty look and said, "I'm here. Let's go mingle."

Stepping into the late morning air Tegh said, "This is my first time in Dunhuang. As you can see, there are lots of tourists from all over the world, which will give us perfect cover."

Betta complained, "Well it better, that's all I have to say."

Steve said, "Ah, Betta, now you sound like Fritz."

As they window shopped just off the town's square, however, it was clear Tegh was right. Hundreds of tourists were in and out of the shops and perusing the market. With its hotels, a cinema and well-paved streets, the town center held the rudiments of urban culture without an abundance of modernity—in essence, the perfect place to remain hidden.

When Fritz saw two soldiers standing on the far corner of the park, however, he turned away saying, "We have to go back. Look across the street in the park."

Seeing the two PLA soldiers, Tegh said, "It's okay, Fritz. They're by themselves. I haven't seen any others since we've gotten here. More importantly, they're PLA and not MSS guards. Most likely they're taking in the sights themselves, just like the tourists."

To Fritz's dismay, Tegh casually asked a man standing nearby about the police presence. They talked amiably for a few minutes, Tegh thanked him, and strolled back to where the others stood.

"No need for concern, Fritz," Tegh said. "The man says that Dunhuang is the site of a regional army barracks."

This put Fritz's nerves more on edge. "What! It's bad enough to see the cops here, but did have to go up and talk to the locals? It just gives people we don't know reasons to remember us."

Steve started to say something to mollify Fritz, but Tegh held up his hand and waved him off and moved them in the opposite direction in the crowd. But as they moved farther along, they started seeing more and more soldiers. Like the two they'd first seen, they simply appeared to be young men taking in the sights, some of them with cameras dangling tourist-like from their necks.

Stopping at a sidewalk café for a cup of tea, Tegh tried again to reassure Fritz the soldiers were harmless and not there to track them down.

"Okay, I'll buy it for now, but I still don't like your talking to strangers," Fritz said.

Betta, looking for a way to break the tension, said, "This tea isn't enough. Let's try one of those food kiosks."

To allow Fritz's anxieties to settle, they bought some fried dough and soft drinks. This seemed to put him in a better mood.

Tegh asked, "What do you want to do now?"

Fritz said washing down his last bite, "What about this place? We worked so hard to get here; well, here we are."

"Fritz, look around you. What do you see?" Tegh said.

Caught off guard, Fritz said, "Well, uh, people."

"That's right," Tegh said. "Lots of people. People from all over the world, not just locals. Dunhuang attracts people today for the same reason it attracted ancient Buddhist pilgrims after crossing the Taklimakan Desert, or Sea of Death. It's a place of relaxation and rejuvenation. What all these people came here to see are what those pilgrims of twelve-hundred years ago left behind."

"Oh," said Fritz, at a loss for something to say for the first time.

Betta raised her eyebrows. "Sea of Death?"

"An ancient term, not mine," Tegh said. "Coming to China, it was the first source of water travelers had seen in weeks. And leaving China, it was the last watering place before crossing the western desert's vast expanse of nothing. This is the Chinese equivalent of Siberia, a place of no return—an outpost on the edge of the wilderness."

"I can relate to that," Steve said.

"Two thousand years ago," Tegh went on, "the emperor recognized its strategic value and commanded that this place where the Silk Road diverged into its northern, central, and southern routes, should be guarded. The remnants of the fort he established still stands. The town's name literally means Blazing Beacon.

"Until the fourth century, the central route was the most frequently travelled, running through the Lop Desert before joining the northern route at an oasis. That route was reclaimed by desert sands by the seventh century after thriving for almost eight hundred years. Its existence remained unknown to the western world until the Lost City of Loulan was rediscovered in 1899 by western explorers. They found mummies there—the most famous being the Loulan Beauty, a female mummy with long red hair."

"Humph. Will wonders never cease," Betta said.

Tegh continued. "Dunhuang was the exit from the Hexi Corridor, the last caravan stop before crossing the Lop and Taklimakan deserts. Genghis Khan conquered this area in the early thirteenth century."

"No kidding? Genghis Khan?" Fritz said.

Tegh was glad he'd finally intrigued Fritz with something. "The Great Wall was finally extended here in 1372, marking the western boundary of China. The wall's west gate, or Gate of Sighs, was where those exiled from the empire—political prisoners, disgraced officials, and criminals—were sent to fend for themselves in the 'outer darkness'."

"Ancient China sounds fascinating, Tegh," Betta said.

Tegh smiled. "Thank you, Betta. It's one of the reasons I was studying Asian history. Every Chinese schoolchild learns of the ancient Empire."

Fritz surprised them all by saying, "I can see you take great pride in that heritage."

"Well, Fritz, technically, I'm Chinese," Tegh said. "I was born in western China. But our move to Mongolia when I was a toddler marks me as an exile in the government's view. The China of today is a police state, that is, it's intolerant of anything contrary to their system of government. They consider my family's leaving as a rejection of their system. And when they find anything displeasing…" Tegh stopped to collect his emotions.

Finally, Betta said, "But you're okay now. So, let's all be compliant tourists and not do anything foolish to attract attention."

Tegh said, "Well said, Betta." Then clearing his throat, he said, "Dunhuang became a trading crossroad where north, south, east, and west met. The Taklimakan Desert is the only geological feature for the next thousand miles, a most formidable barrier. Its Uighur name means 'you go in but you don't come out'. Marco Polo referred to some of its thousand-foot sand dunes as Singing Dunes. You can still hear that singing sound, though today we know it's caused by grains of sand being pushed about by the wind and not simply the stuff of legend."

"Wow. Marco Polo and Genghis Khan. Right here?" Fritz exclaimed.

Steve gave Fritz a friendly pat. "Hard to believe, isn't it?" Turning to Tegh, he asked, "So trade urged the ancient peoples to brave all the dangers?"

"Trade, as well as religion, which probably played a bigger role. Dunhuang was a Buddhist stronghold for centuries. Pilgrims left cultural artifacts and sacred writings right here in the Mogao Caves."

"What's the big deal with the caves?" Fritz asked.

"The Mogao Caves were carved by pilgrims starting in 366. They created almost five hundred caves containing thousands of wall paintings, sacred scrolls, and carved Buddhas. These treasures, unknown for centuries by the west, were rediscovered in the nineteenth century by a German archeologist."

"German?" Fritz blurted out.

Steve said, "You're really getting into this, Fritz."

Tegh smiled. "So now you're interested?"

Fritz's cheeks reddened.

"That's okay. Now, where was I? Oh yes, in addition to discovering the art treasures in the caves, the German archeologist coined the term Silk Road."

Fritz beamed and puffed out his chest. "See, I'm not the only German to take an interest."

Tegh chuckled as he continued. "He also uncovered a sealed chamber at the back of one cave, inside of which were hundreds of perfectly preserved sacred documents written by Buddhist pilgrims from India. He purchased these ancient manuscripts, including the Diamond Sutra, the oldest printed book, dating to the year 868.

"You asked why caves, Fritz. Scientists discovered these paintings, manuscripts, and figurines had survived in such pristine condition because of the perfect climate inside the caves—heat, low humidity, and lack of direct sunlight. Until their rediscovery by the German archeologist, this region was completely unknown to outsiders.

"Unfortunately, many of the artifacts were removed by robbers, warlords, Muslim fundamentalists, and eventually Mao's Red Guards during China's Cultural Revolution. Fortunately, the artifacts removed by the Europeans were taken to western museums where they're..."

Tegh stopped, his attention drawn to a small crowd gathered around a stage in the town square where actors were giving a performance. Tegh put up his hand and motioned for them to stay put, saying, "I want to hear what's going on. I'll be right back."

Watching him leave, Betta said, "I can't believe I never read about any of this in school."

"Me neither," added Steve. "If we only had the time, I'd love to learn more."

Tegh returned shortly. "Fritz, you asked me before if

Marco Polo were real. Well, that's him up on the stage right now, the one with the gray cap. The two men with beards are his uncle and father. They're explaining something to Emperor Kublai Khan, the fat one sitting on the chair."

Fritz strained on his tiptoes to see over the crowd.

"What's the matter, Fritz? Can't you see?" Taller than Fritz, Betta was having fun at his expense.

Seeing Fritz willingly withstand her playful jibe, Steve wondered if their relationship was simply one of business partners or something more personal.

Frustrated, Fritz said, "Enough about Marco Polo. Let's do something else."

Betta said, "Why don't we try those camel rides I read about on the hotel poster? I'm betting none of us has ever done that. Come on, whadda you say?"

The men readily agreed.

The camel corral was located not far from their hotel. Tegh paid the proprietor eight yuan apiece and his helper brought balky beasts over.

"Oh my," Betta said. "I didn't realize how big they were."

"And smelly," Fritz added. And try as he might, Fritz couldn't get past that horrendous smell and saw none of the fascination Betta had about these ships of the desert.

Stepping aside, Fritz said, "I'll watch from here." He plopped down on a bench and grabbed a smoke.

The proprietor held three camels steady by the raised wooden platform so the intrepid riders could approach their rides at double-hump height. They each straddled a camel saddle, an X-shaped, folding wooden frame covered with padding of horsehair-stuffed leather. Once seated, their guide mounted a large male camel and took Betta's reins. Tegh explained he would hold the reins until she got the hang of it. As it turned out, hang was the operative word.

Caught unaware by the camel's gait, Betta was immediately thrown out of her comfort zone. Though the guide merely walked the camel, its long strides and insistent rhythm moved much more quickly than she felt comfortable with. Within minutes, her lack of anticipation of the camel's herky-jerky motion made her nauseous. The pitching created an uneasy sensation in her gut, which heaved in unsyncopated rhythm. Each sideslip and corkscrew of the beast's ass moving up, sideways, and jarringly downward unmercifully repeated itself. Now-and-again weightlessness accentuated the animal's risings and fallings. The combination of stink, heat, and uncertain motion caused her to salivate.

A series of disembodied jerks jarred Betta's head, sending an insidious message to her inner ear which her brain desperately tried to interpret. She unsuccessfully attempted clamping her legs, hoping beyond reason to stifle her urge to throw up. The mounting pressure of accumulated bile triggered her brain to a state of upheaval that she couldn't hold back. She vomited with several gut-wrenching purges.

With no stomach contents left, other than discontent, she draped herself formlessly across the pommel, certain that her bones no longer functioned, as her chest hopelessly tried to sustain what little life she retained.

At her signs of distress, Tegh spurred his camel alongside Betta's and reached for her reins. At the same time, he waved to get the guide's attention, who was enjoying Betta's reaction. Tegh shook his head as a signal for the guide to stop, which he did.

"Betta, I think this is one adventure you may not become proficient at," Tegh said.

Woozy, she said, "Ugh, I'm sorry. I don't know what happened."

Steve came along her camel's other flank. "I think you're suffering from mal-de-mer, or at least mal-de-mammal."

Betta simply glared.

"Okay, bad pun. Let's just chalk this up as a bad idea?" Steve said.

"Please, get me down," she pleaded.

Tegh motioned for the guide to have Betta's camel kneel. He brought his camel around, grasped Betta by her waist, and held her steady. With her firmly in his arms, he said something that his camel and the beast pitched forward to his knees before lowering his rump to the ground. With the guide's firm grasp on her midsection, she burped loudly, but remained in place. The guide slid to his feet onto the ground, never losing hold of her. Tegh and Steve dismounted and took charge of her.

Tegh led her, wobbly kneed, back towards the hotel. "You need some tea and flat bread, young lady. You'll feel better."

As she sipped and nibbled, color slowly returned to her cheeks and Betta bravely claimed she felt better. But her facial expression said otherwise.

Trying to be sympathetic, Steve said, "Just imagine how difficult a trip across the desert on camelback would have been."

But Betta wasn't in the mood for conjecture.

Fritz pointed towards town center. "Not to seem insensitive to her plight, but what's happening in the central square?"

Tourists and street performers had gathered near colorfully covered stalls and food carts. Curious, they went closer. While watching a juggler, Fritz noticed Tegh approach and then engage a young soldier, who was obviously enjoying himself, in conversation.

A moment later, Tegh returned to the others. Before Fritz could vent his frustration, Tegh said, "The soldier says the only thing we need to worry about is pickpockets. That's why his barracks commander put him and some of his buddies at the park on duty. He's here specifically to ensure the tourists aren't bothered by riffraff."

But as Tegh spoke, the soldier walked over to them. Steve and Betta drew themselves alongside Fritz to make sure he didn't say or do anything as Tegh greeted the soldier and asked him something. They talked a moment and Tegh thanked him and walked on. Tegh motioned for the three to follow him as he led them in the opposite direction.

Once they'd gone a safe distance the soldier, Steve asked, "What was that about?"

With no apparent concern showing, Tegh said, "He just wished for us to have a good time and enjoy ourselves. That's all."

Betta sensed he was holding back, but didn't want Fritz to make a scene by asking a question. Instead, she said, "Good idea. Let's enjoy ourselves. We haven't had a chance to do that for…"

She caught herself. "Well, for a while."

Fritz and Steve agreed as they strolled among the tourists enjoying the tempting sights and smells. Braziers were roasting nuts and grilling meat skewered on bamboo sticks. Piled high dishes of multi-colored spices gave off tantalizing aromas. At one kiosk, vegetables sputtered in oil as cooks added chunks of mutton or lamb, skillfully flipping their delicacies in the pan to heat them. Street performers entranced small groups with pantomime, dance, and song.

Onlookers meandered from venue to venue, or simply strolled with friends, chatting at the end of a busy day of tours, work, or school. Everyone was vested in having a good time and no one seemed to mind, or even notice, the inescapable body odor brought on by the stifling heat and the press of the crowds. Soon enough, the four had worked up an appetite and headed towards the market that bordered one end of the square. With Tegh's help in describing the offerings, they chose shashlik, shish-kebobs, and fried lujabee, ground meat-stuffed pastries. Delicacies in hand, they sat at one of the many outdoor tables and ate.

"Is this a festival?" Steve asked.

"The soldier said they hold this festival once a week during the summer," Tegh explained. "He said it's a good opportunity to make money from the tourists."

"Whatever the reason, I'm having a good time." Steve said, raising a bottle of local beer.

But Fritz was still bothered and said, "I can't believe you attracted his attention to us after I told you I didn't like it. Is that all he said? Is that why he came back over?"

Tegh looked at them and said, "Okay, I didn't want you to worry because you were having such a good time."

A wide-eyed Fritz said, "Worry? I knew it!"

"Calm down, Fritz. He was just here doing his job looking out for people harassing the tourists. But, he said his unit is expecting a squad of special MSS tomorrow. Rumor has it they're searching for fugitive subversives from the eastern provinces."

Fritz jumped on his words, "Did you—"

Betta elbowed in his ribs. "Keep your voice down."

In an exasperated stage whisper, Fritz said, "But he's hiding crap from us again."

Steve had to agree on that count and came to Fritz's defense. "I know you're trying to protect us from worrying about things over which we have no control, Tegh, but it's our lives too. You need to keep us informed. Three more brains working the problem has to be better than one."

"Okay, but I wasn't trying to befriend the guy. I was just trying to get information we can use."

"But when you do get the information," Betta said, "You have to share it. Now, what else did the soldier say?"

"He told me the unit arriving tomorrow is searching for the plane crash survivors."

"What!" Fritz blurted, but his outburst was absorbed by the merrymaking in the park, and no one seemed to notice.

Betta looked at Fritz and then Steve. "What are we going to do? Are they looking for us?"

"Of course they're looking..." Fritz started.

Tegh cut him off. "We don't know it's us specifically. All he said was 'survivors of a plane crash'. He didn't mention names or nationalities."

Fritz said, "Who else could it be?"

Tegh said, "Look, we've done nothing to draw attention to ourselves."

"Except talk to every goddamn soldier and policemen you can find," Fritz said, taking out a cigarette and lighting up.

"That's not helping, Fritz," Steve said. Then looking at Tegh, he said, "Go ahead, you were saying?"

With some deference, Tegh continued. "They can't be looking for us specifically. We haven't used any credit cards and I'm the only one who's used his passport, and then only here at the hotel and when buying our bus tickets. With all these tourists, we still blend in."

"That may be true," Steve said. "But I think we should leave just in case."

Tegh shook his head. "I know how you feel, but I'm not so sure leaving Dunhuang now is the right idea. If they're looking for people on the run, we should stay put and blend into the crowd. We can hide in plain sight. It might look funny if tourists who just arrived left the minute MSS investigators showed up."

"So how the hell do we do that… you know, blend in?" Fritz elongated the last two words. "We don't look like you."

For the first time, Tegh added vehemence in his voice. "But you do look like tourists, so act like them." Then more calmly, "There are plenty of Europeans here."

Betta squeezed Fritz's hand. "We can do this, Fritz. Tegh's made some good points."

"Tegh's always right!" Fritz threw his half-smoked cigarette down, unable to hide his frustration.

Betta pleaded with Steve. "How about it, Steve?"

But Steve didn't answer right away. Instead, he gave another look at the throngs of festival goers and realized they truly didn't stand out among the glut of foreigners. Looking back at them, he said, "Tegh has the best idea. Let's stay put for now."

Fritz glowered but said nothing. He lit another cigarette and puffed away in silence, this time standing apart from his colleagues.

No longer hungry, they walked, pretending interest in the vendor tables, occasionally picking up items local merchants had for sale. At one vendor's stall, Betta saw some scarves and stopped to look more closely. But the men hadn't notice her and continued walking until they heard her scream. "Fritz!"

The men turned.

Twenty-feet away, Betta was struggling with a man pulling at her backpack. Steve bolted towards her and forced himself between Betta and her attacker, breaking the assailant's grip on the backpack.

"Get away from her!" he yelled.

The man, who'd apparently thought he'd seen an easy mark, released his grip and dashed away, running right past Tegh and Fritz before they could react.

Visibly shaken, Betta asked, "Did you catch him?"

"No, he was too fast," Fritz said. "No sense in trying to follow him in this crowd. Are you okay?"

"Yeah, just shaken up," she said.

"That's a relief," Tegh said. "You're right, Fritz. There's not much we could have done. Anyway, it would have involved the police, and we definitely don't want that."

Fritz said, "We gotta move. Let's get out of here."

Tegh glanced around and saw a uniformed guard

heading their way. Tegh tugged at Betta's sleeve. "Start walking this way like nothing's wrong."

The four of them disappeared deeper into the multitude of festival merrymakers.

"You can't just let him get away," Betta pleaded.

Steve said, "Keep moving, Betta. Making statements to the police will only attract attention—passports, travel papers, and the such. You're okay, aren't you, Betta?"

Growing slightly out of breath and feeling a twinge in her ankle, she said, "I'm… fine. Let's go… to the hotel. I've had enough local color for one day."

Walking up to the second floor where their rooms were, Steve said, "You going to be okay tonight? If you want, we can take turns sitting in your room while you sleep."

Betta waved him off. "That's gallant of you, but I'll be fine. I don't think anyone followed us here. You guys get your rest and we can regroup in the morning."

Chapter 16

MOGAO CAVES, DUNHUANG, WESTERN CHINA

AFTER A QUICK breakfast in the morning, they booked a tour of the Mogao Caves from the hotel. Emotionally, Betta had recovered from the mugging, but Fritz had decided he was going to stay closer to her for moral support, if not physical protection. He and Betta sat together on the bus, while Steve and Tegh went to different seats a few rows back, again trying not to appear as a contiguous group. Tegh looked around at the other tourists and felt confident his plan of remaining inconspicuous among the tourists was the right tactic to avoid being discovered.

Their tour guide started her presentation while they drove to the caves. She explained that ancient Buddhist pilgrims from India had stopped in Dunhuang to recuperate after surviving the arduous trek across mountains and deserts. The convenient oasis gradually became a place where merchants came to cater to the monks who carved out and decorated the caves in the surrounding cliffs.

Their bus pulled into a parking lot at the base of an escarpment, which was covered with scaffold walkways and fronted by a pagoda entrance. Tourists jostled up the stairs to the elevated wooden trestles that allowed access to the caves.

When Fritz stopped at a kiosk to buy a guidebook, Tegh cautioned him. "Buy one printed in English. The special army unit is probably looking for two Germans. No sense in waving a red flag."

While Fritz was paying for his book, Tegh looked back toward the parking lot. Suddenly, he gasped in alarm.

"What is it?" Steve said.

Tegh motioned for him to keep his voice down as he turned to see if Betta or Fritz had seen it. They hadn't, both intent on looking through their guidebook.

"Steve, get them going. Move." Tegh all but pushed him.

Betta, recognizing she was being hurried, "Said, hold on. Fritz and I are trying to…"

Tegh gave up and said, "Head up the ramp to the first cave."

Fritz said, "What's the…?"

Tegh said, "I just saw the soldier from the town square, the one I was talking to. He's in the parking lot."

Fritz said, "Did he see us?"

"I'm certain he couldn't. He's well on the other side by some busses. But we need to get moving."

Betta followed some people she'd seen on their bus up a ramp towards one of the caves. Following close behind, the men were right behind her and the group soon turned into the cave, out of sight of the bus marshalling area where Tegh had seen the soldier.

After listening for a moment to their guide's explanation of artifacts and wall murals, Tegh whispered, "I think we did it. I don't see any soldiers following us."

By the time another half hour had gone by, they were on their fourth cave and still, there was no sign of soldiers. Fritz said quietly to Betta, "All the Buddhas look alike."

She gave him a not so gentle squeeze of the hand and he remained quiet. At least he went through the motions of being a tourist, though he voiced a mild protest when their guide reminded him that smoking wasn't permitted.

Betta pushed him towards the back of their group and said softly, "Are you trying to get her to kick us out? For once, will you play well with others?"

Fritz mumbled something and wouldn't look her in the eye. Instead, he refocused on their tour guide and at least looked like he was paying attention. Steve turned to look at the two and saw them whispering. Catching Betta's eye, Steve saw the exasperation on her face. He eased his way back to them and asked, "You guys okay?"

Fritz said, "For being as old as they are, these paintings are in pretty good shape."

Betta put a finger to her lips and nodded for him to pay attention to their guide.

Seeing Betta cringe, Tegh took a moment to scan their tour group to see if anyone was paying attention to Fritz. No one was. Relieved, but still on guard, Tegh returned his attention to their tour guide who was telling the legendary story of the Monkey King, "arguably" as she put it, "one of the greatest novels of Chinese literature ever written."

One woman in the group said in Italian accented English, "That sounds interesting."

Fritz mumbled to Betta, "No, it doesn't."

Either not hearing or ignoring Fritz's comment, the guide obliged the woman. "It's based on the travels of Xuan Zang, the Monkey King, as a fictionalized fool rather than a heroic traveler. Monkey King, Pigsy, and Sandy encountered treacherous…"

Tegh looked around again and saw everyone in the group's attention fixed on the guide. He took this opportunity to work his way to the back of the group to look for any sign of soldiers. He didn't see a single uniformed person.

Maybe that's a good sign, he thought, and returned his attention to his group, this time standing a few people back from Steve, Betta, and Fritz. When the guide mentioned something about the Flaming Mountains, shifting sands and apparitions, he heard Fritz whisper to Betta, "Oh good, a ghost story," which prompted another muffled "shush" from her.

Betta's admonishment did the trick and Fritz remained silent. In fact, after a few minutes, Tegh noticed Fritz was actually paying attention and, from his body language, enjoying what she said. At one point, though, he tried to raise his hand to ask a question, but Betta tugged his elbow, shook her head, and glared at him.

Not seeing his aborted gesture, the tour guide continued. "A more modern find, if one hundred and thirty years ago is modern, was the discovery of the Oracle of the Yellow Door and the Wiseman of Dunhuang. This sage was a man so enlightened that he would only reveal all if asked the right question. At least that's what the partially decoded, faded scripts painted on the wall murals tell us.

"The oracle lived a floor above this cave in a secret room. The entrance to his final resting place was hidden by a yellow door, finally discovered by a nineteenth century Spanish archeologist. Because of his facility with ancient Arabic and Persian texts, he established a loose association with a German archeologist working in the western Chinese deserts."

This time, Betta wasn't quick enough to stop him, and Fritz asked, "The same one who found the Diamond Sutra?"

"Ah, a very good question. We have a scholar among us," the tour guide quipped. "No, this was a different German, but a colleague nonetheless. While probing this cave, the Spaniard found a back passageway leading to a hidden staircase ascending two stories inside the bedrock. Upon reaching the top, he discovered a yellow door sealing off any further progress. His analysis eventually dated the door's origin to the tenth century.

"What he discovered behind the door, however, was an even greater find—a meditation chamber. On the hidden chamber's back wall were three rectangular niches centered four feet above the stone floor and facing three same-sized openings, or windows, carved through the two-foot-thick exterior cliff face, open to the outer world.

"For five midday hours, shafts of sunlight progressively shone through these windows and brightened the room's interior. Over the centuries, successive exposure to the brilliant sunlight, which directly illuminated the back-wall murals, faded an arc across the murals' message, accounting for some of the mystery we have today. You can still see the faded arc the sun made as its rays transited the paintings and forever bleached their once bright pigments, shrouding the full message.

"Even more astoundingly, the Spaniard found the remains of fourteen men mummified at the base of the mural. He speculated the mummies were those of successive monks, based on radio-carbon dating of their funerary shawls. Each monk succeeded his mummified predecessor over a period of 234 years from the seventh to the tenth centuries. According to the wall mural, the reigning oracle held court for supplicants, answering pilgrims' questions. Supplicants in turn brought the oracle sustenance as payment for his imparted wisdom.

"As each oracle died, his body was anointed, wrapped in silk bindings, propped against the wall next to his departed predecessors, and a new sage was enthroned. Inexplicably, when the fourteenth and last monk eventually died, the apartment was sealed by a sturdy yellow door and the ascending staircase was barred from below with rock and plaster. Why this action was taken remains a mystery still debated today.

"What adds to the mystery is that scientists haven't been able to reproduce the yellow pigment of the door. Renowned artists have examined the door, but none has ever claimed to have ever seen such a beautiful hue, much less duplicate it.

"You have been a kind and patient audience. Now if you will all move to your left, we'll proceed to the next cave."

But as the others moved, Tegh said to his colleagues, "Let's get back to the parking lot. If our original group is gone, we can get a ride back to town on another bus."

Fritz said, "Aren't we going to run into that soldier again?"

"If you recall, Fritz," Tegh said, "we didn't run into him when we got here. I just saw him as well as a whole lot of other people in the parking lot."

Steve added, "Best I could tell, he had no interest in the tourists up here in the caves. I think he's here for parking lot security, not looking for us."

But as they made their way down the entry ramps leading to the parking lot, Tegh got the attention of his three companions and motioned them to the back of the venue ticket building.

Steve said, "Why are you stopping us here, Tegh?"

Fritz didn't wait for a reply. "It's soldiers, right?"

Tegh said, "Yes, it's definitely the same soldier we encountered during the street festival. He's standing by a crowd control barrier, and I'm pretty sure he spotted us."

"Oh no," Betta cried.

Chapter 17

"I THINK WE'RE okay, though, because he waved to me," Tegh said. "Remember, he said his job was to help the tourist, not harass them. He said his assignment was to look for street kids and pickpockets."

As he said it, Tegh thought, *I hope I'm right because he said the MSS were on their way to look for survivors from the crash, which means us.* He didn't share these thoughts, however, fearful of upsetting his colleagues and further.

Trying to lighten the mood, Tegh said, "The way he was eyeing you, Betta, maybe he's just bored with crowd control and wants a break from the tedium by meeting a pretty girl."

"I doubt that," she said, holding out the sides of her oversized trousers.

Steve gave a soft laugh. "We can't wait here. We might as well head for our bus and brass it out."

Fritz looked at him with a questioning expression.

"Brass it out," Steve said. "It means to face the music, meet the situation head on."

"Oh," Fritz said.

"That's a good idea," said Tegh. "He's been nothing but friendly so far. Okay, ready?"

They nodded and walked as casually as they could towards where the buses were parked.

Almost right away, the soldier saw them, waved, and began walking towards them.

Betta looked away. "Oh no."

But Tegh grinned and greeted him with a handshake. "Stuck with tourist duty?"

The soldier smiled, looking first at Betta and then at Tegh. "Once a week I pull duty at one of the tourist stops to keep the ruffians in check. Did you enjoy the caves?"

Tegh translated as Steve and Betta politely voiced their appreciation for the cultural experience. Fritz stood back, concerned that the soldier was paying them too much attention. The others exchanged pleasantries but Fritz remained aloof, content with his cigarette.

Seeing the soldier eyeing Fritz as he put his pack back in his shirt pocket, Tegh asked, "Do you smoke?"

The soldier seemed embarrassed, having been caught watching Fritz so closely, but Tegh new the appeal of foreign cigarette brands to everyday workers like him. When he nodded, Tegh said, "Fritz won't mind sharing one cigarette, will you Fritz?"

Caught off guard, Fritz pulled out the pack and tapped up. The soldier readily took the offer and Fritz held out his lighter. As they talked, now in a more relaxed atmosphere, their tour bus's engine revved up, signaling it was time to return to Dunhuang proper.

On an impulse Betta said to the soldier, "Why don't you meet us back in town. We'll be looking for someplace to eat. Maybe you can suggest somewhere good."

Fritz couldn't believe her and fought the urge to protest.

But the soldier answered, "I recommend Feng Yi Tung as a place to eat. It has spicy food." Turning his head in the direction of a guard shack at the edge of the parking lot, he said, "I have to go now before my sergeant thinks I'm not being diligent in my duties."

They waved goodbye and then worked their way back aboard the bus. Once seated, Fritz let loose at Betta. "You didn't have to go and invite him."

She fired right back. "He's harmless, Fritz. He's more afraid of his boss than he is of turning us in, that is if he even suspects something. He's looking for pickpockets, not international fugitives."

Fritz silently fumed all the way back to the hotel.

In the hotel lobby, while waiting for Betta to come down, Fritz harangued Tegh about what a bad idea this was to meet with a local—and a soldier no less. "And another thing, while we were driving those first few blocks in the city coming here, is it just me, or are there more police around them now?" He pointed towards the lobby entrance where a policeman was talking formally to the hotel manager.

"I think you're right, Fritz," Steve said. "I saw them, too. When we passed the train station, there was an army troop carry-all truck. Something's up."

Tegh said softly, motioning for them to keep their voices down, "This confirms what our soldier friend told us at the festival."

"Soldier friend?" Fritz mocked.

Just then Betta came down the lobby stairs. "Are we ready for something to eat? I can't wait for some authentic Chinese food."

"I can't believe you just said that, Betta," Steve said, trying to lighten the mood. "We've been eating nothing but Chinese food for the past two weeks."

"Well, I hope for the sake of your soldier friend," Fritz continued, "he's on the up-and-up and isn't setting a trap for us."

Steve said, "Fritz was just commenting on the extra police presence, Betta."

"You really think so?" Betta said.

As they stepped outside, Fritz pointed. "See?"

Three regional policemen stood talking on the opposite corner. Farther down the street stood a group of four soldiers were being instructed by the one who had just been in their hotel lobby.

They looked to Tegh for an answer. This quickened all their pulses. Tegh pointed and said, "Go that way, away from them."

As they headed in the opposite direction, Tegh knew they were struggling to keep their anxieties in check. Tegh thought, *This is a police state—notorious for harsh treatment of outsiders—and not one of us has proper travel documents.*

After three blocks, he had them turn up a street and then make their way to the Fen Yi Tung restaurant. There, outside the establishment, their soldier friend was waiting for them. Thoughts of betrayal raced through Fritz's mind as he said not exactly softly, "Is that the same soldier Betta invited?" But he pulled up short as he saw the soldier's smile in recognition.

Temporarily relieved, Tegh slowed their pace and said to his colleagues, "It's best these people think of us as friendly. So be nice." Waving to the soldier, he said, "Good you made it."

With their new friend in tow, they took a seat away from the restaurant's entrance and ordered a round of the local beer, naan, spiced mashed beans, and a nondescript black liquid which Fritz thought was soy sauce, but which turned out to be not as mild. Taking an aggressive bite, Fritz chewed for a few seconds before he dropped his bread on his plate. He gulped some beer before giving a long and loud exhale. Fanning his mouth, he let out, "Yeow, that's hot!"

The soldier slapped his knee and tilted his head back laughing. The men did too, but it was Betta who commiserated. "Oh Fritzee, are you all right?"

The soldier said something and Tegh translated, "You should have asked me. I would have told you it was very spicy."

Fritz held both palms out, tears rolling down his cheeks. "I don't recommend the black sauce, whatever it is."

The soldier replied, "The sauce contains Szechuan peppercorns and brown mustard seeds. It's very popular, but we don't use nearly as much as you did." Touching his thumb and first two fingers lightly to his tongue, as if taking a small bite, he said, "Like this."

Fritz drank some more beer and motioned the waiter for another. "Now you tell me. It would have been nice to know that beforehand."

As the five ate, the soldier introduced himself as Feng. At Betta's urging, he told them a little about himself.

"I'm from southeastern China, near the Laotian border."

"Ah, near Vietnam," Steve said.

His comment surprised Feng. "Yes, very good. I joined the army last year and requested service near my home province. But the PLA saw fit to ship me here, at the other end of the earth."

Tegh noticed the others' expressions of sympathy and figured they, in turn, were further endearing themselves to the young man, which wouldn't help their anonymity.

Steve quipped, "I think all armies do that as a matter of course." He was careful, though, not to reveal he was an American.

Betta giggled and the men looked at her. Embarrassed at the unwanted attention, she put her hand to her mouth.

Fritz asked, "What is it, Betta? What's so funny?"

"I… I just realized that Feng has the same name as the restaurant."

Steve and Tegh grinned, but Fritz just looked at her.

Tegh translated for Feng and he said, "No, no. Feng is a very common Chinese name."

After another round of beers, they ordered bowls of noodles in broth. The beer and food kept coming at regular intervals at Tegh's urging. His alternate purpose, besides affording his colleagues a thorough sampling of regional cuisine, was to ply young Feng with enough beer to lower his inhibitions and fog his memory of the occasion. After more drinks than young Feng was used to, Tegh's ulterior motive became apparent to the others. It was then that Tegh began digging for the information.

"Are you part of the army unit standing guard around town tonight, Feng?"

"No, that's a special MSS unit, the one that just arrived. They're searching for the survivors of a plane that crashed several days ago. It must be important—the MSS sent their First Director out with his boss, and the police have sent their regional administrator to help. That's why there were seven of us at the caves today. Normally it would be just me and one other policeman."

Betta couldn't resist asking, "Have the police had any luck finding who they're looking for?"

Fritz froze.

Feng tapped a fist to his chest to stifle a burp and then said, "I don't think so. Otherwise there'd have been a big to do when that special unit's boss flew in. General Wu Xi is famous. On more than one occasion, he's made headlines by tracking down undesirables at large in the Chinese interior."

He took another pull on his beer and belched. "First Director Lin Chu, his subordinate, reportedly does anything the regional administrator tells him to. Then again, don't we all simply do what our bosses say?"

Tegh chuckled, noting Feng's sound judgement was seriously impaired. He was giving them information which they sorely needed to plan their next moves.

Fritz, finally seeing what Tegh was up to, joined in. "What happens to escapees when they're caught?"

The tipsy soldier said, "The world will never see them again. I guess they go to prison or worse. They just disappear."

Tegh could see his comment disturbed Betta, so he simply smiled as spoke softly to Betta. "Don't mind what he just said, Betta. Just look at me and smile. I must squeeze this soldier for more information and need you to distract him. So, look pretty and give him eye contact."

Betta swallowed and did as Tegh asked. She knew that concentrating on this simple charade would distract her own fears from the dangerous game she was playing.

Turning to Feng, Tegh raised his glass in salute to encourage his talkative mood. "So where and when do the MSS personnel go next?"

"Tomorrow, they return to their barracks in Jiayuguan. The general and first director will fly west to Turpan and search using a fresh detachment from the barracks stationed there. If that fails, I think he said they'll continue to Urumqi, Yining, and Khorgos on the western border."

Tegh pressed him. "Why, do they believe the fugitives are heading west?"

Feng shrugged. "I only heard my sergeant talking about how long this unit would be here and what we must do in support." He took a swig on a freshly arrived beer that had come as quickly as he'd put down his empty.

Seeing Feng's eyes glazing, Tegh figured he had all the information he could coax from him. But to dispel any suspicion Feng might possibly harbor should he happen to remember, Tegh kept up an idle conversation through another round of drinks and some flaky pastry dough drenched in honey accompanied by red grapes. When that was gone, he gave the sign to the others that they should head back to the Feitan Hotel.

"It's been a long day, Feng. I suspect you're tired," Tegh said, offering more than a suggestion to the drunken man. "Do you need help getting to your barracks?"

Feng waived him off. "No, I've got it," he said stumbling a bit as he stood. "Good fortune in your tours tomorrow. Maybe we can meet again?" His question was more suggestive than a casual goodbye.

Tegh patted his shoulder and said, "Maybe. Just look for us at the caves."

Feng cast a hopeful glance at Betta and Tegh wondered that perhaps he was expecting more than a simple goodbye. But Betta put an end to his speculation by excusing herself for the lady's room.

Tegh and Steve walked with Feng to the door of the restaurant to make sure he could get by on his own. As Steve opened the door, Tegh was troubled by Feng's last bit of information about the security force's plan to continue west from Turpan. Urumqi was the gateway to Yining and the border crossing at Khorgos, where they'd planned to cross into Kazakhstan. All these places were in the direction they were heading.

As Feng walked unsteadily away, Tegh noticed the extra police presence was still in evidence, a fact that kept his alarm bells ringing. Just then, Betta came back from the restroom. Tegh said, "Come on, we have things to discuss back at the hotel."

Heading in the opposite direction from two guards at the end of the block, they took another circuitous route from the restaurant, reaching the hotel without incident.

Upstairs in the room the three men were sharing, Fritz began. "So they know that we survived the plane crash and are unaccounted for. I mean, I'm sure they checked the manifest against the recovered bodies and know it's us who's missing."

"That may not be entirely true," Steve said. "For all we know, they have a bunch of bodies all jumbled up and burned to a crisp. Even if they recovered recognizable body parts or DNA, it would take weeks to identify everyone. So, they might not know exactly who's missing, just that some bodies are unaccounted for."

Fritz blurted, "But they know who was assigned to which seats and that our seats were empty."

Steve shrugged. He had to hand that one to Fritz.

Tegh knew Fritz's logic was accurate and, knowing that Chinese officials were searching for them in particular was a real problem. "We should give them a moving target. That makes it much harder to track than a stationary one." His logic seemed to calm some of their apprehension.

"We've slipped past the authorities for now," Tegh continued, "and avoided suspicion because Feng took a shine to you, Betta. He never once asked to inspect our travel documents.

"If you remember when we first headed to Dunhuang, we always had the intention of doubling back to the east. I think that's the tactic we should stick with. I've studied our map. We should buy bus tickets destined for Zhangye, that's well to the east of the crash site. When we reach the intermediate stop at Hongliyuan, we'll get off and buy train tickets north to Hami.

"That way we'd be changing direction as well as our method of transportation from a bus to the train. Even if they figure out we headed east on the bus, it's unlikely they'd discover we'd switched mid-trip until the bus arrives in Zhangye two days later and we don't get off. That will buy us both time and distance. By then, we will have travelled northwest a good five hundred miles from Zhangye. It will take the authorities even more time to sort things out."

"Where the hell is Hami, again?" Fritz asked.

Tegh indulged him. "It's a city west of Anxi where we caught the bus to Dunhuang. That gets us over half way to Urumqi, which is the direction we need to travel to get out of China. If the MSS should be tracking us, they'll have to chase bus tickets west to Dunhuang and then east again to Zhangye. By the time they realize we didn't go all the way to Zhangye, we'll be almost to Kazakhstan."

Fritz grinned and Tegh figured he liked the subterfuge.

Tegh added, "In our favor, Xinjiang Province is a predominantly Uighur region, rather than Han Chinese. With a greater mix of ethnic people, we have a better chance of not standing out. On the other hand, there's a large PLA and MSS presence in Urumqi because it's a huge city close to the western border. The large military presence is required to discourage a recurrence of a Uighur independence movement. Maybe the guards will be preoccupied watching them and not necessarily looking for us."

The others were silent as they thought about what he'd said. Then Steve spoke. "I say we do it. If you're going to be a bear, be a grizzly."

The others looked at him, not understanding the American cliché.

"I mean, if we're going to do this, we should be all in."

Now understanding and realizing he made perfect sense, they nodded their approval.

"I need a cigarette," Fritz announced. "I'm going outside to grab a smoke before I turn in."

Thirty minutes later, Fritz hadn't returned.

Tegh said, "Fritz should be back by now."

This sent her imagination reeling and Betta cried out, "Tegh, Steve, what are we going to do? Do the Chinese have him?"

Chapter 18

A Long Night in Dunhuang, Western China

Tegh went over to where she sat on the bed sobbing and put his arm around her shoulders. "Betta, it's probably nothing. Most likely, he's standing on the corner sulking and smoking his third cigarette right now. At this hour, I wouldn't think he'd attract attention."

She looked at him hopefully.

Tegh said, "Tell you what, I'll check the front of the hotel. You guys wait here."

Five minutes later he was back, but no Fritz.

"I didn't see him." Slipping on a light jacket, he said, "Steve, you take Betta back to her room and stay with her while I walk around."

"No, I should go," Steve started to say.

But Tegh stopped him. "If either of you were to accompany me outside this late at night, it might draw attention. Me they won't notice."

Betta's voice wavered. "Don't be gone too long,"

Tegh could hear the anguish in her voice and said, "I promise I won't." With that, he headed out into the night.

Out of curiosity, Steve watched from their window at the main street activity below. Two groups of security guards were coming down the street, one on either side, conducting a door-to-door search. As they passed one establishment's doorway, two of them pushed inside while the rest continued along until they reached the next doorway, where two more went inside that building. The soldiers on their side of the street were about to reach their hotel entrance.

Steve let the curtain fall and said, "Betta, quick, we've gotta leave the room!"

"What?"

"The police, or soldiers, or whoever they are, are making door-to-door searches. They're coming into our hotel right now. We can't get caught. Grab the backpack with our passports and money and follow me."

He grabbed her hand firmly and she followed him into the hall. As they took the first two steps towards the hallway corner in the direction of the elevators, they heard the universal ding announcing one's approach to their floor. Steve made an about face and tugged her in the opposite direction. They reached the stairwell exit at the opposite end and he pushed open the access door. He headed them up the stairs towards the roof.

Checking that the door's crash bar wasn't alarmed, he eased open the roof access door and glanced outside to make sure they weren't walking into a trap. Not seeing anyone, he led her onto the tar and gravel surface towards the elevator hoist and ventilation utility enclosure. They crouched on the opposite side of the housing, well clear from the line of sight to the roof access door, and caught their breath.

Betta put her weight on her thighs with her forearms and rested her head on Steve's back, making as small a profile as possible. From her rapid breathing, he could tell she was terrified. Without facing her, he whispered, "Take deep breaths. We're okay now. Try not to worry."

She snaked both arms around him and he clasped her hands around his midsection. "What if they've found Fritz or Tegh? They'll know we're nearby and come for us."

Steve knew he couldn't allow her to become hysterical. Putting his other hand on the roof's gravel surface for support, he eased down from his crouch and put his butt flat on the roof gravel, with both legs extended.

"Here, sit like this next to me."

She gripped him as tightly as she had after regaining consciousness in the plane crash. They rested their backs against the elevator housing and waited. Steve could feel the hoist's vibrations and hear the electric motors whine as the elevator worked its way from the lobby to intervening floors. Each stop produced an audible clunk, adding to their anxieties. Suddenly the pattern set up by the cable reeves stopped. The elevator had reached the roof.

Alarmingly, a thin shaft of light spread across a section of the roof, not forty feet from where they hid. Someone had opened the access door. Steve heard careful footsteps in the gravel. Then the crunches stopped. They were standing stock still now, listening. Steve squeezed his one arm tighter around Betta's shoulder, pressed a finger to her lips, and mouthed, "Shhh."

He heard the guards speaking in short, clipped sentences, but they weren't moving. Their back and forth discussion lasted for an agonizing minute. The entire time, Steve felt Betta scrunching closer to him, valiantly choking back her fear. He squeezed her as firmly as he dared to help slow her breathing.

Finally, Steve heard feet grind into the tar and gravel,

as if the guards were turning. He held his breath, waiting for the footsteps to get louder. But they didn't. Instead, he heard a few short steps, saw the light cast from the stairwell go out as the roof access door's closure mechanism hissed, and the door finally clicked shut.

Thoughts raced through Steve's mind. Had they both gone back down? Was one still there waiting because he suspected someone was up here? With the piercing light from the stairwell gone, the rooftop was again pitch dark. Neither of them moved for a whole five minutes. Steve felt her breasts pressed against him as they sat perfectly still except for their breathing. Ever so slowly, the tension left her grip on his hand, but her body pressure on his arm remained.

Having heard no moment since the door went shut, Steve figured they were alone and safe—for the time being. He relaxed his hand and whispered, "It's okay now."

She turned and put both arms around him, buried her head between his neck and shoulder, and sobbed. Her tears trickled against his skin. For the first time since their ordeal had begun, he felt a closeness to Betta, both comforting and awkward. Though he'd never established the precise nature of her relationship with Fritz, other than being business partners, he assumed that as a lovely, young woman, she probably had some romantic attachment to the man she travelled and worked with.

Steve put his hands on her shoulders and pushed her back slowly. "I'm going to look over the edge to see what the security guards are doing. You're okay sitting right here, so don't move. I won't let anything happen to you."

She slowly released him, her fingers not wanting to let

go. Leaving her with her back against the equipment housing, he duck-walked his way towards the edge and then sneaked the last five feet on his hands and knees before peering over the side.

The phalanx of guards was moving farther down the street and continuing their house-to-house inspections on the next block. Directly below him, several curious hotel residents stood on the sidewalk having animated discussions. Steve noticed Tegh across the street talking with a guard. After a few seconds, Tegh raised a hand to the guard in a friendly gesture of thanks and turned back towards the hotel.

Steve jerked back from the edge. *Did he look up? Did he see me? If I didn't know better, I could have sworn Tegh knew that guard from the way they both acted.* Was Fritz right along in his assessment of Tegh? Had Tegh given Fritz up to the guards somehow using soldier Feng as a messenger? His thoughts were coming too fast and were too difficult for him to answer.

In a quandary, he returned to Betta and took her hand. "Let's go back to your room."

They carefully made their way down the stairwell and entered the corridor on their floor. Just as cautiously, they peered around the corners to check the coast clear. Once in the room, it was obvious the guards had been there because chair cushions were tossed and a closet door stood open. But the backpack she'd left behind with her spare clothes was untouched.

Steve said, "I guess they were just looking for people and not evidence. I'm glad you grabbed our valuables, though."

Betta came up behind and wrapped her arms around

him, pressing close to his back. He felt her body heat radiating through his shirt. This was a different feeling, one he hadn't suspected he'd have towards her, one he hadn't felt towards a woman in a while.

"Thank you," she whispered. "I'm afraid I wasn't much good up on the roof. At least you kept your head."

He turned around, still in her arms, and gave her a reassuring look. She didn't attempt to push back. Instead, she hugged even tighter.

"Well, I'm glad I was good for something." They stood like that for a moment before he said, "Hey, look at me, Betta. You're going to be all right. Tegh will be back soon and so will Fritz. Then we can work on our plan to get out of here." He chose not to tell her of his fleeting thoughts at seeing Tegh talking to the MSS guards.

She didn't react at the mention of Fritz's name, holding onto Steve for a long moment. He could only wonder if something had changed.

As Fritz aimlessly looked in a closed shop window, smoking a cigarette, he heard a commotion coming from two blocks up the street. Looking up, he saw several uniformed guards turn the corner and head down both sides of his street. Crushing out his cigarette, he turned away, walking slowly in the opposite direction. Several yards further along, he came to an alley and turned in. It was the service access for the hotel and ran adjacent to the shops, mid-block between the buildings.

Trash cans, empty pallets, and stacks of broken-down cardboard boxes lined the alley next to the buildings. It was dark, except for the dim light spreading down the alley from the adjoining main streets at either end. Fritz walked part way down the alley and hunkered behind a pile of boxes. He was in full shadow, in a position that commanded a reasonable view in both directions. He waited.

Within ten minutes, the soldiers or police, he still wasn't sure, moved past the alley entrance. One of them stopped to shine a flashlight down the length of the service driveway, its beam passing slowly above where he sat. Seeing nothing but refuse and trash bins, the guard turned back to his colleagues and continued down the street.

Fritz dared not move for fear of encountering a straggler lagging behind his fellow guards or, worse yet, another group moving down the opposite parallel street who might happen to walk past the other end of the alley.

He remained still, all the while craving a cigarette. It was foolhardy to risk striking a match and letting the unmistakable smell of cigarette smoke waft to the main street and reveal his whereabouts. After several minutes, which seemed forever in his fear-heightened state of mind, all grew quiet.

He walked to the opposite end of the alley, peeked around the corner, then glanced at his watch. It was almost one A.M. There wasn't another soul on the street. Convinced the coast was clear, he hurried directly across the street and headed down the opposite alley way, which was just as cluttered as the one he'd left.

Fritz continued for several blocks, travelling back alley to back alley before he tried to double back and return to the hotel. But as soon as he ducked into a third alley, he heard a truck engine. At first it got louder and then died away. He flattened himself in the shadow of a building and looked to the cross-street alley where he'd just come from.

A truck had turned down it and was moving slowly, away from him, the occupants clearly searching for somebody. It wasn't a garbage truck on late night rounds, because no one left the truck to pick up the overflowing trash cans. It had to be a police carryall searching for someone—searching for him.

He thought, *Have they captured Betta, Steve, and Tegh?* Just as quickly as he'd thought this, he dismissed it, reasoning that he hadn't heard police sirens or seen patrol vehicles with their flashing lights converging towards the hotel, which surely would have been the case if they'd caught someone.

Convinced the police truck was searching for him, Fritz walked cautiously in the opposite direction, distancing himself as much and as rapidly as he dared from their search zone. As he moved with purpose, he desperately looked for a safe spot to hide.

He hadn't gone more than fifty yards when he pulled up short at the sound of a throaty growl. A good-sized, short-haired dog stood defensively over something on the ground. It was guarding some offal, probably gleaned from a garbage can, and had taken a protective, threatening stance. Fritz took slow side steps, displaying submissive disinterest in whatever it was the dog was defending, and skirted his way around. The dog gave a menacing growled, then barked.

Fritz stopped. *Do I stand still while the dog barks, or run and risk being chased by the dog? Shit, I'm betting on the dog.*

Fritz ran. After a few strides, it was clear the dog had been more interested in what it had dragged from the garbage than in pursuing him. Evidently, the mongrel's possession of choice kitchen scraps outweighed any instinctive urge it might have felt to enforce a territorial claim.

Reaching the main street at the end of the alley, Fritz turned left and slowed to a fast walk. Thankfully, there were no patrols in sight. Within a few strides, he slowed to a less conspicuous pace, just in case someone stuck a head out a window. He maintained random movements down streets and back alleys for another half hour until he found a sheltered doorway part way down an alley that was shielded on one end by a dumpster. He eased himself behind the dumpster, sat with his back against the building, and waited for the first glimmers of dawn to appear, fighting his incessant urge to smoke.

It was half past one in the morning when Tegh knocked on Betta's door. Steve answered. Betta, who had finally fallen asleep, looked up with a start. Not seeing Fritz, she began crying.

"I walked around for over an hour and didn't see him," Tegh said. "There were only a few businesses open, and I checked inside each one. I even went over to the police station, where dozens of guards were coming and going."

Steve said, "But no luck?"

"No. I didn't actually go in or even talk to the police. I just listened to hear what I could pick up."

"And?" Steve said.

"And nothing. They were just talking about what a waste of time their search was. Several of them talked about it but the conclusion was that all crash victims were probably dead and scavengers probably got the bodies."

A quick thought ran through Steve's mind. *Do I ask him about his encounter with the police outside the hotel?* Deciding against it, he told Tegh of their experience on the roof during the guards' search of the hotel, all except the part of seeing him talking with the guards and of his suspicions.

Betta, still fighting sobs, said, "Where can Fritz be?"

"My guess is he was scared by something, went in a direction he didn't know, and got lost. Something made him leave the immediate vicinity. Hopefully he found a place to hide until the morning. I suspect we'll see him at first light, when he can recognize a familiar landmark and make his way back to the hotel."

Betta looked plaintively to Steve. "What do you think scared him?"

"It could have been anything, a vagrant, a thief on the prowl, or one of those roving patrols like we saw. I don't know. But I'm certain it wasn't a security force issue, or we'd have seen a big reaction."

His explanations, as reasonable as they were, brought her no consolation. She could only imagine her friend lying hurt and bleeding somewhere in a back alley, in a strange town, in a foreign country. Her tensions running high and fear still haunting her, travel fatigue and worry finally overwhelmed her as she climbed on the bed and hugged the pillow. Within minutes, her breathing steadied and she fell asleep.

Steve and Tegh took turns remaining awake in Betta's room in case they heard something, while the other one got some sleep.

Just before 6 A.M., sunlight streamed through their one curtainless window and roused Tegh, who awoke with a start. Steve was nudging his foot. "Shit, I must have dozed off," Tegh said.

Steve motioned him to be quiet, then whispered, "I heard something moving in the hall."

They listened with an ear to the door and heard the distinctive sound of a door being pushed shut in the hall. Steve said, "That's the door to our room across the hall."

Wary that perhaps the authorities were back, Steve slowly cracked the door and peered into the hall—nothing, no sign of life. But he was certain he'd heard a door gently close. Both men tip-toed out. Steve put his ear to the door and heard some movement coming from inside the room. Taking a deep breath, he thrust open the door. Both men were surprised to see Fritz sitting on the bed taking off his shoes.

"What the..." Steve stopped, mouth agape.

"How'd you get...?" Tegh started.

Calm as could be and puffing a cigarette, Fritz looked up. "I was wondering where everyone was."

Betta burst through the open door. "Where have you been?" She threw her arms around Fritz and hugged him, tears of relief streaming down her face. It was all Fritz could do to move his cigarette from harm's way.

Steve and Tegh both clapped him on the back.

"Welcome back," Steve said.

Not waiting for him to speak, Tegh said, "So Fritz, what kept you so late?

Fritz spent a few minutes recounting his events of the evening, out-foxing the guards, hiding in alleyways, and being scared into running farther away by a foraging dog. "At first, I moved away from the hotel to evade the police patrols. When I finally thought I was free of danger, it was too late and too dark to move. And besides, I didn't have a clue where I was. So, I took refuge behind a garbage can in an alley and waited until the sun came up and I could see my way back."

Betta balled up her fists and pounded his shoulders. "You should have thought of doing something else instead of worrying us to death all night. You had us fearing the worst. All I could think of was that you were in jail, or had been robbed, or were lying dead in a gutter somewhere."

Fritz, grinning the whole time, grabbed her hands and held them until she stopped struggling. "Gee, Betta, I didn't know you cared. I'll have to stay out late more often."

The other two laughed, which only frustrated Betta more. "Oh, you!" She threw her arms around Fritz and hugged him. "Just don't do that again, okay?"

A bewildered Fritz said, "Okay."

Standing back, Steve could tell Betta was angry at Fritz for almost getting caught, but overwhelmed to see her friend safe—happy glad, not happy love. Though she hugged him knowing he was safe, she stepped back, not standing close any more, nor holding his hand, nor making any attempt to maintain contact. Steve took comfort that her emotion was simply collegial.

Tegh looked at the three of them. "Okay, guys. Time to make our next move. We're out of options here."

Chapter 19

THE ROAD TO HAMI, WESTERN CHINA

RUNNING ON LITTLE sleep, they were too wired emotionally to rest. With backpacks in hand, they checked out of their hotel and made their way to one of the restaurants down the street for breakfast.

As they waited for their food to arrive, Tegh said, "The bus depot is only a short walk from here. I'm going to go get tickets for the fourteen-hour trip to Zhangye and then be right back."

Fritz looked at him and said, "Yeah, I wouldn't want to have to come looking for you."

When Tegh returned, they were already eating and his breakfast was waiting for him. Sitting down he held up the tickets. "Got them, one hundred ten yuan apiece, not bad."

"We still have that much money?" Betta asked.

Taking a bite, Tegh said, "And then some. Don't worry. Look, we're all set. Our bus leaves in just under four hours. It's scheduled to reach Hongliyuan five hours after that. We'll disembark there, and purchase train tickets north to Hami. This change in direction, means of transportation, and the person making the purchase will ensure the authorities have a difficult time unravelling what we've done. That is, even if they have cause to question depot employees."

With several more hours to kill, they bought new clothes to further confound anyone who might be watching them. There wasn't much they could do about their facial features, but at least they wouldn't be dressed the same as they'd worn the day before. Fortunately for Betta, she found a pair of sturdy, over-the-ankle boots, which greatly improved the support for her nearly-healed foot.

Seeing her lace up the boots, Fritz observed, "I guess that horrible smelling salve worked."

Steve looked at everyone in their new clothes and said, "Let's hope this works."

"I'm thinking it would be good to have one of Marco Polo's golden passports," Fritz said.

"Well, Fritz, I'm honored," Tegh said. "You were paying attention."

As the bus pulled out of Dunhuang, the road eastward soon changed from oiled gravel to macadam. Steve noted to himself they were leaving the edge of the wilderness and heading back towards civilization.

Their trip through long stretches of desolate countryside was broken by short stops at unremarkable, arid outposts. Not exactly towns, these small clusters of humanity consisted of a few buildings and perhaps a bivouac for soldiers, rail, or highway workers.

From his bus window, Steve could see army personnel sitting about at these sidings, appearing not nearly as intimidating as those he'd seen prowling Dunhuang the day before. Like the few people who got on or off their bus, the soldiers looked as if abandoned in the hinterlands of the most populated nation on earth.

Disembarking passengers carried their possessions gathered in a bed sheet or pillow case, or sometimes in a battered suitcase, making Steve realize how little these people possessed. The newly arrived passengers sometimes stood momentarily, seemingly in the middle of nowhere, amidst surroundings which sighed centuries of sorrows, before trudging towards nothingness, their intrepid souls evaporating into the hot, sparse landscape. Neither did anyone greet these arrivals nor take notice of their departure down the road. Staring curiously out the window, Steve opined, *these are worn out people in a worn-out land.*

For most of the trip, they had nothing to do but talk, play cards, or look out the window at an unchanging, parched countryside. The other passengers, who were anonymously trying to get from one place to another, didn't interact with them or each other: no exchanges of pleasantries, gossip, or matters of opinion exchanged among these countrymen, all seemingly satisfied to remain strangers.

There was no idle talk, until a man from another section walked up and asked a question. Fritz froze, as did Betta. Not understanding the man and not knowing what to do, Fritz looked to Tegh for help. Tegh, however, spoke right up in the man's native tongue and seemingly satisfied whatever the man wanted.

As the local returned to his seat, Fritz said, "What the hell was that? Does he suspect we're foreigners?"

Tegh motioned his hand for him to lower his voice and said, "All three of you, right now look at me and smile. All he wanted to know was if he could help us, since he realized we weren't from around here. I said I was your guide and gave him the story we agreed to about being German journalists covering Chinese culture."

Steve and Betta relaxed, but Fritz still wasn't convinced of the innocence of the encounter. And then his suspicion was confirmed. "Are you sure he wasn't asking because he saw the authorities back in Dunhuang looking for us? How come he just shows up out of the blue?"

Tegh slowly shook his head. "Fritz, when will you ever believe me? We saw him get on the bus an hour out of Dunhuang at one of those rural stops. He's travelling with his wife to visit relatives somewhere east of here. And, if you took time to notice his clothes, he's a farmer and a poor one at that. He probably spent a good deal of any money he has for these bus tickets, so I doubt seriously that he's in the secret employ of the PLA or MSS."

But Fritz wasn't buying it. "I just don't believe in coincidences, that's all. I guess I just have to wait and see if at the next stop or two, he doesn't get off to make a call to report us."

Betta grasped his hand and said, "Fritz, sometimes you just have to trust that it's human nature to want to help others. I think that's all this was."

Lighting up a cigarette and exhaling a cloud of smoke, Fritz said, "We'll see. I'm just not as trusting as you."

The others sat back in their seats and didn't say anything else. Fritz finished his cigarette and then turned in his seat, back to them, and closed his eyes.

"Just ignore him," Betta said. "I agree with you, Tegh. My guess is that the average Chinese person's lot in life is such that they're willing to help each other out to survive in this remote part of the world."

It was early evening, almost two hours behind schedule, when they disembarked from their Zhangye-bound bus in Hongliyuan. From the immense size of the railyard situated only a few yards away, it was obvious to Tegh that this was a railway town whose purpose was dedicated to supporting railroad operating and maintenance crews. His guess was that the only purpose for the bus service was to provide people living in the surrounding area access to the east-west running trains. The town's infrastructure was mundane in almost every aspect.

While Steve, Tegh, and Betta stood at one end of the rail platform, Fritz approached the dual-purpose bus and train counter and purchased four soft-seat tickets for the next train to Hami at eighty yuan apiece. Tegh had instructed Fritz to order second-class tickets to avoid the chance of being noticed if they travelled in the more expensive first-class sleepers. It also avoided the press of people found in the more affordable third-class section.

As Fritz came back, Steve asked, "Any problems with the tickets?"

Fritz held them up. "There weren't any guards standing around, but I'm not convinced this changing from a bus to a train is going to fool the police."

Steve said, "You have to admit, though, it's better than doing nothing."

Tegh looked at the tickets and said, "If the schedule is to be believed, we have at least a four-hour wait until the north bound train departs for Hami."

Tired from sitting so long on uncomfortable train station benches, they finally boarded their train, only to be confronted by straight-backed seats. Seeing the three of them look at the uncomfortable wooden seats, Tegh explained, "The designation 'soft seats' doesn't refer to an upholstered seat like on European trains. It's merely a differentiation between the not-so-crowded confines of their second class carriage and the congested accommodations of a third-class conveyance."

Seeing Betta react to the smell of passenger sweat, foul breath, and unwashed clothing, Tegh asked, "You okay?"

Betta nodded, resigned to her situation, but Fritz said, "What about this place we're headed to? Is it a big city?"

"Not by Chinese standards. Hami began as an ancient caravan stop on the original Silk Road, sort of the gateway to what today is called Xinjiang Province."

"Why'd people stop there?" Betta asked.

"Sitting well below sea level, its oasis is the only water between the Lop Desert to the south and the Goshen Gobi Desert to the north." Looking at his watch, Tegh said, "It's going to take a while to reach Hami. Try to get some rest."

Though tired, the three slept uneasily in the wooden seats. Tegh, on the other hand, slept without interruption through the night.

Just before 5:00 A.M., they were awakened as the train slowed. Their steam engine pulled the train to a stop next to a pagoda-styled, one-story terminal framed by ramrod straight poplar trees. Tegh scanned the building looking for a sign telling them where they were. *This can't be Hami already; it's too early.*

Just then conductor came through the car saying, "There's was a problem with our engine and we have to wait until afternoon for a new locomotive to be brought in. Everyone's tickets will be honored once we're ready to go again. Now please disembark the carriage."

Standing on the platform and looking around, Fritz exclaimed, "Great, here we are, stranded in the middle of nowhere."

Betta added, "What are we going to do now?"

Chapter 20

FLYING WEST OVER Xinjiang Province, General Wu Xi called First Director Lin Chu and his three lieutenants into his private cabin. The aircraft, a perk only general officers had at their disposal, had the trappings of high rank which he enjoyed flaunting. This demonstrated to his subordinates his superiority and reinforced the imperative of the message he wanted to deliver. He conducted himself as if holding court, rather than exchanging ideas, and he wanted to insure First Director Lin Chu bore the brunt of his frustration.

"Why haven't the escaped exiles been brought to ground yet?" the general said. "I'm absolutely certain the four unaccounted persons from that China East Airlines flight survived and are running unchecked around the country. I'm just as certain, First Director Lin, that the reason they haven't been captured yet is because of your laxity and faulty leadership. Need I remind you that it was you who insisted on taking personal charge of the investigation at the crash site? Well, that hasn't worked out to well so far, has it?"

First Director Lin sat still in his chair.

"The only thing I know for sure is that their bodies weren't found in the wreckage and there have been vague reports from two towns west of the crash site that strangers, two or four—the numbers have varied—have been sighted. The exact timings of those sightings are imprecise as well. Details have been inconveniently vague, like an unattributed report that they stole a farmer's horse.

"How do you explain, First Director Lin, that the local population has failed to grasp the importance of this mission to our national security? Why don't they cooperate? If we had a way to prove the locals' complicity, I would put them all under arrest. All you've managed to unearth has been a nondescript sighting and an incomplete registration form at a Dunhuang hotel, which referenced three men and a woman. All this information confirmed was that they could have been any one of four women and nine men yet to be identified from the plane's wreckage.

"Chu, when we get on the ground in Turpan, I want you to lead the detachment immediately to check every hotel, restaurant and to apprehend these fugitives. By my calculations, we're a half a day ahead of them. I want no excuses this time, do you hear me?"

First director Lin Chu bridled at his boss's use of his first name. It made him feel like a child. "Yes, General, I fully understand the significance of the mission."

When their aircraft touched down in the intense heat of Turpan, the local PLA commander met them on the tarmac with a platoon of men and transportation. The commander had dealt with General Wu before and had no desire to incur his wrath. He surreptitiously handed a dispatch to First Director Lin, whispering, so the general couldn't hear, "I received this not an hour ago from my

Dunhuang counterpart."

The telegram reported that the police chief in Dunhuang had questioned a soldier assigned to tourist security at the Mogao Caves who was certain he'd seen three men and a woman, all in their twenties or early thirties, at an outdoor festival. He had witnessed them the next morning at the bus station, just about the time an eastbound bus was to depart, but wasn't certain they had boarded. The police chief had followed up with the station master and found that a foreigner had bought four bus tickets to Zhangye, which was due to arrive at that eastern city late tomorrow.

Lin pocketed the dispatch, choosing not to tell the general. Instead, he'd hold it until he could check out the Turpan stores, hotels, and eating establishments as he'd been directed. By then, the general was sure to tire of the miserably hot environs of Turpan, and depart for more comfortable surroundings.

With access to a plane, First Director Lin thought, *I'll fly east and be hot on the fugitives' tails while the general remains none the wiser. I'll apprehend the fugitives and any animosity General Wu might have about my withholding information will be lost in the news of the capture. On the other hand, if I have no luck, nothing will be lost.*

Chapter 21

THE ROAD TO HAMI, WESTERN CHINA

STANDING ON THE platform, Tegh stared down a dusty main street only to notice the town, such as it was, appeared to be devoid of population, except for a few citizens and a single shepherd herding his flock towards a sparsely tufted pasture behind one of the buildings. In no time, all four of them were sweating.

Steve said, "Whew, it's still early morning and I'm sweating through."

"Where are we?" Fritz asked trying to make sense of what little he could see in the dim light of dawn.

"I don't know the name the town," Tegh said. "But, see that minaret and mosque down the street? That tells me there's a Muslim population here, or at least there used to be. I'm thinking we've got time, so let's head that way, find somewhere to eat, and figure things out."

"Good idea," Fritz said. "I could use some food."

As they approached what looked like a mosque, Tegh said, "It looks like they turned it into a parking garage, judging by all the vehicles in its forecourt."

"How'd that happen, I mean turning a church into a parking lot?" Steve asked.

Tegh said, "For years, the government has discriminated against the Muslim culture. We're near the boundary of Xinjiang Province, predominantly the home of Chinese Muslims, or Uighurs. We'll see more debasement of the Uighur culture the farther west we travel."

Somewhat skeptically, Fritz said, "I can't believe a government would do that to an entire culture."

Tegh looked at him for a moment, then chose not to comment, simply saying, "I can assure you, Fritz, their campaign isn't a subtle one."

The sparse shops were closed this early in the morning, but they came across a hotel. Needing a rest, they registered, not bothering to ask for separate rooms, being too tired to consider deception. For thirty-two yuan, they got two rooms with beds, functioning in-room sinks, and a communal bathroom with a shower. Too tired from travel, they fell in bed to sleep.

Tegh woke just before 11:00 A.M. and roused the others. "We'll take sponge baths here using the sink, Betta. You go ahead down the hall and use the communal bathroom."

Feeling as decent as they could while still wearing yesterday's travel clothes, they left the hotel in search of a restaurant. The main street, no longer empty, bustled with bicycles and shoppers. At a small café, they ordered *manti*, a meat-filled dumpling topped with yogurt, sweet potatoes, boiled eggs, melons, grapes, pomegranates, and tea. At last feeling full, if not refreshed, they walked back to the hotel.

Fritz asked Betta, "Did you get enough sleep?"

"I don't think I've ever gotten enough sleep on this trip. But I must admit, it wasn't bad."

Steve fidgeted all through their lunch, uncomfortable at being marooned for the time being and, at least temporarily, sidetracked in their plan to move west. "Tegh, how are we going to proceed? I don't want to stay here longer than necessary. We need to get to Hami, if not beyond."

Not wanting to upset them, Tegh didn't want to reveal what Feng had confessed to him in Dunhuang about the MSS's destination for Turpan and Urumqi, the two major cities to the west. By the same token, he didn't have a reasonable solution yet as to how they'd get around those cities. Until he did, there was no sense in burdening them with the worry.

Instead, Tegh said, "I agree. We should push all the way to Urumqi as quickly as we can. Right now, the police are busy questioning locals at stops on the main line east of here, all the way to Zhangye. In about a day, they'll figure out we didn't get off there. Then, they'll backtrack to Dunhuang and rework the problem until they determine that we got on the train and headed north. That will take a few days as the very least, so we've got a window to make as much distance as possible."

Fritz took a drag from his cigarette. "I bet they'll never figure out we got stuck here. It's so small, it can't possibly be a destination for anyone."

They laughed, but the levity was short-lived as they realized that staying put wasn't an option and they still had no solution.

"The one thing we do have going for us," Tegh continued, "is that the police, MSS, and PLA are famous for not coordinating. But, if they discover soldier Feng in Dunhuang and question him, the authorities will surely realize it was us that he talked with at the caves and during the festival. That will put them back on track.

"I have an idea. You three stay here while I find the bus station. If security personnel are around, that's where they'll be. If they're there, I'll try to learn what they know."

Fritz looked up and started to say something, but Betta pulled on his sleeve. "Not now, Fritz. Let him do what he says. He's good at it."

Steve heard Betta cautioning Fritz and that made him think of the night Fritz got lost and he'd been trapped on the roof top with Betta. When he crawled to the ledge, he'd seen Tegh talking with the MSS authorities on the street below. And then in Dunhuang, it was Tegh who befriended the local policeman at the festival. Each time, he'd said it was to get information about what they knew. And now he was going to do the same thing. Maybe Fritz was correct.

Before he could carry his thoughts further, Betta asked, "You seem lost in thought. What are you thinking, Steve?"

He hesitated long enough for Fritz to lean in to hear his answer. "Oh nothing. I was just thinking it must be difficult living where, if things break down, it probably takes forever to get help."

Fritz eyed him warily as he took a drag on his cigarette.

Realizing there wasn't anything to do but wait, they ordered some tea from the front desk. They were in the lobby when Tegh returned half an hour later.

"There were two MSS guards walking around the bus station," Tegh said. "They questioned a few people in the waiting area, but I don't think they got much cooperation from what I could gather by the passengers' body language and the frustration on the faces of the guards.

Most of locals I saw were Uighurs, and they don't like Han Chinese, much less the MSS. When I checked the train station the next block over, the only employee I could find said he still didn't know when the replacement engine would arrive.

"On a hunch, I went back to the bus station and the guards were gone. I bought four bus tickets. We leave in about an hour for Xingxingxia."

"Where the hell's that?" Fritz asked.

"It's about a six-hour ride, on the way to Hami, northwest of here. At least it'll get us closer to Urumqi and, most importantly, keep us moving."

Still not grasping the importance of what Tegh was telling them, Fritz said, "So we're dumping our train tickets to get on a bus? What's in Zingzing?"

"Xingxingxia," he corrected. "It marks the start of the Autonomous Region of Xinjiang and will put us much farther away from the central government-dominated areas. From there we can make our next decision. I also bought us some new clothes and, just in case someone should remember Westerners arriving on the train from Hongliyuan, some hats. This will offer any pursuers another complication should the authorities get this far."

"Why so many new clothes? Not that I'm interested in laundering these," Fritz said, picking his sweaty shirt away from his body.

Tegh said, "Clothing norms and styles change significantly from region to region in China, owing to differences in local cultures."

"I don't care about the reason," Betta said. "I can't stand myself much longer, or you guys for that matter. These rags smell pretty ripe. Give them to me, Tegh."

He passed out Uighur caps—embroidered off-white skull caps called *doppa*—longer coats, and pantaloons.

"Betta, you don't wear the cap, but everyone wears the same type coats and trousers. I'm hoping this gets us through any police checkpoints or roadblocks."

She snatched up her new clothes and headed for the communal bathroom while the men changed.

Within a few minutes Betta returned and stood in front of the men, her arms out as she made a slow twirl. "Whadda ya' think, guys?"

"What do we do with the things we've been wearing?" Fritz asked.

"Give them to me," Tegh said. He took the bundle and disappeared through a door at the end of the hall, only to reappear a moment later empty handed.

"What did you do with the clothes?" Betta asked.

"I found the maids' quarters and left them there. The locals don't have much. They'll take them home. No one will question them for wearing something a little different. Besides that, police following up on descriptions of what some outsiders were wearing will realize they were mistaken if they see locals wearing outfits matching what they've been told."

Checking at the depot an hour later, they found the spare locomotive still hadn't arrived, so they opted for the bus, which pulled out as scheduled. Once again, they took separate seats in different parts of the bus, Betta and Fritz next to each other on a bench seat. Steve sat opposite Tegh further in the back. Fortunately, there were no other foreigners on the bus who might possibly see a potential compatriot and strike up a conversation, drawing unwanted attention.

Steve leaned close to Tegh and said, "I hope this changing back and forth is working."

Chapter 22

URUMQI, WESTERN CHINA

GENERAL WU XI was furious as he crumpled the hours-old telegram he'd just been handed. "First Director Lin," he shouted, "you should have shown me of this as soon as you received it! I've lost even more time in this backwater town and the fugitives have gained more time to hide. Now you tell me the four escapees are heading back east!

"I should have you permanently stationed in this forgotten part of the world to reward your incompetence. It's plain to see, even for the most severely afflicted with insufficient reasoning ability, that they're heading for their embassies in Beijing to seek repatriation. Must I show you how to stop them?"

But he didn't wait for, nor did he expect an answer. "I will fly east to Lanzhou and establish an eastern perimeter blockade. As for you," and now he was shaking his head. "As for you, start here in Urumqi. Search it as thoroughly and as quickly as you can. Then take the train east to Jiayuguan, questioning every train depot master between here and there, and I mean every one of them. Find who's seen them and who bought tickets." He balled up a fist. "We will squeeze them between us. Send me an update when you have confirmation of finding them.

"And for the guard in Dunhuang, who had them and let them go, tell your counterpart there to arrest him for incompetence and abetting espionage."

Lin had mixed feelings as he suffered the criticism stoically, never daring to show his deep-held disdain for the general. If there was any good part to the verbal abuse he was receiving, it was that he wasn't being immediately dismissed. There was always the chance he could ride out General Wu's fit of anger when he invariably would turn his attention to something he deemed more important in advancing his career.

But, Lin had been given an important chance to redeem himself. Unfortunately, if he failed, he might never again see his ancestral home in the east. As far as telling the security detachment commander in Dunhuang of the general's order to incarcerate the young soldier, he thought, *I will conveniently lose track of that communication. The unfortunate lad, whoever he is, is no more responsible for our failure to detain the crash victims than is the rabbit in the moon.*

Chapter 23

XINGXINGXIA, WESTERN CHINA

BY EARLY EVENING, the beleaguered travelers' bus approached Xingxingxia. As they neared the outskirts, Tegh pointed out a prison on a hillside. Illuminated by klieg lights, it was hard to miss. Surrounding the two-story structure was a high chain link fence topped by coils of concertina barbed wire. And barely visible beside the complex was a rail line leading through what had to be the prison's own terminal.

Struck by the oddity of having its own rail siding, Steve thought that the planners had built a certain efficiency, if not foreboding, into the construction of this facility. Looking more closely, he could see prisoners walking in the floodlit exercise yard. Their faces were expressionless, not from a lack of hope, nor even lost hope, but rather, their faces were of men who had never known hope at all. They shuffled in each other's footsteps along an elliptical path, stripped to the waist, their bodies adorned with tattoos.

Betta followed his gaze and noticed it too. Betta asked, "How do they acquire such bold tattoos locked up in prison?"

Tegh offered, "Tattoos are a hallmark of prison culture, a prisoner's rite of passage bestowed on them by fellow inmates. They're forever set apart from the outside civilization, even for the ones who may eventually be released. Their body-prints depict the nature of their offenses and punishments. Those who are hardened criminals will eventually be shot, perhaps once their internal organs are harvested for medical use. Those incarcerated for religious or political reasons are kept here for reeducation."

Steve picked up on that last comment. "Reeducation?"

"The state doesn't tolerate protests against civil policies or laws. You only have to look at my situation for an example. They persecute Muslims because they've resisted Beijing's dictums for years, if not centuries. Uighurs are rounded up and reeducated as to what good citizenship entails."

Tegh noticed Fritz was looking, too, and said, "Perhaps, Fritz, now you will believe what I've been telling you about the plight of the Uighurs."

Fritz looked at Tegh as if he wanted to say something but stopped.

Tegh continued. "The prison is guarded by the Ministry of State Security. When we get into Xingxingxia proper, we probably won't find any MSS on public duty, since they leave that to the local constabulary."

"This is very unsettling," Betta said.

"It's just the way things are in the People's Republic. The central government has many methods of keeping tabs on its citizens and monitoring their movements," Tegh said.

"You mean spying on their own citizens?" Fritz asked.

"Yes," Tegh replied. "And to keep track of foreigners, they have the Public Security Bureau, or PSB."

"So this PSB is trying to find us?" Betta asked.

"No," Tegh said, "that's only for their own citizens."

"Talk about Big Brother," Steve said. The others gave him quizzical looks and he explained, "I was referring to what a British author wrote a long time ago. Never mind."

As their bus progressed, they saw a series of long, low barracks illuminated by more klieg lights. Tegh pointed to a sign above the entrance gate. "That's the regional rehabilitation center I mentioned before. It's a halfway house for released prisoners at the end of their sentences, a place of reflection, work, and preparation for repatriation. Prisoners sent there have no travel papers. They can work locally, but are unable to return to their old homes. In essence, the system forces them to acclimate to the new region where they'll live out the rest of their lives."

"You mean like in exile?" Betta said.

"Exactly," Tegh said. "It's part of the government's forced colonization policy. In fact, many of the released prisoners are Han Chinese. As they reenter society, their numbers add to the minimization of the indigenous Uighur Muslim population and further perpetuates the seeds of conflict between the Han and the Uighurs. The communists' goal is to dilute the Muslim culture's hold with a policy of massive resettlement by ethnic Han."

Fritz shook his head. "That just seems inhumane. I can understand not liking someone, but to do that just to phase them out of existence. That doesn't seem right."

"And that's the reason your parents emigrated to Mongolia?" Steve said.

Tegh nodded. "That, and a business opportunity for my father."

"That doesn't seem right," Betta said, "to just up and displace people. Isn't there something they can do, or say, or something?"

Tegh shrugged. "Now you see firsthand what life in a police state is like. Everything's controlled and dissent isn't allowed."

"But how can they just persecute one class of citizens with another?" Betta retorted.

Tegh said, "You see the fallacy and so do I, but the government claims modern China is classless. But all the while, their bureaucracy strictly categorizes citizens by their social, cultural, and geographical backgrounds as appended to their identity papers. This perpetuates a party policy of bloodline guilt that descendants of the well-to-do must bear. Thus, Han Chinese consider themselves superior to any other culture in China."

"So this is the system you were up against?" Betta said.

Tegh said, "No, it was my university roommate who was up against it. I didn't like it, but knew better than to express that openly in China proper."

Steve, Betta, and Fritz could only stare out the window.

When their bus finally pulled up to the Xingxingxia terminal, it was almost 10 P.M. Most of the passengers disembarked, including two soldiers. Looking at the people on platform from his bus window, Steve wondered if these soldiers were reporting for duty or were just returning from time off spent in more hospitable environs. Three porters offloaded the cargo lashed to the roof, while passengers, the native Uighurs readily identified by their embroidered doppa caps, waited patiently on the platform, oblivious to the army personnel.

Noticing Steve's interest, Tegh said, "The locals don't openly express resentment of soldiers and others in authority. Theirs is a passive defiance ever since the central government forcibly cracked down on their attempts at independence several years ago. Guards are an unpleasant but constant reminder of those days."

"You're speaking from experience, Tegh?"

"Somewhat," he replied. "The government puts up with the Uighur opposition attitude as long as it's not too vocal and it remains confined to Xinjiang Province."

"Sort of like isolating an epidemic outbreak," Fritz said.

"Exactly," Tegh said.

Steve couldn't help adding, "It's their version of peaceful coexistence."

Tired and hungry, the travelers had three hours before their next bus left for Hami, which lay another seven hours to the northwest. They headed up the dusty street towards a lighted window sign above the only restaurant open at that hour. Unlike Dunhuang, there was no nightlife apparent in this windswept outpost. They passed several shuttered shops and saw a few parked vehicles—old model Opals, Peugeots, Toyotas, and even a Ford.

"I think cars and trucks come here to die," Fritz quipped.

"Vehicles are like people in this region—every ounce of usefulness gets squeezed out," Tegh said.

In a six-table restaurant, Tegh translated and they ordered. When their server came back with grilled chunks of pork, slivers of carrot and peas, all covered in a savory ginger and saffron sauce, they dug in with gusto.

"This is delicious," Betta said, taking her first mouthful.

Even Fritz agreed, demonstrating journeyman facility with the chopsticks. Hungry from travel, they ate quickly. Other than snacks on the bus, they hadn't had a full meal in almost a day. Soon, they pushed back their empty plates.

"Whew, sorry for pigging out, but I was hungry," Steve said, patting his tummy.

"What do we do now, Tegh?" Fritz asked, lighting up a cigarette. "Looks like we're at the end of the earth in a land time forgot—a long way from home."

"But, to paraphrase Chairman Mao, we're hiding amidst the minnows in the sea," Tegh replied. "We're among a population descended from outcasts. So, we'll be ignored as long as we remain quiet."

"How do you mean, Tegh?" asked Betta.

"Xinjiang was once called Tartary, and Turkestan and has been dominated for centuries by Turkic Muslims. As Islam spread east after the seventh century, Uighurs became the oasis dwellers, the middlemen of the Silk Road. Today, the Kazakh, Kyrgyz, and Tajiks are the descendants of those central Asian steppe nomads. Within such an ethnic mix we'll draw little attention among the locals. My only concern is the PLA barracks we passed just before arriving at the bus depot."

Steve said, "It can't be too much of a concern. I saw a lot of out-of-date armored vehicles, and their whole camp looked more like a backlot movie set than a modern army camp."

Fritz focused on the mention of an army camp. "I hear what you're saying, Tegh, about how the locals don't get along with the army. But trying to blend in with the locals to avoid the authorities is a tall order. There was a lot of security activity in Dunhuang. The authorities are obviously looking for someone. The sooner we leave China, the better I'll like it."

"I agree with, Fritz," Betta said. "We've been pressing our luck. Tegh, how long till we reach Urumqi, what do we do once we get there, and how do we reach to the border from there?"

Tegh sensed their anxiety, but wasn't about to reveal his real concerns with the answers to Betta's questions. Indeed, what to do next weighed heavily on him. Then he said, "Let's take things one at a time. I know this is unsettling, but plan has done us well so far. Urumqi is a huge city, much easier for us to blend in until we figure out how to cross the Kazakh border. The best thing we have going for us is that we've kept our heads down and gone in directions the authorities never dreamt we'd go."

"Yeah, yeah, yeah," Fritz stood in disgust. "It's not like we had a choice. I'm going to find a bathroom." As he walked away, he mumbled, "Wait, blend in, something good will happen. Like shit it will."

Steve followed him to the restroom, while Betta and Tegh waited at the table. By the time Steve and Fritz returned, no one was talking.

Finally, Tegh broke the silence. "I know you're worried. So am I. Do I know exactly how we'll get across the border? No. But I've crossed the western Chinese border before. Not under circumstances like this, but I have. The four of us are smart; we'll figure it out. Four heads are better than just one."

The others didn't say anything and Tegh was glad that

at least they didn't balk at what he'd said. He thought, *maybe my appeal to their own ingenuity will work in our favor.*

They boarded the bus to Hami well after midnight. Surprisingly, the bus was almost full. Fritz thought it odd that a bus in the middle of nowhere was at near capacity. They pulled out and continued their odyssey. If they were apprehensive, it didn't show; the strong Chinese beer they'd had with dinner soon took a merciful toll on their eyelids.

With one bathroom stop at breakfast time and one more for gas, the bus pulled into Hami at the Bogda Shan foothills just after noon. There were no ominous signs of prisons or rehabilitation centers to greet them. The town was more than a wide spot in the road, with modest trappings of civilization, albeit limited in its resemblance to urbanization.

What immediately caught Steve's eye was how green everything appeared. The arid landscape of the last several days had given way to shade trees and orchards. Although the heat was nearing oppressive, the houses had flower gardens with grape trellises, their vines twisting upwards towards a high sun.

"If I didn't know better, with all this green, I'd think I was in New Jersey," Steve said.

"Remember the story of the Monkey King?" Tegh asked. "Well, this is where he almost died of thirst until his horse found water. Underground cisterns are fed from the run off from the Bogda Shan and irrigate everything you see."

"So what now?" Fritz said. "History lesson aside, I'm feeling exposed standing in broad daylight outside this bus depot, especially since two policemen are standing at the other end of the platform and I don't like the way they're looking this way."

"Don't panic, Fritz," Steve said. "We haven't done anything except get off a bus."

But about the time he'd gotten his words out, the policemen began making their way down the platform towards them.

As if the approaching policemen were the Prophets of Doom, Fritz turned excitedly towards his friends. "Tegh, think of something," he yammered through clenched teeth, barely under his breath.

Tegh decided instead to go on the offense. He stepped forward to ask something of the older of the two policemen, while at the same time gesturing towards Betta. "Do you know where there are toilets for my friend here? She's not a good traveler and is in a little, uh, distress right now." He put his hand to his mouth, as if embarrassed to say such things to another man, much less a stranger, catching the policemen off guard.

The younger of the two stepped forward and pointed to the backside of the station, so that Betta would understand his gestures while speaking to Tegh.

Tegh said, "Betta, you should go to the bathroom now, even if you don't have to. And stay in there a few minutes. I told him it was your time of the month."

"For real?" Betta scowled and then changed to offer mock indignation to help sell Tegh's ploy.

Next, Tegh asked Fritz for a couple of cigarettes. "You don't smoke," Fritz protested.

Annoyed at Fritz's comment, Tegh said, "But they do and I'm going to offer them some of yours."

Fritz understood. "Ah, right. Good thinking."

The guards readily accepted the smokes and shared the light that Fritz offered. Recognizing the rapport this gained them, Tegh handed the remainder of the pack to the older one, thus giving him psychological leverage and cementing a friendly bond.

"Where are you headed?" the soldier in charge asked.

Tegh realized his gambit had worked. The guard could have asked where they were from, which would have been more intrusive. Instead, his question was idle curiosity, an icebreaker. Pointing to Steve and Fritz, Tegh said, "My friends are looking for a barber shop. We've been on an academic tour for three weeks. We're headed to a symposium of Chinese artifacts in Urumqi and need to clean up a bit. They're presenting papers on—"

"Tegh, what are you saying?" Fritz interrupted. "We don't want to be their friends. We just want to fade into the woodwork."

This prompted Steve. "Fritz's right. We don't want to stand out, one way or the other."

"That's what I'm trying to do, fellas. If I get these guys to show us the town, then they'll forget all about us, just like Feng did in Dunhuang."

Instead of pointing out where the barber was, the younger guard took Tegh by the elbow and motioned them towards a shop down the street. There, next to a bank and a florist, was a two-story structure, with an older Chinese gentleman sitting out front wearing a white lab coat. With a rapid fire but friendly exchange, the policeman explained this was his barber and he would be only too happy to accommodate them. Tegh told Fritz and Steve to follow the policeman and fend for themselves in explaining how they wanted their hair cut.

Fritz complained, when he saw Tegh not following, "You're not going with us?"

Tegh said, "I have to wait for Betta and follow."

By the time Betta and Tegh reached the shop, Steve had finished and the barber was working on Fritz. Steve's hair was cut evenly in length on top and tapered towards his ears. The barber was buzz-cutting Fritz's hair to a quarter-inch stubble.

"That looks very good, Steve," Betta said.

"You think so? I wasn't sure, I had to use sign language."

But as the barber finished Fritz and he stood up, she burst out laughing.

Unfazed, Fritz said, "I couldn't stand it anymore and I wasn't sure what to say, so I decided this was best."

Tegh rubbed his fuzzy head as if patting a Buddha for good luck. "Practical is usually the best choice." He thanked the barber and paid him with the yuan equivalent of a half-euro apiece. Judging from the smile on the barber's face, this was above scale for the service.

The older policeman was waiting for them outside and invited them to visit their station. This set Tegh's alarm bells ringing, but with no ready-made excuse not to, he had no choice.

Though they didn't understand what Tegh and the policeman were saying, the others couldn't help noticing Tegh's anxious expression.

As they walked along, Tegh thought, *what possible motives can he have? Is he just being friendly to gain my confidence before he springs the trap to apprehend us? Maybe Fritz has been correct.* Reluctantly, he realized he had no choice but to play along. As they approached the police station, Tegh assured the others the policeman was simply curious.

What ramped up their anxiety, however, was when the policeman bid them to sit in chairs under the trees in front of the station. They did so, but remained wary until Tegh explained, after asking the policeman what was going on, "He says he just wanted to talk. He doesn't get to meet many visitors to the region and their policy forbids them from socializing in town while on duty."

Tegh told the policeman that he and his friends were looking for some sundries after being on the road and could he offer suggestions as to where to look.

Unable to understand what was being said, Steve noticed that other police coming and going at the station didn't even take notice. *Maybe this isn't such a bad tactic after all,* he thought.

Finally, Tegh convinced the policeman they had to leave, saying, "We're meeting a colleague in Urumqi and don't want to miss our bus."

The cop bid them good journey and they left the station as casually as they could.

Once far enough away, Fritz muttered under his breath, "Now we've been seen. There's no way they won't remember us. They may not know much about our past, but they now know our future. If the state security police question them, they'll know they spent time with outsiders today."

"But our cover story explains all that," Tegh protested. "Think about it. We were stopped, but not detained."

"Yeah, but I for one want to keep a lower profile," Fritz insisted.

"That's hard to do with that silly haircut," Betta snickered.

But Steve agreed with Fritz, saying, "For sure, we've been noticed."

"Okay, that's settled. Let's go get train tickets for Urumqi," Tegh said.

"But, I thought you said bus to the… Oh I get it," Steve said.

"That train station isn't going anywhere and neither is my appetite," Betta said.

"Hear, hear," Steve seconded.

They sat at the restaurant counter seats leaving several empty places between them and a local man who already had his meal in front of him.

"I didn't realize how hungry I was," Betta said, breaking off a piece of flatbread their waitress placed in front of them.

"So what's the special this afternoon?" Fritz asked Tegh who was looking at the menu.

Tegh pointed to the slate chalk board on the wall behind the waitress and said, "It's *plor*, which is rice, meat, onions, carrots, raisins, and chickpeas. Your other choice is *samsa*, which is a meat pie, probably mutton."

"They both sound good," Steve said.

Fritz said, "I'm okay either way. What's bothering the hell out of me is that we don't have any idea what we're going to do next. Take a bus, take a train… I'm worried about leaving traces for the police. Sooner or later, with these tickets we keep buying, they'll catch on to us."

"But we've been careful to have someone different buy them each time," Betta said. "And I can't believe there's that much checking of that sort of thing anyway."

Tegh nodded his head and said, "Betta's correct. We have every advantage right now and should..."

But a sudden blast from air brakes startled them as a stake truck stopped abruptly out front. Shortly, the driver, a smallish man wearing heavy-gauge canvas trousers and a sturdy cotton shirt, with a weathered visage most likely due to spending years in the sun, entered, taking a seat at the counter two down from them. Tegh thought he was shorter than Fritz, but more ruggedly built, with arms and a chest well-developed from lifting heavy things over a lifetime. Tegh's estimate was that he was in his early fifties.

Without asking, the waitress dished him a bowl of the special from the large pot on the stove. She pulled a brown bottle from a plastic cooler at her feet and opened it. They jabbered a bit before she returned to her work behind the counter in preparing the other meals.

Focusing more on the meal the newly arrived man was eating rather than Fritz's concerns, Betta said, "That smells good, Tegh. I think I'll try it."

Taking her suggestion, Tegh gave the waitress their order.

Fritz resumed his objections. "Do you really think we should risk the train again? The MSS is bound to discover who's getting these tickets and be there waiting for us."

Frustrated with Fritz, Tegh said something in Chinese under his breath. Then, calming himself, Tegh said, "I think we're okay, Fritz. I know we've seen a lot of security guards, but we haven't detected the slightest hint that we are the ones they're looking for."

The newly arrived truck driver stopped eating when he heard Tegh's muffled epithet and looked at him. "You seem upset, my friend. What bad thing can possibly be on the minds of four good looking young people such as yourselves?"

Tegh was taken aback by the driver's intrusion. "Oh, I just won a bet with my friend here on what was in the stew today. I think he's gotten too used to beef."

The older man smiled.

Fritz immediately noted the stranger's sudden interest and was about to ask Tegh something when Betta butted in. "What's he saying?"

Tegh ignored her, turning his full attention to the truck driver. Several times the driver grinned at something Tegh said, and after a moment, their discussion became more animated, as if two old friends had just run into each other after a long absence.

Finally, Tegh turned to his anxious compatriots and introduced them to the driver, who nodded politely. "This is Otarbai. He services the sheep ranches on the lakes to the northwest, transporting livestock and delivering supplies. Right now, he's taking a load of fodder to his friend at a lake near Turpan, east of Urumqi in the shadow of the Flaming Mountains."

"Flaming Mountains?" Betta said.

"Remember the Monkey King and his search?" Tegh started and then stopped. "Anyway, the driver's willing to let us ride and—"

Fritz exploded, "Ride! We don't know this guy. He just shows up and wants to help?"

Tegh, in as stern a voice as he could muster said, "Fritz, I explained were trying to get out of the country but we've lost the visas in our passports and are trying to avoid the police and—"

"And!" Fritz said.

"And," Tegh continued, "he just laughed because he also tries to avoid the police every chance he gets. He says the authorities are always harassing the ranchers in the area for money, so he'd be glad to help us. I figure if we ride with him, we won't risk having to buy tickets, which we are all worried about, Fritz."

Fritz considered this. Still skeptical, however, he asked, "What's he want? Money? How do we know he's not going to turn us in?"

Tegh said, "Nothing. He just says he's more than willing to help us."

Fritz looked at Betta and Steve, then back to Tegh. "There's got to be a catch. It's too good to be true."

Tired of mollycoddling Fritz's outbursts, Tegh swallowed his exasperation and was about to respond when Steve said, "Fritz, just hear Tegh out. I think we have an honest opportunity to get out of here without being noticed."

Calmer now, Tegh said, "Fritz, I don't ask for these things to happen, they just do. I'm trying to make the best of a bad… no, dire situation. You may not fully appreciate what could happen if the authorities catch us, but I do."

Then, lowering his voice so as not to alarm Otarbai, who was as pleasant and agreeable as anyone Tegh had ever met, he said, "For the last time, will you, all of you, get on board with me, or do I go it alone and let you figure out how the hell you get back to New York, or Stuttgart, or wherever it is you think you want to go, on your own?"

Steve started to say something, but Betta cut him off. "Does he want anything?"

Tegh looked at her and then the two men. Seeing they were of a mind to listen now, he asked Otarbai how much he wanted in exchange. The driver raised an open hand dismissively, which they all understood as, don't bother. Tegh exchanged a few more words until the driver nodded his head.

"He said it's a long drive and he's just happy to have some company. I told him we insisted on paying for his gas, so he agreed."

Betta, warming to the proposition, said, "His name is too awkward for me to pronounce."

Tegh tried coaching her in pronouncing the Kazakh name. "Come on, Betta, you can do it. His name means 'rich in sheep' and it would do a lot to win his confidence if you were to at least try."

But she wouldn't relent. "Tell him I've nicknamed him Benny, after my beloved uncle on my mother's side."

Tegh translated and Otarbai's eyes lit up, honored to be named after a revered member of her family. And Benny he became.

Tegh asked Benny to show them on their dog-eared railway map where he was headed. He indicated an area northwest of the Bogda Shan Mountains which was labeled as the Junggar Pendi, a high, arid plateau which extended west to the border.

Tegh explained to them, "This gets us to Kazakhstan, exactly where we want to go. So finish eating and let's get moving."

Several minutes later they paid their bill and went outside where the truck was parked. Benny reluctantly accepted the equivalent of twelve euros in yuan and motioned for them to get into the truck bed, which was strewn with hay, remnants of sheep dung, and rivulets of blood in one corner, the sight of which had Fritz wondering again what had they gotten themselves in for.

Chapter 24

TURPAN AND LANZHOU, WESTERN CHINA

FROM HIS TEMPORARY headquarters in Turpan, First Director Lin suffered in silence as Ministry General Wu rebuked him on the phone. Hearing that Lin had missed the fugitives in Jiayuguan, Dunhuang, and now Turpan, the general was apoplectic.

"Lin, I'm getting inquiries from the Minister of Security himself in Beijing as to why we can't find these four people. He called it an embarrassment of the first order and said that it wouldn't go well for me, or anyone who works for me, if we don't resolve this, and quickly. Do you understand?"

First Director Lin didn't reply. Instead, he waited for the general's tirade to continue.

"Listen carefully, Lin. Your career is on the line. Get you and your people back to Urumqi and work east one more time. I'm in Lanzhou and will work west. I sent orders to the Dunhuang garrison commander to scour the city again, since that's the last known place where the fugitives were seen. The Dunhuang commander will work his way northeast until he meets up with either you or me."

This time, there was no mention of an arrest order for the Dunhuang soldier who had seen the fugitives. Lin decided not to point that out to the general. There was no use in invoking more verbal abuse.

When the general hung up, Lin turned to the local Turpan commander. "Please bring up the lead vehicle of your convoy. We must make best possible time in getting to Urumqi."

Not afforded the luxury of flying, First Director Lin would travel in a three-truck convoy for the 180-kilometer trip to the western city, a two-and-a-half-hour journey across the waste of the Turpan Depression in forty-three-degree heat. It would be pleasant compared to the criticism he'd just received from his boss.

Chapter 25

THE LIVING ROOM phone rang and Warren Applegate got up from his couch to answer it. His was a modest home, one he'd come back to many times during his three-decades-long career in the Marine Corps. Home to his wife and where his son Steven and daughter Julie had grown up, now it was where his wife of thirty-eight years lay in hospice care and he waited for news of his missing son.

The voice on the other end said, "Warren, this is General Gearity again."

"Good afternoon, General. Have they found Steven?"

"No, but I do have some intel that will interest you. Our security det commander at the embassy in Ulaanbaatar caught wind of something yesterday. It seems his Mongolian counterpart was talking to some of their guards stationed on their southern border with China. He reports the MSS have made several inquiries about whether any suspicious Westerners may have tried to cross into Mongolia from China."

"Did they identify who these Westerners were, sir?" Warren asked.

"The det commander didn't say. But he did say the Chinese were looking for a Mongolian dissident, most likely a Uighur, under an expulsion order from China for subversive activity. He was manifested on the same CEA flight that Steven was on. The implication being this dissident might be traveling with the others, presumably our missing Westerners—that is, Steven."

"Did they specifically mention Steven?"

"No, but the NSA did go back and took another look at some MSS chatter they picked up based on this embassy report. Sure enough, the People's Ministry of State Security is looking for two Germans and an American in Urumqi. And evidently, this is causing quite a stir inside the Ministry headquarters in Beijing. We've got indications some very senior officials are more than embarrassed that their security personnel can't locate them. They've now expanded the search all the way west to Urumqi."

"Urumqi. That's one shit-pot-full of a long way from where the plane crashed, sir. Besides that, it's got nothing to do with Mongolia."

"I know, Warren. You know how raw intelligence is. It takes a while to fit the pieces together. We've got a lot of very talented people working the problem.

"Oh, and one other thing. It seems the Chinese government has put an MSS general in charge of this investigation in western China, which means it's important to them. Even though the Chinese won't let our NTSB people in, we do know for certain they still have four persons unaccounted for, in addition to thirteen sets of remains they have yet to identify from the crash."

"Well, thank you, sir, but I'm not getting my hopes up. I don't suppose we have any assets in that part of the world?"

"Even if we did, Warren, I couldn't confirm it for you.

But I'll keep you cut in."

"Thank you, General. Oh, and by the way."

Every military man hated a statement that started, "Oh, by the way."

"Yes, Warren, have you got something?"

"Well, General, it's the strangest thing. Shortly after you last called, I went back and checked my answering machine and a brief message was recorded."

"Go on."

"It was from Steven. And the time stamp put it several hours after the crash."

"Hmmm. That's all?"

"I'm sure it sounded like his voice."

"What did the message say?"

"All it said was, 'I'll call later when I can'. Then it ended."

"Okay, not much to go on, but I'll get NSA on it ASAP and see if they can make anything of it."

"Thank you, sir."

Chapter 26

TURPAN, WESTERN CHINA

BY THE TIME Benny topped off his jerry cans with water and bought a bag of apples, it was nearing five P.M. Shadows were elongating and Benny told Tegh he had about another hour or so to go before dark. They settled in the back of the truck bed and made themselves as comfortable as possible as Benny pulled away from the small restaurant.

Benny drove to within two hours of reaching Turpan before he pulled onto a roadside turnout. The sun's last rays lit up the ochre-orange mountainsides to the northeast, the Flaming Mountains. Tegh jumped down and talked with Benny.

Turning back to the others, Tegh said, "Benny's stopping to get some sleep. He says one of his headlights is out and his eyesight isn't what it used to be, so he prefers not driving in the dark. I suggest we make ourselves comfortable in the back of the truck and follow suit."

Fritz, as usual, started to object until Betta said, "I don't think you have a choice, Fritz. It's either on the truck or alongside the road."

Fritz looked around at the barren landscape. "What, out there? What if he should drive off?"

Steve laughed, "Now why in the world would he do

that, Fritz? He's going out of his way to help, not kidnap us."

But Fritz wouldn't let up. "Well, what about the blood in the corner of the truck bed? Where'd that come from?"

Tegh looked at him and said, "He's a rancher and hauls sheep and goats. The animals jostle around and sometimes kick each other with their hooves. You can argue all you want, but I'm going to get some rest while I can. Fritz, let me know what you decide."

"Me, too," said Betta as she staked out her spot on the truck. Turning her back on Fritz, she pushed her backpack to a corner, lay down with her backside to a hay bale, and pulled her coat over her.

Steve shrugged his shoulders and motioned for Fritz to do the same.

When dawn filtered through the eastern sky, Benny awakened them in the truck bed. Tegh was the first up and asked Benny how far they had to go. Benny figured it was about a hundred and sixty kilometers to reach Turpan and he wasn't planning to make any more stops except for fuel.

Seeing Fritz smoking a cigarette a few feet from the truck, Tegh asked him, "You okay this morning?"

Fritz, not looking directly at Tegh, simply said, "Yeah, but in case you haven't realized it, I'm nervous as hell about everything that's going on. I don't know where we are or who any of these people are we keep running into. And the way you talk, I worry that the Chinese Gestapo are going to round us up any minute."

Tegh looked at him, thinking, *at least he's sharing what's really on his mind.* "Fritz, it's okay to be wary, even afraid.

I'm not comfortable with this situation either. But we can't let it get us down. We must keep looking for a rational way to resolve the issues confronting us and not let them get the better of us. If we don't, we'll get discovered by the wrong people and I guarantee you won't like that. So, you on board?"

Fritz drew the last puff on his cigarette and flick it into the scrub. "Yeah, I'm all set now. Let's get going."

They resettled among the hay bales and Benny pulled his truck back onto the highway, heading west-northwest, the most direct route to the Kazakh border.

Finally reaching Turpan, Benny pulled in to fill up with gas. Tegh helped Betta down and they welcomed the chance to stretch their legs.

Steve looked around. "Everything is so green, not exactly what I expected after looking at barren landscape for the past few hours."

Tegh said, "Just like Hami, it's another geographic oddity. Though Turpan is over five hundred feet below sea level, it sits in a natural basin at the foot of the Bogda Shan." He pointed to the range of mountains rising sentinel-like just to the north. "Some the hottest summer and coldest winter temperatures in the world have been recorded here."

Betta wiped the sweat from her brow and the back of her neck with her sleeve. "I bet it's over forty degrees right now."

"Easily," Tegh said.

"So where's the water come from to keep everything so green?" Fritz asked.

"The mountains," Tegh said. "It rains very little here,

so over the centuries, the settlers here, as in Hami, built underground channels and cisterns beneath the desert floor to distribute the snow melt from the Bogda Shan to prevent its evaporation. There's such an abundance of water that the city is sometimes referred to as the Venice of the Taklimakan. Turpan's a major supplier of fruits and vegetables for China."

"You're a walking encyclopedia," Steve said.

"I travelled a great deal of western China, including the Turpan Depression, during summers off from secondary school in Almaty, Kazakhstan. That's also when I picked up a working knowledge of the Russian and Kazakh languages."

"You should be a college professor, Tegh," kidded Betta.

When Benny rounded the corner of the filling station, he motioned that he needed to get going. They clambered back aboard. As Tegh went to climb up on the truck, Benny said something and Tegh nodded agreement. Satisfied, Benny went around and got in the cab.

Tegh said to the others, "Benny needs to make a quick stop at a friend's home before he delivers the hay north of town. He says it should only take a few minutes."

This set Fritz's alarm bells off. He tried to stand, but the jostling of the truck as it backed out and headed down the rutted street required him hold on to the staked side rails. Maintaining a precarious balance, he said over the noise of grinding gears, "Am I the only one who thinks it all too convenient that now he mentions this extra stop, especially after he's been inside getting gas and out of our sight? For all we know, he could have been calling the police."

Betta was caught up in his reasoning and looked pleadingly at Tegh. But it was Steve who voiced the reality to counter Fritz's argument. "Don't you think he's had plenty of time to have called the authorities since we left that diner yesterday? And just exactly would be this jovial rancher's motive for turning us in?"

Fritz said without thinking, "Reward."

"Oh come on, Fritz," Steve said, "if he—"

Tegh interrupted, tired of the exchange, tired of Fritz's moods, and tired of playing the peacemaker. "Fritz, for once in your life you must recognize that not everyone is out to get you. More often than not, the people you meet in life are simply good folks, like you. They have no ulterior motives and they aren't trying to hide some inner evil nature behind a benign façade. Otarbai is exactly what he says he is, a rancher. He's too short to be in the army, he's got way too many calluses on his hands to have done anything but lug heavy hay bales and equipment all his life, and he's so bowlegged, he could never keep up with a platoon in a marching parade."

Steve snickered, but Tegh wasn't done.

"So cut the crap," Tegh went on. "Be inquisitive but not accusative. Recognize an ally when one comes along. Now sit back down before you get bounced off the truck. You look ridiculous hanging onto the side rails."

Stinging from the rebuke, Fritz sat down in a huff.

With the emotional outburst settled, they passed through a residential area, where they got a firsthand view of lush flower and vegetable gardens. The modest homes had fences with bowers in bloom supporting ripening grape arbors. When they reached town center, Tegh pointed to hotel marquees with names written in

Chinese as well as in the Latin alphabet.

Betta looked down a side street where people sat at tables amid shops and under grass-mat awnings, shielded safely from the intense sun.

Seeing her interest, Tegh said, "That's the city bazaar. It's said to rival the one in Istanbul."

The market teemed with women shoppers, all wearing headscarves, being enticed by merchants dressed in long coats, tall boots, and embroidered doppas. Seeing how the locals were dressed, Betta was glad for her own billowing shirts and pantaloons they'd gotten when their train had broken down on the way to Hami.

A block beyond the bazaar, Benny parked next to a mud-brick house and went inside. While they waited, Steve found a worn soccer ball lying under a rusted basketball hoop tacked to a weathered clapboard building. Within minutes, the neighborhood children had gathered to watch this strange looking white man shooting the ball at the metal hoop. Noticing his audience, Steve motioned for one of the older boys to join him. Reluctant at first, he was goaded by his younger cohorts, themselves too shy to take up the offer. Before long, several were playing a pickup game. The boys rattled on in their native tongue, with the only words Steve could glean being Shaq, Michael, and LeBron.

Done with his business transaction, Benny came back outside and called Tegh over to discuss where the group should be dropped off. Tegh listened and then gathered the others.

"Otarbai must drive back into town before he heads towards his relatives living near Lake Barkol, north of the mountains. He offered to take us all the way into Urumqi,

229

but after discussion I realized that was about a hundred and sixty kilometers out of his way. Turpan has both a bus depot and train station. We've been off public transport for a while, so it's probably safe for us to try it again. So, we've got a choice to make, ride along with him or, buy bus or train tickets. Either way, we get to Urumqi."

"I for one would like to rest for a day before sitting in one of those backbreaking seats in a swaying bus or riding across clacking rails," Betta said.

"Is there even anything to do in Turpan?" Fritz asked. "It's so hot, I can't believe anyone does anything for recreation, excluding playing basketball."

Steve gave a slight bow.

"I asked Otarbai about hotels," Tegh said. "The way he described them, the Hotel Jiaotang comes closest to being a European hostel, which I think would best suit our needs. It's inexpensive and probably a place where we can blend in with other travelers. The other hotels are more upscale, with amenities like internet, attached restaurants, and air conditioning."

"A/C would be nice," Steve said, who was sweating profusely after his impromptu workout.

"We'd draw less notice by staying at the cheapest place," Fritz said.

"So what do we do while we wait for tomorrow's bus to Urumqi?" Steve asked.

"We could visit the Gaochang Ruins," Tegh said. "It's a ghost town today. All that's left are remnants abandoned in the time of Charlemagne. But within Gaochang are the Bezeklik Thousand Buddha Caves, which—"

"Oh boy, more caves," Fritz remarked.

"They're really fascinating," Tegh said. "The well-preserved frescoes and the like."

"Any more yellow doors?" Steve asked.

"No, but the caves do contain silk paintings and bits of manuscripts—"

Fritz cut him off. "Are we tourists or are we trying to avoid soldiers and get out of China?"

"Fritz makes a good point," Betta said.

"I think laying low for a day or two would be a good idea," Steve countered. "Security forces have probably figured out we're moving. If we stay hidden for a few days, wherever our trail has led them will be that much colder. I vote for staying put."

"Whatever we do, we can't make friends like we did in Dunhuang," Fritz said, glaring at Tegh.

Betta said, "Fritz is right. I've liked visiting caves, but I can't believe they're much different than what we've already seen. By staying put, we allow the authorities to catch up. By moving on, we stay ahead of them."

"Or perhaps run into a trap," Steve offered.

They were at an impasse.

Feeling the peer pressure, Tegh relented. "Okay, we'll rest here a day and then press on to Urumqi. The caves are a tourist attraction, so we'll at least be less conspicuous."

Tegh saw two of them nod, but Fritz seemed skeptical.

Steve kidded Tegh. "Do we take a tour like in Dunhuang, or are you our guide?"

"I know something about the caves," he said. "They contain—"

"Here we go again," Fritz said, eliciting a laugh from Steve and Betta.

Fritz scuffed a shoe in the dirt and then removed a cigarette from the pack with his teeth. He turned his back and cupped the match in his hands to shield it from a hot breeze.

Tegh didn't take offense. "Cultures mixed, traded, and were created here in Turpan, as goods and ideas flowed east and west. These pilgrims were in a state of bewilderment in this strange land—"

"No shit," Fritz said.

Tegh could see Fritz wasn't in the mood to listen. So instead of going on he said, "Fritz, I thought we were agreed we wanted to rest here a day. If we do, then we can't just sit around. We should at least put on a show as tourists."

Fritz said, "As fascinating as this stuff sounds, how about moving closer to our goal of getting out of this country? Maybe we should leave Turpan tonight and check out Urumqi. Maybe they've got caves there we could play tourist in, Tegh. At least we'd be closer to the border."

Steve gave Fritz an exasperated look.

Tegh raised his hand in a peacemaking gesture. "In fairness to Fritz, there's a good bit to see in Urumqi. It's a huge city, one easier to hide in than Turpan. But, that means there's a larger police presence."

"Maybe we should skip Turpan and Urumqi altogether," Betta said.

They looked at each other, dismayed that their survival logic had gone full circle. Sensing their frustration, Tegh offered a conciliatory suggestion. "Let me talk to Otarbai. He might have some advice on the best way to avoid either Turpan or Urumqi."

Fritz started, "But what about—" He stopped when Betta squeezed his arm.

With no more suggestions, they watched silently as Tegh approached Benny. The two talked at the front of the truck's cab until suddenly Benny looked up in alarm. He waved them back into the truck bed. Not hesitating, they scrambled onto the truck. Benny remounted the cab and started the engine. Pulling out quickly, the truck rattled past storefronts. They desperately held on as Benny drove it up a side street and then turned deeper into a neighborhood.

As they careened around the corner, Tegh explained. "Benny saw an army truck loaded with troops pull into the market while we were talking."

Betta took a sharp breath. Before she could say anything, Tegh said, "Quick, everyone sit down. There are several national police over there in front of the hotel." He leaned around the driver's side of the cab and yelled something to Benny.

"What'd you tell him?" Fritz yelled over the noise of the air rushing through the truck's side slats.

"I told him to head beyond the bazaar and then find a place to pull over so we can talk. We need a plan."

As they passed backyard gardens on a secondary street off the square. Tegh slapped the top of the cab and Benny pulled over behind a series of tall grape arbors.

They huddled in the shade and caught their breath, the odors of rich soil and ripening fruit doing little to calm them. Acutely aware it was paramount to avoid the police at all cost, they set about to agree on a plan that put as much distance between them and the police as possible. Much to their surprise, it was Benny who offered a viable alternative which would bypass both population centers completely.

He told Tegh, "There's a northern spur road east of Turpan that crosses the mountain divide before turning west again. Then it follows the northern slopes of the Bogda Shan, leaving Turpan and Urumqi well to the south. I assure you, only herdsmen and locals use this road on the edge of the Junggar Pendi, the Kazakh grazing lands. The road's not well known by outsiders, so it probably won't be patrolled by the police or army."

Fritz, unable to suppress his anxiety, said, "What if the police we just saw weren't a random sweep? What if they're part of a network of road blocks set up to intercept us going west? Maybe it's safer for us to backtrack to Hami and regroup."

The others listened as Tegh translated and waited for Benny to respond.

"Benny says that even if there is a patrol, the authorities will think I'm just a rancher with his field hands on the back road making a supply delivery. I was planning to visit my uncle at Lake Barkol sooner or later. Right now, I'll go back into town, buy the supplies I was going to deliver to him and return for you in a few hours. Winter is just around the corner, so stocking up now isn't out of the question for my uncle."

Tegh suddenly remembered the soldier Feng's comment about MSS sending detachments specifically to search Turpan and Urumqi. Maybe Benny's idea was a blessing in disguise. "Benny has a great idea. I think we should do it," Tegh said with all the persuasiveness he could muster.

Betta and Steve nodded.

Then Tegh added, "What Benny says makes more sense than anything we could have come up with."

Fritz took a long drag on his cigarette, but said nothing.

To win him over, Steve said, "Fritz, it's not a given these police are looking for us. Blending into the countryside with the local population like Benny suggests is a good idea. I vote we go to Benny's uncle's house and figure out where to go on from there. At least we'll be among people we can trust, we'll be that much closer to our goal, and we bypass the big population centers."

Fritz kept working his cigarette, unable to come up with an objection.

Resigned to a decision, the they settled on their haunches while Benny went for supplies with 350 yuan, or about €50, Tegh gave him. An hour and a half later, much to Fritz's outward relief, the truck returned. Benny configured several crates of vegetables and melons and several hay bales in the truck bed to form a makeshift windbreak for them, as well as a barrier to separate the three sheep he'd picked up from the human passengers. Almost as an afterthought, he threw a bundle of newspapers tied with butcher's twine into their little apartment.

They clambered aboard the truck and situated themselves the best they could, comfort not being the foremost quality of their accommodations. With a hefty slam, Benny shut the cab door and headed east, back down the main highway. It took him thirty miles to reach the detour road that headed north across the mountains.

Chapter 27

BYPASSING TURPAN, WESTERN CHINA

IT TOOK AN HOUR to reach Benny's turnoff to the north. Unlike the national highway, this spur road heading into the mountains was filled with ruts, potholes, and washouts, which significantly slowed progress. Those in the truck bed endured the jolts in the heat, holding tightly onto the side stakes for security while the sheep bleated. After about three miles, the grade increased as the truck climbed, slowing their progress even more, however, it eased the impacts on their spines significantly. The truck engine groaned as Benny used body language, invective, and epithets to coax his truck in the struggle to ascend the switchbacks in the ever-thinning air.

The views were dizzying when the truck bed leaned beyond the shoulder in the sharp turns. For those sitting on the outside of these turns, they could see the mountain drop off hundreds of feet below them. "Definitely not for the faint of heart," observed Steve, who noticeably scooted closer to the center of the truck bed and hunkered down with Tegh and Betta, while Fritz just tried to ignore the vertiginous vistas altogether.

As they climbed, they were pleasantly surprised to feel relief from the intense heat of the earth's depression they had left behind. Within the first hour, the temperature lost its oppressiveness, still hot, but tolerable, thanks to the air flowing by and through the truck's slates.

Though the temperature was better, breathing became more difficult. The altitude not only affected the riders' breathing, but the truck's engine began to labor and the truck perceptibly slowed as the grade and altitude took their tolls. But their spirits were buoyed because every minute meant they were distancing themselves farther from the limelight of a big city and the chance to be discovered. By the time they reached the road's last set of switchbacks, the weather had become pleasant, sparse evergreens replaced leafy trees, and perspiration no longer soaked their clothing.

The hard-packed dirt road leveled out as they reached the crest of an 11,000-foot ridge. Patches of snow, even in early September, frosted the exposed ridgeline. They had a grand view of the plateau that spread below them, all the way to the northern horizon. In contrast to the beige-gray featureless terrain of the desert depression just on the other side of the mountain ridge, this panorama was tinged with green and dotted with brownish-red rock outcroppings. This was the Junggar Pendi.

The descent of the northern slope, more gradual than the upward climb, passed scattered, high-elevation pastures that became more expansive the more they dropped in elevation. The scrabble road ran through sparse pines that offered little refuge from the freshening gusts of the exposed slope to the prevailing winds. Trees here were much shorter than those on the northern slope, their trunks bent by an ever-present wind and their needles offered up a piney-resin scent in the air.

On the "morning" side of the range, as Benny referred to it, a cloud front pushed its way over the mountain ridge behind them and began its descent to the plateau below. Urged by winds aloft, a gentle, late summer rain fell. As the truck began its S-turn rumblings downward, with brakes groaning and chassis creaking, it was inevitable—those in the back of the truck, animals and humans alike, got wet. The truck and the rain shower were in a contest to reach the tabletop of the plateau.

The shower finally dissipated when they reached the open steppe and Benny headed the truck across the southwestern edge of the Junggar Pendi's arid landscape. Their respite from the rain was brief, however. Three miles farther along, the road bent westward towards the mountains again, and they reencountered a diminished drizzle. Those in the back huddled closely, but no one complained, except the sheep. They weren't cold—just wet.

Betta daydreamed as the altitude transformed alpine foliage from small clusters of short evergreens into bushes more suited to a dryer, hotter clime. "It's so different from Bavaria," she mused to Fritz.

He squeezed her hand. "The higher elevations are more like what we're used to. This dry scrub would require a long time for me to take a liking to. I wouldn't want to trek for too long out there," he said to the expanse of the steppe. "At least back home, this rain made the heat more bearable."

Benny's windshield wipers streaked in protest until enough droplets provided sufficient wash for clearer vision. Eventually, the rain stopped, unable to overcome the heat reradiating from the floor of the Junggar Pendi.

In the distance, Steve pointed to a column of circling birds.

"Vultures," Tegh said, noticing Steve's interest. "Something died and they'll glean the carcass. Nothing lasts too long out there. In relatively short order, the Junggar Pendi reclaims everything. Life has to be tough."

At one point, they encountered a five-camel caravan whose herder waved a greeting. The camel driver was alone, except for his Mongolian Mastiff that commanded the respect of people and the fear of the camels. Benny pulled the truck over to honor the teamster's offered greeting. Hobbling his camels, the herder invited them for tea, the traditional form of hospitality.

As they dismounted the truck, ready for a break from the constant jostle of travel, Tegh explained, "You'll get used to the hospitality afforded strangers in this part of the world. Whether you want to or not."

"Nice custom," observed Betta.

They sat cross-legged in the sandy gravel near a quickly built fire while the herder brewed tea in a battered pot. Tegh translated as their host explained that his cargo was yurts, disassembled for transport. He was on his way from the high meadows to set up his winter camp in the valley. All his family's worldly possessions were loaded on his five camels. He explained that the rest of his family was a day behind him and would catch up by the time he made camp.

In addition to the tea, he shared a bottle of dark red liquid he kept in a suede pouch. Taking a swig, he said it was the blood from the antler velvet of the native deer, a powerful aphrodisiac. He smiled at the men and winked at Betta. Fritz and Steve politely refused the offer, but Benny and Tegh readily accepted. But each of them happily joined in when the herder poured a chaser of home-distilled vodka, a surprising bit of familiarity in the middle of nowhere.

Hospitality concluded, the travelers gave their thanks and parted company to resume their separate journeys.

Shortly thereafter, Fritz drew their attention to ominous black clouds blossoming over the mountains. Tegh slapped the top of the cab and Benny stopped beside an outcropping of boulders and shouted to Tegh.

"Benny says get down and help."

Fritz looked confused. After trying to avoid the hooves of the sheep with their constant scrabbling in the truck bed, he had just gotten comfortable in the corner. "What now? Another camel herder wants to drink tea?"

"Come on, Fritz," Steve said with urgency. "Give a hand."

Benny hustled to the rear of the truck and backed the sheep out, hobbling and tethering them together.

"He wants us to wrap a shirt or coat, anything we can find, around the animals' eyes and noses," Tegh said, his voice tinged with the same excitement Benny voiced in unloading the sheep.

Steve and Betta pitched in to help.

Fritz stayed off to one side to finish his cigarette. "What's the big deal?"

Benny pointed to the angry clouds, now getting larger and darker, and shouted to Tegh.

"Fritz, get a move on," Tegh yelled. "This looks bad, not only for the sheep, but for us if we don't get battened down. It's a sandstorm! We have to get everything secured to ride it out."

Steve looked anxiously at the clouds. "I'd say we've got fifteen minutes at most before it hits."

Fritz threw down his cigarette and joined the struggle. Within a few minutes, they had the sheep shielded by whatever cloth they could find. Next, the five wrestled a huge canvas from the back of the truck and strung the flapping tarp lengthwise along the side of the truck, tucking one edge in the door jamb and stretching it along the truck bed where they weighted it down with hay bales, the water trough, and rocks from the roadside. They pulled the other edge away from the truck and weighted it with more rocks, creating a lean-to beside the truck.

With the sheep secured and their makeshift shelter in place, Benny motioned them into the tent.

Tegh translated. "It's a *bara whakan*, a dry thunderstorm. There's too little moisture for rain, but the updrafts pick up sand as the storm rolls over the desert. Benny says it won't last long, but the choking winds are deadly."

Steve uttered something which was lost in the howling of the ever-building wind.

Betta shouted, "What about the animals?"

Benny made some hand gestures and Tegh replied for him. "They'll butt their backsides to the wind and huddle together between the boulders and the truck. Benny says they'll be fine with their noses and eyes covered. They can breathe. As long as they can't see anything, the noise won't bother them."

"I wish I could do that," Betta said. "I'm not sure..."

A tremendous blast of air roared over the top of boulders and the truck and one edge of their tarp flapped loose. Benny grabbed a rope hanging from a grommet and struggled to hold it taut. He motioned for Fritz to do the same on the other side.

Betta screamed. Steve pressed close and put an arm around her. Fritz saw him but was too intent on keeping his grip on the tarp rope to comment, much less object.

They finally relashed the tarp's hold-down ropes as the noise grew louder and sand blew in from the sides. They turned their backs to the lean-to's openings and faced each other, huddled against the elements. The wind tried mightily to wrench their shelter canvas away as it filled the air with the fine, powdery sand.

Benny removed his shirt and wrapped the sleeves around his nose and mouth. Tegh and Betta followed his lead, while Steve and Fritz tucked their chins in the hem of their undershirts to cover their noses. All of them shut their eyes to keep out the flying grit.

For twenty long minutes the wind howled and buffeted them with a vengeance.

Between fighting the wind to keep the canvas in place and keeping their breathing pathways clear, they were exhausted when the fury finally lessened and the undulating canvas finally lay still. After waiting a few minutes to make sure it was over, they stepped from their hideaway to an eerie scene. Sand had drifted everywhere, several inches thick in the lee of the rocks. A strong breeze persisted, which sent dust devils scudding across the hard scrabble of the Junggar Pendi in the storm's wake.

Betta shuddered as she took in the view. "That was scary."

Tegh said, "It's a good thing Benny knew what it was and got us to shelter. Had we been caught in the open, it could have been disastrous."

Fritz was nonchalant. "Really? I didn't think it was that bad."

Tegh looked askance at him, not sure if he were kidding. "If you talk to the shepherds and horsemen in this area, you'll know these storms are no laughing matter. Every year, unlucky people and their livestock are lost to sandstorms."

Betta said, "I think he's pulling your leg, Tegh," prompting a laugh from Steve.

Fritz calmly pulled a cigarette out and lit it.

Benny went to the front of the truck where, between the left front fender and the huge boulder, his sheep huddled, placidly pressed together, their backsides to the rocks.

Tegh called to the rest of them, "Benny needs help getting them back on board. Fritz, he wants you to take down the water trough from the truck bed and put it on the ground for them. Wet the cloths wrapped around their heads and wipe the sand from their snouts. When you're done, dump the water and refill it with clean water from the jerry cans under the truck. They're going to be thirsty."

"I could use a lager myself," Fritz said, clinching his cigarette between his teeth as he hefted the heavy trough to the ground.

Steve, who was breaking down the tarp, gave him a thumbs up.

Soon enough, the group had the truck bed swept out and the sheep safely back aboard. Benny climbed back behind the wheel and headed them down the road. Overall, they'd lost almost two hours, but they weren't on a schedule. For five miles, they dodged hummocks of wind-blown sand. Off to the east, they could see the roiling cloud of sand receding across the Junggar Pendi.

As they their emotions settled, Tegh said, "One good thing about the sandstorm. It hampered the PLA and MSS searching the roads just as much or more than it did us."

Chapter 28

A FEW MORE hours down the road, high-pasture shepherds' yurts came into view. Several of the circular, felt-covered structures were pitched on the verge, each with smoke rising from the tent's center-roof oculus. Benny pulled off the road and pulled to a stop in front of one of the yurts.

Hobbled horses grazed behind the yurts and older children busied themselves milking the family sheep and goats. One of the youngsters carried a full pail into a yurt just as a woman stepped through the doorway for fresh air, wiping her hands on a colorful print apron. She wore a baggy shirt, long pants, and a knit cap, its ear flaps framing her face.

"The girl's mother processes the milk into cheese," Benny said.

A man stepped from the closest hut, smiled broadly, and motioned for the four in the back to step down from the truck bed. A woman, presumably his wife, and three children joined him in the entryway. Benny grinned and bellowed a greeting and the men clutched in a bear hug. After Benny hugged each family member, he turned to Tegh and made introductions. There were more handshakes as residents appeared from the neighboring yurts to greet the visitors.

Tegh said, "Otarbai says this is his friend, Duzhendi. He's delivered him supplies and taken his products to market for twelve summers now. The man from the neighboring yurt is named Abai Shokan, his partner in their enterprise, and a friend of Duzhendi's mother. As a chaban, or traveling herdsman, Abai Shokan has tended horses, goats, and sheep in these summer pastures for over two decades. Soon they'll break camp and move to their winter pastures further down the valley. Duzhendi, or Duz as Otarbai refers to him, wants you to come inside for refreshments while the older children unload what Otarbai's cargo."

The yurt, surprisingly large inside, had finely patterned, woven rugs on the floor and a fire burning in a free-standing, cast iron stove in the middle. A slender stovepipe carried the smoke out through the hole at the top of the yurt, which also admitted an abundance of sunlight. Packing cases, an old wooden bureau, and boxes formed the interior sectional walls, separating two sleeping areas from the central communal space.

The children made quick work of offloading the truck, leading the three sheep to pasture behind the yurts, and soon rejoined the group. The youngest held up the bundle of newspapers. Benny, seeing the youth's confusion, pointed to a spot near Tegh and the child dropped them there.

"What good will those do us?" Fritz said, noting they were printed in distinctive Chinese calligraphic writing.

Steve snapped the twine, separating what turned out to be three complete newspapers. "These may not be the *Washington Post* or the *Wall Street Journal*, but look here, they've got photos."

As Steve paged through the papers like a subway commuter, Benny passed around sweet pastries to share. Duz's wife served tea and fresh cheese, which Tegh pointed out was the household pride, as well as being a major source of their income.

Betta took a bite of the soft cheese and winced, fanning her mouth and scrunching her nose. "Whew, that's tangy. It may take some getting used to, but I like it."

Everyone turned to a sudden outburst from Steve. "Will you look at this?" He pointed to two photos on an interior page. One showed Russia's leader talking with his Chinese counterpart, and the other was of several warships sailing in the open ocean. "Those have to be American. We're the only ones with aircraft carriers like that. Tegh, what's the caption say?"

Tegh read carefully, then let the paper halves crumple together as he translated. "The first one shows the presidents of Russia and China in discussions regarding Russia's invasion of Ukraine. And in the other, it seems, the US has sailed a contingent of its Seventh Fleet into the Taiwan Straits, which the Beijing government claims is a clear provocation of their peaceful relations with its Taiwanese neighbors. The US is conducting war games with the Nationalist Chinese, causing the People's Republic to file a protest at the UN claiming the straits are waters to be used only for peaceful purposes and not violated by warships."

"Well, we know that's bullshit," Fritz said. "Nothing the communists say or do is peaceful."

"Shhh," Betta warned him. "You'll embarrass us in front of our hosts. Besides, you don't where their loyalties lie."

Fritz replied quickly, "Look at him. I don't think—"

Before he could finish, Tegh said, "You'll find that international politics for these people is as foreign to them as would be space aliens, only much less interesting. Remember where you are. You're a long way from the seat of government, and the government controls the press. For all we know that picture could be years old. It's just something the Chinese government uses to feed their propaganda mill. It serves them by building a sense of nationalism among citizens enlightened enough to read, who care about such things, and provides a warning to outsiders, in this case America, to stay clear of the People's Republic."

Fritz interrupted. "Like I said, bullshit."

"No, far from it." Tegh smoothed and folded the paper before adding it back to the stack. "It serves the purposes of the Central Committee. But there's nothing we can do about it, so I recommend we enjoy ourselves." He grinned, which was a signal to Benny and Duz that whatever they had been talking about was amusing. He held up his cup for more tea and asked Duz if he could try some of his homemade cheese.

But Steve couldn't dismiss Tegh's explanation. "What the hell is going on in the world out there that we—"

But Betta interrupted him. "Are Benny's friends Uighurs? They aren't dressed like the folks we saw in Hami and Turpan."

Tegh said, without asking Duz or Benny, "No, they're Buddhists of Kazakh descent. You'll find that religion and politics among these people is secondary to tending their flocks and selling their enterprise products, cheese and felt cloth, at market."

Steve couldn't help but remember his father's advice when Steve called him from Irkutsk with the news of the State Department's evacuation warning and of his plan to come home. "Not everyone likes Americans, despite what you may think."

Judiciously, Tegh didn't translate for this host's benefit.

Otarbai stood and told Tegh to have Steve and Fritz follow him. Betta got up to join, but Tegh motioned for her to stay put. "This is for men only, Betta."

Betta bristled at his overt sexism, but realized where she was. The two wives gestured to her with open arms and smiles, either not bothering to notice her distress, or dismissing it outright. They ushered her towards the door with their children in tow. Betta gave a finger wave to her colleagues with a furtive glance over her shoulder as she flashed a wish-me-luck look.

The women and children led Betta to a much larger yurt, which seemed to be the social center for this small, mobile village. Inside, an older woman handed Betta an over-garment, much like a western apron, and motioned for her to put it on. In no time, the women had her engaged in preparations for a celebration, a celebration of what she wasn't sure.

From the transportation cases stacked inside this grand yurt, they pulled colorful tablecloths and serving platters. The central stove, larger than the one in the smaller residential yurt, smoldered from a bank of coals, which one of the girls was stoking. Betta busied herself with braising mutton chunks while another woman boiled water for a stew. Betta accustomed herself with her hostesses, a social exercise made much easier by their laughing and carrying on, as if they were lifelong friends.

Names didn't matter, which Betta found to be a good thing because she couldn't have pronounced them anyway. The women were expressive with their sign language and Betta soon grasped the gist of what they were saying. Duz's wife was the nominal woman-in-charge as the group busied themselves, for what purpose she still wasn't sure.

Betta found it difficult to determine the ages of the women. Constant exposure to the steppe's relenting sun had weathered their features and darkened their skin. The persistent hard physical work of tending livestock, making cheese, repairing clothing, and moving their homesteads every few months had transformed whatever feminine figures they may have once possessed into the blocky forms now engaged in nonstop industrious motion.

While Betta cut up meat and vegetables with two older women, the five girls, teenagers to a six-year-old, brought skillets and pans from storage, arranged spices and flour on the work table, fetched water, and restocked fuel for the stove. The efficiency and timeliness were all at the flick of a hand, a cluck of the tongue, or a single word from Duz's wife. All the while, the women and girls kept up a persistent chatter. To Betta's amazement, she followed along from these mannerisms alone.

Meanwhile, Benny, Duz, and Abai Shokan ushered the three men inside an adobe building, the only permanent structure in this village, which was situated a hundred yards from the cluster of yurts. On the inside, three more men were seated at a table playing cards. The acrid smell from their cheap native brand cigarettes seemed as strange to Fritz and Steve as was their habit of spitting frequently on the floor. The seated men looked up and nodded acknowledgement of their two neighbors, Benny, and the three strangers.

As way of introduction, Duz announced that these were his friends who'd travelled a long distance to visit. This provided assurance enough for the card players that tranquility would prevail. Their nonchalant expressions transformed to eager anticipation when Fritz removed a cigarette pack from his front shirt pocket. Fritz pushed a few cigarettes part way out of the pack and held them out as a gesture to share. For these frontier herdsmen, this was an unexpected treat. The men quickly indulged themselves, with genuine smiles that exposed yellowing teeth. Convinced of their friendly nature, Fritz placed the half-empty pack on the table, an open invitation to help themselves.

Tegh translated as Duz introduced his local acquaintances. Two of them were herdsmen from a nearby valley and the third was a Kazakh herder friend from another village.

Fritz chuckled as he turned to Steve. "Duz says he's a cowboy, like in your American western movies."

Steve gave a belly laugh as Duz beamed, glad that he'd made a connection.

With a friendly gesture, the largest of the three card players beckoned for them to join. With no more chairs available, they arranged pillows on the rough wood-plank floor and the new arrivals crossed their legs and sat. Duz produced a large jug he'd brought for the occasion, which engendered a jack-o-lantern grin from one of card players. Another host rummaged in a saddlebag hanging from a wall peg and produced additional earthenware mugs. Duz's jug lasted just enough to fill everyone's mug and they settled in for a few rounds of storytelling.

Cigarette smoke thickened the air thanks to Fritz's donations, and another jug appeared from the saddlebag stash for their next round of cheer. Tegh explained it was home-brewed ale, a regional specialty. In no time, they were the best of friends, swapping stories of the American wild west and the Asian steppe. The Kazakh horsemen couldn't get enough information from Fritz and Steve about Western life, and in turn, the three travelers became engrossed in the horsemen's descriptions of their lives scratching out a living in this sparse grassland. By the time the fourth jug was emptied, Steve, Fritz and Tegh had forgotten what had brought them there—looking for a way out of China.

Finally, Duz's friend stood and gestured for them to follow. Outside in the gathering twilight, he led them in a communal effort to bless the steppe as they relieved themselves. Then he bellowed down the line of yurts for Duz's wife to assemble the village in the grand communal yurt. Tegh shook off Fritz's and Steve's queries as to what was going on, explaining, "It's all new to me."

When they reached the meeting yurt, the three of them almost didn't recognize Betta, who was busy working with the women setting out food and drinks and stoking the central stove's fire. She wore an embroidered apron over her blousy shirt and pantaloons. Wisps of her hair peeked from beneath a head scarf and her flushed face had random smears of whatever they had been preparing during the men's card game. As she bustled about, she explained she'd been working the entire time they'd been gone, putting the finishing touches on a feast and listening to the women's stories, but not understanding a word.

Tegh, soberer than his two compatriots, asked, "Betta, what is going on?"

Not stopping her busy pace, Betta said, "The best I can tell, this is a birthday party, except it's no one's birthday. They just like to party. By the way, be careful how much you drink from those clay jugs. I had a cup and had to beg off on the refill it was so strong. Anyway, I gathered from the ladies that, because we're visiting as Duz's friend, it's time to celebrate."

"Good enough for me," Fritz said, mellow from having finished off the better part of a whole jug.

Sixteen people settled onto cushions arranged around several low tables. With everyone cross-legged, the feast began. There were platters and bowls holding fruit, salted fish, salami, stew and *baotse*, or steamed dumplings, flat bread, cakes, cream, orange juice, and vodka, along with more jugs of home brew, which the men had sampled liberally in the adobe hut.

Tegh sat between Steve and the Kazakh horsemen to translate. As the beer and vodka toasts took a toll on their sobriety, not to mention their inhibitions, Steve told them of their efforts to reach Kazakhstan. He explained that their biggest concern was how to get across the western border.

Normally, Fritz would have bridled at Steve's revealing so much of their personal business, but he was beyond caring, having imbibed more than his share of home brew. In all his blathering, Steve had been careful not to mention the airplane crash.

The chaban listened to Steve's story without comment, other than to offer a gap-toothed grin of understanding or produce an occasional loud burp. But he paid close attention because Steve's story intrigued him. While the rest of the Kazakhs partied for several more hours, getting further in their cups, the chaban maintained a clear enough head so he could understand what the visitors were searching for, though none of them noticed.

Chapter 29

TEN THOUSAND MILES away, the phone rang in Major General Warren Applegate's home in Ohio. "Warren, this is Brad Gearity. I hope I'm not calling too early. I know you're taking care of Gladys. How is she?"

"She's doing the best as can be expected, General. Thank you for asking. What can I do for you? You have more news on Steve?"

"No, but NSA was able to recover the phone call he made to your answering machine. They could only fix the source to a region of western China, more specifically about ten miles west of the plane wreckage. The phone's been offline ever since. Make of that what you will.

"But they've intercepted a lot of chatter among Chinese PLA and MSS forces who are spread along the length of their east-west national highway, which runs parallel to the mountain range where the plane went down all the way to their western border with Kazakhstan. They definitely have a manhunt going on, but I'm afraid they're not looking for survivors. The term they're using is 'fugitives'."

"Shit."

"Exactly. And to make matters worse, my friend Charlie Kinkaid is sailing elements of his Seventh Fleet through the Formosa Straits in a freedom of navigation exercise, as we speak. We do this periodically to impress upon the world no single nation owns the oceans. We did it to Qaddafi in the Eighties off the Gulf of Sidra."

"Yeah, I know, I was a platoon commander on the Sixth Fleet flagship at the time."

"Then you know we don't necessarily know how these dictators will react when it comes to matters affecting the countries concerned."

Warren paused. "You mean like when they find Steve?"

"If they find him, Warren. If. Your son's pretty resourceful and it looks like there are four people missing. The rest of those on the manifest are now confirmed dead. We can only presume the four that are missing are survivors and are travelling together, but we don't know that for a fact. What we do know is that the PLA and MSS are looking for four people, and one of them is an American.

"And to throw a little more shit in the game, the president's sending more military aid to the Ukrainians in their fight against Moscow. So, if they do get out of China, that will limit whatever safe haven they may seek."

"We're not sending troops?"

"Doesn't look like it. Just wanted you to know what the whole situation may look like from the bad guy's point of view. Anyway, I promise to keep you cut in on what I know. Keep it close hold."

"I will, and thanks, General. I'll be here."

Chapter 30

ZHANGYE AND HAMI, XINJIANG PROVINCE, CHINA

FIRST DIRECTOR LIN was more than reluctant to pick up General Wu's call, but he cleared his throat, took a deep breath, and said, "Good afternoon, General. How is our search going?"

"Our search? It seems I'm the only one working your problem. I'm in Zhangye at the train station. What a godforsaken town. I've checked every train depot east of here all the way to Lanzhou. There's not a shred of evidence the fugitives ever came this way. You've been wasting my time, Chu. I'm tired of doing your job. What have you discovered? Tell me you've got something worth my while to report."

First Director Lin, though accustomed to his boss's badgering, didn't like it one bit. He especially didn't like it when the general addressed him by his first name. How could this over-the-hill bureaucrat turn this around on him? He took another deep breath. "Yes, General Wu, I do have news of their whereabouts."

"What?" General Wu was taken aback. "Well, why are you waiting? Get to the point! Where are they?"

"Right now, I'm in Hami. There's been no public sighting of them west of here to Urumqi. What brought me here was that four foreigners bought bus tickets from Hongliyuan to Hami five days ago. That means…"

General Wu interrupted as he looked at his railway map. "Hongliyuan? That's on the train line from Dunhuang to here in Zhangye. But they never got here!"

"That's what I'm trying to tell you, General. There is a record they bought bus tickets to go north to Hami. But the best I can tell, they never got here, either."

"What the hell's between Hami and Hongliyuan? They didn't just stop. They must be headed somewhere. First they're in Xi'an, then in Jiayuguan, then Dunhuang, only to disappear somewhere near Hongliyuan. What are they doing?"

First Direct Lin let the general's frustrations die on the line. Then he said, "General Wu, if I may? I think between your excellent efforts in the east and our combined sweep of Urumqi and Turpan, we now know within a few hundred miles where they are." He stopped for a reaction.

"Go on," the general said, calming only slightly. He wouldn't admit it to Lin, but his underling was making sense. And right now, he could use a plausible idea.

"Yes, sir. They didn't continue east, and we know they just left Dunhuang. So, the only place they can be heading is northwest to Urumqi."

"But..."

"But we just came from there. I know, General. That means they must be riding in vehicles other than the public buses or trains and just haven't reached there yet. I believe they're trying to leave the country via the route west of Urumqi on the road to Almaty, Kazakhstan. To prevent that, I will travel by road to Urumqi checking for any signs of their hitchhiking. I respectfully suggest you, sir, fly ahead to Urumqi and organize our network there to intercept them. Together, we'll force them into the open."

Lin detected a shift in the general's tone, almost of acceptance, when next he said, "You're trying my patience, Lin, but I think you have come up with the best-least alternative."

First Director Lin found the pause that ensued interminable.

Then the general spoke. "All right, I'll do it. But you had better be correct."

The line abruptly went dead. A broad grin broke across First Director Lin's face.

Chapter 31

The festivities finally wound down and the families left for their respective yurts, with wives holding up their men. Steve, Tegh, and Fritz stood to follow Benny, but when Betta started to follow them, Duz's wife tugged at her shirt and motioned she must sleep in the women's section of the tent.

Betta watched as the men staggered away and sheepishly followed Duz's wife and the girls. When she stepped behind the curtain that secluded the area, there was a pallet already laid out for her. But before she could bed down, she needed to visit the outside toilet facility.

As Betta started to reenter the communal tent, she was startled when she heard her name whispered from nearby.

"Betta."

It was Steve. She stumbled as she stepped towards him, and a strong arm caught her.

"Easy, girl."

Grabbing Steve's arm, she said, "What are you doing here?"

"Waiting for you. I knew you'd be out here sooner or later. That beer was getting to me."

She giggled. "And I thought we Germans were

drinkers, but these folks are serious."

Still half in each other's arms, they looked at each other for a moment, not saying another word as the insects chirped and a night owl suddenly took flight from the nearby shrubbery.

He led her to the adobe hut where the men had played cards. As he motioned her inside, all she said was, "But what if…"

Steve put a finger to her lips and said, "Shhh."

His hand shifted her blouse from her shoulder and Betta said, "But, the others. What will Fr…"

His mouth covered hers before she could say another word.

The next morning, Steve and Fritz awoke when Betta stood outside their yurt's entrance flap and called softly to them. Bleary eyed, Fritz came outside.

"Fritz, you look like you really had fun," Betta said, pointing to his disheveled hair and bleary eyes.

"I don't know what we drank, but it was potent. And, there was lots of it. What did you ladies do?"

She curtsied and said, "That's my little secret and wouldn't you like to know? Suffice it to say, I had fun. Right now, however, you need to get the others up. We need to decide what we're doing today. Being stationary for too long isn't healthy for our cause."

Within a half hour, they stood with Benny and Duz warming their hands around cups of hot tea. Sharing a furtive glance with Betta, Steve said, "That was quite a party last night."

Tegh translated. "Duz says he's happy you enjoyed it."

"That must have cost them quite a bit. We should pay something to help out," Fritz said, reaching for his wallet.

Tegh put his hand out to stop him. "You shouldn't do that. When receiving Kazakh hospitality, offering to pay would offend them. Besides, they wouldn't accept it in the first place."

"How can we show our appreciation?" Betta asked.

"By having a good time, which I think each of you did, judging from your bloodshot eyes this morning," Tegh said.

Steve and Betta tried not to look at each other.

Duz began speaking and the Westerners listened. Finally, Tegh smiled and turned to them. "Duz and the chaban heard what Steve said last night about trying to reach Kazakhstan."

"What?" Fritz said. "What did you tell them?" He overcompensated with his show of concern to hide his embarrassment at not being able to remember.

"Don't worry, Fritz," Tegh said. "They're offering to help. Being Kazakhs, they have no love for the Han Chinese, or Uighurs for that matter. They harbor deep-rooted, bitter feelings towards the Chinese, who have confiscated their pasture lands and levied taxes on their livestock. They're proud descendants of Cossack cavalrymen—an independent, noble people. Kazakhs are measured by the number of sheep and wives they own, not by their connection to the government."

"Own?" Betta cringed. "They own their wives?"

Tegh cautioned her. "Be careful, it's not clear which has a higher status in this culture, wives or sheep." His serious expression suddenly broadened into a grin. Betta looked at him and wasn't sure if he was kidding or not.

"In any case," Tegh went on, "these men go back and forth across the border all the time without a second look from the border guards. Duz said he could stand to visit the pastures west of Lake Barkol and pick up some stud horses for his herd. The lake is just beyond the Borohoro Shan Mountains."

Duz smiled, as if he understood what Tegh was saying and expected that they would accept his offer. When he saw their eyes brighten, he and Abai Shokan walked over to shake hands. Benny joined in the congratulations, intrigued by the small conspiracy and the chance to be a thorn in the side of the Chinese in the only way they knew how.

With Tegh translating, Benny said, "It sounds like fun, and I may make some money hauling hay for new customers."

Just like that, the compact was struck. Under Duz's and the chaban's direction, their trucks were loaded. Balky truck motors finally caught in the chilled morning air, and the throaty engines roared to life, breaking the pastoral stillness of the camp.

The north slope of the Bogda Shan descended to an inland sea of pasture land called the steppe, which was dotted with scattered yurt clusters and sheep. Their two-truck convoy passed several villages with permanent standing structures, which Duz explained were laid down by the Soviets seven decades earlier before the Sino-Soviet ideological split. Abandoned by the Russians, the resident locals, ever experts on making good use of anything at hand, had converted these structures into storage bins for winter fodder.

They drove all day, stopping only to refuel the trucks and take comfort breaks. They ate from a basket of food left over from the feast the night before, which Duz's wife had packed for them. As dusk settled, Benny and Duz stopped their trucks by a yurt, with a caution from Tegh that they were in for more hospitality.

"I don't know if my system can take another internal assault," Steve said.

"Yeah, their hospitality can get aggressive," Fritz said.

"You'll do fine," Tegh reassured them.

There was a horse whip mounted upside down by the yurt's portal, or *ger*, as Duz called them. He explained that the orientation of the whip was a Mongol tradition. "If the whip points down, the man of the house is home. Up, and he was away in the field tending the flock or herd."

The man of the house stood in the doorway, legs astride, hands on hips, and sporting a broad smile. Keeping up the translated dialogue, Tegh told them their host's name was Dzhigits, Benny's uncle by marriage. Once again Betta simplified his name, this time to Ziggy.

Steve whispered to Tegh as they entered, "Ger, yurt, what's the difference?"

"They're the same thing," Tegh reassured him. "Yurt's a Russian word and ger is what the Mongols call them."

The inside of the ger was carpeted and the walls were covered with gray-blue felt mats, which served as both decoration and insulation. Ziggy ran a propane generator to light the four bare bulbs hanging from the ger's roof arches. A dung-burning stove sat in the center with a sheet metal exhaust flue extending up to the central hole in the roof. The furniture consisted of stacked storage trunks and repurposed packing crates.

Ziggy invited them to spend the night, indicating they should bed down in a small area set off by two hanging rugs. Not wanting to over crowd the situation, Duz,

Benny, and Abai Shokan indicated they'd sleep in their truck cabs.

Introductions complete, the group got down to what Kazakh hosts loved best, the business of eating. Ziggy's two wives served a supper of sour-milk-softened crusted bread and cheese. The pungent flavor took the westerners some getting used to, but Duz, Benny, and Abai Shokan relished it. Much more to the tastes of western palates were the braised chunks of lamb the women served next with roasted almonds, new potatoes, and squash.

Fritz dug in, saying, "I could get used to this."

Seeing Fritz's enthusiasm, Ziggy clapped his hands and urged Fritz to help himself to more.

When dinner was done and the two women had cleared away the serving pieces, Tegh once again served as translator. Ziggy made an overt, welcoming gesture for Betta to remain seated as they talked.

Tegh whispered to Betta, "This is a great honor he's bestowing upon you."

Dropping into a cross-legged seat on the rugs, Betta said, "Honor? Why?"

"Tonight, you aren't just a woman to be relegated to the cleanup, but a guest."

Betta said under her breath, "Be still my heart."

As conversation ensued, the Kazakhs became accustomed to the translation pauses and mastered the knack for nodding their heads as visual cues to their guests that they were listening and interested. For his guests' benefit, Ziggy explained he made his living making cheese, selling wool, and marketing the felt the women manufactured by beating and pressing wool into a useable fabric. In addition, he harvested hay and sold off an occasional extra sheep or horse. In a few years, his sons would take wives from nearby regions and then follow in the family tradition.

Steve noted that despite the differences between his and their material conditions, they seemed perfectly happy. He was even more surprised when Tegh said that, although Ziggy relished life on the steppe, he was impressed his guests had been to Xi'an, even if only to the airport. Apparently, that was the limit of his geographic understanding of the world. He marveled at their revelations about life in distant European cities and was amused in listening to Ziggy ask seemingly endless questions about their travels.

To satisfy their host's curiosity about where the four travelers had been, Steve described a few highlights of their sojourn to date, leaving out the portion about being pursued by Chinese authorities, much to Fritz's relief. But he did make clear their desire to reach Kazakhstan.

Hearing this, Ziggy eyed his guests, as if taking their measure before sharing a confidence. Then he began.

"My people are nothing like the Uighurs who maintain a difficult relationship with the Han. As loyal Kazakh nomads, everyone, Uighur and Kazakh alike, joined the Uighur conflict of a decade ago for a time. But, we found we couldn't match modern Chinese warfare. We nomads split with the Uighur coalition and returned to our herds on the Junggar Pendi, which the central government was only too happy to let us do.

"But, we understand how the Uighurs in Xinjiang have had to endure strict controls at the hands of the eastern Han Chinese. Fortunately, the bulk of the central government's attention is devoted to those living south of the Bogda Shan, and has yet to reach us here on the Junggar Pendi."

Ziggy sat back on his haunches and motioned for more tea. The travelers nodded thanks as their cups were refilled. Then he continued.

"We are a proud and old people. We don't care about modern international boundaries. The Soviet regime's collectivization led to confiscation of our livestock and grain. By 1933, famine had taken almost two million Kazakhs and just as many fled here, to China."

He paused and Betta could see him wipe a tear away.

Composure restored, Ziggy continued. "However, the Han didn't protect the Kazakh immigrants. Instead, they imposed their own brand of persecution. Which is why we briefly joined with the Uighurs. But, we have learned to mind our own ways here on the steppe and now lead prosperous lives."

Again he stopped and the guests were quiet for a solemn moment, astonished by Ziggy's revelations.

He continued. "So you see, we're not friends of the communist regimes who have plagued us over the years. We listen to what the authorities say, but we don't hear them." Then in a surprise to his guests, he clapped his hands loudly and said, "So now you understand my sincerity when I ask, what can I do to help you?"

Steve and Fritz sat back flabbergasted. They hadn't seen that degree of sentiment nor gesture of friendship coming. Betta simply chose not to react, not sure how this proud male Kazakh would receive a comment from a woman, compliment or not.

Steve was the first to speak. "I appreciate your willingness to help. But I'm not sure how."

Ziggy's smile was genuine. "I'm sure there is a great deal I can do. I know the area; I know the demeanor of the police; and I know how the MSS operates. To go west from here on your own would not only be difficult, but also dangerous—to your health and your political well-being. Avoid the well-travelled crossings along the national highway and rail lines. You should cross north of here, north of Urumqi. When you reach Lake Ebinur, follow the river through the Dzungarian Gate. This will allow you to avoid Urumqi and the southern crossing at Yining to Khorgos." He paused while Tegh caught up.

Once again the three westerners were without words. Steve thought, first the chaban and now Ziggy are willingly to offer their assistance. They're perfect strangers in an even stranger land.

Ziggy dismissed his wives, making a concession to allow Betta to remain for what was clearly to be a male-only discussion. In a hushed voice, he bid his older son to bring them some fermented mare's milk. "A serious drink for serious talk," as he put it.

With Tegh translating, he said, "Now let us make our plan."

Cross-legged on the carpet, the Westerners leaned onto their cushions to hear what he had to offer.

Tegh said, "Ziggy wants us to take his proposal for consideration, although there's some risk to him. If for nothing else, he wants to show up the authorities if they should ever come asking. He has a friend who can escort us to the Kazakh border and into Kazakhstan, but it will take a few days to set up. Tomorrow, he will send his thirteen-year-old son to his village, a day's ride from here, and ask his friend to return with his truck."

Steve was amazed at the offer and even more so that Ziggy would send his young son alone, on an overnight trip through the wilderness on horseback, to summon someone. "Won't that be dangerous?"

Ziggy scoffed, "He's made such trips alone across the steppe before. Besides, what could happen?"

Oh, I don't know, wolves, a broken leg, Betta wanted to say, but didn't.

Tegh continued the translation. "He says it's the least he can do for us. His friend makes the trip to the border three or four times a year to take sheep and horses to the Kazakh livestock markets. Whether the animals are for mounts, food, or breeding, the auctions in Kazakhstan are more lucrative than the local ones. There, he can get 1,200 yuan for one good breeding stallion. In return he can buy a sheep for 225 yuan and a brood mare for 530 yuan. For one good stud horse, he can get two mares.

"The border crossing will be unremarkable, since livestock auctions are a common venue for herders from both sides of the border. China and Kazakhstan both benefit."

"How will we get across?" Fritz asked.

Tegh relayed the question and the reply. "We'll ride in the back with the livestock. The guards will think we're farm hands. Most likely they won't even check our papers."

Fritz quipped, "But we don't look anything like the locals, plus we don't have any papers."

Tegh spoke up on his own. "Don't worry about your looks. There's lots of Western blood in the local population. The Russians have stomped around these parts for decades and many of them took local wives. You won't be as out of place as you might think. Your clothes are authentic. Just don't speak.

"Ziggy says it's a little over four hundred miles to the Kazakh border and another seventy or so to the livestock market. Once we're there, it will be easy to get the train to Almaty, the Kazakhstan capital where we'll be able to reach our embassies and arrange travel home. So, we should get some rest while he fetches his friend."

Fritz said, "Oh boy, more time in the back of a truck. How long is this going to take?"

Betta gave him a cautionary stare. "Fritz, it's uncomfortable for everyone, but it's what we have to do. You can put up with it."

Steve interjected, "Come on, Fritz. This can't be any worse than your camping trips back home. Think of it that way."

Fritz stood and went out into the night air for a smoke.

The rest, seeing that the discussion was done, left to their respective quarters.

When she got ready to bed down on the ger's surprisingly soft carpet, Betta couldn't believe their good fortune. Restless with anticipation, she heard a stirring from the other side of the tapestry partition separating the women's sleeping area from the men's. She gathered a jacket around her and went to investigate. When she pulled back the entry flap to the ger, she saw Steve standing some thirty feet away.

"Couldn't you sleep?" she whispered, stepping closer.

"No, I'm pretty keyed up by Ziggy's offer. I mean, I figured we'd have managed to get across the border somehow, but I didn't think we'd have been handed a chance like this."

"My concern," she said, "is how closely the border guards will examine the papers he's giving us. Our passports won't do us any good, and I don't really look like the local girls. For one I'm taller and I'm, uh, better... you know—stand out more than these women do."

Steve laughed. "Really, is that what's got you worried? It didn't seem to bother you last night."

She was glad he couldn't see her blush in the dark. "That was different. And in case you hadn't noticed, my good sir, we women do think of things like that." She gently pushed him away as he leaned in.

Steve didn't press the issue. "Well, just so you know, I don't regard that as your best asset."

Betta wasn't sure if she should inquire as to what was, but was glad to know that Mr. Steadfast and Reliable had noticed her. "And just what would that be?" She could kick herself as soon as she'd said it.

He answered right away. "You're the steadying influence in our group. When Fritz goes off the deep end with one of his conspiracies, you're there to calm him down. When Tegh launches into one of his history lessons, you have a nice way of letting him know that his talks are appreciated, even if they are desperately long."

She chuckled. "And you? What about you? How do I complement your obvious faults?"

"Why madam, faults? Whatever ever can you be referring to?"

She wanted to reach out and hug him tightly, like the night on the rooftop in Dunhuang when Fritz was chased by security guards. But she wouldn't let herself succumb. *Maybe I'm simply responding to the artificial attraction that befalls people confined during times of stress. Maybe I'm*

271

worried about being found out. Circumstances have a way of altering one's perception. Or maybe I'm worried about the professional image I've cultivated for so many years to perfect.

Steve broke into her thoughts and steered her back towards the women's side of the ger. Without thinking, she leaned into him.

He gave her a peck on the cheek. "I think we should both try to get some sleep. We have a long road to travel in the next few days."

Suddenly, they heard a faint rustling from close by, but couldn't see what it was. They stood still for a moment and then Steve motioned her into ger entryway. As they ducked in, they both caught an unmistakable whiff of cigarette smoke.

Steve thought, *How long had he been there?*

Chapter 32

THE JUNGGAR PENDI, WESTERN CHINA

THE NEXT DAY, after his son embarked on horseback across the Junggar Pendi, Ziggy mounted them up and led them for a twelve-mile horseback trip to a ridge overlooking Lake Barkol. The best Steve could tell looking at Fritz, he gave no hint of having heard nor seen anything from the night before. But the thought that he'd overheard him and Betta haunted him.

As the village disappeared behind them and they rode onto the steppe, Steve took in the extraordinary pastoral beauty. The steppe was a patchwork of light greens and sandy tans spreading for miles. "I can see why you raise so much livestock," Steve said to Ziggy. "You have all this free pasture land."

"I wouldn't say it's free," Ziggy said. "For the time being, maybe, but the Chinese don't value the open steppe and our way of life as we do. Our lake is fed by mountain runoff and it's the primary reason this area is self-supporting.

"But the more the government expands into the region, the more they rob the water before it can be re-fed from the streams. You will see what I mean when you get to the Dzungarian Gate."

Steve thought, this was the second time he had heard mention of this mysterious structure guarding the passage out of China. What could this architectural wonder be?

Early the next day, a rickety, Soviet-era truck rumbled up to the ger and Ziggy greeted his son and an old friend. Leaving Betta to amuse herself with Ziggy's wives and daughters, all the men sat cross-legged next to a fire pit outside and discussed the coming journey. Over tea served dutifully by Ziggy's wife, the two Kazakh herders came to an agreement.

Tegh turned to his three friends. "Ziggy's friend will lend us his truck and load it with eight sheep for shipment to the livestock market in Kazakhstan. He wants us to sell his two prize rams and six ewes and thinks they'll fetch a good price this time of year. In return, he's agreed to split the proceeds 70-30 in his favor, because it's his truck."

Fritz, thinking this sounded fair and mutually beneficial, nodded his head.

Steve said, "And it gets us that much closer to leaving China—great news. Is there anything we can do to help, like at least pay for the gas? After all, he's renting us his truck for a few days. That's the least we can do."

"Keep your money," Tegh said. "There are two things you must learn. First, don't let anyone know you're carrying that kind of cash. These men you can trust, but for others we'll encounter on the road, you won't be able to. Secondly, this falls under hospitality. Remember what I told you earlier."

Steve said, "Okay, I guess we're in for the ride. Let's tell Betta and get our things ready to go."

But as they were putting backpacks onto the truck bed,

one thing gnawed at Fritz's sense of fair play. Now seemed like the right moment to voice his concern. Tegh was talking with the herdsman and it was just him, Steve, and Betta. Fritz saw his chance.

"Not paying for the trouble these people are going through for our benefit doesn't sit well with me. Hospitality culture or not, they're undertaking great risks for people they don't even know."

"What do you propose?" she said.

"I want to figure out a way to give them some of the money we have," Fritz explained. "Goodness knows we've more than enough from what we took from the plane."

"You're right, we've been spending that money freely," Steve said, "on bus and train tickets, clothing, and hotels. In my mind, though, I can justify that."

"What do you suggest?" Betta asked. "Give it back? Come on Fritz. This is no moral crisis. It's not like we stole it."

"Actually, we did," countered Fritz. "It wasn't ours and now we have it. What would you call that?"

"I wouldn't call it stealing, that's for sure," Steve said. "Call it ours by right of salvage, abandonment, or chance encounter. But what we did wasn't stealing."

Betta spoke up. "Fritz, Steve's right. We're benefitting by necessity from that money. It's no different than the other things we salvaged from the plane: food, clothing— your cigarettes. We wouldn't have survived this long without all of those."

"So it's two against one again. Fine."

The way Fritz had said it, Steve, could see that Fritz wasn't placated. "Oh, Fritz, one other thing, who knows how much of it we'll have to hold on to or not use to get out of China."

With something still gnawing at his sense of conviction, Fritz nodded his head, but he didn't like it—losing the argument or keeping the money. Then he thought of a perfect compromise. "Okay, I'll grant you that. I'll agree with you as long as we get rid of whatever excess money we might have if and when we get out of here."

Steve and Betta looked at each other and then nodded to Fritz.

With agreement finally reached, Steve went to Tegh, who was standing with Ziggy and his friend. "Tegh, I know what you said about hospitality, but I don't think that extends to business deals. I want to make an offer to Ziggy."

Tegh looked curiously at Steve. "What is it?"

"Tell Ziggy's friend I want to buy a ram and one of his ewes. Also, ask him if I can keep them here with him until I return to claim them."

"But you're never..." Tegh stopped, smiled, and translated.

Hearing the offer, Ziggy eyed Steve cautiously but understood what he was attempting to do. This young foreigner was avoiding an open effrontery to custom by offering to buy into their enterprise. Ziggy shrugged and explained Steve's offer to his friend. The herdsman gave Steve a broad grin and they shook hands all around.

Seeing a new side of Steve which she had to admire, Betta squeezed his arm and then quickly stood back, not knowing if Fritz may have seen her. If Fritz had, he didn't react. When she got the nerve and looked in Fritz's direction, he was hiking himself up onto the back of the truck.

They loaded the livestock onto the truck, Betta and Tegh headed for the truck cab while Steve and Fritz made themselves as cozy as possible, separated from the sheep by strategically positioned hay bales. Steve's anxiety was piqued when Tegh cautioned him, "Ziggy wants you to be mindful of the ram. Two of the ewes are in heat."

"Good for them," Betta said.

"Oh, wonderful," Steve muttered.

With the truck loaded, Tegh noticed Ziggy's friend wasn't making ready to board the truck. He asked Ziggy, "Isn't he going?"

"Oh no. He'll ride one of my horses back home and I'll return the truck in a few weeks when I get back. We'll have to settle up accounts, anyway."

Benny, Duz, and Abai Shokan came to say goodbye. Benny assured Ziggy he'd return in the spring with another load of fodder. Turning to the four travelers, he wished them well on their continuing journey.

"If it is the will of God, then it will come to pass," Ziggy replied.

Steve took notice of his reference to God, something he hadn't heard so far in this land of Buddhists and Muslims, and wondered which deity he referred to.

As Ziggy pulled the truck out, the four of them waved farewell to Duz, Benny, and Abai Shokan, three wonderful human beings whom they happened to meet on the Silk Road. The truck with its cargo of livestock and four fortunate plane crash survivors moved steadily westward towards. It wasn't long, however, before Fritz and Steve discovered that no amount of hay bale separation was sufficient to avoid the stench from their shared space with the ewes and a randy ram.

About an hour later, Ziggy slowed and Tegh leaned out of a cab window and told Steve and Fritz, "Get low in the truck bed. We're coming to a roadblock. The guard manning the barrier will want to see our papers. Ziggy says he's used to these roadside shakedowns and not to worry. Just stay down."

Tegh and Betta sat quietly in the cab as Ziggy handed his identity documents to the young cop, along with a few yuan tucked within, while at the same time he berated the young official. With a cursory glance, and having been modestly intimidated by Ziggy's sharp remarks, the lone security man waived the truck past with a semi-official gesture, never even bothering to look in the back.

Sufficiently down the open road now, Tegh asked Ziggy, "What was that all about?"

He listened to the reply and chuckled.

"What?" Betta asked,

Tegh laughed and explained, "The guard is the son of an old acquaintance of his, a fellow herdsman. Ziggy shamed him for not having a real job and for relying on the government for his salary, but still gave him thirty yuan because he knew he didn't make much."

Betta, "I don't think it's funny, Tegh. I'm still worried when these local arrangements won't serve us well."

"The important thing, Betta, is that it did."

They made camp that night several miles north of the highway in a pasture situated by a stream bed. Isolated from a view of the road by distance and trees, they avoided even the remotest chance at encountering impromptu security patrols. Ziggy had assured them,

"Patrols are rare, but I want to be cautious."

They broke camp in the pre-dawn light to get as early a start as possible. Shortly after 10 A.M., as they bounced along the poorly maintained road, Tegh saw Ziggy's usually jovial expression suddenly change. With visible concern on his face, he pulled over to the side of the road and killed the engine. Not sure what he was reacting to, Tegh started to ask a question, but Ziggy motioned for silence and rolled his window down so he could hear better.

After sitting still a moment and letting his senses acclimate to the countryside quiet, Ziggy explained, "I hear another truck. I can't see anything behind us, and the road ahead is hidden by the mountain beyond a curve. The rock walls can do funny things with sound."

"What are you going to do?" Tegh asked.

"We must get off the main road and onto that secondary road that runs below us."

Tegh opened the cab door, stood on the running board, and explained to those in the back of the truck. "We're going to leave the main road. Ziggy thought he heard heavy trucks coming from ahead. He suspects an army patrol or police detachment may be approaching. The last thing we need is to deal with another roadblock, official or not. He's going to back up to a turnout we passed a few hundred yards back and then take the secondary road that heads along the valley floor. He wants our truck off the main road until whatever and whoever is ahead of us goes by."

Fritz looked at Betta and saw fear in her eyes. He reached for her to say something comforting, but Tegh interrupted. "We'll be all right. Just sit still and stay quiet.

Ziggy will get us out of this." But Tegh thought, settling back in the cab with Ziggy, *I wish I felt as confident as I sound.*

Ziggy restarted the engine and backed the truck until he reached the dirt track turnout. The bad news was that he could only make about ten mph going in reverse and what he thought might be truck engine noises up ahead were getting louder. Tegh could also hear the unmistakable throbbing of heavy diesel engines and rattling chasses, but Tegh figured, with all the potholes and ruts in the main road, the noise the still-invisible trucks were making would mask whatever noise Ziggy was making to get off the main road.

He backed their truck flush to the hillside, turned his wheels, shifted into first, and pulled ahead about fifteen feet. He repeated the maneuver on the narrow road until he'd negotiated the truck onto the descending secondary road. He headed the truck down the hillside, until the road turned left to parallel the main road. As Ziggy negotiated the secondary dirt road, it gradually descended below the line of sight from the main roadbed above them. Finding a small copse next to a stream, Ziggy stopped and killed the engine. He motioned them to get out, to get across the stream, and to hide in the cluster of trees.

While they hurried to become as inconspicuous as possible, Ziggy had Tegh place a rope bridle on one of the rams and back the balking beast off the truck. Tegh led it to a narrow patch of grass behind the truck and tied him off to a tree. The ram was only too happy to partake of the unexpected chance to graze. Ziggy in the meantime hunkered down on a nearby rock, in full view of the road above, and puffed on a cigarette, motioning Tegh to join him. From this vantage, they had a full view of the main road above.

Reaching the stand of brush and birch trees that blocked a direct view from the upper road, Steve, Betta, and Fritz got as far into the foliage as possible.

"Take off that blue coat, Betta. It stands out like a neon sign," Steve said.

"I can't see what's going on with Ziggy," Fritz complained.

Shedding her coat, Betta said, "That's the whole point of what we're doing."

Steve dropped to all fours and crawled to a fork in the trunk of a birch tree and peered out.

"See anything?" Fritz asked.

"Shhh, don't let your voice carry," Steve whispered.

They only had a moment or so before they heard the screeching of air brakes from above on the main road. Steve said softly, "I see the tops of four army trucks stopping on the high road. Ziggy's tied one of the sheep to a tree and is letting it graze while he smokes a cigarette."

"I could sure use a cigarette about now," Fritz said, drawing a swift nudge from Betta.

Steve continued. "Three of the trucks are loaded with military equipment, which I can see poking out from beneath a tarpaulin. One truck has soldiers riding in the open back. It looks like seven, eight, hmmm, maybe a dozen soldiers. Their uniforms look like the ones the MMS guards at the airport wore. Wait a minute, Ziggy's waving to the lead truck."

"What?" Fritz gave a muffled cry, and Betta gave him

more than a nudge eliciting another yelp.

Steve continued, "The leader's getting out of his truck. He's talking into a walkie-talkie and heading towards Ziggy."

"What's Ziggy doing?" Betta couldn't stifle her anxiety.

"He's just sitting there. Wait a minute, now all three of them are talking. Looks like the soldiers are not all that excited about anything. From the way Ziggy's pointing back down the road they just came from...wait a minute, now he's pointing ahead of them. I think Ziggy's giving him directions."

"Does he have a gun?" Betta asked.

"Of course he's armed. He's a soldier," Fritz said, and Betta skewered him with another elbow.

"Will you two be quiet," Steve whispered. "The soldier just motioned for Ziggy to step back with him towards his trucks. Maybe to get a better view of what he's trying to explain to Ziggy. Damn."

"What?" Betta and Fritz said in a hushed chorus.

"I can't see them now. They're out of view, somewhere back up on the main road. I'm guessing that's good because they looked like they were talking about which way the highway goes."

Steve crawled back from the fork in the tree and faced his friends. "I guess we'll have to wait and see."

They heard heavy truck doors slam, followed quickly by truck engines rumbling back to life. Steve rolled over on all fours and pushed his head back through the vee of the tree trunk. "The convoy's moving out. They're continuing in the direction they were headed."

"What do you think they wanted?" Betta asked.

"Whatever it was, it didn't have anything to do with a

herdsman taking a smoke break," Steve said.

They stayed put and waited for Tegh to give the okay signal to come out. Finally, Tegh said, "All right, you guys, the coast is clear."

Scrambling from their concealment, they quickly made it across the stream and back to Ziggy's truck.

Fritz asked, "What the hell did they want? Were they looking for us?"

Ziggy explained, "They were looking for the bypass to Urumqi. I told them they weren't far from the cutoff road that leads across the ridge to the outskirts of Turpan, about twenty-five miles from here. My guess is they're an MSS patrol heading to Urumqi to organize a search for you guys."

Betta gasped.

Ziggy gave her a paternal smile. "I wouldn't worry about those men. They're gone, but I don't want to chance that upper road just in case there should be more of them. It's best we travel this lower road to the northwest. In another mile or so, it will ford that stream and start angling away from the main road. This route will put distance between us and the mountains. Though the trip will be longer, it's more isolated."

Unable to ward off his nicotine craving anymore, Fritz took a cigarette out, lit it, and took a welcomed drag. Exhaling, he said, "I certainly don't want to go through that again." Noticing Ziggy eyeing his cigarette, Fritz offered him one of his.

"Good move for once, Fritz," Betta said.

Ready to get started again, the Kazakh coaxed the reluctant ram from his late summer grazing and reloaded him onto the truck. Steve and Fritz remounted the truck bed, with Tegh and Betta joining Ziggy in the cab. As predicted, about ten minutes later the road forded the stream and flattened out to become a hard-packed byway.

Ziggy said, "We're on a beeline across the southern edge of the Junggar Pendi. It's hard-panned desert, covered with the sand and grit that encompasses the southwestern third of a basin formed by two mountain ranges, one to the north and one to the south.

"Doesn't this country have anything besides desert?" Betta asked.

"That's why we'll stay on the southern rim of the dunes," Ziggy said. "That way, we'll be on hard pack gravel and will still be able to find occasional water."

"Well, at least there's that," Betta replied.

For the next 160 miles, they were in the shadow of the Bogda Shan, which receded in the distance to the west. The road was studded with bumps, ruts, and chuckholes, making travelling at more than 35 mph impossible. Ziggy stopped once to top off his gas from the jerry cans stowed beneath the truck bed.

Periodically they passed small clusters of peasants along the roadside, most of them walking, though occasionally they encountered men leading horse-drawn carts. They passed several encampments, all situated well off the road, where an occasional stream ran. Every so often, they saw one or two gers looming out of the middle of nowhere.

Tegh explained shepherds established these temporary camps, places where shepherds stayed for a few days, before moving their sheep to yet-to-be-used grazing spots. During their midday stop, they paused at one of these ger camps to partake of some ready hospitality.

Chapter 33

XINGXINGXIA AND URUMQI, XINGJIAN PROVINCE, WESTERN CHINA

GENERAL WU XI all but screamed into his radio handset. "What do you mean, they haven't come west? I flew all the way here to Urumqi and there's no sign of them. Where the hell are they?"

First Director Lin reluctantly replied, "I mean, General, we have confirmation from our own people they were in Dunhuang a week ago. Now I have credible intelligence indicating they were here in Xingxingxia, having arrived by bus from Dunhuang the day after the soldier's sighting. Prison guards here report seeing four persons matching the descriptions of the missing crash victims who boarded a train bound for Hami. So, this all seems very plausible."

"Don't get flippant with me, First Director Lin! I'm in no mood." Wu knew he had his subordinate worried that his career was spiraling towards an ignominious end.

Lin replied, "By all means, no, sir. By process of elimination, this can only mean they're heading to Urumqi to reach the western border crossing into Kazakhstan at Khorgos, west of Yining."

"You were just in Urumqi. Why didn't you detect them?"

"Sir, for some reason, they are moving more slowly

than we estimated. By my calculations, they are most likely not far from Urumqi. They definitely weren't there when I was there a few days ago. I was checking for bus passengers travelling the national highway and didn't know they'd switched to the train."

"Well your intelligence, as you call it, isn't worth a..." The general was too mad for words, and grew silent, his anger having gotten the better of him. In that moment, he was more than surprised by First Director Lin's next statement.

"Right now, General, I'm in Xingxingxia. Since we don't know how they're travelling, but do know they're heading for the border, I propose that I fly directly to Yining, west of you, and convoy to the border crossing to get ahead of them for certain. In the meantime, I'll send a message to our western border detachment at Yining to be on the lookout for four undocumented persons travelling by either bus or train, and to detain them until I arrive."

Hearing the suggestion, the general paused a moment and thought, *Of course, I could organize such a roadblock, but why should I sully myself with grunt work when I have a lackey like Lin to do it for me?*

Hearing nothing and deciding to press his luck, Lin said, "If I might suggest, General, you could liaise with your senior associates and let them know of your plan."

General Wu grunted something unintelligible into the phone. Then, uttering an epithet that belied his pre-communist conversion to atheism which abandoned his Catholic missionary upbringing, he said, "Listen carefully to me, Lin. You had better pray to God you don't mess up again. I'll authorize your flight, but I expect when I see you next, you will have captured them. Do you understand me?"

General Wu didn't wait for an answer as he terminated the call, slamming his handset back into its cradle. Then, venting his spleen further, he said to his near empty command post, "I don't relish having to spend more time in this western outpost. It isn't Beijing, where I rightfully belong. I'm tired of putting up with the incompetence of the likes of First Director Lin."

Only the mail clerk was within earshot to hear his protest, and she said nothing.

Chapter 34

JUNGGAR PENDI, WESTERN CHINA

THE SLENDER SOUTHWESTERN crescent of the Junggar Pendi spreading before them had yet to be claimed by desert. It was a tufted, relatively fertile basin stretching to the northern Altai Mountains. Surprisingly, the nearly deserted road they travelled was smoother than what they'd found closer to civilization. Though only slightly better than an improved horse trail, it hadn't been rutted by motorized traffic. They encountered only two other vehicles all day.

As far as the sheep in the truck bed were concerned, the condition of the road made no difference to them. They simply shit, peed, bleated, and humped. It was a captive audience for the rams, who filled the air with an inescapable, nauseating foulness for their human roommates to endure. By now, animal urine had soaked beneath the bale barrier separating man from beast and had become problematic. All Fritz and Steve could do was lift their feet to the top of the bales.

"Couldn't we have bought some housebroken ones?" Fritz complained.

They camped that night at the base of a dune, two hundred yards from a meager stream, which nurtured sparse grass for the hobbled livestock to feed on.

The next morning, they rejoined the northwest-bound

road that followed a nearly dry stream bed towards the town called Shehezi. Tegh explained to them, "Ziggy claims he has a friend there, a cousin, or a cousin of a friend, where we can spend the night."

"Oh, good, maybe I can get a bath and a bed," Betta said.

"I wouldn't count on it," Tegh admonished. "At least we'll receive a hot meal in a settlement that hopefully has no inquiring police."

Ziggy's acquaintance, as it turned out, was a widowed friend of his mother, a woman he'd never personally met. Her home was a gray concrete structure, typical Soviet-era four-wall, cement construction with an outhouse in back. Fortunately for them, her home, on the edge of the small town, offered moderate isolation from any curious passersby who might take notice of strangers. In this part of the world, outsiders were welcome as long as someone known to the group vouched for them.

Their good fortune held and the widow rolled out the red carpet, or more specifically, a hand-knotted Oriental one, to cover her floor as she spruced up for her old friend's son and his companions. She offered them tea with sugar-coated baked dough balls. After a half-hour of pleasantries, their hostess ushered them outside to an open area behind three similarly constructed houses.

Tegh interpreted while Ziggy explained. "We're in for a treat. Her neighbor's daughter is getting married and we're invited. I for one have never been to a Kazakh wedding, so this should be fun."

Fritz said, "This isn't going to take a day or two, is it? I'm all for hospitality, but the longer we're still in China, the more likely it is that we'll be discovered."

"Don't be a poop head, Fritz. Can't you ever learn to relax?" Betta chided.

But Tegh understood Fritz's concern and tactfully asked Ziggy if this would delay their departure in the morning. Reassured that this was only to be a one-night stay, he relayed the news to Fritz, who, though remaining sullen, voiced no more objections.

In the meantime, the old woman explained to her guests, "The bride is our oldest daughter, the first of the girls to wed. Her groom comes from a family living several miles away."

Steve and Betta smiled, and Fritz, as usual, wasn't paying attention.

Betta said softly to Steve, "What's gotten in to him?"

Steve said, "I think I know."

But before she could ask, the old woman began explaining their marriage traditions. "The groom has already built a small house for his bride. Next, he'll offer a dowry, probably some sheep and a horse, which her father will accept. We women will roast one of the sheep for the feast, which everyone, including you, will be honored to share."

Betta, mindful of Fritz's obsession with delays, asked, "How long does this last? The sun is almost down."

Fritz, who had been listening said, "Gird thy loins, my dear. You're in for another long night."

Betta, excited at seeing the wedding ceremony, joined in the clapping as a man in traditional Kazakh garb strummed on a many-stringed guitar accompanied by a man on a synthesizer plugged into a propane-powered generator amplifier. Papa apparently had accepted the offered dowry, because the gathered clans gave a great cheer and the music began in earnest. The women paraded in a freshly spitted animal and laid it over a long bed of coals. When Betta turned around to comment to Steve and Fritz, she didn't see them anywhere.

After a short ceremony, the music picked back up and merriment ensued. Food was brought out and laid on two large tables. Revelers danced and ate, ate and danced in a seemingly endless stream of excitement. But Betta still had no sign of her two friends. For what could last several hours, Betta couldn't relax.

She was about to ask Tegh to go look for them when Betta saw the two missing men sneaking back into the area, but keeping their separate distances. They looked disheveled. Steve had good-sized scrape over one eye, and both looked like they'd been rolling around in the dirt. They took up positions on opposite ends of the tables and satisfied themselves with mugs of homemade beer.

Satisfied that her two friends had returned, Betta joined the rest of the celebrants to the fresh fruit, horse sausage, dried cheese curds, pastries, salads, nuts, *baursak*, deep fried dough, *beshbarmak*, meat in boiled pastry squares with cooked onion, grilled dowry mutton, and of course, vodka.

When the festivities finally came to an end well into the night, once again Betta had lost track of either friend. Not able to check on them in the men's quarters, she had to let things be.

Ziggy was the first up in the morning. Putting on his sheepskin-lined boots, he nudged the other men. "If we want to make the Dzungarian Gate before dusk, we best get going."

Tegh rubbed his throbbing head and slowly sat up on

his mat. It took him a moment to awaken fully. His first realization was of a cottony dryness in his mouth and an overwhelming urge to lie back down. Seeing Ziggy already dressed and disappearing out the back door, he reluctantly got up.

He coaxed Steve and Fritz awake with his toe while he buttoned his shirt. "Get up, you two. We need to get going or Ziggy's going to leave us." Seeing each of them get up, not saying a word of greeting and looking like they'd gone a round or two, he was about to ask a question as to what happened when a clank sounded. One of the wives opened the scuttle on the standing dung-burning stove in the middle of the room and added another fagot to the coals.

Tegh nodded to her, though she seemed not to notice. Forgetting Steve and Fritz for the moment, he walked over and greeted her. "Good morning, mother," he said, the proper salutation to an elderly Kazakh woman. "Would you wake up our companion, Betta?" He motioned with a hand to the back of his head, as if he were pulling a ponytail. She nodded and disappeared behind the stacked wardrobe and felt curtain separating the sleeping sections.

Fully awake and ready for a new day, if not just a little hung over from the wedding festivities, the four huddled with Ziggy and finished their morning tea. The only departure from the norm was that Steve and Fritz stood on opposite sides of the huddle as Ziggy explained, "Be glad you aren't taking the longer route on the main highway from Urumqi. It runs much further south and crosses the border some seventy miles from Yining at the Kazakh town of Khorgos. And from there it's another four hundred miles to Almaty. Because it's the main highway linking Urumqi and Almaty, it's heavily traveled by police, as evidenced by that convoy we saw. They do have a livestock market in Khorgos, but it's of secondary importance, and…"

Fritz heard his voice tail off as he turned his back, stepped away to light a cigarette, and stare into the distance. Seeing the dirt and grass stains on his jacket, Betta chose to leave him to his solitude. She turned back to the group where Ziggy was still talking.

"…and from experience, I couldn't get nearly as high a price for my animals as I can at the market where we're headed. In thirty-five miles, we reach Jinghe. There, a secondary highway goes north and the river cuts through the elevated plateau at a natural pass called the Dzungarian Gate. That's…"

Steve's ears picked up at the mention of the mysterious facility stuck out in the middle of nowhere.

"…where we'll cross the border. This eliminates almost three hundred miles from the trip if we'd left from Urumqi."

"All right, then let's get going to this gate thing," Steve said.

Fritz grumbled, "I'm just glad we're getting out of here."

Betta, looked at both of her friends and thought, *They look like crap. What the hell got into them last night?*

With that, Ziggy clapped his hands for them to herd the animals back into the truck. Steve and Fritz simply stared at each other, undecided as to who was to get into the truck bed and who would ride in the cab. Seeing the impasse, Betta said, "Steve, you ride up front in the cab with Ziggy. The rest of us will make do with the sheep and the hay bales."

As the truck pulled onto the road, the villagers assembled in front of their homes, all except the honeymooning couple. Everyone waved and Fritz said, "I guess the bride and groom are too busy to say goodbye."

Betta punched his arm in rebuke.

Chapter 35

THEY PULLED INTO a truck stop on the outskirts of Jinghe for fuel and to use the restrooms. While they waited for Betta, Tegh handed Ziggy a hundred-yuan note to pay for the gas. As he stood near the back of the truck, Steve noticed an elderly couple selling fruit and flatbread. Unsure as to how long it would be until they reached the border crossing and what delays they might encounter, he bought some of their offerings, while Tegh and Fritz busied themselves helping Ziggy. With travel essentials complete, Ziggy headed the truck back down the road.

"Right now, we're only eighty-five miles from the Kazakh border," Tegh said. "Ziggy tells me he was stationed in Jinghe years ago as a policeman. He agreed to that remote posting because he was told it would be good for his résumé, that he would be promoted more quickly. But he soon realized that, for most guards stationed there, it was a way for the system to move them out of the mainstream of a successful career pattern, not a step towards advancement. After four years, and seeing no future in working for the police, he resumed his family ranching business. And being a Kazakh, he was perfectly fine with that.

"He says the border region is full of failed officials, rank-and-file bureaucrats, and former army personnel who have committed minor infractions elsewhere, making many of these repopulated inhabitants denounced, disgraced, deported, demoted, or dishonored by the greater Chinese society. Those who came west in the hopes of finding economic improvement had no means to return east. Regardless of their status of origin, Han, Kazakh, or Uighur, everyone here is under the thumb of Chinese officialdom. Ironically, the Chinese authority prevails by using the same inherent social and bureaucratic hierarchical system that displaced most of them in the first place."

"What a depressing set of circumstances," Betta said, "to be isolated in a strange land, far from home, with no say in the matter."

Tegh nodded. "But, by necessity, the exiles have been forced to live and mingle. The remnants of many languages are found in the local dialects and are a gift from two millennia of travelers, deportees, and exiles. Ironically, those who were banished must now serve the newly arrived exiles. Everyone in Jinghe, served and server alike, has been released from bondage to this forgotten mélange. The road and rail lines constantly remind them that these main arteries of communication only meet their most meager needs."

"Jinghe doesn't sound like the greatest of hometowns."

"Sadly, you're right, Steve. No one else in China claims the people here," Tegh said.

Betta asked, "So tell me why we're heading for this Dzungarian Gate?"

"Because Dzungaria is hundreds of miles north of the main highway leading west through Urumqi," Tegh said.

"But don't the Chinese have guards at this gate?" Betta asked.

Tegh and Ziggy laughed. "The term gate describes a geographic anomaly carved by a major river that cuts the mountains and bisects the plateau that rises hundreds of meters above the plain on either side."

"You mean it's not a real gate, like we saw at the end of the Great Wall?" Fritz asked.

Glad to hear him finally participate, Betta said, "I know you're disappointed, Fritz, but try to follow along."

Tegh said, "I'm proud of you for remembering something I've mentioned during our travels, Fritz."

Fritz looked hard at them. "Let up. I'm tired of hearing it. I didn't ask to be here." But his grin belied his acceptance of the good-natured ribbing as he lit a cigarette.

Betta looked hopefully at Steve to see if he would say anything. But he didn't.

Reaching the town's outskirts, they saw dozens of locals driving donkey carts loaded with people and products of the local commerce. The term donkey was merely a euphemism, since the carts were pulled by whatever mammal was at hand, including man.

The energy these residents exhibited seemed oddly robust to Steve, who found the scene invigorating as he observed, "These entrepreneurs are the local teamsters and taxi drivers of the Junggar Pendi."

Hearing their comments, Tegh wondered if Steve and Fritz were back in the group from wherever they'd been brooding.

As they passed through town, Tegh pointed out the businesses, which seemed to cover all the essential trades: farriers, cartwrights, clothiers, butchers, and food vendors.

The people's dress and town center's buildings matched the dun of the surrounding Junggar Pendi, but what they lacked in color was more than made up for by a multitude of aromas from the small open market place. Mounds of brown, yellow, and red spices blended with the raw smells coming from the butcher's stall with its quarter sections of sheep and goat hanging in the sun. The bustle of patrons mixed with dozens of ongoing, tonal conversations among merchants and shoppers who were intent on striking a purchase price.

One indigenous ethnic group seemed oddly out of place to Steve, with their tanned white faces and Slavic features of narrow-set eyes, prominent brows, and blocky jaw lines. Steve asked Tegh, "The Western-looking people are dead ringers for the Russians I knew in Siberia. Why are there so many?"

"They're remnants of the pioneers abandoned here by the tsar, joined by later additions thanks to Stalin. Urged to go east and settle the frontier, they were marooned here with no means to return. The Russian immigrants and their descendants never integrated with the Mongol and Kazakh locals, building separate neighborhoods instead. That's why you'll see weathered Orthodox churches alongside fields of horses tended by an enclave of fair-skinned, blue-eyed herdsmen. But they're numbers are dwindling. They'll most likely be absorbed by the general population within a few more generations.

"The Kazakhs, on the other hand, are a gregarious people, eager to meet outsiders. Those who are Muslims are the Uighurs of western China. Visitors offer them a welcome break to their routines. Most locals have been to Urumqi, but returned to live in the unhurried lands of their ancestors." Tegh pointed down the street. "You can see the minarets of their mosque over there."

Driving into the town proper, Ziggy pulled the truck to a stop at the home of a horseman he knew, yet another Kazakh host, who greeted his friend warmly. Ziggy introduced him as Zhylkyaidar and asked if they could rest there before continuing north to Lake Ebinur.

"Of course, I would be dishonored if you hadn't asked," Zhylkyaidar insisted.

"We have known each from years of attending livestock auctions to buy and sell horses, goats, and sheep." Eyeing Ziggy's truck, he said, "I see you have two good looking rams in the back. Those ewes seem to be in very good condition, too. Are you selling?"

"You need new breeders?" Ziggy asked, always on the lookout for a sale. They began an earnest back-and-forth bartering session, friendly banter that Tegh didn't try to explain. But the body language and expressive faces of the two elder herdsmen told the others of their good-natured exchange. They soon agreed on a price for the entire lot of Ziggy's sheep.

Zhylkyaidar's wife brought out an earthen jug and passed around drinks to seal the deal. It was fermented mare's milk, something the three Westerners had agreed, from the last time it was offered, was an acquired taste.

Seeing their scrunched faces after tentative sips, the Kazakhs laughed heartily. Zhylkyaidar took a healthy swig straight from the jug, exhaled in satisfaction and said, "Now we should eat."

His wife served a typical shepherd's fare: kabobs, flat bread, black tea, noodles, and home-brewed vodka distilled from whatever grain or fruit was at hand, in this case, apples. Their host drew a few drops of the clear hooch right from the still's condensing kettle onto an overturned saucer. With the liquid pooled in the saucer's depression, Zhylkyaidar lit it with a match.

As he did, Ziggy explained, "If the flame is invisible, it's ready to drink."

The flame flared a diaphanous blue and then turned transparent. Zhylkyaidar exclaimed with the pride of a new father that it was ready. Fearful of the alcohol content, Betta took only small sips, but Fritz and Steve took a few fingers full in their glasses and soon had a buzz on.

Betta noticed and thought, *Whatever it was, they've resolved their differences.*

Now that the mood was convivial and not encumbered by business, Tegh explained to their host the real reason for their trip to the border. Normally, Fritz's alarm bells would have sounded, but he was already on his second glass of vodka and well on his way to becoming wasted. Besides, with a full beard and weathered look, Zhylkyaidar didn't strike him as the type who was looking to confide with the local authorities.

With their bargain struck for the sheep, Zhylkyaidar observed, "Your truck will look conspicuously empty if you cross the border with nothing but human cargo heading for a livestock market. I happen to have two brood mares in foal I'd be willing to let you take to auction for me. In return, you could pick up some milking goats. I had to thin my stock earlier this year and it's time to build it up before winter sets in."

Fritz, now in his own purple haze, thought this was a wonderful idea. Maybe horses wouldn't stink as much as sheep. Horses certainly couldn't be worse than sheep. He motioned to his host for another shot.

Stroking his beard, Zhylkyaidar surprised them when he said, "On second thought, I'll go with you. It's been a while since I attended an auction."

To consummate the bargain, they sat down to enjoy the lunch Zhylkyaidar's wife had prepared.

Having outlasted the heat of midday and now under a pleasant afternoon sky, they loaded the mares into the truck. Steve and Fritz rearranged their hay bale apartment to keep the horses from shying into them during the trip. Seeing the two men cooperating at least, Tegh thought, *I hope their disagreement is behind them. But maybe I'm just seeing the effects of the vodka.*

Zhylkyaidar bid his wife goodbye and hauled himself into the back with Tegh and Steve, leaving Fritz to ride in the cab with Betta. The truck roared to life and Ziggy pulled back onto the highway. Within an hour, they'd reached a blue-green river. Zhylkyaidar pointed out that the fields of flowering clover and rippling short grass were the beginnings of the winter pastures. Tegh thought they looked more like a turquoise brush stroke on the dun-colored canvas of the Junggar Pendi.

The pastures formed verdant strips extending miles. A truck garden, situated a hundred yards away from the river bank, appeared as alternating brown and green stripes of vegetables and wild flowers. Tegh could smell the musty scent of turned earth and ripening fruit that hung in the air. Beyond that, the hard scrabble pan was dotted with tufted grass. Solitary gers punctuated the expanse in the distance.

The truck drove on until dusk when Zhylkyaidar pounded on the roof of the cab, signaling Ziggy to pull up to a ger just up ahead. The hut was almost bleached white from years of exposure to the sun.

As the truck shut down and the passengers dismounted, yet another friendly Kazakh herdsman emerged with open arms and a broad smile to greet Ziggy and Zhylkyaidar. Seeing the beefy hands and the stocky Kazakh's barrel chest, Tegh thought this guy could have stepped off the set of a grade-B western movie as an extra. *I wonder if there are any ranchers in this part of the world these men don't know?*

Zhylkyaidar introduced the bear of a man as his longtime friend, Akhmet Shulgin, and assured them that they were in for a treat in his home. Tegh could see the other three were in awe at how close-knit the Kazakh community seemed to be. Inside the ger, beautifully woven wool carpets covered the floor. The circular interior walls were backed by the now familiar sight of stacked trunks.

Learning that his guests were from distant lands, and therefore unfamiliar with his Kazakh homeland, Akhmet offered tea, flatbread, and a soured cream spread. With everyone settled, he proposed a toast. "Welcome to my home in a land where we are free to tend our herds and graze anywhere the rich grasses grow and the streams flow."

Tegh asked his three companions, "What do you think?"

Steve said, "He's definitely patriotic."

Having taken in the relative luxury inside a home that was packed up and moved every few months, Betta said,

"I'm impressed with its simplicity. But how do nomadic people accumulate so much?"

Akhmet saw her skeptical look and said, "Ah, you are wondering about us Dzungarians."

Seeing Fritz sitting cross-legged and leaning on a cushion, Tegh wasn't sure if he were disinterested or still hungover. Rather than give offense to their host, Tegh answered for them, "Perhaps you could enlighten us."

Akhmet, only too glad to oblige, began. "Centuries ago, Chinese explorers came looking for Heavenly Horses for the emperor. It was—"

Recognizing the thread of a familiar tale, Fritz, suddenly showed interest and interrupted. "I remember your mentioning those horses, Tegh. But what exactly were Heavenly Horses?"

Tegh looked at his host, explained Fritz's question, and asked, "May I?"

The burly man shrugged. "Please, go ahead. I'm anxious to hear what such a young outsider could possibly know of my history?"

Tegh nodded. "Two thousand years ago, the emperor sent an emissary, Zhang Qian, west to find and bring back a sturdy breed of horses known as Heavenly Horses. Zhang Qian journeyed to what we know today as today as the Fergana Valley of Tajikistan. He returned with the horses for his emperor, who immediately grasped the strategic value of the route he'd travelled, a route that happens to pass directly through where we stand now."

When Tegh paused, Akhmet clapped his hand in glee, saying, "Go on, go on. You're doing well, young man. I'm impressed."

Tegh nodded and continued. "Successive emperors

established military garrisons along the Hexi Corridor to control the trade and bind the western lands to the empire. Eventually, China governed commerce clear to the Caspian Sea. Begun only as a vision for extraordinary horses and salvation from an enemy, the Silk Road came into being."

Akhmet applauded. "I couldn't have said it better." Reaching for a clay jug, he offered a toast as his wife filled their cups.

Betta eyed the jug warily, remembering the last time the men had succumbed to its temptations, but Fritz's eyes lit with obvious joy. As the hostess poured the first drink, Fritz said, "Sounds an awful lot like that Monkey King story."

Tegh nodded. "And it should. The fictitious Xuan Zang's adventures were, in part, the allegorical tales of the real Zhang Qian's travels. Historical fact begat a fictional legend."

As the drinks were poured, Fritz leaned over to Betta and whispered not so softly, "I sure could use something to eat. This stuff's making me hungry."

Akhmet saw the four laughing and asked Tegh what he'd said. When Tegh translated, he gave a belly laugh, stood, and stepped outside the ger, where he barked something to his wife. When he retook his seat, Tegh said, "Akhmet begs your pardon for not offering you dinner right away. His wife will bring something shortly."

Betta nudged Fritz with her elbow while looking directly at her host. As demurely as she could, she said, "Oh, you don't need to go to any trouble."

The Kazakh herdsman replied, "No trouble." He nodded to Tegh. "Please continue."

But as Tegh was about to continue his story of the Silk Road, the ger's flap flew back and the herdsman's wife and teenage daughters brought in the food. The travelers widened their circle and the women served a meal of mutton, onions, and a ground wheat paste cooked into flat bread. In addition, several more jugs of home-brewed ale were produced and passed around.

Remembering her previous experience with soured mare's milk, Betta gingerly tasted the contents of the jug to make sure it was ale.

As they ate, Akhmet and his wife smiled all the while. When the last morsel was eaten, his wife and daughters whisked away the trays. As another gesture of friendship, the herdsman took out a pack of local cigarettes. But before he could offer one, Fritz offered his own pack, knowing full well this was an offer the Kazakh couldn't refuse.

"I see you've learned how to make friends," Steve said to Fritz.

Betta held her breath, fearful if whatever had led to their row before might erupt again, but she was surprised when Fritz replied, "Consider it Western hospitality."

Tegh smiled and thought, *Looks like their disagreement's behind them.*

With everyone refreshed and enjoying the unexpected camaraderie, Tegh thanked their host.

The hardened veteran dismissed his thanks with a wave. "It's the least I can do for those kind enough to honor my home with their presence. In fact, I would insist that you spend a few days visiting so I can show you around the Dzungarian countryside."

Hearing the translation, worry crowded Tegh's face, as

he was not exactly sure how to refuse his gracious offer.

Catching site of Tegh's expression, Steve asked, "What did he say?"

When Tegh told them, Fritz muttered something in German and made as if to stand. Betta grabbed him by an arm and hugged him to her. Fritz, confused by her sudden show of affection, said in English, "But we can't hang around here?"

Betta placed her mouth next to his ear and whispered, "Don't mess this up, Fritz. Let Tegh handle it." Then releasing him, she smiled to the others saying, "Sorry, not sure what came over me."

At Tegh's urging, Steve ushered his two friends outside as Tegh explained to Akhmet, "You'll have to excuse him. He drank way too much last night, and now he's feeling out of sorts. I assure you, it has nothing to do with your gracious hospitality. It's simply that he has trouble holding his drink."

Akhmet gave a paternalistic smile and said, "Ah, is that common among Westerners?"

Tegh replied, "I'm afraid so."

Akhmet chuckled and Tegh, seeing he'd diverted Akhmet's attention from his offer of several more days of hospitality, quickly said, "I think we'd best get him to bed so he can be rested for our continued journey tomorrow."

Akhmet said, "Yes, you must attend to your friend. If you like, I can provide him some herbs that will settle his..." He stopped looking for the correct word.

"Hangover?" Tegh offered.

"Yes, hangover. I have just the thing."

Tegh thanked him profusely and said, "I think he'll be all right with some rest." Then, turning to Ziggy and

Zhylkyaidar, he said, "We're calling it a night. We have an early day tomorrow."

Zhylkyaidar replied, "We're going to visit with Akhmet for a while longer. Go check on your friends. We'll see you in the morning."

The next morning, the chill reminded Tegh that winter wasn't far off for this region. Breakfast was fast: dry bread and hot tea. Zhylkyaidar and Ziggy unhobbled the mares, loaded them onto the truck, and refilled the truck bed's galvanized water trough. The travelers thanked Akhmet and his wife, who stood by their home's entrance to bid them farewell, last night's incident apparently forgotten. The truck's engine groaned as it cranked a few times in protest before roaring to life. Just that quickly and the intrepid group was off.

The road angled slowly away from the Bogda Shan as it wound its way across the western Junggar Pendi. They had a forty-mile stretch to cover before they'd reach the shores of Lake Ebinur.

When the truck surmounted a switchback at the crest of a low ridge, Zhylkyaidar pulled the truck to a stop. Tegh nudged the other three who were dozing on propped up hale bales.

"Look out there." He pointed to a panorama of the grayish-brown, rocky scrabble of the broad Junggar Pendi with an occasional pale ribbon of green. In the western distance was a sky blue lake in a narrow valley between two mountain ranges.

Tegh said, "That pass in the distance is the Dzungarian Gate."

Ziggy, who'd climbed out of the cab to enjoy the view,

said for the travelers' benefit, "Once through the Gate, you'll be in Kazakhstan, clear of your Chinese worries." As soon as Tegh translated, he could see Steve's and Betta's faces brighten.

Ever one to question, however, Fritz asked, "How far away is it, I mean the lake and the border?"

Ziggy said, "About another twenty miles, my friend. The only Chinese you'll encounter now will be the border security guards."

"You mean there aren't any patrols in this area?" Fritz asked in clarification.

Ziggy shook his head, "Not in this valley. They don't bother the herdsmen and the herdsmen don't give the Chinese authorities reason to."

Finally, Fritz relaxed as he lit up a cigarette, offering one to both Zhylkyaidar and Ziggy.

Taking the goodwill gesture, Ziggy said, "The Dzungarian Gate is only twenty miles wide. Those white patches you see along the northern lake shore near the marsh are mineral deposits left by evaporation. As the Chinese build more settlements, they draw down the lake's water level faster than it mountain runoff can replenish it. Among other things, the valley is the evolutionary home of the apple, which was first cultivated here before it spread to the rest of the world."

"No kidding," said Steve.

Before they got too engrossed in more history, Tegh reminded Ziggy that they needed to get going.

As he headed for the truck cab, Ziggy added, "On the other side of the border is the Kazakh town of Dostyq. That's where the livestock market is."

Climbing back onto the truck bed, Fritz said, "I'll be

so glad when we get across the border and don't have to worry about running into Chinese police anymore."

"That's why we avoided Urumqi," Tegh said in a half-truth. "It's not just foreigners the police harass, but the locals as well, given half an excuse. So, feel good that we're getting that behind us. All right, folks, it's time to get this over with."

Ziggy and Zhylkyaidar cranked up the truck for the descent into the valley. In a little under two hours, as the truck rounded a bend, a cluster of buildings swung into view. For reasons unknown to those in the back of the truck, Ziggy pulled to the side of the road and got out.

"What's wrong?" Fritz asked.

Chapter 36

Dostyq, Kazakhstan

"Nothing," Tegh said. "Ziggy and Zhylkyaidar want to review with us the plan for crossing the border. He wants to insure we'll understand what's going to happen and how to react. Let them to do all the talking, since they've crossed dozens of times."

Zhylkyaidar said in a confident manner, "I have the papers not only for us, but also the horses. These guards all know the two of us; they've seen us crossing many times." He pointed to Ziggy. "And it's not uncommon for border guards to see extra people riding along who work with us as wranglers."

"How do we explain Betta?" Fritz asked.

"For the crossing, she'll ride in the back, too. Chances are the guards will only pay attention to the horses," Zhylkyaidar said. "The guards probably won't even bother to step up onto the truck bed. But just in case," he pointed to Fritz, "give me a couple of packs of your cigarettes. If I offer them money, a conscientious guard may get suspicious. But for Western cigarettes, they'll look the other way. Cigarettes aren't a danger to the state the way a monetary bribe is."

As he fished in his pack for more cigarettes, Fritz asked skeptically, "Will this really work? How many times have you crossed the border?"

Zhylkyaidar looked at Fritz with veteran confidence. "Trust me, we know what we're doing. Besides, it's the end of the month. They've probably met their impound quotas by now, so scrutiny will be less strict."

"You better be right," Fritz said, handing over the smokes.

"Or what?" Steve said. "You'll turn them in?"

That earned a small laugh from Ziggy and Zhylkyaidar when Tegh translated.

The border crossing was marked by a yellow concrete portal spanning the road that caught the full brightness of the sun and reminded the three Westerners of the tour guide's story about the yellow door.

The truck pulled up to the first crossing station, a modern structure with a long pullout parking lot for trucks. They were waved forward to a counterbalanced, striped gate. Because they drove a stake truck, the Chinese guards could easily inspect the cargo.

Ziggy spoke through the open cab window, giving the guards the story he'd rehearsed earlier. One guard casually glanced at the papers Ziggy handed him, which included two packs of cigarettes. Another guard, standing ahead of the hood, waved to Zhylkyaidar in the passenger seat and smiled.

A third guard, who displayed an unfaltering stern look and cradled a menacing automatic rifle, walked around the truck where he bent over to look underneath. Straightening up, he poked the rear-most hay bale, which moved slightly. One horse nickered and stomped a hoof.

Betta pulled her hat lower on her head and held her breath while squeezing Steve's hand. It was everything the three of them could do to keep their gazes downward and not stare as the guard made his interminable way around the truck.

Not in a hurry, the stern looking guard continued his circumnavigation, taking no note of the people in the back. Finally satisfied, he went up to the guard with the papers and whispered something. The senior guard seemed to accept the report as he slipped something into his pocket from beneath the papers. Then he reached up to the cab and handed the papers back, minus the cigarettes. Zhylkyaidar nodded to the pleasant guard who had waved to him and the gate swung up.

"You can let go of my hand, Betta," Steve whispered, a comment fortunately unnoticed by Fritz who was peeking through the slates at the goings on outside the truck.

Ziggy slowly pulled ahead a few hundred yards until he stopped at the Kazakh gate, where the scene was markedly different. The initial armed guard waved hello to the driver like two old friends running into each other. The captain of the guard asked Ziggy something and was immediately satisfied with his answer. Neither guard bothered to look in the back, trusting what he could see through the truck bed rails matched the invoice just handed to them. The crossing gate lifted and the truck pulled ahead.

Ziggy didn't gun the engine. Rather, he accelerated slowly and drove 350 yards farther down the road to a rest area, where they could tank up and refresh themselves.

Once inside, the travelers broke into broad grins and hugged each other in jubilation. Ziggy and Zhylkyaidar stood back to observe before cutting in to offer them congratulations.

Finally, Tegh said to his fellow celebrants, "You'd best use the facilities and get back on the road. We can't loiter here, or the officials, friendly or not, will think something's up. After all, we're supposed to be heading to a livestock auction. We can celebrate more when we're finally on the train to Almaty."

As they went into the men's room, Steve asked Zhylkyaidar if he knew one of the Kazakh border guards, the friendly one that waived.

He laughed. "Know him? He's my brother-in-law. He's worked here for fifteen years."

But Fritz, having only heard part of the conversation, noticed concern cross Zhylkyaidar's face, as if he was holding something back. Before he could ask, Ziggy was shooing everyone back to the truck so they could get moving down the road.

Chapter 37

Dostyq, Kazakhstan

THEY ENTERED THE small, dusty Kazakh border town of
Dostyq, whose inhabitants, from the looks of the scarcity
of shops, made a living providing services to transiting
merchants and herders. Seeing their curiosity, Tegh
explained that semi-nomadic people passed back and
forth through the Gate at will, seeking whichever grazing
lands offered the best forage for their horses, sheep, and
yaks, regardless of political signposts. "There's a river
flowing through Dostyq which provides animals with
adequate winter forage."

Ziggy kicked up a cloud of trailing dust as he pulled
the truck to a halt at the auction site's livestock pens.
Those in the back got out and stretched.

Tegh remarked, "Now you've been through the
Dzungarian Gate. That border crossing is so frequented
by herders travelling to and from market that authorities
rarely examine papers for people or livestock with much
rigor."

"No one smuggles sheep," Zhylkyaidar observed.
"Serious contraband, such as drugs or arms, doesn't come
this far north to cross the border, since this area isn't near
a major consumer population center. Smugglers more
frequently cross the border farther south at Khorgos, west
of Urumqi."

Leaning on a livestock pen fence, the travelers looked over the busy enterprise. Tegh said, "I see Ziggy and Zhylkyaidar aren't the only herdsmen there to buy or sell animals. Looks like there's quite a few other ranchers walking around corral rails to get a first had view of the arriving livestock."

While they took in the sights, Ziggy and Zhylkyaidar backed down the two mares to the ground, tied them to a hitching post, and put feed bags on their muzzles to give them something better than the hay and grass they'd nibbled during the trip. The entire time, the two herdsmen were in serious discussion about something, but were out of earshot. Finished with tending to the horses, Ziggy came over and said something to Tegh, then the two herdsmen headed towards the auction crowd.

Tegh turned to Fritz, Steve, and Betta. "Zhylkyaidar is off to meet the auctioneer while Ziggy's looking up a friend he knows."

Steve said, "Of course he has a friend here. He knows everyone."

Tegh noticed that Ziggy hadn't ventured too far down the fence line before he stopped to talk with a bow-legged, wiry man who looked like he'd be more comfortable on horseback than standing. After a few minutes, he tipped his hat to the man and returned to where the four travelers stood, one foot resting on a fence rail, leaning with their arms hooked over the top rail and watching all the activity. Ziggy went up to Tegh and discussed something for a moment.

Finally, Tegh turned to the other three and said, "Ziggy says that his friend he just talked with knows a colleague in Semey who can help us."

"Semey?" Betta looked confused.

"Semipalatinsk. That's close to where you'll cross the border into the Russian Federation," Tegh explained.

"Russia!" Steve's voice was like a thunderbolt.

Hearing this, Fritz slammed an open palm on the fence railing. "I thought we were going to Almaty in Kazakhstan, not Russia. What's going on?" His voice got louder as he spoke.

Seeing his anger building, Betta needed to do something. She was upset, too, but knew this wasn't the place to make a public scene. She put a hand on Fritz's forearm and said, "Come on, Fritz. These people have been accommodating to us so far. Let's hear what they have to say."

Fritz turned away. "I thought Zhylkyaidar looked worried when we were celebrating after we crossed the border. Look, we don't know Ziggy's friend, much less his acquaintance in Sem...whatever the name of that place is. I want to know what's going on." He pulled a cigarette from his pack with his teeth and lit it, tossing the match on the ground.

Not fully understanding the angst of his foreign guests, Ziggy felt compelled to give them all the information he'd learned to ease the situation. He stepped forward, and with Tegh's help said, "Zhylkyaidar's brother-in-law told him at the border crossing that the Chinese guards were talking about a significant effort by the MSS to check the border crossings farther south at Khorgos. The word is that the Chinese authorities have convinced the Kazakhs there to keep a special lookout for four foreigners heading for Almaty, which is the nearest major city in Kazakhstan.

He didn't say why the Chinese were looking for them except to say it seemed to be a big deal. That tells me that the rail and bus lines south of here towards Almaty are being heavily searched."

Fritz exploded. "So you're telling us this now! That's incredible. It would have been good to know this before we got all the way to the auction site!"

Tegh said, "And had you known, what would you have done, gone off on your own?"

Steve didn't give Fritz a chance to answer, for once agreeing with him. "If it's such a big deal, why didn't he turn us in? And who's making the decision to switch our destination to Russia? I'm not keen on going into Russia with a war going on in Ukraine backed by the US. Why not stay put here for a few more days until the heat dies, and then go to Almaty?"

"Lower your voice and soften your tone, Steve," Tegh warned. "These people are on our side. Family connections mean a lot to them—a heck of a lot more than kowtowing to the Chinese government. Zhylkyaidar's brother-in-law said that with all the attention focused to the south, he figured our best bet would be to head north to the Russian border. We can cross at Semipalatinsk and be in Novosibirsk within a day and a half. The train makes a daily run from Almaty all the way to Moscow. Novo is a big city, and both Germany and the United States have consulates there. Once there, you three can get home without a problem."

"Without a problem!" Steve exclaimed. "I just had to leave Russia three weeks ago because my State Department said it was no longer safe for Americans to remain there. Now you want me to sneak back into that fucking country and escape again! How the hell am I going to do that?"

Tegh held up his hands.

Fear spread to Betta and Fritz as they realized the predicament their friend now faced. "What are we going to do, Tegh?" Betta pleaded.

"What we've done successfully so far," Tegh said. "We'll rely on the good graces of the men we've allied with to get us to safety."

Having heard the explanation before and not liking it, Fritz tossed his cigarette butt to the ground and said, "Easy for you to say, Tegh. You're basically in your homeland now. Your problem's solved. You were kicked out, and now you're out of harm's way. But we're still hanging out here in the wind, looking like lily-white tourists."

Tegh kept his face impassive. "Look, I know the bind you're in. But Ziggy and Zhylkyaidar are good people. They've faced plenty of tough situations like this in the past. They're committed, and they're your friends. In this culture that means everything. So, calm yourselves, accept their good will, and listen to what Ziggy's proposing."

The three said nothing, their anxieties running rampant. Then, as the heat of the moment subsided, Tegh went on. "Steve, the Russians didn't force you to leave, your State Department did. In fact, I'm sure you still have a valid Russian visa in your passport. That at least keeps you on the proper side of the law, if not abreast of the world situation, whatever that is right now."

"So I should bet on the come, is that what you're saying?" Steve said.

Tegh looked at him, not understanding the expression.

During the momentary pause, Steve felt no reason to explain. "Never mind. Okay, Tegh. Let's just hope our friends are up to the task. Everything depends on it."

The four brooded as Ziggy walked the hundred feet or so down the corral fence line and retrieved his friend. As the two herdsman walked towards them, Tegh noticed how similar they were in dress, stature, and swagger.

Ziggy introduced Tegh to his friend and they exchanged a few words before Tegh turned to the other three and said, "Ziggy's dealt with his friend here many times at livestock auctions and vouches for him. He still has to finish some transactions at today's auction. But he'll be ready to drive to Aqtoghay tomorrow morning. That's where you'll catch your train to Semey. If you meet him here about ten o'clock tomorrow morning, he'll drive you to the train station and make sure you get on the proper train."

Fritz was quick to interject. "How do we know we can trust him?"

"There's no intrigue with these men," Tegh said pointedly. "The men you're dealing with are colleagues. They do business together, entertain each other's families, and would do nothing to jeopardize their own livelihoods or homes. Accept their hospitality, smile at their stories, offer them a cigarette every now and then, and they'll be happy. They don't meet outsiders very often, other than Chinese and Russians, and they trust neither. Westerners are like a breath of fresh air, and you they trust. They would no more turn on you than they would one of their own family, and in their culture, family means everything."

Seeing their acquiescence to his sobering words, Tegh

said, "Additionally, he set the meeting time to coincide with the big fun event of this week's auction. Thirty men on horseback will be in this paddock in two teams vying to capture a stuffed goat hide ball with rawhide loops sewn on. Each team attempts to get it across the other team's goal. It's been a sport enjoyed by Kazakh herdsmen for centuries."

Ever the cynic, Fritz asked, "How does that affect our leaving at ten A.M.?"

Tegh said, "The contest attracts the attention of everyone at the auction, including the security guards assigned. A great deal of wagering will dominate their interest and no one will notice four strangers leaving amidst all that excitement."

"Well, what do we do until tomorrow?" Betta asked.

When Tegh translated this, Ziggy simply smiled and said, "I know a—"

Steve couldn't help chuckling, cutting Tegh off. "I think this man knows everybody."

"Actually," Tegh said. "He's pretty well connected."

Tegh saw the glum look on Fritz's face, as the uncertainty of their situation out-weighed Steve's attempt at humor. He said, "Trust me, Fritz. It will be all right."

But Fritz wasn't buying it. "We just reached what's supposed to be a safe haven in Kazakhstan, yet now we're facing another wait and another chance at being discovered, stuck at the mercy someone we don't know."

Betta gave him a sympathetic look and patted his shoulder, which seemed to put him at ease.

Seeing that objections had died out, Tegh gestured to Ziggy and then had the other three get aboard the now empty truck.

Ziggy drove along a street that bordered train tracks along the edge of the town. He turned north, away from the stock and freight yards, passing a few rows of small shops and modest homes until they reached the surrounding countryside. About a mile out of town, on a slight rise in elevation, Ziggy pulled to a stop at a home. It was an unremarkable slate-gray house with an asphalt-shingled roof, situated above the small river that flowed north of Dostyq. Motioning them from the truck, he explained he had known him the owner, a successful businessman, for years.

Inside, in sharp contrast to the drabness of the surroundings, Bekzat, as he was introduced by Ziggy, had decorated the living quarters with rugs, artifacts, and furnishings from the region. Betta could have taken all evening to ask about each item, rich in colors and designs. But Tegh told them they should freshen up because Bekzat was cooking on the grill out back of the house and would be serving soon.

"I'd love to have his wife give me a tour of the house," she said. "I've never seen anything so interesting."

"Well," Tegh informed her, "that's not possible, since Ziggy tells me Bekzat is a lifelong bachelor."

"Now Betta, I'm sure I could get a good price for you, in terms of sheep, if you want to marry this guy and set up house so you can learn all about his furnishings," Steve kidded.

Betta balled up a fist. "Steve, there's no hope for you."

Ziggy was parked outside the next morning, waiting. He returned them to the stockyards to meet up again with

Zhylkyaidar. Upon arrival, as Tegh had predicted, everyone was poised on the paddock rail, attentions fixed on the contest in the arena, and took no notice of them. The two herdsmen walked them over to a parked truck and the owner stopped loading hay and greeted the two men warmly.

When Tegh told the three the man's name, Betta immediately said, "That's way too hard to pronounce. Let's settle on John, which should suffice for the one day we'll deal with him."

Tegh explained, drawing laughs from the three Kazakhs.

Not quite as tall as Fritz, John's face was sunbaked nut-brown. As he removed his gloves, the travelers saw his hands were heavily callused from years of manual labor. He pointed to the truck bed, where he'd fashioned an alcove out of hay bales where they could ride. He'd even stretched a canvas top to keep out the high sun.

Hearing the cheers in the background as the modified polo match played on, Zhylkyaidar and Ziggy made their goodbyes, saying they had to return to Ziggy's truck to load some newly acquired goats and depart for home. Ziggy was adamant about not accepting any more money, but he willingly accepted Fritz's offer of a carton of cigarettes. Zhylkyaidar, however, wasn't squeamish about pocketing the three hundred yuan Tegh handed him for gas. Handshakes from Steve and Fritz and a hug from Betta completed their farewell and the two Kazakhs were off.

Climbing aboard John's truck, Tegh took the cab, relegating the others to the stake bed. John quickly drove from the livestock grounds and Tegh saw that none of the spectators along the paddock fence appeared to notice their departure. John followed a road leading northwest for the eight-hour ride to the town of Aqtoghay.

Reaching main the road, John reassured Tegh, "You'll gather less notice buying a train ticket from a small town such as Aqtoghay than you would in the capital of Almaty. Besides that, it's closer to the border and is less expensive."

"All good considerations. Thank you," Tegh said.

Once at the depot in Aqtoghay, Tegh bought tickets on the Almaty-Moscow train for the 210-mile ride to Semipalatinsk. It would depart late that afternoon and arrive early the following morning.

"Why not get a ticket all the way to Novosibirsk? It's in Russia, where we're trying to get to," Fritz complained. "I don't see why we're delaying. Didn't someone say there's an American consulate there? I'm sure they can put Betta and me in touch with German authorities. We're allies and all that."

Tegh knew Fritz was anxious and had to complain about something. "John says that because Steve's an American, there's too much risk in crossing into Russia by train. It's too well guarded. Considering the current state of political differences between the US and Russia over the war in Ukraine, he thinks it best we cross in a manner where there's less scrutiny."

But this brought an equally nervous question from Steve. "So now we're getting on a train only to go as far as Semipalatinsk? How does that help?"

"Yeah," Betta said, "Cross how?"

John explained. "I know someone in Semey who

crosses into Russia on business in his private vehicle all the time. That will draw less attention than by using a public conveyance."

Steve stammered, "This is getting more and more complicated. I'm not sure I like it."

Betta spoke directly to Steve. "Russia may not be our favorite place right now, but it's our only shot, unless we want to camp out in Kazakhstan for a year until the world situation improves. And besides that, this part of Russia's a long way from Moscow and Ukraine. And I'm thinking that's where all Russia's security focus is now, not looking for possible survivors from a three-week-old Chinese plane crash sneaking across their Siberian border."

Fritz said, "I don't like it at all. It's another delay. Every time we switch transportation, it's another chance for discovery. And, can we really trust this guy?"

Tegh looked exasperated as he said, "I've talked with him and John's known Ziggy and Zhylkyaidar quite a while, just as long as his friend in Semipalatinsk. I'm confident he's helping us in good faith."

Tensions were running high, and none of them spoke for a moment. Finally, Betta and Steve acquiesced, but Fritz grumbled, "I don't see how it's possible to hitch a ride across the border into Russia."

Tegh countered matter-of-factly, "That's how we entered Kazakhstan." But to no avail.

John, after hearing Tegh explain away Fritz's reluctance, said, "My friend in Semey has been making that crossing every few days for years. If anyone knows how to do it, he does. Of more immediate concern for you is that your train to Semey doesn't leave until morning and railway amenities aren't all that good on the Almaty-

Moscow run. So, you should eat well before you board."

As a show of good faith, John treated them to dinner in a small restaurant frequented by locals. When they finished, John wrote out the name and address of his friend in Semey.

He said, "This man will make sure you don't get lost. Semey's a large city built up by the Soviets to support their nuclear bomb testing. My friend was never a fan of that old Soviet regime and says, in general, the locals see themselves as rather independent of Moscow. He's much like me, endeared to the free and easy life of the horseman. He knows how to get you across the border into Russia. Have no fear."

"Easy for him to say," Steve mumbled under his breath."

John drove them to the train station and dropped them off. But as he drove off, his assurances did nothing to quell Fritz's anxieties. "I don't know if I'm willing to trust a total stranger anymore."

"It's not like we have a whole lot of choices," Betta observed.

"I think it's as good a plan as we can get, considering the circumstances," Steve added. "It's time to trust the experts."

Betta knew Steve's conviction was hollow, but surreptitiously squeezed his hand to let him know she agreed.

Fritz saw Betta's gesture and whirled in her direction. "Still taking his side?" he barked. "I guess all these years between us has meant nothing. Times get tough and you turn to the pretty American for comfort."

Betta looked aghast, too shocked to say anything.

Steve took a step towards Fritz and said, "Fritz, let's not get into this again. It's not—"

"Spare me," he fired back. "I know what my eyes see. All I can say is good luck, you two."

Before anyone else could speak he walked to the other side of the platform and started another cigarette in earnest.

Not wanting to draw attention, not a word was spoken by anyone until it was finally time to board the train.

Chapter 38

SEMIPALATINSK, KAZAKHSTAN

Tegh watched as the others slept fitfully in uncomfortable second-class seats, Steve and Betta next to him, and Fritz across the aisle. In the enduring morning twilight of the northern latitudes, he caught a glimpse of modern tall buildings as the train approached Semipalatinsk. It was by far the largest city they'd seen since leaving Xi'an almost a month before.

They stepped onto the platform, with Fritz still maintaining a notable distance from them. In the background were the sounds of urban bustle: car horns, the rumble of traffic, and the hissing of steam from nearby locomotives.

Betta said. "I vote we find a hotel where we can clean up."

"Hear, hear," Steve agreed. "I don't think we have to find the Ritz. I don't know about you guys, but I haven't slept well in over a day."

They turned to Fritz standing several feet away, looking for some acknowledgement, but none came.

Breaking the uncomfortable silence, Betta said. "Right now, I'd settle for a simple room with a bed, a bathroom, and a shower, and not necessarily in that order."

Fritz crushed out his cigarette on the concrete and said, "Then you'd better make sure you and Steve get a room to yourselves. You don't want anyone barging in."

Steve was about to respond, but Tegh said, "First things first. Right now, we need to look up John's friend before we do anything else. Without him, we are on our own."

Betta, still wounded by Fritz's comment, ignored Tegh's suggestion. "Fritz, you need to be an adult. There's nothing going on behind your back. We've talked about this before. You and I have been good business partners, but that's it. And as far as Steve or Tegh is concerned, we've all been thrown into this mess by circumstances beyond our control. So, grow up and cope with it."

They stood frozen on the platform, each looking at the faces of the others to see who would react first.

Finally, Fritz said, "All right, Tegh. The sooner we make contact and get out of the public eye, the better I'll like it."

Keeping the focus on their mutual situation, Steve said, "Maybe we should convert our foreign bills to rubles. I got rid of all of mine when I left Irkutsk. There's no sense in drawing more attention to ourselves than necessary by flashing foreign money, or worse yet, trying to convert currency in Russia—you know, presenting passports and IDs and all."

"Won't a hotel convert money for us?" Betta asked.

"They will," Tegh said, "but Steve's right. It's safer to have John's friend convert it for us, rather than risk the scrutiny of a hotel. We should keep our euros and dollars just in case, though. And, we should only get a few rubles; they're no good anywhere else in the world."

Fritz said, "If we're going to find John's friend, let's get on with it."

Tegh found a street map written in Cyrillic posted inside the train depot. Though they were in Kazakhstan, public transportation still brandished leftovers from the Soviet days. He and Steve put their combined knowledge of Russian to the test and found the name of the street for their contact. "Come on," Tegh said pointing to an exit. "It's this way."

The residence was a several-block walk from the train station. Tegh knocked on the door and they waited anxiously under the dim glow of the front porch light, trusting in fate. The door opened to reveal a short man who apparently had weathered the same outdoor life that John and Ziggy had, most likely as a herdsman.

Tegh introduced himself and produced the piece of paper on which John had written the man's address. The resident waved if off and extended a hand in greeting. "I got a call from our mutual friend last night. He told me to expect you."

"We don't want to be a bother, but we could use a little help until we board the train tomorrow," Tegh said.

The man sat them down while his wife served tea. He introduced himself as Kylyshlbek. Betta couldn't help herself from laughing when she heard him pronounce his name, another tongue twister. Their host looked at her, unable to appreciate the humor.

She put a hand to her mouth. "I'm sorry, it's just I couldn't pronounce that if I tried. I'm going to have to come up with something to call you that's easier on my tongue. How about Roger?"

For their host's benefit, Tegh explained Betta's penchant for assigning nicknames. "I hope you don't find this insulting, Kylyshlbek."

Kylyshlbek, or Roger, slightly tilted his head and shrugged his shoulders. "That will be fine."

While Tegh was explaining Betta's foible, Steve's eye wandered the room and then settled on a framed memento on the wall. It was a sepia photo, faded and mildew stained along the edges—an aged portrait from the shoulders up of a man in a Soviet military uniform wearing a Soviet army officer's high-peaked cap. Details of the man's features were grainy, but his array of military medals was impressive. Steve thought, *Where the hell did this Roger guy get those medals? Who have we been hooked up with?*

Seeing him daydreaming, Tegh asked, "How about you, Steve? Any trouble pronouncing it?"

Hearing this, Steve turned to pay attention. "Huh? Oh yeah, Roger's fine with me."

The name stuck.

Relieved at Roger's good nature, Betta asked, "Is there an inexpensive hotel nearby where we can get rooms?"

"There is," Roger said, "but let me suggest you freshen up here. Then I'll take you to a youth hostel only a short ways from here. They have restrooms and beds, and aren't sticklers for things like passports and visas the way a hotel is. But their bathing facilities aren't up to Western standards. Tomorrow morning, I'll collect you and purchase your train tickets, which will be for the journey from the Russian train station in Rubtsovsk to Novosibirsk, not from here in Semipalatinsk."

"But why not buy the tickets and board the train at a station here in Kazakhstan?" Fritz asked.

"The trip from here across the border is short and easy by car. If you took the train from here, it adds a good deal to the price of the ticket, plus it would require you to cross the border into Russia on the train." He dropped his voice, as if passing on a close-held confidence. "A much riskier proposition. And I take it, risk is something you folks want to avoid."

Fritz said, "I don't think the cost is a problem for us."

Tegh didn't translate, but said instead, "And it would add yet another twist to unravel for anyone who might be trying to follow us. If they should track us to Semey, they certainly won't easily follow our trail across an international bounder in a private vehicle."

Roger nodded. "Also, we should make your booking for the train leaving from Rubtsovsk two days from now, not—"

Betta interrupted. "Two days from now? Why not tomorrow?"

Roger nodded, acknowledging her confusion and said, "Because Semey is a crew rest stop for train workers. The crew that served your train today disembarked when you did and is resting tonight in Semey. That crew will change out with the crew arriving from Almaty tomorrow. So, if you were to board tomorrow's train you'd be served by the same crew that brought you here. There'd be a chance one of them might recognize you, which could lead to questions not worth the risk.

"Day after tomorrow, I'll drive you across the border to Rubtsovsk, where you can board the Almaty-Moscow train without fear of encountering a crew who knows you by sight. You'll have tickets in hand, there'd be no need to risk buying tickets there in Russia. This way, you'll draw less scrutiny from border guards or ticket agents."

Steve thought Roger's scheme was quite clever. He

certainly wouldn't have thought of it. But the picture of the Soviet soldier on the wall still bothered him.

"Just exactly how are you going to get us across the border without drawing suspicion?" Betta asked.

"I run a blacksmith and tractor repair business now," Roger replied. "It's much easier on my body since my horseback days are over. I routinely cross the border to Rubtsovsk, Russia, to pick up machine parts. They're easier to obtain there and are less expensive than those available locally here in Kazakhstan. Because I frequent the border, having workers with me with temporary work visas won't draw suspicion. The border guards are used to seeing me with different people in my crew."

He paused to let his explanation sink in and then continued. "I'll take my wife. That will make it more convincing when I explain that you two," he said, pointing to Betta, "are shopping while I am buying parts. The Russian border security will be only too happy that I'm spending money in Russia."

"We are obviously Westerners and not Asians," Fritz said, pointing out what he thought would be an obvious attention-getter.

Roger dismissed his comment. "Many Russians come from the European part of their country. You won't look as out of place as you might think. Besides, we're a long way from the central governments in both Almaty and Moscow. This border is a provincial Siberian outpost and the guards are used to handling long-haul trucks and local merchants, both of which consist of ethnically diverse people. The Kazakh guards don't care who goes into Russia. They still regret the old Soviet occupation, and with good reason.

"And as far as today's Russian border guards go, they think they have a most undesirable posting, being stuck in the remote eastern Asian steppe with little hope of transfer to a city in European Russia during their lifetime. Both realities result in relaxed border scrutiny of either cargo or workers. Once in Rubtsovsk, you'll board the Moscow-bound train to Novosibirsk via Barnaul without the additional risk of having to purchase tickets."

"What time of day do we drive across the border?" Fritz asked.

"The Moscow train is scheduled to depart Rubtsovsk at 11:30 each morning," Roger said. "That is, if it's on time, which it usually isn't. We should be at the border crossing about 7:00 A.M., when it opens. There will be an overnight backlog of vehicles waiting to cross. The more vehicles in the crossing queue, the less likely for us to be questioned."

While Betta showered, Roger's wife brought out a tray of cheese and Kazakh beer. Steve told Tegh, "Ask Roger if there's a phone I could use. Now that we're no longer in China, I'd like to call my father."

If I know my father, Steve thought, *he'll have any number of people turning over rocks looking for me. I have to get word to him, if for nothing else, to give whoever he has working on finding us a location to work with.*

The look on Tegh's face told Steve that he didn't think it was a good idea. But surprisingly, Roger agreed.

"Use my cellphone, not my land line. The telephone exchanges aren't private. But making the call in Kazakhstan is still much safer than doing so once you cross the border."

Steve said, "I'll keep it short."

He stepped onto the patio and called. To Steve's amazement, the international call went through in less than a minute. But after several rings, the answering machine kicked in. He purposely kept his message cryptic. "Hey, Dad, it's me. I'm okay. The four us will be back in the country I started from a month ago in a few hours. I'll let you know when I get there."

He hung up thinking, *Here's hoping that helps.*

After they showered and ate, Roger walked them the few blocks to the hostel. He told them to sit tight until he came by to pick them up the next morning. Tegh thanked him and then added, "Oh, can you change some money into rubles for us?"

Roger didn't hesitate. "I'll do that first thing in the morning. Give me what you want to change out. People on this side of the border readily accept rubles, so no need to purchase any Kazakh currency. I'm thinking you'll need enough for breakfast, the hostel room charges, and your train tickets."

Steve and Tegh did some figuring and handed Roger five hundred euros, which Roger agreed would be sufficient. "I'll be here at 5:30 to collect you for breakfast."

Seeing him leave with their money, Fritz groaned.

Tegh anticipating Fritz's comment said, "Yes, we can trust him."

Too nervous for bed, Fritz said to Betta, "I need to unwind. Let's get a drink at that café down the street."

"Oh, we're talking now, are we?" she said.

"Come on Betta, it's important."

As they listened to the odd exchange and watched them leave, Steve said to Tegh, "You know, I'm not tired yet, Tegh. Want to join them?"

"No, I think they need some time alone to sort out their differences. They certainly don't need us there to do that."

Steve said, "I agree, but I've got something I need to clear up. But not here. Let's go talk out in that park up the street."

Heading in the opposite direction from Betta and Fritz, they found a bench in the small park by the hostel.

"You sound apprehensive, Steve," Tegh said.

"We've been worrying about Chinese state security up to now, but Russia's not an open society either. And with the world situation the way it is and me being an American, I'm not sure what I'm going to run into."

Tegh said, "But heading this way has one big advantage."

Steve looked skeptical. "Yeah, what's that?"

"No one expects us to do it. Hey, I get it. Russia is still a police state, perestroika, the fall of communism, and the new world order notwithstanding. But heading towards Almaty isn't an option anymore."

They sat quietly, contemplating what still lay ahead of them. Then Tegh broke the silence. "But we've already been through this, Steve. What's really on your mind? I'm sure it's not world politics."

Abruptly, Steve stood and paced. "I'm just anxious. I guess there's nothing to do but move ahead with our plan and hope for the best. I certainly didn't do anything to upset the Russians. At least they didn't tell me to leave, like the Chinese did with you."

Tegh looked up at Steve, thinking that something else was bothering him but that he was reluctant to bring up. Deciding not to probe, he said, "I'm pretty sure with Roger's help, we'll be able to get safely into the country and to an embassy. Then you'll be fine."

"That's it, Tegh. I'm not sure we can trust Roger."

"What? Where's this coming from?"

Steve thought of staring at that photo in Roger's living room and wondering if their benefactor was a secret FSB or SVR agent and they were only steps away from taking them into custody. "I have to know something before we go any further. What about those Soviet medals and that framed picture on the wall at Roger's home?"

Tegh furrowed his brow. "And that's what's got you upset?"

Steve's voice was all business. "Humor me, Tegh."

Shaking his head, Tegh said, "First of all, if you'd read the Kazakh inscription below that picture, that's not Roger, that's his father. You forget, until 1991, Kazakhstan was part of the Soviet Union. And the date on the picture's plaque was 1938 to 1942. His father was killed at Stalingrad fighting in the Soviet army."

The creases in Steve's brow disappeared. "Oh."

"Take a deep breath, Steve. I can only imagine the concerns you have as an American about to make a clandestine trip across the border back into Russia. But, if Roger is who you fear he is, that is, someone working within Russian security, he's had plenty of opportunity to turn us in.

"He wouldn't have harbored us in his home. He wouldn't have shown us where to stay for the night or have suggested inconspicuous restaurants for us to use. And he wouldn't be exchanging our money—he would have simply confiscated it."

Steve looked as his colleague. So far, Tegh had done right by them during their entire ordeal and he was making good sense now. "Okay, I guess were in this to the end, however that may turn out."

Betta and Fritz sat quietly at a small table in the café as Fritz smoked his cigarette. Finally, Betta said, "So, are we okay, or are you still bugged by whatever you think is going on between me and Steve?"

He snuffed out his cigarette in his cup's saucer and said, "Yeah, it hurts, that's all. And before you try to say something to make me feel better about it, let's just drop it."

Betta gave him a moment and then nodded.

A waiter came and they ordered a latte for her and expresso with two shots for Fritz.

After a bit more silence, Fritz said, "I can't believe we're almost out of here. I admit I'll still be nervous until we get home. I'm just not sure all of this was necessary. I mean, the Chinese surely wouldn't have treated us harshly if they had rescued us, or even brought up the matter about the photos I took at the trade show. We didn't actually steal anything."

"You know," Betta said, "there's such a thing as intellectual property, even in China. You took a lot of pictures, enough to upset that Sunku manufacturing rep at the booth across from us. I'm pretty sure he's the one who turned us in."

"Still, it's not like we were dealing with state secrets. Besides, we're Germans, not Americans. That's who the Chinese really have a problem with." He thumbed his hand towards the hostel where they'd left the others.

Betta disregarded his gesture and his attempt to inveigle her into discussing Steve. Instead, she put the onus back on him. "Still, it upset the Chinese enough to cancel our travel visas and take us to the airport. I for one didn't want to stick around that crash site to find out if they were in a charitable mood. And who knows, they might even have..." She paused a second. "Look let's not rehash this. I'm just not the cynic you are. We've got a good group. We couldn't have made it without Steven and Tegh and their—"

Fritz interrupted. "Tegh and Steve are the reasons we needed to make this mad dash for the western border. If we had—"

"Tegh and Steve are probably the reasons we survived, Fritz."

"I just didn't want to chance running and having the Chinese thinking we were in the same category as them." Fritz stopped and took a long drag on his second cigarette to keep from saying anything further.

The waiter brought their drinks and they sipped quietly.

Betta could see he was holding something back, so she waited before finally saying, "Without Tegh, we'd have never found our way with the locals. From what I could tell, the local Chinese and Kazakh citizens didn't treat us poorly. In fact, from the way they acted, none of them was a real fan of their government. We'd have never found that out without Tegh."

Fritz took a last drag off his cigarette and stubbed it out. *I still don't trust Tegh, but I'll never convince her.*

"What's on your mind, Fritz?"

"I'm thinking it doesn't make much difference now. It's almost over. With just a little luck, this all ends in a couple of days."

"Do you miss home?"

"Yeah, I do. But what I miss more is being able to do what I want to do, when I want to do it. I feel like I've been on pins and needles since Xi'an, always looking over my shoulder, hoping the next Chinese person I see isn't the one to turn me in."

Betta squeezed his hand.

Fritz crumpled the empty pack. "We best get some rest. I'm not sure what Roger has in store for tomorrow."

As they reached the doors to their rooms, Betta hesitated. "I'm going to use the ladies room before bed. I'll see you in the morning."

On the way back to her room, Betta hesitated outside her door. Then she went down the hall, stopped at Steve's door, knocked softly, and waited. After a half-minute, she was contemplating knocking again when the latch turned and the door opened slightly.

Steve squinted looking into the lighted hall from a darkened room. Clearly he'd been asleep. She started to speak but averted her eyes, realizing he was standing there in his undershorts. "Oh, I'm sorry."

Still clutching the door's edge and half hiding himself, Steve said. "No that's okay. Is something wrong?"

Turning away towards the direction of her room she said, "No… I was just talking with Fritz… I mean…"

Steve eased the door open.

"Betta, what is it?"

Still facing away, she said, "I'm worried about tomorrow."

Steve reached from behind the door and put his hand on her shoulder. "Come in and have a seat. Let me get some trousers on."

She sat in the straight-back chair next to a bedside table and lamp, which Steve switched on. He slipped on his trousers, zipped, and buckled up. Sitting on the edge of his bed, he smoothed the rumpled sheet and blanket. "Okay, what's got you upset?"

"I just had a long talk with Fritz and I'm worried about what's going to happen tomorrow. We don't know these people. Roger is a friend of Ziggy's and Zhylk...oh, however you say it, who's a friend of Duz, who's a friend of Benny's, who we met at a roadside restaurant in western China. That's not normal, and you ask me why I'm upset?"

"Look, Betta, I know it sounds crazy, but there were plenty of opportunities for the authorities to find us and they didn't. We're already out of China, and in a few hours, we'll be out of Kazakhstan, too. Russia's not the friendliest country in the world, but both our countries have consulates there and maintain diplomatic relations, at least they did. I personally think we're going to be all right."

Steve thought of his unwillingness earlier to bring up his concerns regarding Roger's picture of the Russian soldier. Despite Tegh's assurances, he still harbored misgivings he couldn't shake. But now wasn't the time to burden Betta with his lingering doubts about Roger's goodwill. The former cowboy, now would-be repair-mechanic, seemed legitimate. Roger's saving grace was that he'd already done a lot for them.

He clutched her hand in both of his and she squeezed back. "I know that telling you not to worry isn't much consolation, but that's all I have to offer right now. I believe in Roger because I have to. Trust me?"

She gazed into his eyes as unsaid words passed between them. She put both her arms around his neck, leaned her head on his shoulder, and pushed her breasts against his chest. His mind flashed back to the times he'd held her this closely. For a moment, he hesitated, then reached with his other hand and clasped her shoulder and held her, desperately resisting the urge to pull her closer. For the longest time they said nothing, but simply sat there in an unchaste embrace.

She pressed closer and said in his ear, "Thank you. I feel better." She kissed his ear and stood up. "I'm okay. You're right. This was foolish of me."

They both stood and she took a hesitant step for the door. Before he could do anything, she turned back to him, this time without embrace, and kissed him full on the mouth.

"Goodnight, Steve. I'll do fine tomorrow."

She padded down the hall to her room. Steve stood there, bewildered with the realization that a very beautiful woman had just set the boundaries they both required. Only a few feet away, she was all alone and they both held strong feelings for each other. Then he gave in and went and knocked softly on her door.

Steve awoke first and slipped quietly from the bed, not want to wake Betta. Back in his room, he got fully dressed, and ventured outside for some fresh air where he was surprised to see Fritz already there smoking.

"You couldn't sleep either?" he asked.

Fritz held up his cigarette. "I needed one of these. Besides, I've got a lot to think about."

"Like what?" Steve asked.

"Like what's going to happen today. You know me, I'm worried."

"What about?" Steve didn't want to reveal his own concerns.

"For one thing, it's Tegh."

"Tegh?" Steve hadn't seen that coming.

"Yeah, I thought all last night about how he's been able to get us to one safe place after another. He just seems to be one step ahead."

"So you're thinking Tegh's...Fritz, that's farfetched. I mean, why'd he go through all the trouble to get us out of China?"

"I know, I know. I was just thinking there were lots of coincidences, like when that shepherd kid showed up and—"

"Listen to yourself, Fritz. What you're thinking is preposterous."

Fritz hunched his shoulders and cupped his cigarette to his mouth. "Remember that time I disappeared all night when the police patrols were looking for us? The reason I hid down the alley in the first place was I saw the guards coming down my side of the street. When I turned to come back to the hotel, I saw Tegh talking with the guards on the other side of the street. I ducked down that alley and kept going. I kept hiding because I thought he was telling them one of us just left the hotel."

Steve started to respond and then remembered spotting Tegh from the rooftop talking to the guards, just as Fritz had described. But Fritz can't be right. Too much had gone in their favor, and much of it because of Tegh's doing, for his suspicions to be correct. Tegh was always the one making the correct decisions.

"Fritz, I think you saw what you wanted to believe. This ordeal has been totally out of your comfort zone. I'll admit, we've been fortunate so far, but it's all made sense. I think Tegh is exactly who he says he is.

"I'll tell you, though," Steve continued. "One thing that has me worried—the most dangerous part of our trip is coming up. I don't know what awaits us when we get to Russia, especially for me. Shit, I might have gone through all of this only to end up in a holding cell in Siberia. But I for one want to see it through."

Before Fritz could say anything, Steve saw movement out of the corner of his eye as Roger pulled up in his car.

"So what's it going to be, Fritz? Are you in or are you out?"

Fritz dropped his cigarette and ground it out with his shoe. "Okay, let's get on with it. Let's see what happens."

As Betta and Tegh came outside, Roger held up an envelope with their rubles and handed it to Tegh.

"This should be enough for your needs. There's a café nearby. Why don't we get breakfast?"

While they ate, Roger sensed from their fidgeting that their nerves were on edge. To put their minds at ease, he said, "We've got a few hours. Why don't I show you some of the city while you're waiting? If you should think of any last-minute thing you need, let me know."

Betta tugged on her field jacket. "I'm tired of looking like a field hand. If I'm supposed to be shopping with your wife, I'd best look the part."

Her three companions followed her lead in shopping for clothes. Soon they'd purchased European styled apparel, much more appropriate than the pantaloons and blousy shirts they had become used to.

As they walked in the crisp air, Betta said, "I'm really disappointed I couldn't find a good pair of blue jeans."

Tegh replied, "You might have found some in St. Petersburg, Kiev, or Moscow, but not here."

After an hour, and not wanting to spend more time exposed on the streets than they had to, Roger dropped them back at the hostel to wait. In the late afternoon, he returned to check on how they were faring.

"How are you set for cash? Do you have enough for dinner tonight? That café we ate at this morning is open late."

Tegh counted their money. Figuring one more meal and the hostel bill, that left them with over a hundred euros worth of rubles for incidentals on the train. "I think we're okay, Roger."

"Good," Roger said. "In that case, there's nothing else for me to do. I'll see you early tomorrow morning."

As he lay in bed, Steve contemplated going to Betta's room. Then, thinking about what was at stake for them, he decided not to risk Fritz's finding out and creating a problem just as they had their goal in sight. The thought of what else could possibly go wrong kept him awake for a while.

Chapter 39

KHORGOS BORDER CROSSING, WESTERN CHINA

FIRST DIRECTOR LIN CHU sat nervously in the MSS local commander's armored personnel carrier. He'd driven from Yining the day before and had set up surveillance of the Chinese border crossing at Khorgos. He'd watched all evening and through the night as every vehicle and bus passenger was checked for foreigners who could possibly match the descriptions of the fugitives he so frustratingly sought.

But he'd had no luck—not a single possibility. By the time 5:00 A.M. came around, Lin was dreading having to contact General Wu, who he knew was waiting impatiently in Urumqi for his report.

The local commander on surveillance with him said, "You seem worried, First Director, like you're in dire straits. If it's General Wu, I don't envy your dilemma. I've had personal run-ins with him myself." Then remembering something, he said, "The daily bus to Almaty is due to cross the border at 7:20 A.M."

Lin's face brightened with the hope that not all was for naught. Perhaps he'd begun the surveillance too early and the fugitives were in fact on this morning's bus. "Yes, you're correct, Commander. We should wait until the bus to Almaty reaches the border crossing before making a call."

His colleague added, "Also, a train is scheduled to arrive about 9:00 A.M. They could always be on that."

"Another good suggestion." First Director Lin was more than willing to accept any additional delay in having to deal with General Wu.

The local commander and Lin Chu waited and watched, but their quarry was nowhere to be found at the Khorgos crossing that morning. Finally, Lin reluctantly placed the phone call. When the general picked up, it was all Lin could do to keep the earpiece near his head.

"What do you mean, they haven't crossed the border?" General Wu all but crawled through the receiver to levy his invective. "Did you inspect the hotels and truck stops to see if they were there?" He was beside himself with rage.

"Yes, General, I double-checked last night. It seems they haven't crossed the border here."

"Seems? Seems! You mean they haven't. So, where the hell are they? They certainly aren't here in Urumqi! At least I know how to conduct a competent search."

Silence ensued. Lin could only contemplate that General Wu was at a loss as to what to say next and was letting his apoplexy dissipate. He knew his general hated being in the field, away from the comforts of headquarters. The general had already told him how he abhorred being in the Xinjiang provincial capital with its overflowing "Islamic culture".

"Excuse me, General." First Director Lin interrupted the general's silence. "I didn't mean to imply you didn't know how to conduct a search. But if those we seek aren't in Urumqi, and there's no evidence of their having crossed the border here, that leaves only one other option."

"This had better be good, First Director Lin. Your future in the MSS depends on it."

As does yours, First Director Lin thought. But unlike his feckless boss, Lin was working on a solution. "Sir, they had to have gone north to cross at Dostyq."

General Wu barked into the phone, "That's hundreds of miles north of us and means they could already be in Kazakhstan, you idiot! There's nothing we can do about that."

Lin heard the general's voice change in timbre, no longer sounding confident. Rather, his voice bordered on a pleading tone, as if asking him for a suggestion with merit.

"Yes sir, but there is something we can do," the First Director said.

"Go ahead, I'm listening."

"We know they didn't cross here, and that leaves only the northern crossings."

"Yes, yes, get on with it!"

"They aren't headed all the way south again to Almaty, General. They're going north. And you have friends in the north."

After a brief pause, Lin heard the general say, "Yes, and I know someone there who owes me a favor."

Chapter 40

BRIGHT AND EARLY the next morning, Roger and his wife rolled up to the hostel in their delivery van and gathered the four travelers. The sun was rising, casting progressively shorter shadows.

Roger said, "It's about forty-five minutes to the border crossing. Here are your work visas and train tickets." He passed out their documents and they inserted them into the passports they hadn't used since boarding their ill-fated plane in Xi'an.

Tegh held the door as the other got in.

"I hope these work," Steve said, giving Tegh a furtive glance.

Roger replied, "Please, set your mind at ease. I do this all the time with my workmen. One of the Kazakh guards is my sister's nephew by marriage. Trust me, it will be all right."

But Betta held back. "I guess I'd never have been a good secret agent. I'm too nervous."

"But you aren't hiding anything," Steve said. He looked carefully at Betta to see if his word 'hiding' had elicited some recognition from her of their encounter. He saw none.

"No, but I'm concealing my identity," she said.

348

"You aren't even doing that," Fritz observed. "That really is your name on the passport."

"And when they ask me why an out-of-work outdoor clothing designer from Dresden is buying used tractor parts in Siberia, what am I supposed to say?" she retorted.

Tegh knew he should say something before Betta lost it. "That's just your nerves talking, Betta. I'm sure you'll never be asked. But, if they do, tell them you're trying to see how the working classes of the world dress. This is just a summer job for you. Consider it research so when you get home you can design clothes using the ideas you've gained from your travel experience."

"That works for me," Fritz said.

They pulled up to the border crossing behind three tractor trailers and two livestock trucks. A low set of buildings stretched to the left and there was a pull off for semi-tractor trailer inspections on the right. Apparently, the crossing wasn't manned around the clock and drivers had to wait in a queue at the gate. The backlog was working its way to the crossing guards as the border control personnel methodically handled the morning's steady business. Delays were running about five minutes a truck.

When Roger handed over their papers, the Kazakh guard only checked for the required stamps, which Roger had arranged for the day before. The guard also found some folded money, thirty euros worth of rubles, tucked neatly inside one passport. Deftly moving the money to his pocket, he made a show of looking at the passengers through the window, examining them with feigned interest, then stepping back. He motioned for the gate officer to raise the bar and handed back their papers.

"I hope you had a pleasant stay in Kazakhstan. Please, enjoy your time in the Russian Federation." He waved them forward.

Roger let out the clutch, disengaged the brake, and rolled forward through the few hundred feet of no man's land that separated the two nations' border control stations.

From the back seat, Steve said, "You're right, Tegh. They don't care who leaves to go to Russia."

Tegh sat patiently and checked his watch. It was a quarter to nine. They had plenty of time.

Major Victor Karelchenko had arrived at the Russian Border Control building at 8:41 A.M., almost an hour after the morning shift began. He was still thinking of the night he'd spent with his young mistress and wasn't focused on the work that awaited him. For the major, his work was of no importance; he was the boss in this small oasis of Russian authority. In actuality, he was arriving about two hours earlier than he usually came to work. The sergeant of the guard noticed his unexpected presence and wondered, *What's got him up so early this morning?*

The major drew a cup of hot tea from the samovar and dropped his two hundred and fifty pounds into a chair, mildly irritated at having to leave her apartment so early. Mostly, however, he was upset because of the unwelcome phone call that had awakened him after he'd rolled over to catch some recovery sleep when she'd left for work as clerk in an office complex.

He fidgeted with the calendar on his desk and stirred his tea, his only signs of urgency. Tea was the only compensation he had for getting to work at this ungodly hour, the seriousness of the earlier phone call from his commander in Novosibirsk notwithstanding. Evidently, a Chinese Ministry of State Security general wanted Russia to be on the lookout for four escapees. The Chinese official's call to the Russian regional commander had nearly accused the Russians of planting the four as spies on Chinese soil. Victor's superior had relayed to him, in no uncertain terms, that the Russian Federation would cooperate in apprehending these people should they attempt to enter Russia.

The major disliked his regional commander so much so that he briefly considered doing nothing. But the bureaucrat had been insistent and Victor had resigned himself to at least put on a good show, just in case the boss managed to get off his fat ass and drive down to his border post, something he rarely did.

Mind made up, Victor strode from his office and asked the sergeant of the guard if anything unusual had happened since the morning crossings had begun.

With a truck working its way across the border in the background, the sergeant assured him, "Just the usual traffic, sir."

"Did you see a group of four men holding suspicious papers?"

Brakes squealed as the next tractor-trailer pulled up to the barrier and stopped.

"Nothing that stood out, sir. Most everything has been long-haul transport goods coming from or going to Almaty. Pretty standard, sir." The lead crossing guard couldn't understand his boss's unusual interest in the mundane matters of their work.

The truck in front of Roger released its air brakes and

picked up speed as the guards waved it across the border into Russia. The gate lowered and a stern-looking Russian guard motioned Roger forward. It had only taken a few minutes. Not bad, Roger thought, glancing at his watch. 8:53 A.M.

"What is your business in the Russian Federation today, sir?" the Russian guard demanded as he extended his hand for papers.

"I'm headed to Rubtsovsk for some repair parts for a tractor. My neighbor's hay-baler broke down and he must get the field cleared before the weather turns. My wife is going to do a little shopping with a neighbor while I pick up the parts. You know how that is; she spends it as fast as I can make it."

The guard gave a conspiratorial smile to Roger, as if husbands around the world felt the same way.

Roger looked at the two other guards standing off to one side on a smoke break and called to the younger one he recognized as his sister's nephew.

"Dmitri, how goes it this morning?"

The young man stubbed out his cigarette and walked over to the passenger side window, recognizing his uncle.

Seeing him approach, Tegh whispered to Fritz, "Give me two packs of cigarettes," which he surreptitiously handed to Roger.

Roger exchanged pleasantries with his nephew and slipped him the cigarettes along with a small cloth bag. The senior guard examined the work visas and took his time to match the people seated in the van with the paperwork. The fact that the driver knew one of his young guards wasn't lost on the older guard.

The sergeant said, "Dmitri, if you are done gossiping

with men trying to get to work, would you let them proceed?" He handed the visas back to Roger and motioned for the guard controlling the gate to raise it.

Roger let out his clutch and pulled ahead. Steve, Betta, and Fritz held their breath. As their car moved slowly forward, Roger heard a phone ring in the guard shack and the older guard walked over to answer it.

From the administrative building set back fifty yards from the Russian border gate, Major Karelchenko spoke calmly on the phone to his guard at the barrier. "Tell the sergeant I want him to put a man up in the tower with field glasses to survey the Kazakh side's truck marshalling area. We're to look for a group of four men who the Chinese claim are trying to sneak into our country."

"Of course, Major. For how long should we do this?" The sergeant watched the sedan with the tractor repairman and his passengers ease ahead.

"I want two three-hour shifts, then you can bring them down." Victor thought, *That should be sufficient effort to satisfy my boss.*

Victor heard the sergeant give an order to one of the guards manning the gate. "Dmitri, get your ass up into the tower. Take your field glasses."

Victor thought to himself as he hung up the phone, *Six hours, good. That way I can always report I gave it my best shot.*

Chapter 41

KHORGOS BORDER CROSSING, WESTERN CHINA

FIRST DIRECTOR LIN waited on edge at the Khorgos border crossing from China to Kazakhstan for a return call from his Russian counterpart some 440 miles farther north in Semipalatinsk. He was certain his Russian colleague would come through with good news.

General Wu Xi sat equally impatiently 360 miles to the east at his MSS command post in Urumqi and tapped a pen on his desk, waiting to hear from Lin, his incompetent subordinate. He was equally certain, but of failure, not of success.

The general's phone rang. When he heard the First Director's voice, it took all the self-control the general could muster to say, "Tell me some good news, First Director Lin."

"Actually sir, that's what I have. It would seem the trap we set for our fugitives at the Russian border was mismanaged with typical Russian inefficiency."

"And just how is that good news?" the general bellowed.

Lin waited a before continuing and stretching out his next words, "My Russian contact who controls the border crossing between Dostyq and Rubtsovsk couldn't believe it when he contacted his border guards this morning and discovered that the major in charge was late in arriving to work. From what I gathered, the major had other interests in town that distracted him from his state security duties."

"Get to the point, Chu. What about the fugitives?"

"The Russian regional commander assures me they are doing everything they can. But so far, there's been no sign of them, sir."

The ensuing silence was palpable. Lin heard the general mumble, more like thinking out loud. "Yes…yes. I can work this to my advantage. We tracked them down, but it was the Russians who were unable to snap the snare shut."

"What was that, sir, I couldn't quite make it out. Our connection isn't that good."

"Oh, nothing, Lin. Uh, so you say my plan would have worked had it not been for this Russian's lack of attention?"

Lin smiled. "That's correct, General." He waited for a reply. When there was none he said, "Then I take it sir, all is satisfactory as far as we're concerned?"

First Director Lin heard the general's voice turn positive. "It would appear so, for now, Chu."

This time, the general's use of his first name didn't carry its usual demeaning undertone.

Chapter 42

THE RUSSIAN FEDERATION BORDER

FOUR MILES FARTHER down the road, well into Russia, Roger pulled over.

Tegh asked, "What was in the bag you gave the border guard?"

Roger said, "A pound of Kazakh cheese, some of the best in the world. Like a good son, he'll pass the cheese on to his mother. The cigarettes will go to his sergeant. With a little luck, in a year or so, that young man will be promoted to sergeant and take over from the one there now. Then I'll have a most reliable border contact. But right now, we need to get a move on. Rubtsovsk is still forty more miles away. With still two hours to catch the Moscow train, we shouldn't waste any of it. Of course, that's if the train's on time."

Cheers erupted as the weary travelers, survivors of a plane crash and architects of a journey of a lifetime, realized they'd made it.

"What's wrong, Steve?" Fritz asked, noticing him holding back from the celebration. "You should be rejoicing, we're home free."

Steve forced a smile. "Sorry, I guess it just doesn't seem real. I don't think it will sink in until I'm back home."

Roger's van reached the train station at 10:45 A.M. They got out and said their goodbyes. Standing back from

Roger and his wife, Fritz hoped any onlookers wouldn't notice that they had only backpacks for baggage.

Roger and his wife waited with them until the train came, just in case there was a problem. When 11:30 came and went, Tegh and Steve went to the ticket counter and checked on the train to Novosibirsk. They got the stationmaster's plaintive explanation and a shrug. When they returned smiling, Betta let out a sigh of relief and said, "This has to be good news."

Steve said, "Not to worry. The train's running late, but it's on its way." Seeing her relax renewed his confidence. He pinched himself, almost as happy as if he had just landed at JFK. He thought, *We've done it; almost to our destination.*

The four of them hugged and then finally settled down. Tegh turned to Roger and his wife, who were grinning from ear-to-ear at seeing their jubilation.

"I don't know how to thank you," Tegh said. "I speak for each of us. We couldn't have possibly done this without you."

Tegh pulled the last carton of Fritz's cigarettes from his backpack, much to Fritz's token objection. "Hey, I've only got two packs left."

Along with a €100 note, Tegh handed them to Roger, saying, "I know what you offered was hospitality, but I figure when I come through here again, I'll probably need a new oil filter for the tractor I'll be wanting to buy. This is my down payment."

He winked at the wiry Kazakh and Roger grinned an uneven toothy smile as he accepted both gifts. He shook hands all around before he and his wife got back into his van and drove off.

The four stood there on the platform, alone now in a precarious and upside down world.

Looking around the station, Steve spotted a universal sign for restrooms. "I don't know about you guys, but I gotta use the head. All this standing around and waiting has done a job on my kidneys."

The rest fell prey to the power of suggestion and followed him. One by one they emerged and stood on the concourse edged by a small food kiosk and a newsstand. A lead headline on one newspaper caught Steve's eye. He picked up the paper to read it, drawing a suspicious eye from the old woman behind the counter.

Tegh prompted him. "She wants you to pay for it."

Steve reached into his pocket, then realized that Tegh carried the money. Tegh gave him a coin and said, "Make sure you hold your hand out for change. They don't tip in this part of the world."

Pocketing the change, Steve snapped the paper open and took a closer look at the picture spread across the fold. It was of a Ukrainian village with several destroyed buildings in the background and a tank and armored personnel carrier, painted with white Zs and Cyrillic letters, in the foreground. He read the caption out loud.

"Our compatriots in the Donbas make quick work of hapless defenders." He crumpled the paper and shook his head.

Seeing his dismay, Betta asked, "What's wrong?"

"I can't tell from this article if the Russians are winning or losing, but there's one hell of a fight going on in Ukraine."

"So what's the problem? How does that affect us?" Fritz said.

"Me, not us," Steve said. "You guys aren't Americans. Somehow, I'm sure we're mixed up in this mess." *Maybe this is a mistake.*

Fritz pressed. "So you shouldn't be in Russia? Is that what you're saying, go back across the border to Kazakhstan?"

Tegh saw their solidarity slipping and said, "Of course not, it's a concern for the diplomats and not for foreigners, even Americans, ten thousand miles away from where the fighting is. Steve, you have a consulate in Novosibirsk. The sooner we get you there the better off we'll all be. If we press on, you'll be home free in less than a day."

Steve dropped the paper in the waste bin and said, "I hope you're right, Tegh."

They boarded the northbound Moscow train without a problem, finally rolling out of the station at 1:42 P.M., nearly three hours late. Once again, their seats were in second class, meaning no reserved seating. They followed fellow passengers through the cars until they found four empty seats. Tegh and Steve sat on one side facing forward, with Fritz and Betta opposite the aisle, one facing backward and one looking forward. They were situated among working class Kazakhs and Russians.

As the four talked softly among themselves, the other passengers knew right away they were foreigners. Instead of ignoring them, as had been the case on the Chinese trains and busses, the locals relished in asking questions. Tegh and Steve tried their best to keep up with what they were saying, but Fritz and Betta, not speaking the language, were lost.

Somehow, a mutual understanding emerged without translation and a general conversation ensued. Dialogue followed, as locals took interest in their new-found source of outside information.

For the next 275 miles, lasting a little over six hours, the locals smiled, nodded, and took a legitimate interest in them. When the female conductor checked tickets, she was almost apologetic, as if she were interrupting a family reunion. For the remainder of the trip, she was the only symbol of authority the four saw.

At Barnaul, the train stopped for thirty minutes to take on cargo and exchange some passengers. The locals urged the four of them to disembark and explore the gypsy merchants hawking foodstuffs and souvenirs on the platform. One of the ladies took Betta in tow to the lady's room. Betta later confessed to her male companions that the facilities weren't westernized, but at least she didn't have to share them with the men. When they reboarded, the burliest of the locals ran off some usurpers who had just boarded and had mistakenly taken their seats.

Just before 7:00 P.M., they rolled into Novosibirsk under the waning daylight of a late September sun. They looked at a piece of paper upon which one of the young men from the train had drawn a map showing where many of the foreign consulates were located.

Optimism grew as they followed the makeshift directions. The weight of their month-long worries over imminent capture no longer plagued them. Doubts some of them had harbored about each other were gone. Their conversations, for the first time, dwelled on plans beyond the immediate. As they walked up the avenue, they revealed some of their burgeoning thoughts.

"School," Fritz said. "I think I'll go back to school and get a graduate degree."

"In retail management?" Steve asked.

"No, I'm tired of that. It has too many roadblocks."

Steve thought he saw a questioning glance from Betta at hearing his comment.

Fritz continued. "There's an alpine school in northern Italy. I've read it specializes in outfitting expeditions for mountain adventures, both winter and summer trips. Leading treks, that's more in line with my true interests. Clothing is simply too confining for me."

The others laughed at his unintended metaphor.

"How about you, Betta, will you still pursue making your own brand of outdoor clothing?" Tegh asked.

"The first thing I'm going to do is check into a spa and soak in a bubble bath for as long as I can. When I come out, you won't recognize me; I'll look like a prune."

"Will you go back to Bavaria, or do you have somewhere else in mind?" Steve asked.

She searched his face for a hidden message. Seeing none, she said, "Yes, back to Germany. I'm done with trying to find partners. I'm an ideas person when it comes to design. I'm sure I can find someone who knows manufacturing and can handle that aspect. I'm still of the mind that there's a market for the kind of clothing I want to make."

"You might want to consider the large American outfitters like Cabela's or L.L. Bean," Steve offered.

Betta wondered, *What's he trying to say?* "That sounds interesting, but I'm thinking of a specialty market. My interests are more in line with providing for those who are serious about exploring the out of doors."

"So, dreams of a combined company between you and Fritz are finished?" Tegh asked.

Without hesitation, the two of them said "Yes," prompting laughs from Tegh and Steve.

"All right, Tegh, what are you going to do?" Fritz asked. "Teach tourists Chinese history?"

He laughed. "Not on your life, Fritz. It seems you were my one and only test pupil. And I failed miserably."

This brought a good-natured guffaw.

Tegh said, "I haven't talked with my parents in almost six months. I don't even know if they knew I was on board that CEA flight, much less knew to worry. I'll find the Mongolian consulate, tell them my story, and ask for a visa to return to Ulaanbaatar. Then I'll give them a call."

"But what then?" Steve asked.

"After a few days to enjoy being home, I'll look for a graduate program and continue studying the Silk Road. Who knows, maybe I'll end up being a college professor after all."

Just as Betta was going to put Steve on the spot about his future, they turned a corner and saw a large American flag flying above a building. A large bronze plaque mounted on the perimeter wall next to the security gate read, "Consulate of the United States of America."

They stopped short to take in the scene. It had been a grueling few weeks. After enduring little chance to bathe, incessant desert sun, inexpert haircuts, and wearing dirty, ill-fitting clothes, they were a sight. Steve, Betta, and Fritz were sunbaked by over three weeks in the high, arid wilderness. Betta's ankle had fully healed and all their bug bites were in remission. They stood tall. Each of them had lost weight and it showed in the hollows of their cheeks. But other than those outward appearances, they were in fine shape.

Finally, Steve said, "Let me check with the Marine guard."

Tegh raised his hands, palms out. "I can't go any further."

The others looked at him, for the first time recognizing that he was the odd man out here, the non-Westerner in their group. It was a difference they hadn't dwelt on, though Fritz had to overcome a few latent biases.

To avoid anything awkward, Tegh said, "I wanted to make sure you got here safely. But it's best I repatriate to Mongolia. There will be too many questions to answer if I try to go through the American consulate. I'm sure that being essentially right next door, my country maintains a diplomatic legation here. Don't worry about me. I've managed to cross international borders many times, both legally and illegally."

Uneasy smiles crept across their faces.

Tegh reached into his backpack and pulled out their remaining wad of money. Pulling off several large euro bills, he handed the rest of the money to Steve. "This should do me until I reach Ulaanbaatar. You guys still have a long way to go to get home. You'll need it more than me. Keep in touch, you guys."

Remembering Fritz's comments earlier about using the salvaged money for other than their own purposes, Steve said, "You keep it, Tegh. Use it to take a closer look at your heritage, maybe even to help the herdsmen and their families back home. The money will do better staying in this part of the world than it would coming with us. Consider it not as a payment for hospitality, but as a down payment on your tuition."

Tegh was impressed by their generosity.

"Are you sure? We could just split it."

"No, Tegh," Betta said, "there are a great number of people here who should benefit from it more than we could."

They stood awkwardly, not saying or doing anything for a moment, as the enormity of what they'd just endured settled in. In just under four weeks, they'd traversed over 2,300 miles, in some cases only a few steps ahead of people who could have done them irreparable harm. They had learned a great deal about the goodwill of perfect strangers and even more about each other. It had been a shared experience of a lifetime; one they'd never forget.

Taking in the moment and gathering around, they exchanged hugs and handshakes. At last, Tegh stepped back and watched his three friends of the last several weeks walk across the street to the building behind the gated wall. He reached in his pocket and found the piece of paper with Roger's address and phone number in Semipalatinsk, and thought to himself, if worse comes to worst, I can always go back to Rubtsovsk and give him a call. And if not, there's always more than one way to cross a border.

On the sidewalk outside the reinforced enclosure, Steve said to his German colleagues, "Put your passports at the bottom of your packs and don't speak until we get inside. I'll explain our situation, that we're survivors from the CEA plane crash, and that you two are seeking asylum and safe passage to your country's embassy."

"Will that work?" Fritz asked.

"It will if you believe what's written on that plaque the Statue of Liberty holds," Steve said.

In over-worn clothing and sporting several weeks' worth of beard, he stepped towards the Marine guard. He held up his passport and said, "Lance Corporal, good evening. My father is Marine Corps Major General Warren Applegate and I'm his son Steven. I'm an American citizen from Cleveland, Ohio. I was in a plane crash several weeks ago in China, and I would like to go home."

The Marine, dressed in crisply starched battle-dress utilities, didn't break his stoic expression. "Stand right there, sir. May I have your passport?"

Taking it, he entered his reinforced guard shack and picked up the phone.

A few minutes later, a woman in her thirties, looking very officious, arrived to speak with the Marine guard. After exchanging a few words Steve couldn't hear, she walked through the gate.

"Mr. Applegate, I'm Cynthia Simpson, Consular Assistant to the American Chargé d'Affaires. We heard of a plane crash in China a few weeks ago and were informed that all fourteen of the Americans on board had died."

"Well, ma'am, it seems that at least three people survived. We didn't want to get detained in China, so here we are."

She looked at his companions, noticing one was a young woman. She motioned for them to come forward. "Will you please follow me? It sounds like you have an interesting story and I would love to hear it."

Récession

A PRISON IN GENOA, 1296 CE

IN THE DARKNESS, he could just make out one barred window positioned well above the hard floor, set high enough that it was impossible to see anything outside. Judging from the scant light, he reasoned it must face north and dawn was not far away. As his eyes adjusted to the shadow-softening of a new day's light, the cause for the dankness he'd smelled during the night was now obvious from the foul water he could see seeping through the mortar along one wall.

He heard movement coming from deeper in the room, which was still shrouded in the darkness he'd been reluctant to explore after being summarily incarcerated by his Genoan captors the evening before.

"What brings you here, my friend?" A deep voice came from the dungeon's fetid recesses.

Feeling a sudden apprehension at conversing with the likes of a prisoner, but realizing a common kinship with someone suffering his fate of imprisonment, the merchant said, "It seems I was foolish enough to risk my wealth in defense of Venice. I armed a small galley for the fight and was captured by Genoan forces off the Anatolian coast."

"Ah, we have something in common then. I am from Pisa and was captured in 1284 during our war with Genoa."

"Oh my! That was twelve years ago," said the newest prisoner.

"And the accommodations haven't gotten any better. Tell me, you don't look like a sea rogue. How came you to become bold enough to join the navy of Venice?"

"I returned from Cathay after being absent from my home for twenty-five years of travelling."

"Were you in captivity there? I heard the khans are barbarians."

"Far from it, my friend. I was under the Grand Khan's protection. But why are you interested?"

"I'm the writer, Rustichello, or at least I was until I became foolhardy enough to get captured. So, tell me… what did you say your name was?"

"Polo. Marco Polo."

The long-term prisoner with the deep voice stepped from the shadows revealing a bearded derelict of a man, and extended his hand. "Then tell me, Marco Polo, about this fantastic adventure of yours."

Author's Note

I wish to thank those who have helped me in what I have learned can be a lonely endeavor.

Once the drafts are done, then the real work begins. Without the patience and encouragement of my fellow members of the Writer's Studio at the Midwest Writing Center (MWC) in Rock Island, IL, and my fellow writers at the Writers on the Avenue (WOTA) in Muscatine, IA, bringing a work of long fiction to fruition would have been much more difficult.

Also, I wish to thank my beta readers, Mary Davidsaver, Carly Dawson, Xixuan Collins, Martin Connor, Jennifer Wieland, and my wife, Kathy, for their thoughtful (and sometimes brutal) criticism as they plowed through early versions of this work. Their honest appraisals and comments were immeasurable.

I especially want to thank my editor, Misty Urban of Pearl City Press, for her professional assessments and timely urgings for things to consider to make *Silk Road* a better work.

About the Author

Dan Moore is a graduate of Duke University and a retired US Navy captain. He has published nonfiction in the *Naval War College Review*, award-winning short stories with the Midwest Writing Center; short stories and poetry in anthologies for Writers on the Avenue, and poetry in Iowa Poetry Association's *Lyrical Iowa*. His submarine novel *Westpac* was featured on the WVIK 90.3 FM radio "Scribbles." He lives with his wife in Davenport, Iowa. His first published novel was *The Last Voyage of the Marigold*, also released through Pearl City Press.

www.ingramcontent.com/pod-product-compliance
Lightning Source LLC
Chambersburg PA
CBHW051242270626
47162CB00001BA/243